THE PROPHECY

THE PROPHECY

Kim Sakwa

Taggart
Press

ISBN 978-1-7336172-0-8

Library of Congress Control Number: 2019907657

Published in Clarkson, Michigan

To the greatest Highland clan, he is born
From a different time, first she must mourn
Two souls forever joined, still so far apart
Yet the reason is clear, she mends his broken heart
A great storm will rage, the eve of his thirty-third year
On her twenty-eighth, when the path is then clear
Once they touch 'tis forever, their bond is the key
Once together, they shall remain…for infinity

❧ CHAPTER ONE ❧

APRIL 25, 2016

"*You're what?*"

Gwendolyn Reynolds could only stare at her superior. She'd told him three times already. *Three.* And of the many qualities she possessed, patience with people who refused to see exactly what was in front of them wasn't one of them.

What didn't the man understand?

"I'm leaving, Frank. Surely you know the meaning… the act of removing oneself, the—"

"Don't get smart with me, Gwendolyn," Frank Sutter returned through clenched teeth.

"I'm sorry, Frank. I know this comes as a surprise, and I understand your unhappiness with my decision, but I've made up my mind." Gwen kept her voice calm and steady, contrite for the moment, as she tried a different approach.

She smoothed her hands across the tabletop in front of her, then fingered the silver bracelet adorning her wrist. A touch for courage. Her white blouse was tucked perfectly into charcoal trousers, her legs beneath the table, crossed. Her foot, encased in a sinfully expensive black pump, rested on the floor and tapped uncontrollably. It was the only gesture that belied her steadfast composure.

"You have a responsibility, Gwen, not to mention a contract," Frank continued, red-faced and angrier than before.

The man looked like he would have a coronary at any second. Gwen's eyes narrowed slightly. Was it possible he was having one now? Would it be her fault if he did?

Gwen had called Frank last night. Late last night. It had taken her two weeks to build up her nerve and another twelve hours to dial his number. She knew now she shouldn't have told him of her decision over the phone, but she couldn't seem to help herself.

Another quality she possessed: honesty. Unfortunately, to a fault. She'd expected a fight from Frank. And she knew that was the reason she'd waited. Now that her mind was made up, however, she couldn't be swayed.

Unless Frank dropped dead, of course. Maybe then she'd reconsider.

Gwen looked him directly in the eye and counted to five before responding. "I'm leaving, Frank, contract or not." Determined to deliver only short, decisive statements, she bit the inside of her cheek.

Frank turned to the two men who sat to his left, Mark Ingersol and Gary Ackerman. Gwen almost groaned aloud. *Crap!* When she entered the boardroom earlier, those men sat facing her. Frank had been seated at the head of the table, drumming his fingers impatiently on the stack of papers in front of him.

Gwen knew Frank would try to intimidate her. And bringing in Mark was intimidation. Everyone knew she had dated him. And they knew how it ended: badly.

Gwen tried to keep everything in perspective, which wasn't too difficult. Because regardless of the fact that those men made her feel all of twelve years old and truly close to throwing up, what they failed to realize was…she was beyond intimidation.

Now she just had to get through this meeting, and hopefully, with her resolve intact.

Mark spoke, obviously on cue. "Let me explain something to you, *sweetheart*."

Mark. What an ass. What a mistake. Gwen fixed him with an icy smile. "Think ya can?"

"I can explain a lot, Gwen. You have an obligation… the act of binding oneself by a social, legal, or moral tie."

"I wasn't aware you knew the meaning of anything moral," she quipped.

"Weren't you?" he corrected.

Crap again! Score one for Mark.

The man had a point. She'd shown him the door, and he walked. He'd also told anyone who would listen that she'd led him on. The ice queen, he'd said. The term hurt more than she'd admit. She hadn't meant to lead him on, but she couldn't pretend she felt enough to sleep with him. And she wouldn't just give her virginity to anyone. Not when she'd already waited that long.

Gwen turned to Frank. She couldn't look at Mark anymore. Not for the obvious reasons, but because she was so close to vomiting, which wouldn't be so horrible. But it would be one of those spontaneous and uncontrollable moments. A moment in which she knew she'd ruin her shoes. She'd waited two weeks for those shoes. *Two.* She'd never be able to find another pair in her size this late in the season. *And* she'd be out four hundred dollars. Vomiting was definitely out of the question.

"I've only asked for a leave of absence, Frank," Gwen justified. "It's not unheard of." And she had only asked for a leave of absence, but Gwen had a feeling she wasn't coming back.

"Why?" Frank pleaded. "You're finally able to stand on your own. You've accomplished more than any resident I've known, Gwen. Hell, you've accomplished more than anyone I've known."

Gwen didn't have a response. Not one they'd understand. How could she explain something she didn't understand herself?

How could she walk away from everything she'd worked her entire life to achieve?

She'd spent every waking moment since grade school being the best at everything. And she was. Exhaustively cultured, educated to the hilt, and driven beyond reason. One month shy of twenty-eight, she was poised to one day become the leader in cardiovascular surgery. A legacy her parents had all but ensured.

Her perfect life.

Ha! Her perfect life was a frigging wreck.

Somehow she'd reached a turning point. She couldn't hide any longer behind that confident exterior she'd worked so hard to create. For the first time in her life, the rules she lived by had changed. And she was terrified.

Gary, who'd been silent, finally spoke. "Gwen, take a few days, lay off the exercise and relax. I have a feeling you'll see things more clearly. Whatever this is about, running away isn't the answer."

Gwen knew he was trying to be helpful. But he was dead wrong. Leaving seemed to be her only answer. She felt she'd reached her pinnacle. Her goals were attained, and for a reason she couldn't comprehend, it seemed her career drive had come to its end. It was the personal drive she always repressed that called to her now.

Those images she once embraced only at night now filled her days, and a need she couldn't suppress beckoned to her as never before. And it seemed imperative she reach for it. Now.

"For me, Gary, it's the only answer."

"What's that sound?" Frank demanded.

Gwen stopped her foot before it made contact with the floor again. She didn't say anything else. She'd made her point. She was leaving.

"I won't have it, Gwen," Frank stressed indignantly. "This misguided assumption that you can walk away."

"*Misguided?* Are you serious, Frank?" Gwen came out of her chair, her hands on the table as she leaned forward. "You can't keep me here. I don't care about your prized institution anymore. I don't care that I have a contract. And I sure as hell don't care that I'm walking away from my accomplishments. *They're mine.*" Gwen started for the door. Her hand covered the handle as her superior's voice carried from the chair.

"If you walk, Gwen, we'll sue."

Gwen opened the door. "Then I'll see you in court." She didn't look back.

She would never look back.

APRIL 25, 1536

Greylen MacGreggor was aware of the impending dawn. An awareness so acute it bordered on pain. Shadows still played within the last recess of restless slumber, shadows that haunted him for most of his life. 'Twas always in the last seconds of semiconsciousness he found himself reaching into the darkness. A futile hope that something tangible would be within his reach. Yet each day he arose, 'twas emptiness that greeted him.

This day was no different.

Realizing the barren truth, he threw the covers aside and sat on the edge of his bed. Feet on the floor, elbows on his knees, he rested his head in his hands but a moment. Then, as he did every morning, he brushed his fingers harshly through his hair before he stood.

Punishment for fanciful notions.

Pain to ease the ache that never went away.

Barefoot and in breeches, he left his cabin and made his way above deck. The sky was alive with stars and a full moon illuminated the blackened sea. His captain stood at the ship's helm and the few crewmen about left him to his solitude. He walked to the bow of the ship, not surprised minutes later to hear the footfall of the only man who'd dare to approach him now.

"Greylen?" Gavin, his first-in-command, asked.

"Aye?"

"We'll make port by dawn."

Greylen turned his head, raising a brow. "Aye, Gavin, 'tis a fact I'm already aware of."

Gavin gave his commander a crooked smile. "Invaluable, aren't I?"

Greylen returned the smile but refused to answer. He glanced back to the sea, silent again as he always was at the hour before dawn.

This was his second favorite place to greet the day. His first, the shore beneath the cliffs of Seagrave. 'Twas the only time he allowed himself the indulgence of images from his dreams.

The only time he thought beyond them.

"'Tis but a month away," Gavin stated quietly, his stance the same as Greylen's: legs braced apart and arms crossed over his chest.

"You're a wealth of information this morn," Greylen acknowledged with resigned sarcasm. He knew exactly what his first-in-command was referring to, but with each day that brought him closer to his thirty-third year,

Greylen became more reserved.

"I'll leave you to your peace," Gavin offered, dismissing himself as quietly as he'd appeared.

Peace? Had he ever known it a day?

Greylen pondered the sentiment but a moment. He'd felt it briefly the day his mother summoned him. The day she'd told him of the prophecy.

But how could he face the day he'd waited for these past ten years if…if it came to naught?

Would the images go away? Those images that only came in the last hour of what restless sleep he allowed himself. Images of *her*…which forever haunted him.

Nay, he could never let them go.

He would always look back.

❧ CHAPTER TWO ❧

ONE MONTH LATER

"Happy birthday, Gwen."

Gwen smiled into the phone. She should've known Sara would call. "Thanks, Sara."

"How's Scotland? Cold? Rainy? Beautiful? Awful?"

Gwen laughed. "Scotland is perfect. A little chilly but honestly, I haven't seen a drop of rain. How's Mr. MacGreggor?"

"Purring away. He's a great companion. I'm glad you let him stay with me."

"I wouldn't trust him with anyone else."

"Where are you going tonight? Any handsome men catch your eye, invite you to dinner maybe?"

"Hardly," Gwen argued with a snort, though it wasn't truly the case. She had seen plenty of handsome men since she'd been in Scotland over the past three weeks. And, in fact, some had asked her to dinner.

"Haven't found what you're looking for?" Sara asked, as if reading her mind.

Bingo.

"No." Gwen's simple statement was emphasized with a sigh. Maybe she was crazy to think she'd find the answers here. And just what was she looking for anyway?

The man of her dreams. The man *from* her dreams.

Was he what compelled her to leave everything behind? Had he somehow influenced her decision? Was it he who filled her with hopefulness once she'd done the unthinkable?

Could it explain how the end of her residency represented nothing more than completion? Or why her restlessness ended when she purchased her airline ticket? Not the first one she'd booked to London. And not the second she'd booked to Paris. It was only when she'd changed her reservation to Scotland that she knew she'd made the right choice. Was she crazy?

Oh yeah.

"Gwen... *Gwen?*"

"Sorry, what were you saying?"

"Tell me where you're going tonight, and more importantly, tell me what you're wearing."

"A simple black dress and heels," Gwen said in a rush.

"Liar!"

Gwen smiled again. "Does it really matter?"

"Is there a full-length mirror in your room?"

"They don't have mirrors in Scotland," Gwen snapped.

Sara laughed. "Shut up. Go stand in front of it."

"Come on, Sara," Gwen groaned. She wasn't up for this.

"Go...now." Sara paused and gave her time to get in front of the mirror. "Tell me what you see."

"Someone who's pathetic."

"You're far from pathetic," Sara argued on her behalf. "You're gorgeous, smart, and the best person I've ever known."

"I'm not quite tall enough, my chest is too small, and I have no hips."

"You're perfectly tall enough, long on legs, and have a perfect handful. And just so you know, your jeans fit in a way people would die for."

Gwen cupped her breast and frowned at her reflection as she listened to Sara. "The perfect handful, Sara, *is my handful.*"

Sara laughed. "Well, maybe if you let someone get close enough, it would be their perfect handful too."

"I tried that."

"Mark was an ass. I'm glad you came to your senses before it was too late."

"*Too late?* I'm twenty-eight and for the first time in my life, I'm scared as hell."

"You listen to me, Gwendolyn Reynolds. You're the best friend I've ever had. I can't think of anyone more deserving than you to find some happiness. Stop your little pity party and tell me what you're wearing."

"Tank top, capris, Lulu jacket, and running shoes," Gwen muttered, knowing she should've lied again.

"*Gwen*...come on, it's your birthday."

"I'm just going to a pub a few miles from here, and I'm going alone. Besides, I plan on being back in my room early enough to enjoy a great bottle of wine."

"No cocktails?"

Gwen laughed. "I have a stockpile of vodka in my bag. But wine sounds better. I can listen to music while I count the stars."

"Ever the dreamer."

"My one fault." Gwen smiled, listening to Sara choke dramatically.

"One? Ah, Gwen…how about your temper?"

"Temper, schmemper." Gwen scoffed. "It's not *that* bad."

"You're kidding, right?" Sara asked seriously.

"I plead the fifth," Gwen said with courtroom theatrics.

"Speaking of which, have you heard from your attorney?" Sara asked.

"*Oh yeah.*"

"And?"

"I'm going to settle," Gwen said, staring through her terrace window. She fingered the pane of glass in a foolish attempt to soothe—what or whom she couldn't say. "There's plenty of money in the trust, and honestly, I don't know if I can ever go back."

"Don't do anything rash," Sara cautioned.

"*Helllooo*…I walked away from a career I envisioned my entire life. I took the first vacation I've had in years, and I did it all *rashly*."

"That's not true. You agonized for weeks. You agonized your entire life."

"That's not true either," Gwen remarked honestly. "I always felt like I was doing the right thing. I never questioned following in my parents' footsteps." And that was true.

"You didn't just follow in their footsteps," Sara corrected her. "You set the Olympic records for academic, athletic, and professional achievements."

"They'd be so disappointed if they were here."

"Don't give them that power, Gwen. You always said you were their lab experiment, and their prodigy repaid them in spades."

"Well, that prodigy feels like a lost puppy."

"You're lying, Gwen. You sound better than ever."

Gwen's smile widened. "Truthfully, Sara, coming here is the best decision I've ever made."

Greylen arose from his third sleepless night well before dawn. Foregoing his usual bedside ritual, he donned a pair of breeches and made his way through the darkened hallways of Seagrave Castle. Once outside, he nodded to the men who stood sentinel at the keep's main doors and continued to the stables. Then he took the narrow path to the shore.

He would watch the sunrise.

He stood barefoot on the sand, greeting a day that could only be called glorious. 'Twas the day that marked the anniversary of his thirty-third year. His anger grew by the second. His roar of outrage was lost to the waters and cove.

On this day no one would escape his wrath.

Of the many attributes for which Laird Greylen MacGreggor was revered, his barely veiled contempt for this day was not one of them. Few understood the reasoning behind it, and one seemed not to care.

His sister. Lady Isabelle MacGreggor.

Greylen had just returned to the keep, intent to order his mother never to breathe a word of that blasted infernal prophecy ever again, when Isabelle passed him. Obviously in her haste she hadn't noticed he was there. Exuberance radiated from her very being as she hurried down the steps and all but flew through the keep's main doors.

He turned and was about to order her back to her quarters when Gavin at last made himself useful. His first-in-command caught her about the waist just as she made for the first of the steps that would take her into the courtyard.

'Twas at first a comical display. Isabelle's head tilted back, her lips forming an O as she came flush against him. Gavin, too, showed surprise for just but a second before his eyes narrowed and his lips pursed in an angry line. "If you know what's good for you, Isabelle, leave your brother be," Gavin snapped.

Greylen wasn't surprised by Gavin's harsh tone with his sister. Truth be told, 'twas the only way he seemed to address her of late. What did surprise him was that his first-in-command had yet to release her. Gavin must have realized the same, too, for he hastily removed his arm from around her torso and stepped back a full pace. Greylen watched Isabelle adjust her gown, cleverly blinking back tears as she did so.

"'Tis Greylen's birthday. I only wish to bid him good day," she explained, fully composed once again.

"'Tis not a good day he wishes for. He's been at it since the crack of dawn. See you the practice fields," Gavin said, motioning with his hand in their direction. "One fallen soldier after another. Your brother left them long minutes ago and they've still yet to stand."

"Then perhaps you should put him out of his misery," Isabelle suggested.

"'Tis misery he craves," Gavin replied in a softer tone. "Please, Isabelle, heed my advice. 'Twould only blacken his mood more if he is the cause of pain to you."

"Very well, Gavin," she conceded with a sigh. "You'll see, though, both of you. This night will bring what he so desires."

Isabelle left on the heels of her declaration, yet as Greylen joined Gavin atop the keep's step and looked to the sky, 'twas plainly clear—the only storms in the making were those that would be unleashed by Greylen.

Greylen spent the remainder of the day back on the practice fields. Occasionally he saw Gavin on the portico, assessing the damage he wrought. His first-in-command wouldn't think twice that three days without sleep, and swordplay for the last eight hours, hadn't diminished his laird's strength. He was sure that Gavin took note of the number of times Greylen had changed the hand in which he held his sword—but four.

'Twas the gloaming that finally brought a roar from yonder fields. A dusk as clear and calm as the day.

"*NOW*," Greylen bellowed. A demand of such force, it carried across the fields where it echoed for a surprising span of time. He watched as the front doors of the keep finally opened and Gavin's form filled the frame. The cad still wore a crisp linen shirt and looked as if he'd had quite the peaceful day.

Greylen hoped to hell he had.

He knew his first-in-command steered clear of him since he'd seen him that morn, and he knew why.

Only Gavin could give him the fight he so desperately needed. Only Gavin could release the demons to which he wanted nothing more than to succumb.

Ten years of waiting...*for naught*.

He believed with every fiber of his being he would know peace that night. Yet 'twas painfully clear, tomorrow he would face another dawn—and he would face it alone.

Greylen watched Gavin approach as never before. No arrogance, no hint of gladdening malice upon his lips for that which he was about to perform. 'Twas only a man's best friend who came to stand before him now.

God willing, Gavin would beat him to the ground. He only prayed his body would feel the pain that seemed to emanate from his very soul.

Gavin said nothing of Greylen's appearance, dreadful as it must be. He had discarded his shirt hours ago, having ripped it to strips to tie about his forehead. Then he'd changed them every hour as they became soaked with sweat. Now it lay in a pile of tatters. His hair clung to his scalp and the base of his neck, shorn just days ago as he did with the coming of each full moon.

He could no longer feel the weight of his sword. Nor his legs, encased in breeches and what were once polished boots. He wished he felt nothing at all. But truth be told, he felt betrayed.

Betrayed by the prophecy. Betrayed—by *her*.

Gavin at last began to circle him, fixing him with a look that brought even the most skilled of fighters to their knees. Greylen engaged. Steel meeting steel as they repeatedly exchanged blows; barely contained murmurs now grunts released with such force the end seemed nowhere in sight.

After what seemed an eternity, Gavin mercifully gave a nod and their men stood. The only men left on the fields. Five of the best men in the Highlands he'd taken as his own over the past fifteen years. But 'twas Gavin's order that they followed now.

His men would put him out of his self-imposed misery. They'd take him down at last, beat and exhaust him till he ceased to feel. Then he would never feel again. He would never again believe. He knew it as he knew nothing else.

'Twas at that very moment—when defeat seemed so imminent—that the gods showed their grace. Lightning tore through the clearest night sky, and a storm of unnatural force unleashed its power.

And 'twas then that Laird Greylen MacGreggor fell to his knees for the first time in his entire life…witnessing the beginning of his destiny.

❧ CHAPTER THREE ❧

Gwen enjoyed the evening of her birthday more than she ever thought possible. A night usually filled with cold assessments of goals attained during the previous year, that night was met with simple contentment. It was a first and welcome respite from the emotional battle that consumed her day.

Scotland was perfect, just as she told Sara. But for some reason, the glorious day to which she awoke filled her with sadness. As if the day should be anything but glorious. She couldn't put her finger on the exact cause, yet she sensed that the sunshine and warm, calm breeze created a disturbance of some sort. Not an outward one, but one deep within…oddly…*her*.

It was filled with anger. It was filled with betrayal.

It was only when dusk set in, and an unexpected storm of unnatural proportion swept the coastal inlet, that she finally felt better. It seemed to wash all the foreboding away. As if the world, tipped slightly off its axis, put itself to rights.

She sat at a cozy table, savoring a fabulous dinner of sautéed fish, potatoes, and vegetables, along with a glass of incredible white wine the owners had insisted was on them. A band played a variety of soulful acoustic music, which was another reason she'd chosen this pub to mark the occasion. She was having such a nice time.

As she headed toward the door, the same pull she'd been experiencing for weeks heightened. Demanded.

The owners, three patrons, and the lead singer of the band tried to stop her, but Gwen wouldn't have stayed if her life depended on it. Which they righteously told her it did.

In the end, her smile and self-assurance won. It also could've been that she'd felt rather safe in the large SUV she'd rented. Whatever the case, she secured her bag over her shoulder and made a run for the truck. She hugged the wheel with a sigh and smile, knowing she'd made the right choice. If nothing else, she had to go back to the inn. And she had to go there now.

Minutes later she felt like a complete idiot.

Minutes later the worst began to happen.

The storm grew stronger. Its center was above her. Her stomach reeled as the ground beneath gave way. Her screams rent the air as her truck plunged toward the icy waters.

She knew she shouldn't brace herself for the impact, but it was beyond her control. As the hood of her truck crashed into the water and the airbags exploded around her, the truck lurched forward into the turbulent waters.

Knowing she had to get out, she swatted at the chalky smoke and instinctively reached for her bag. She could never part with it; its contents represented everything she'd worked so hard to achieve. It was her life, and sadly, the only thing she had left to value.

She pushed through the driver's-side window, a frantic and futile struggle as the seat belt held her back. She searched for the release button, then pushed through the window again, fear and adrenaline overriding pain as jagged edges of broken glass tore through the palm of her hand and shoulders. The salt water hit her eyes, a hellish sting somehow worse than what she'd already endured. Lightning shot through the sky, and she set her sights on the shore.

Gwen swam with everything she had, an almost impossible feat as the churning waters kept pulling her under.

But no matter how hard she tried, it just wasn't enough. The water was too cold. And when she finally felt the sand and rock with the tips of her shoes—she was pulled farther out to sea again.

Curling into a ball, she willed herself to relax. But when she opened her eyes, the last remnants of hope left her. How she had lasted so long in the freezing water was beyond her.

Damning herself for the choices that brought her here—the foolishness that led to death instead of discovery—Gwen knew her dreams would never be realized. No one could hear her pleas. No one would save her. She would never find what she searched for.

A home. Love. Children.

She would never feel those strong arms wrapped around her body, those of the man whose image haunted her dreams. And she would never hear his whispered endearments, the ones she so longed to hear.

She felt rather than heard her last cry rip from her heart, body, and soul.

It echoed through the stormy night.

Greylen drew upon the reins of his horse. "Gavin," he called through the fury of the storm. "Take Duncan and Hugh and search the perimeter." He turned to lead Kevin, Connell, and Ian toward the cliffs.

Gavin reached his side moments later, his horse dancing upon its hindquarters as he heeded the command to stop. "Greylen—"

"She will come, Gavin." His anger spilled into each word he shouted back.

"'Tis not an argument," Gavin assured. "We swept the perimeter but moments ago." They had in fact swept it for the last four hours. Hours of relentless rain and thunder so loud, the storm's center had yet to move from above them.

"Take the northern trail," Greylen conceded. "I'll—" Lightning tore through the sky, drawing Greylen's attention. 'Twas the only time it distracted him that night, but with the blast came awareness. His entire body tensed—*good God, she was in the waters below.*

He raced toward the cliffs.

'Twas a descent of record time, each second pure torture as Greylen's eyes fixed on a sight far from the shore's edge, each flash of lightning confirming his worst ungodly fear.

He dropped his sword and dagger on the sand as he ran for the water. His boots and shirt lost to the surf as he shucked them while charging through the shallow depths. When the water reached his thighs, he dove into the white-capped waves, his deft strokes closing the distance. Strokes driven by an all-consuming rage. Rage at the peril in which this woman was placed.

His woman.

His eyes never lost sight of her. Finally, a solitary wave between them, but strokes away…she vanished beneath the crest.

She did not resurface.

She did not resurface.

He dove into the wave, and long minutes surely passed before he felt her lifeless body making its descent to the ocean's floor. He grabbed at her with both hands, his fingers twisting harshly through her hair, his arms leashing viciously about her waist. Finally clutched fully in his embrace, an extreme sensation passed through his body.

'Twas as powerful as lightning, intense light and heat. Yet he kicked to the surface above, stunned the force did not take them.

Certain she didn't breathe, and unable to fathom the horrid possible truth of the thoughts that followed, he ceased to think them. He did not live by emotion. He lived with it. But it did not rule him. No one ruled him.

'Twas a lie of such magnitude he would have laughed had this predicament not been his. And if this woman knew what was good for her—this woman whom he held within his grasp, this woman whom he knew to the very depths of his soul was the woman for whom he had waited—she'd better take his blasted breath. And she'd better make a damn good show of it.

As he continued to swim upon his back, willing the hand that held her atop his chest to feel even the faintest of a heartbeat, he realized the storm was gone. No prevailing mist. Not a cloud in the clearest of night skies. Only a full moon and bright stars accompanied the cool, crisp air.

His men waited just beyond the shoreline and formed a tight circle as he straddled her body. He heard their swords drawn in unison, their pledges made to this woman, their oaths sworn as he ripped her shirt in two and tossed aside her satchel that had come loose as well.

Stunned by the vision beneath him, enraged by the prophecy's sadistic twist, he pressed his ear to her chest, praying she had life. And "pray to no one" Greylen prayed as never before. He embraced God with an open heart; he even vowed to attend Father Michael's next Mass.

He suspected that this woman was waiting for just that as the sweet sound of a faint heartbeat whispered in his ear. Then in true overlord fashion, he demanded she take his breath.

Breaths and then strokes as he laid her on her side, harsh upward strokes to remove the water from her lungs.

Breathe, breathe...for the sake of God, breathe! Did she not understand an order?

A good show indeed.

He could've collected a fortune for it, had it been of the theatrical kind. She took his blasted breath all right. And scared him witless in the process, gasping and coughing so violently 'twas painful to watch.

She'd be punished for that.

'Twasn't enough that he had to look at perfection and fight to keep it within his realm. 'Twasn't enough that he had to move his hands over her entire slender frame, cut and bruised but otherwise sound. 'Twasn't enough that he had to watch her violent shakes until he could at last pick her up and wrap her in his warmth. This woman scared him close to death.

'Twas those thoughts that consumed him as he and his men rode back to the keep. He could not live in such fear—with such fear. Yet 'twas that very fear, his need to protect and keep safe, which kept him at pace with Gavin, whom he ordered to ride ahead.

The doors to the keep opened as they took the stairs, and for the first time in hours Greylen breathed a sigh of relief. Home. Lady Madelyn. Isabelle. Anna. Safety. Detachment.

'Twas with this last sentiment that he allowed himself to step back. To distance himself. 'Twas but a farce, this detachment.

Every muscle in his body clenched as he watched his mother and Anna try to remove this woman's clothing. He finally saw to the task himself, ripping the strange garments from her body. Feeling every involuntary grimace and bruise as if it were his own, feeling each of her lacerations as they were cleaned, and in the case of some, tended with needle and thread before being covered.

But the most painful of wounds that he could not understand—the most unthinkable of them—were those that covered her eyes.

Tender skin, raw and exposed. Lids damaged and carefully anointed with thick healing paste. Eyes wrapped with linen strips.

Eyes he'd dreamed of seeing.

He said not a word throughout the entire process. Not as her hair was brushed, then secured, nor as a bedgown of Isabelle's was slipped onto her, followed by a dose of God knows what potion. He merely stood there, his body so tight with tension 'twas a wonder he'd not snapped from within.

Two pairs of eyes turned to him: his mother's and Anna's. But 'twas Isabelle's touch to which he responded. He'd no idea she was in the room.

"Greylen, see to your bath," she instructed softly.

He stared at her upturned face, hearing her words clearly, yet unable to move.

"Greylen, Anna will bring refreshments. Mother and I will stay, I swear to you. Please, Greylen," she pleaded. "See to your needs."

He gave a nod in her direction, then removed himself to the bathing chamber. His needs at the moment were vast. Isabelle, however, had the decency not to throw it in his face. He'd been covered in sweat and dirt when the storm finally broke, then purged of it by the cold waters. Covered with sand from the shore, and then sweat once again as he swallowed true fear.

The bathwater once hot had cooled considerably. He scrubbed his body thrice, his hair more as he rubbed his hands harshly into his scalp. He even shaved. He did everything he could to remain in the tub, when all he wanted was to climb into his bed. With her.

She ruled him already.

Donning a pair of drawstring trews, he left his sanctuary and returned to his quarters. The scene was unchanged. His mother's gentle hand stroked a pale face, Isabelle's supreme glow was barely held in check, and Anna, sewing basket at her feet, worked upon some garment with deft fingers.

Isabelle led him to a chair by the fire where he sat obediently, drinking the wine she'd placed in his hand. Then he cleared the plate she'd set upon his lap. Sustenance. He'd been long without it. So long it seemed to addle his brain. Too late, he realized he'd been given a potion as well. They had better have made a large dose of it, for if not, he would kill them.

He raised a brow as he looked at his mother's profile, willing her to turn. She did, and damn if she didn't look smug.

"By what right do you think to drug me?" he snarled in accusation.

"I know not of what you speak," Lady Madelyn professed with false conviction.

"You lie, Mother," he bit out reproachfully. "And you do it badly."

"Greylen, *drug* is such a strong word." She scoffed, hurrying on when he glared. "You've not slept for days. Think you could do so now?"

"You mean now that you've all but guaranteed it," he qualified. "Or now that she lies in my bed?"

"I meant now that she lies in your bed. I know exactly the dose I administered, and you will sleep, no doubt."

"Gavin," Greylen bellowed from the chair. He knew his first-in-command stood just outside the chamber, and he quickly appeared in the doorway. "It seems Lady Madelyn has seen I receive a proper rest this night. Know you anything of this?"

Gavin's slight tick and barely suppressed smile nerved Greylen to no end, but he took his words that followed as truth.

"Nay, I was not taken into her confidence."

"Keep our guard. Have Duncan check with the border patrols and report to you before he retires."

Having his orders, Gavin dismissed himself, his shoulders shaking with what Greylen assumed must be merriment. The treacherous trio followed moments later.

Greylen made no move once the door was closed; truthfully, he wasn't sure that he could.

He was beyond exhausted. 'Twas the fourth day he'd greeted with no sleep, a day of physical depletion and emotional turmoil. His barely checked adrenaline would have provided another sleepless night. Yet his mother spared him such a fate.

No longer angered and feeling something that must be calm, he moved the chair to his bedside. Bandages did nothing to diminish the woman's looks. Good God, she was beautiful.

He remembered every inch of her skin as if it were branded into his soul, from his meticulous inspection on the shore, and as he held her on the journey back to the keep. Then as he watched her wounds tended. He'd made no comment when Anna gasped at her slender frame. No contrary rejoinder when she implied malnourishment. This woman had a body that bespoke training, sleek muscles atop fine bone structure. 'Twas perfection, and somehow, he knew that she had made it so, as sure as he knew that discipline drove her.

How long had she struggled in the water?

Had she known defeat was in sight?

Did it trouble her as much as him?

He'd not known a day of defeat until the infernal sunshine greeted him that morn, until he watched her struggle end, until she sank beneath the water's surface.

He vowed now—he would never know it again.

That same conviction forced him to admit his pretense of detachment was swiftly fading. With each tremor that ran through her body, each murmur that came from her lips, his anger of the day—the fury she would not, in fact, come—gave way.

It continued until he stood from the chair, pulled aside the bedcovers, and lay beside her. Then he gathered her in his arms and experienced what he never had before.

Contentment.

Soft hair beneath his chin, warm breath upon his chest, and her slender form within his hands.

By God 'twas worth the wait.

❧ CHAPTER FOUR ❧

The dream was always the same.

Gwen pressed deeper into the warm embrace, sighing as strong arms tightened around her. She rubbed her face in the crook of his neck, running her hand over the solid mass of back and shoulders until her fingers tangled in thick, soft hair. Large powerful hands followed her movements, pressing her closer as he cupped the back of her head and gently tilted her face.

She never felt his hesitation before. Tonight she did. She tugged on his hair, a silent demand to be kissed. Then he covered her lips, completely sealing them within his own. A deep sound rumbled through his chest.

This dream was different.

She felt the warmth of his lips and the pressure of his hands, the texture of his hair and the heat of skin. She heard sounds given and returned.

It seemed so real.

His thumb coaxed her chin, and her lips parted as he moved between them. He spent an eternity simply joining their mouths...in every possible way. His tongue, reverent at first, was slow to explore, then became wholly demanding.

She gave in to him completely. In truth, she kissed him back with everything she had. They shared an urgency—taking satisfaction as they'd never been able to before.

She traced her fingers over his face—his broad forehead, straight nose, high cheekbones, his smooth, strong chin—and she pulled him even closer.

My God, it had never felt so good.

She made a sound as he pulled back, a whimper he hushed with slow, passionate kisses over her forehead and cheeks. Then he covered her lips again before tucking her within the crook of his neck. "Sleep, love," he urged in a murmur. "The morn's but an hour away."

Gwen burrowed against him, silent tears wetting her cheeks—oppressive longing crushing her from the inside out.

She'd never heard the sound of his voice.

It would haunt her forever.

It took Gwen thirty seconds to realize something was wrong. Very wrong. Besides the fog filling her head, it was completely dark. She couldn't open her eyes.

Those were the thoughts that occurred within the first ten seconds.

In the next ten, she became aware of the fact she was one giant bruise, some areas more severe than others. Those were the wrong seconds.

The *very* wrong were the last ten.

That was when she felt warmth beneath her cheek, breath upon her head, and large hands spanning her back. Holding her with both tenderness and possession. Sure she was fully conscious but affected by an adverse reaction to her IV, she reached for the nurse's call button. The arms around her tightened, accompanied by a calming whisper.

It was so reassuring, this touch and sound, that she snuggled deeper into the embrace. Indulging in sensations completely foreign to her, she felt safe and protected.

Then she felt panic. My God, she felt fear.

She pushed away with all her strength, scrambling for the edge of the bed, each move hurting more than the last. Each breath she tried desperately to take wasn't quite deep enough. Those same large hands covered her shoulders, gentle on top of her thick bandages.

Then everything came back at once.

Losing control of the truck. The mudslide as she plunged into the ocean. The explosion of the airbags. Pushing through the window. Jagged glass tearing her skin. Fighting to swim to shore. Wave after relentless wave. Defeat.

"Who…?" Gwen tried to catch her breath. Her hands moved forward and stopped against his chest. Smooth, warm skin. Hard muscles beneath her palms and fingers. He was a brick wall—an enormous brick wall. Terrified by the sheer size of the giant who sat in front of her on her bed, *in her bed*, she pushed back.

"Cease."

That one word, spoken with gentle authority, shocked her. *Cease?* Who said *cease?* And who said it like that? A voice so deep, a timbre so rich. It seemed familiar but... "Who"—she took a short breath—"are..." Larger gasps followed.

"Breathe," he demanded in the same tone. "In... out..." He continued his litany, but Gwen couldn't seem to follow. "Good God, not again." It sounded like a curse and a sigh. Then strong lips covered her open mouth. Warm and determined, he stole her breath.

Then he gave it back.

Calm. Steady. Even.

The hands that covered her shoulders moved. One palmed her head, long fingers holding her steady until her breathing matched his own. The other splayed her chest, directly over her heart, as if willing the erratic beat to slow.

It beat the hell out of a paper bag.

He pulled back. But his mouth drew upon her lips, ending his unconventional first aid with what could only be a kiss.

He did not release her. Her head remained in the palm of his hand, her back supported by the circle of his arm, his other hand still covered her chest.

Greylen couldn't have let go if his life depended on it. Too many emotions and not one of them in check. He'd slept as never before. That ache he was so used to was gone.

He awoke as always, in that hour before dawn, but 'twas the first time he had not to reach out. No pain greeted him, no emptiness. Instead he held her closer and kissed her. He felt her sorrow afterward and asked her of its cause, yet she'd succumbed to sleep. Her steady, even breaths, warm upon his chest, lulled him to a light slumber. He'd felt her stir when she first awoke, then sensed her panic.

Anyone else he would have soothed with words. But for some reason he knew she would not have listened. That same awareness told him now that she was bracing for a fight.

He wanted to kiss her again. Instead, he brushed his fingers across her face. Errant wisps, freed from the braid fashioned the night before, swept back once again.

"If you're done being my human respirator, I'd like to see my chart."

Greylen smiled—riled was a very becoming state for this woman. "And just how did you plan on *seeing* this chart?" he asked her.

She obviously heard the amusement in his voice, but her now relaxed facial expression warred with her ridiculous attempts to push him away. "Listen, mister—"

"You will call me Greylen."

"I will *call* the authorities."

"*I am* the authority," Greylen warned, then held back a laugh. She smirked.

"I don't want to hurt you, but if you don't let go of me—" She gasped. "I felt that. *A chuckle*, you repressed a chuckle."

This time he did laugh. "Good God, woman, but I swear I did. You think to hurt me?"

"I'll kick your ass so fast you won't know what hit you," she snapped. "Now let me go and get the goddamn attending in here. *Now*."

Her demand made him tighten his hold. "I've no idea who this *goddamn attending* is you seek, but I can assure you, you're in no condition to kick anything...let alone *my ass*." He spoke with authority. His face an inch from hers. He watched as she started to feel the bed around her. "Tell me what you search for," he demanded, following the motions of her hands.

"The call button," she whispered, what little fight she had seeming to fade.

"What purpose would it serve?" he asked.

"Greylen." A near shout interrupted them. Isabelle sounded the admonishment, stepping into the room. "You're scaring her half to death."

Greylen turned to his sister, but he did not let go. He was, in fact, sorry that Isabelle had entered the room at all. He couldn't seem to help himself but riling this woman could be sport. She inflamed him. And he enjoyed it.

"*Scaring her?*" Greylen argued. "She threatened to kick my—" He shook his head instead. "You'd not believe me."

"I'm sure you misunderstood," Isabelle said with a regal sweep of her hand. "Mother's on her way, Greylen. If she thinks you—"

"Ah...*excuse me*. I need some help here." The plea was directed toward Isabelle.

Greylen set her straight as she seemed to think she needed protection from him. "You are never to fear me, lass. Do you understand?" He hadn't meant to bark. He was just accustomed to giving orders.

"Oh, of course I understand, why would I ever fear you?" she quipped.

Seconds later, Isabelle interrupted. "Enough, Greylen." She made the second admonishment as she reached to pry his hands away from the woman he still held within his grasp. He let her, then watched as Isabelle settled her against the pillows once more. "She's in no condition for...for whatever you're about."

"*What I'm about?*" he asked his sister incredulously. As if he couldn't seem to help himself, he took the little tigress on the bed in his arms again, holding her by the shoulders. "What are *you* about?" he demanded.

"I'll tell you what *I'm* about," the lass returned quickly and with quite a bit of anger to boot. "I'm about five three, long on legs, and short on breasts." She emphasized cupping herself. "*What in the hell are* you *about?*"

Greylen ducked his head to the side, pinching the bridge of his nose so as not to laugh before he looked at her again. When he did glance back, however, he became aware of what now greeted them behind her. If she thought she was riled before, he could only imagine what emotion his words would evoke. "I'm about to introduce you to my mother, sister, and first-in-command," he informed her, taking note of their expressions.

Isabelle looked vastly amused, a blush now reddening her cheeks. And Gavin wore a grin that reflected his own.

His mother, however, appeared shocked. She'd obviously heard the previous comments, or mayhap 'twas distressed at witnessing the display of this woman grabbing her body parts.

This woman pleased him more than she'd ever know.

"Oh God." The lass sighed. "Just knock me out again, please. I can't do this. Drugs, just give me drugs, and wake me up when this nightmare is over."

Greylen took her statement as defeat. His smile vanished as he gently laid her against the pillows. "Are you in pain?" he asked, brushing the hair away from her face again.

"Go away," she pleaded, swatting her hands in front of her. "Please, just go away."

"Tell me your name, lass," Greylen ordered, ignoring her comment.

"Will you leave me alone if I do?"

"Nay, but I'll remove myself from the bed," Greylen conceded.

She snorted. "How gallant, you'll remove yourself from *my* bed if I tell you my name?"

"Nay, lass," he whispered. "I'll remove myself from *my* bed."

"What?" She shot upright. Obviously a poor decision, if the way she clutched her head was any indication.

Greylen reached out, pulling her against him. "Enough! You will cease this at once." He could not endure to watch her suffer. "Mother, for God's sake, give her something."

Lady Madelyn came forward instantly. "Greylen, you must release her. I must see to her wounds." His mother's tone was softer than usual, sensing his distress at the pain this woman was in.

Reflexively his arms tightened, his chin digging a little deeper into the head he'd snuggly secured beneath it. "You will give her something for her pain, Mother. *Now*," he snapped, acting like a wounded animal protecting his young. He'd not release her until he was sure she would suffer no more. And he knew she felt it, too, this woman, for she burrowed against him.

The action sealed her fate, had it not been done already.

Greylen held her head to his chest and placed the cup his mother had handed him to her lips. She drank it entirely. He knew from experience a bitter taste would linger in her mouth, but she stayed completely still. Knowing the potion would work quickly, he continued to hold her. Short minutes later, he felt her begin to relax. Then she gently tapped his chest with her finger. He leaned in, in answer.

She whispered to him, so only he could hear her, "Greylen?"

His eyes closed, calming now as he heard his name upon her lips and the softness in her tone. Then he bent his head. "Aye," he whispered back, keeping their conversation as private as possible with three pairs of eyes staring at them from the edge of the bed.

"My name...is Gwendolyn."

'Twas a surrender. And somehow, he knew surrender did not come easy to her.

Gwendolyn.

She had a name. And a beautiful one. For the first time he could remember, he was beyond words. He knew that if he could speak, his voice would be filled with the same emotion clouding his vision.

'Twas a long minute before he spoke her name. "Gwendolyn, my mother, Lady Madelyn, must see to your wounds. She's a healer and saw to your care last eve. My sister, Isabelle, is here as well, and, Gavin, my first-in-command. Anna is in the room now, too. She's served our family for years, and will see that you have anything you need."

He gently laid her on the bed and watched as his mother brushed the hair back from her forehead. The effects of his mother's potion obviously were working as Gwendolyn remained still while gentle hands unwound her bandages, cleaned her abrasions, and wrapped them once again.

"Gwendolyn, I must see to the wounds on your eyes," Lady Madelyn explained, sitting next to her on the bed. "You mustn't open them; the skin was rubbed raw. I can assure you, 'twill cause great pain if you do."

Greylen watched Gwendolyn wince as the cool air made contact with the exposed skin, but she remained motionless as his mother applied ointment and covered them once again.

"I'll have Anna bring a tray and perhaps later you'll have a hot bath to ease the aches you surely must feel. Isabelle will return shortly, and I will check on you later."

"Thank you, Lady Madelyn," Gwendolyn said.

"You're quite welcome, dear."

As everyone shuffled from the room, Greylen took his mother's instructions for Gwendolyn as well as giving a few of his own to Gavin. Alone again, he sat in the chair he'd brought from the sitting area by the fireplace last eve and watched her sleep. He amended his thoughts seconds later when she rolled onto her side to face him.

"Greylen?"

"Aye?"

"I need your mother again, or Isabelle. Please."

He knew exactly what she needed but wasn't about to let anyone back in his chamber yet. "Can you manage on your own, if I carry you?"

"Yes."

He cradled her before him and carried her to the bathing chamber, leaving only when he was sure she could in fact stand on her own. He waited just beyond the door and when she stepped through, he took her hands and washed them with a cloth before tossing it in the basin. He wasn't sure if her blush was from having to be carried to the garderobe for its use or the intimacy shared by his doing so.

"This is becoming a habit, Greylen," she grumbled sleepily, but her lips curved slightly in a smile.

"'Tis only the beginning, Gwendolyn."

"You sound pretty sure of yourself."

"I am."

"That's it?" she asked, giving his chest a poke. "I am," she mimicked.

"Aye," he drawled, not expounding. He sensed her exhaustion and wished only to see her rest. He carried her back into his chamber and leaned down to place her beneath the covers.

"No," Gwendolyn pleaded, wrapping her arms around his neck. "I don't want to go back to bed." She must have noted his hesitation, because she hurried on. "Please, can't I rest somewhere else?"

Greylen answered, "Aye," at her request and felt her tighten her arms around his neck as he stepped away from the bed. He carried her to the chair by the fireplace and sat with her there.

"I didn't mean on your lap," she said, poking a finger against his chest.

Greylen wrapped his hand around hers, stopping her actions. "Are you always this obstinate?"

"No," she offered with a sigh, laying her head on his shoulder.

"Thank God," he muttered.

"I'm usually much worse," she muttered back.

Greylen shook his head, cursing under his breath. She was nothing like he'd expected. Yet as different as she was, Gwendolyn was perfect for him. She'd not be intimidated or fearful of his power. She had her own strength and he admired her for it. He still couldn't believe she was here. He'd slept the night with her, and had she not been wounded, he would have made love to her.

He could still feel her body as she pressed herself against him last night. Her hands as they brushed through his hair, and the way she'd tugged upon it demanding that he kiss her. She'd been so responsive when he did, it took all of his control to end it. Her tears still bothered him, though, but he'd question her later. For now, he had other matters he wished to have answers to.

"How did you come to be in the water, Gwendolyn?" He felt her shudder and tightened his hold.

"I lost control of my truck. The storm wiped out the road," she whispered.

The term was foreign to him. He had no idea its meaning. "And your injuries, how did you come by them?"

"The airbags caused the burns on my face and the broken glass from the window caused my lacerations," she explained. "Did you save me last night, Greylen?"

"Aye," he answered in a grave tone. 'Twas something he wished to forget.

"Why didn't you take me to the hospital?"

"You're at Seagrave Castle, Gwendolyn."

"I can't stay here, Greylen. I appreciate everything you've done for me, I really do, but I should go."

"You *will* stay here, Gwendolyn. I'd not allow you anywhere else."

"It's not up to you."

"Aye, Gwendolyn, 'tis. You belong here." She muttered a "ha" in response, as if the words were not to be believed. "Where would you go?" *Had she someone?* he wondered.

"Back to the inn, or to a hospital or clinic, maybe," she whispered.

"Who would care for you?" he demanded, still not satisfied with his need to know and clearly unsettled by a feeling of uncertainty.

"I can take care of myself. I've been doing it for years."

"Is there someone—?" He couldn't finish. The possibility infuriated him now.

"No." She made a laugh-like sound. "But I need to call Sara."

He relaxed his hold as her explanation soothed him. "Who's Sara?"

"A friend. She'll be worried, and I'm sure the couple who run the inn will wonder where I am. Will you dial the numbers for me?" she asked. "We'll have to look up the number of the inn. Well, you'll have to, but I can tell you Sara's."

Greylen considered her words. In truth, he didn't understand them. "You'll give me the information. I'll see to it myself."

Finally, he tucked her beneath the bedcovers and sat beside her as she fell asleep. 'Twas a long while later before he reluctantly left, parchment in hand.

❧ CHAPTER FIVE ❧

Gwen awoke to the soft sound of humming and the gentle touch of delicate fingers. She shifted to her side, smiling as the hand that stroked her forehead brushed back her hair.

She couldn't remember Greylen leaving, but he obviously had. He'd carried her back to bed and written down Sara's phone number and the name of the inn. Then he sat next to her, leaning against the headboard.

He'd reached for her hand, seemingly fascinated by it. Brushing his thumbs over her palm and stroking the back. He measured it against his before entwining their fingers.

And he did it again and again. Brushing. Measuring. Entwining.

She'd felt every touch from the top of her head to the tips of her toes.

She could smell his scent all around her now, and if she were alone, she'd bury her face in the pillow to inhale every molecule. She had a feeling she hadn't dreamed last night. She'd slept in his arms and awoke in them too.

She should be terrified by it. But what terrified her wasn't that she awoke in the bed of a strange man, but that waking with him had seemed so right.

Be careful what you wish for, Gwendolyn.

"Gwendolyn, 'tis Isabelle," Greylen's sister said softly.

Gwen smiled. "Hi, Isabelle."

"Hi." Isabelle laughed, mimicking her greeting. "How do you feel?"

"Are we alone?"

"Aye. Anna just left to fetch another tray. You slept through the first, and Greylen insisted we not wake you."

"Is your brother always so overbearing?"

"'Tis his middle name."

Gwen laughed. "Somehow I'm not surprised."

"Oh, she's awake," Anna called as she came into the room. Gwen felt her place something on the bed and shoo Isabelle away to sit herself. "Now let's see if you've become fevered," she said, placing a hand on her forehead. "Cool to the touch, 'tis very good. Let's get you comfortable and I'll help you eat."

Anna began propping up the pillows, hugging Gwen against her plump chest. The gesture almost brought tears to her eyes. She'd never felt so cared for. "Anna, do you think I might sit in a chair instead?" Gwen asked. "I think I should move around so I don't get stiff."

"Are you sure? You've had quite a fright."

"I'm sure. Isabelle, will you help me?" Gwen asked, reaching out.

Isabelle took Gwen's hands and helped her from the bed. "Please be careful, Gwendolyn. If Greylen knew you were out of bed, he'd have a fit."

"Then we just won't tell him," Gwen said mischievously.

"Oh, Gwendolyn, I'm so glad you're finally here."

Gwen stopped at her words. "What do you mean, I'm finally here?" Met with stone-cold silence, Gwen tried again, "Isabelle, what did you mean?"

"We've been waiting for you," Isabelle said quietly.

Gwen didn't miss the way she spoke. Confident in her statement but whispering as if she wished not to say it. "I don't understand. How could you be waiting for me?"

"I've said too much. Come, let's get you settled."

Isabelle started leading her, but Gwen stopped her. "You've really said nothing. Now, I insist, tell me what you meant," Gwen demanded.

Isabelle remained silent a moment as if not sure where to begin, then it all poured out. "We knew you would come last night, Gwendolyn. Well, that's not exactly true. *I* knew you would come," she said with supreme confidence, "but Greylen suffered greatly throughout the day. He was sure he'd been fooled. Well, perhaps *fooled* isn't the right word." Gwen imagined Isabelle tapping a finger against her cheek. "Mayhap *tricked*—nay, not *tricked*—betrayed. Aye." Gwen felt the motion as Isabelle held up her finger. "Betrayed. He all but killed most of the men, and his looks...*good God*, no one wanted to go near him. And no matter how many times I told Gavin the storm would come—" Isabelle stopped midsentence, making Gwen wonder if Anna's mouth was agape like hers.

"Greylen almost killed his men?" Gwen asked. "What men? *Why?*"

"*The soldiers, Gwendolyn*," Isabelle replied in a chastising tone. "Haven't you been listening? They lined up and he beat each one, 'twas quite humiliating...for the soldiers, that is."

"He beat them?" Were her instincts misplaced? Greylen *beat* men? "How?" she asked.

"With his sword, of course," Isabelle returned in the same tone as if chastising her for not paying attention.

"*What?*"

"Oh my, now I've upset you. Please, Gwendolyn, we must sit down. You seem ready to collapse." Isabelle rushed through the words as if she wanted to move on.

"Isabelle!" Lady Madelyn came into the room obviously having overheard most of the conversation.

Gwen heard the censure in Lady Madelyn's voice and immediately took Isabelle's hand. For some reason she felt the need to protect her. Gwen knew Isabelle hadn't meant to upset her. Her honesty and need to please was obvious, endearing even. "Lady Madelyn, please don't be upset with Isabelle. She didn't do anything wrong."

Gwen couldn't see Lady Madelyn's expression soften, but she felt it in the words she spoke. "Gwendolyn, I wish only for your good health and welfare. That you come to Isabelle's defense so quickly, well, it pleases me dearly. Especially with the tension being so thick these past few days, 'tis good to see all is, at last, as it should be." Lady Madelyn held Gwen's hands, leading her in front of a roaring fireplace and then guiding her to sit. She wondered if it was the same chair she sat in with Greylen last night.

Lady Madelyn saw to her wounds while continuing where she left off. "We've waited so long for the events of last night to unfold, Gwendolyn. I've known for years of the prophecy, and I believed with all my heart in its words. I'd been unsure of Greylen's acceptance when I decided to tell him of its existence." She paused as if remembering. "But I made the right decision. If only I'd known how long he'd silently suffered. He'd actually considered himself mad."

Gwen was a little, or maybe a lot, lost with what Lady Madelyn was saying. Warmed by the fire, feeling cared for as Lady Madelyn continued to fuss over her, and of course still affected by painkillers, Gwen continued to listen in silence as Lady Madelyn went on. "I chided myself for my skepticism when I awoke yesterday. The day was as beautiful as a day could be, and Greylen's anger that he'd been a fool was more than painful to watch. Isabelle was the only one who seemed sure that the storm would come.

"Forgive my tone, Isabelle," Lady Madelyn offered in apology. "Gwendolyn, I'll check on you later. I did not realize you hadn't eaten yet. Perhaps after you've rested again, we'll call for a bath."

Gwen smiled, grateful that Lady Madelyn's tone had changed. "Thank you, Lady Madelyn. I would love a bath, but I think I've rested enough."

"Anna will see that you drink a tea infusion. 'Twill tire you, and I insist you rest after your meal."

"May I ask you a question, Lady Madelyn?"

"Of course."

"Greylen said you were a healer. Are doctors in the Highlands referred to as healers?"

"Nay, we have doctors. But as long as you're in my care, I'd not let them near you."

"Is that why Greylen didn't take me to the hospital?" she asked. "Because you don't trust the physicians here?"

"I can assure you, you've received the very best care."

Gwen quickly agreed and thanked her as well. She could tell all of her abrasions were perfectly anointed and wrapped, and though somewhat numb from the medication she'd been given earlier, she knew instinctively she had stitches that were even and tight with no signs of swelling or drainage.

True to Lady Madelyn's words, Gwen was asleep a short time later.

For the second time in less than a day, Greylen tread upon unsure waters. Quite simply, the woman disarmed him. One minute she's threatening to kick his backside, the next she's insulting herself—*with an audience*. She'd turned him upside down in a matter of hours. Especially her comments regarding her need to contact "Sara" and "the inn."

His reluctance to leave her surprised him as well. He, in fact, stayed longer than necessary, content merely to hold her hand. A hand he'd spent at least an hour embracing. 'Twas only when Anna came into his chamber that he'd finally stepped from the bed.

Hoping for a distraction, a much-needed distraction, he went to check on Duncan. He'd been training a new group of soldiers who proved challenging. Their first charge with the boys who came to foster was to unlearn them of the skills they already possessed. The task usually took no more than a fortnight and allowed each a new perspective in applying their technique. Greylen and his men explained repeatedly that if they believed in their own abilities, their proficiencies would naturally follow. This balance enabled his soldiers to become the best fighters in the Highlands.

As Greylen approached the training field, he noticed Duncan's frustration and immediately stepped into the fray. The boys about bowed to him. 'Twas an honor to train with him personally and one not granted by all lairds. Greylen, however, would have it no other way. It gave him pride to watch his boys grow into their skills and manhood.

Today, however, his attention was elsewhere. He took a blow from a sword, splitting the skin of his arm. The boy who dealt the injury instantly dropped to his knees, fear evident on his face. Greylen pulled the boy up and placed a firm hand on his shoulder, demanding that he meet his stare. "A lesson, Michael. Never lose your mental stand in a match—on our fields or in battle. Your life depends upon it." Greylen turned to Duncan and dismissed himself. 'Twas time to seek his mother's needle. She'd not be pleased.

After a pointed look from Lady Madelyn and a regal sweep of her hand, Greylen sat in the chair his mother gestured to. She finished her work quickly and never once mentioned the reason to blame for the wound. "Good luck to you with the rest of your day, son," she'd said.

"I'll be sure to keep my instruments handy should you need my services again." Greylen offered a wry smile and thanks as well, then went to his study.

He'd been consumed the past days, and now needed to address the correspondences atop his desk. Most were letters updating occurrences among neighboring clans. They would become the agenda to be discussed at the upcoming council meeting.

The council, comprised of twelve lairds, convened four times yearly. After years of feuding during his father's reign, Greylen and his peers did their best to live peacefully. Their only fighting now proved to be little more than minor skirmishes or warring at the behest of their sovereign.

Greylen served his king for fifteen years and helped to bring an end to the internal strife which plagued their homeland. Now only a few caused troubles—those spiteful or hungry for power.

One clan in particular was the MacFale. 'Twasn't the father who made trouble but his son Malcolm. Their lands bordered to the south and any disturbances of late, Greylen knew Malcolm had caused. Though he'd not seen him in years, Malcolm's jealousy of Greylen's continued success fueled his hatred.

Greylen began listing the grievances to be addressed but looked to the door when he sensed Gavin's approach. Greylen bid him entrance and waved to one of the chairs in front of his desk. He tossed him the parchment he'd had in his pocket and gauged his reaction.

Gavin studied it, then looked back in question. "What is it?"

"Numbers Gwendolyn wished for me...*to call.* The first is her friend, Sara. The latter, the name of the inn where she was staying."

Gavin shook his head. "I've no idea her meaning, Greylen, nor does this name sound familiar."

"Nor do I." He took the parchment back, staring at the strange sequence of numbers. "She...damn it, Gavin." Greylen stood and walked to the window behind his desk, staring past the garden. "The things she's said...the way she speaks."

"Explain, we'll sort it through."

Greylen gave a wry laugh before turning. "Aye, thank you, *Mother.*"

"Have you a better idea?"

"Nay." Greylen sat again and repeated Gwendolyn's account of what happened to Gavin. The truck accident, the explosion of airbags, and windows with jagged glass. He spoke of her English dialect. Though easy enough to understand, 'twas far different from the one he'd heard. More to the point, the way that she spoke was strange. With authority. Forthright, to be exact.

"And her forthright manner bothers you?" Gavin asked.

"Of course not," Greylen quipped. "I've endured your impertinence for years." And he had. Fifteen years to be exact. They'd fought side by side in service to their king. And shortly after, Gavin gave him his allegiance. They'd forged an unwavering bond over the passing years. Close as true brothers could be, perhaps more so, as they chose their alliance. They antagonized each other continually with caustic remarks and barely veiled insults. But, in truth, one would not be the same without the other. "Nay, 'tis not a bother," Greylen confessed again. "But, what of the other things?"

"What of them?" Gavin offered in a dismissive tone. "The prophecy spoke of—"

"Another time. I know, Gavin." Greylen rubbed his hands through his hair. "'Twould account for her strange clothing, the accident she spoke of, her dialect and manner as well. I…" He cursed instead of continuing.

"I've other news, Greylen," Gavin said as Greylen walked back to the window. Greylen raised a brow in wait, and Gavin continued, "Our southern border was breached before dawn. Five cattle were slaughtered."

Greylen shook his head. Just what he needed right now. *Damn.*

Resigned 'twould be night before he could return, he gave Gavin his orders. "Kevin and Hugh will remain. If Gwendolyn's somehow able to move about, they're to shadow her."

"They assume their posts outside your chamber," Gavin informed him.

"Then we ride. I wish to see the carnage myself."

"Your plans…for Lady Gwendolyn?" Gavin asked.

"Nothing's changed, Gavin. I'll not wait."

Greylen considered the significance of the question as he watched his first-in-command leave. He rubbed his hands through his hair, the scene playing in his mind.

The one in which he informed Gwendolyn of the role she would assume.

❧ CHAPTER SIX ❧

Instead of the courtyard, Greylen found himself within his chamber. 'Twas the last place he should be at the moment, yet there he was. Loath to admit it, he was anxious to see Gwendolyn. And, oddly, as soon as he laid his eyes upon her, the tightness within his chest subsided. She seemed to be resting fitfully beneath the covers while Isabelle sat beside her.

"Leave us," Greylen commanded, standing at the bedside.

Gwendolyn rolled over but waited until the door shut before she spoke. "You sound angry, Greylen."

"I thought you to be asleep."

"Just resting. Is something wrong?" she asked, sitting up. "Or when you said *leave us*," she mimicked in a deep voice, "was I supposed to go too?"

"How do you feel?" he asked, disregarding her comment.

"Your mother said the bandages could come off tomorrow."

"I'm aware of your progress, Gwendolyn. I asked how you felt." He said it more harshly than he intended, angered with himself for what could only be a loss of discipline on his part.

"Your mother keeps plying me with liquid painkillers," she said, gifting him her first true smile. "You obviously have an awesome and very lenient pharmacy. And please, call me Gwen."

"Gwen, I..." Disarmed by her smile, he truly had difficulty continuing.

"Are you going to take me back, Greylen?"

He waited a moment to answer. "Gwendolyn, you'll not be going back." As he looked upon her upturned face, he wondered how she could even think such a thing. There were of course still many unknowns; however, relinquishing her was not one of them. Based on his physical reaction, and attraction to her, as well as this odd internal awareness that Gwendolyn was in fact the "she" of the prophecy, the thought of "taking her back," as she just stated, was preposterous.

"Was there a problem at the inn?" she asked, a slight puzzle to her lips. "Did they let my room go? I could have sworn I paid for two more nights." She said the last almost as an aside, then turned her head from left to right as if considering something. "They have my credit card on file, too, Greylen."

"I've not spoken with them, Gwendolyn."

"You didn't call?" The reprimand in her voice was unmistakable. She reached for his hand. "But you said you'd take care of it." Her slender fingers worried over his. "What about, Sara? She'll be concerned if I don't check in."

He knelt in front of her, covering her hands with his own, and he told her quite honestly, "I've no means to call, Gwendolyn."

"You don't have a phone?" she asked, sounding surprised.

Her brow furrowed above the bandages and he wished to reach out and smooth it, but instead, continued to rub her hand. "Nay, Gwendolyn. I have not a phone."

"Not even a cell phone?"

Truly grateful she offered questions that he could seemingly answer, he repeated her words, "Not even."

"Greylen, it's the twenty-first century. *Everyone has a cell phone.*"

'Twas a statement he would remember for the rest of his years and a life of training that kept him perfectly still. While shock and curses ran through his mind at what she'd just revealed, moments later, he was smiling. Of the many reactions one might have to such a statement, what he felt most was relief. Gwendolyn was his. This beautiful creature he'd plucked from the waters was in fact his. "Gwen..." *Gwen what? Holy mother of God—glad tidings aside—what?*

"Did you lose power? Did the storm wipe out the lines or something?" she asked before he could continue.

Bless the woman for making it so easy. "Or *something* would suit," Greylen implied.

"Well, I guess I'm stuck here."

He was grinning as she shrugged while making that last declaration. "Aye, Gwendolyn," he drawled. "I guess you are."

'Twas dusk by the time Greylen and his men approached the sight of the attack. Greylen listened to the report of the men who awaited their arrival as he inspected the heinous display.

He knew MacFale was to blame and cursed him for taking his hostility out on helpless animals. Without a word, he grabbed a shovel. His men silently followed his lead. Having to ensure the carcasses wouldn't contaminate the surface, it took two hours before the trenches were deep enough. By the time the task was finished, they were covered with dirt and blood.

New patrols relieved the men who rode the perimeter throughout the afternoon. They would remain till dawn when the guard would be turned over again. Confident his men would hold off another attack and assured by Gavin that all of their patrols had been doubled, they rode back to the keep.

Consumed by thoughts of Gwen, the time went quickly. Her words nearly rang in his head, *twenty-first century*. Good God, 'twas astounding. Gavin, too, had been shocked when Greylen told him and said little in response. In truth, what could they say?

Thankfully, Gwen had worked everything out herself, justifying the things he couldn't explain with assumptions. He was happy to go along. He'd not had to lie, though he'd have done so easily.

He was relieved too. No man waited for her, and she spoke nothing of her family.

He would be her family now.

'Twould be done on the morrow.

Gwen awoke sometime in the afternoon, knowing once again that Greylen had left. He was turning out to be a serious distraction, especially her reaction to him. She meant to ask him about the strange things Isabelle and his mother had spoken of earlier. What they'd said about them waiting for her and knowing that she'd come. It didn't make sense, and although her head was truly fuzzy, there was something really odd about it all. She just couldn't put her finger on it. And just when it was on the tip of her tongue to say something, Greylen sat next to her on the bed and asked her if she needed anything.

What she needed was some distance from the man. Well, not really. She'd been thrilled when he told her the storm had knocked out their power and phone lines. She didn't want to leave. She couldn't explain it, but being near him seemed to be the only thing she did want.

She knew it was ridiculous, but, what the hell. If she had to get stranded somewhere, why not here? She obviously wasn't in any danger. Greylen had saved her last night. He'd taken her back to his home to recuperate, and his family was taking care of her. It couldn't be clearer, they were only doing what was appropriate under the circumstances.

Of course, it didn't explain why she was in his room. Shouldn't she be sleeping somewhere else? If they didn't have an extra room, shouldn't she be in Isabelle's bedroom instead?

And what about last night? She was almost certain she'd slept with him. Worse, she had a feeling her dream was no dream. She'd remember that kiss for the rest of her life. My God the man had a powerful mouth and he definitely knew how to kiss. She'd never kissed like that. Well, she'd kissed like that but…she'd never felt consumed by a kiss. She'd never been held like that either. He must think her ten kinds of a hussy, but she hadn't been able to help herself.

It felt so right and his body…his body was so…well, the man was built. He was so large he engulfed her, and his muscles were so defined they were amazing. When she ran her hands along his back, his skin was so hot she felt like she was being seared. And she wanted to feel his hair again too. It was thick and soft, longer than it should be. But she liked it on him.

Oh my God, what in the hell was she thinking? She hadn't even seen him yet.

If she had the chance, though, she knew she'd do it again. Somehow, deep down she knew Greylen was what she'd been searching for.

The rest of her day was spent in bed. Hiding blushes when she thought about that kiss and enjoying her recuperation more than she ever imagined. Anna sat by the fireplace while Isabelle sat next to her reading. When Gwen wasn't sleeping, Isabelle chatted endlessly.

Greylen's sister was delightful. She had a dry sense of humor and seemed quite mature for someone who'd just turned eighteen.

Before supper Gwen had a bath in front of the fireplace. Why there, she couldn't be sure, but it helped immensely. Anna rubbed the aches from her body, using a soap that smelled of wildflowers. And Isabelle leaned against the rim and brushed her hair, then tied it in a ribbon. Lady Madelyn returned and removed her bandages, commenting on how pleased she was with the progress of her wounds.

Since she wasn't used to being cared for by others, she sat quietly wrapped in a towel in front of the fire. Lady Madelyn and Isabelle put ointment and gauze on all of her cuts while Anna instructed the servants to remove the tub and bring up a tray for dinner. But when she heard Anna ask Isabelle to fetch another bedgown, Gwen finally spoke up. "Anna, is there something else I might wear? I'm not really comfortable in long nightgowns."

There was an extremely long pause and Gwen thought she'd be refused. Thankfully, Lady Madelyn saved her. "I see no harm," she finally said. "No one's about but us, and you might rest easier."

Relieved, Gwen thanked her and asked for a shirt to sleep in instead.

They laughed.

"Gwendolyn, we possess no shirts ourselves but if you wish, you may use one of Greylen's," Lady Madelyn offered.

Gwen couldn't resist. "That would be great, thank you."

Anna replaced her towel with a very large shirt. Isabelle laughed the second it was on and continued to do so as she rolled up the sleeves. Gwen didn't care how big it was. It was made of the softest linen she'd ever touched. And it was Greylen's.

"Is there somewhere else I should be sleeping?" Gwen asked, wishing at once that she'd kept her big mouth shut. She didn't want to leave Greylen's room. But staying meant that she would sleep with him again, like she did last night. And everyone in this room knew it.

Lady Madelyn spoke those words again. The ones she'd always dreamed of hearing. The same Greylen had spoken earlier. "This is where you belong, Gwendolyn. My son would have it no other way."

Gwen didn't ask Lady Madelyn to explain, and honestly, she didn't want her to. She had dinner with Isabelle by the fire while Anna fussed about the room. And later, when Anna pleaded with her to rest in bed, Gwen stood her ground. She was going to sit by the fire until Greylen returned.

Then she would ask him about the things that had bothered her all day.

❧ CHAPTER SEVEN ❧

He was going to hell.

Over a blasted promise.

He'd burn for eternity.

And it'd be worth each infernal second.

Damn but the woman caused trouble. Tempted him to heights so unfathomable, he cared not of the consequence. He cursed himself a fool—a thousand times. Then added another.

Had she any idea? Had she a care?

Nay!

Had she, he'd not be in his current predicament—which at the moment was dire, and entirely Gwendolyn's fault. He cursed again, aloud this time, a litany in seven languages. His muscles were so taut now, he feared his skin would split. His eyes narrowed as she began to stir. He scowled.

She had the nerve to stretch.

His erection, now painful, throbbed as he watched her. She might as well deliver him to hell's gates herself.

"Greylen?" Gwendolyn whispered.

"Aye." It came out as a growl as his hands fisted at his sides.

"Bad day?" she asked.

"Bad day? *Bad day, Gwendolyn?* Have you any idea what you're doing to me?" he shouted.

"Me?" she shouted back, sitting up straighter. "What in the hell are you talking about?"

"I made a promise," he yelled again.

"I take it promises make you grumpy?"

"Nay," he argued, kneeling before her. "Lasses with flawless skin and honey-colored hair, wearing *nothing* but my shirt, make me grumpy."

"All of them? Or just me?"

"Just you, Gwen," he whispered, lowering his head to her knees. "I swear, just you." He sensed her smile and felt her relax as she placed her hands on his head and tangled her fingers in his hair. 'Twas a reflexive gesture, yet intimate as well. It felt amazing.

"Speaking of swearing, I didn't get the fifth one. What was it?" she asked.

Greylen lifted his head, sorry that he had when her hands fell away. "Persian," he answered. "Know you the others?" he asked curiously.

"As a matter of fact, yes," she all but boasted. "Do you know only the colorful words, or are you more versed?"

"I speak each fluently," he bit out, unable to return her playful tone. 'Twas the absence of her touch aggravating him so.

"Are you going to keep growling at me? Or are you going to tell me what's bothering you?" she asked as she reached out to him. Her hands landed on his shoulders and her fingers at once started kneading into his muscles. "God you're wound tight—what happened?"

"I can do no more than growl at present." Though, he was thankful for her touch once again. "And as to what happened? *You* happened. And you *happened* to be wounded. The reason for my current mood."

Her hands stopped. "You're angry that I'm wounded?"

Greylen moved his shoulders until she began massaging again. "I'm angry your eyes are covered," he grumbled. "Otherwise, I'd not have given Lady Madelyn my word I'd leave your bandages till the morn."

"And the significance of my bandages," she asked him, digging deeper with her fingers, "if you don't mind?"

"The significance is simple, Gwendolyn. I've every intention of making you mine." His hands encircled her wrists and moved them to her shoulders. "I've every intention of making love to you till you're reduced to nothing more than whimpers." He leaned forward, placed his lips against her ear, and whispered in a dark promising drawl, "Till I've had you so many times, you'll be able to do little more than lift a finger...if that." He paused before leaning back. "But I'll not have you with your eyes covered. So keep your hands removed from my person before I lose what little control I have left," he snapped.

A blush stole across her face, at least up to where the bandages covered her eyes. "Hmm, I see your problem." She burst out laughing, hiding her embarrassment in her hands.

"Oh no, you shall suffer as well," Greylen warned, though he, too, smiled now. "And if you saw my problem, you'd take pity on me, not enflame me."

"Excuse me for being direct, but well, with your last sentiments and all, I think we've moved past the formalities. My intention was to wait by the fire," she explained. "So we would have a chance to talk when you returned. I didn't mean to upset you by wearing your shirt."

"I'm not upset you're wearing my shirt. I'm upset I can't rip the damn thing off."

"And I thank you for that. Very much at the moment, I might add."

"Because you'd not like me to touch you…or because you're not wearing anything beneath?"

"I am not going to answer that," she said, holding up her hand in emphasis.

Greylen took her hand and kissed her palm. Then using his teeth, he grazed her wrist. "I've ways to make you talk, love," he whispered suggestively before carefully scooping her in his arms. He groaned again. She was light as a feather and her body seemed even more slender against his.

"I think I have it all figured out, Greylen," Gwen said as she pressed her face to his chest. "I'm really in the hospital, on an IV drip, and you're just a hallucination, a magnificent one, of course." Greylen offered a quick "thank you, love" at the compliment and she continued, "And in this fantastical hallucination of mine…well, I really didn't think I would've come up with it myself, but I guess you've decided to make me your love slave. Is that about right?"

Greylen grinned. "I'd not thought of it, and the idea has merit. But just so you know, I'd have wed you," he offered with a squeeze. "Father Michael was to come at dawn."

"See, now I know it's true. I really am in the hospital. I never imagined unconsciousness would be like this," she said, waving her hand about the room. "You must be the doctor who's caring for me, and I guess you're taking me off life support in the morning."

Greylen froze in place. Whatever Gwen was working out in her mind, he'd not let her assume she was somewhere else and under someone else's care. And he sure as hell wouldn't let her think what he thought she implied. "Explain yourself, Gwendolyn."

"He's coming to give me my last rites. I'm going to die tomorrow. That's why the priest is coming. I hope I remember you, Greylen. I hope I can find you next time… before it's too late."

"Ah, Gwendolyn, I swear to you—you're not going to die in the morning. And Father Michael is coming to see us wed, love. Not to give you last rites." He made the assurance as he placed her back on the bed and tucked her beneath the covers.

"Oh my God." Gwen started laughing hysterically. "I'm really dying."

"I just told you, you're *not* dying." At his words, she became very quiet. Her fingers worked furiously at the bedcovers. Good God, what was going on in that mind of hers now?

"Greylen, can I ask you something?"

"Aye," he answered, wondering what foolishness she'd come up with.

"Last night, when I was dreaming…it was you, wasn't it? I mean, I know I'm dreaming, but in my dream, the one I'm in now, you kissed me. You really kissed me, didn't you?"

"Aye, Gwen, I kissed you."

"Will you do it again…please?"

She was doing it again. Tempting him back to the gates of hell. Thank God she was beneath the covers. He cursed as she threw them aside…and again as she crawled over to him. He cursed the very same litany as before. Didn't she know he could see down her shirt? She found her way to his lap…and straddled him!

Open the gates, he was a dead man.

Her hands tangled in his hair and she whispered, "I'm probably going to hell for this, Greylen, but right now, hell's looking pretty frigging good."

Greylen's arms snaked behind her, tightening until she was pressed fully against him, and his hand gripped her head. "It appears to be frigging Eden, Gwen," he agreed, using her word.

Then he kissed her.

No niceties this night. No slow explorations. He fed off of her like she were his last morsel. Holding her as if she were his lifeline in the world. And he could not get enough. No matter how he tried, it simply was not enough.

He tugged Gwen's chin, deepening their kiss when she opened for him. His tongue swept inside, and he swallowed the sound she made, returning it with a growl as she joined him. Good God, she kissed him back with such abandon, pressed so hard to his body, he felt her every measure. He continued his feeding, his need of her such that he'd never experienced. Her legs tightened around his waist as her hands moved through his hair, urging him deeper. Then he was standing, with Gwen in his arms and her long, bare legs wrapped tightly around his waist. She seemed not to notice as he laid her upon the mattress, never breaking their kiss. He lay completely atop her, supporting his weight with his arms, feeling her entire body beneath his.

'Twas as close to heaven as he'd ever been. And he was going to hell when he was done.

Greylen felt Gwen's hands move across his back, pressing him closer. Her hips moved against him and he growled in response. He tried not to move with her, but 'twas beyond his control. He was lost. Lost in an intense haze as he settled between her thighs. Then they were moving together. A slow, torturous grind he could not stop. His hand ran down the length of her body, and as he brushed past her waist, 'twas only bare skin that he felt… bare skin from her hip down to her foot.

He was going to take her.

His hand wrapped around the underside of her thigh. He growled as his fingertips glanced warm, moist heat. He tugged on her lips with his teeth…scraping past her chin…her long, delicate neck.

His face brushed the swell of her breast through the material of the shirt. Then he covered her with his mouth.

She gasped, her body tensing as she tangled her hands in his hair. His teeth closed over her nipple, gently tugging... then his mouth covered her again. Closing with infinite slowness as teeth scraped—

"Oh God...Greylen...take them off. Please, help me take them off."

Greylen lifted his head. Gwen was reaching for the bindings covering her eyes. Something was amiss.

"Help me, damn it," she snapped.

Sanity was like a full-frontal blow when he wished to be witless. But he said a silent prayer that Gwen had brought him to his senses. He reached for her hands and wrapped them behind her back. Then he could do little more than rest his head on her chest.

"What are you doing?"

"Have a care, Gwen. I need a moment."

"You need a moment? Take off the damn bandages. *Now*," she demanded, trying to break free.

"Nay." He sighed. He leaned back, taking Gwen with him. She sat on her knees, and he wrapped his legs around her, adjusting the shirt to cover her from his view.

"*Nay*," she mimicked in a shout, poking a finger at his chest. "I'm going to die in the morning and you're depriving me of my *last wish*?" She didn't wait for a reply and reached for the edge of the binding.

Greylen cursed again and covered her hands. "You are not going to die." Good God, the woman had a thick skull. "And I've already said, you'll not remove them. I promised."

Gwen snatched her hands back, then pushed against his chest with both of them. "Break it."

"I never break my word, Gwen," Greylen replied.

"Oh my God...you don't want me." As Gwen whispered those words, she realized she'd never been more humiliated in her life. Too many firsts and his rejection was the worst of them. Tears filled her eyes and she wanted nothing more than to leave. Dream or not, she was out of there. She began scooting backward, feeling for the edge of the bed with her feet.

"Where are you going?" Greylen asked in a chiding tone.

"Don't touch me. I'm leaving."

"You'll go nowhere."

"This is my dream. I can do whatever the hell I want," she shouted as she slid from the bed and moved along the side. Truthfully, she had no idea where she was going, but she couldn't stay any longer. And she would not cry in front of him. She would not. But then his hands were on her.

"Don't push me away, Gwendolyn—ever." His warning came with a squeeze to her shoulders.

"In case you've forgotten, you're the one who stopped, Greylen. Excuse me for feeling rejected, but *I was*."

He pulled her closer. "I did not reject you. How could you even think such a thing?"

"How—*how?*" She pushed him away again. "If you didn't notice, we were moving from appetizers to the main course, you giant idiot," she snapped. "But you obviously don't want me."

He grabbed her again, his voice angered. "I want you so much 'tis killing me." He brought her closer to his body. "For more years than I care to remember, I've wanted nothing more, Gwendolyn. But when I take you, I'll have the pleasure of looking in your eyes. Which leads us back to my promise. I gave my word, Gwen. Once given, 'tis a solemn vow—I will not break it. Understand."

Oh this was priceless. The man who rejected her, humiliated her, and made her feel like a fool, wanted her to accept *his* word. She wished she could stare him down. Instead, she made a sweeping motion with her hands and broke his hold.

"Listen, *Greylen, whatever your name is.* I don't give a rat's ass about your word. And I sure as hell don't have to stand here taking your sanctimonious bullshit. The message was loud and clear, buddy, *now hear mine.*" She paused, feeling for his chest. Finding her mark, she used her finger and nailed his center with it every few words. "Dream or not, I would've made love to you tonight. Do you know why? Don't answer that," she hissed in his face. "It was rhetorical." She qualified it all the same. "You made me feel things tonight, things I've only dreamed about—*with you,* I might add. And, maybe, before I died, I wanted to believe that I did belong somewhere." Tears of frustration ran down her cheeks now, but she had to finish. She, unlike some, did not run away. "I'd have taken it, Greylen. I'd have unabashedly reveled in those feelings," she confessed, mortified that her words caught on a sob before she could continue, "even for one night."

Greylen didn't say a word, in fact, it seemed the man was utterly still. Well, bully for you. But then he grabbed her and she must have been only inches from his face. "First, that move you used to disarm me was brilliant. 'Tis pride which fills me that you used it." He must've been done complimenting her, because he squeezed her and brought her even closer. "Now let me make myself clear... *Gwendolyn, whatever your name is*. I don't give a *rat's ass*, as you've said, what you believed before, and I sure as hell didn't feed you sanctimonious bullshit. And by the way, who in the hell taught you to speak such filth?" he yelled. "Nay, don't answer that," he warned her when she opened her mouth. "*'Twas rhetorical.*" She could only imagine his great satisfaction in the fact she remained silent. "Mouth *and* temper aside, I'll have you, Gwendolyn, I swear I will," he hissed. "And when I swear to anything, you'd better believe I make good on it. Do you understand?" He seemed to wait for her to respond, and when she didn't, he gave her a squeeze. "Answer, Gwendolyn. *Now.*" Even with bandages covering her eyes, she knew they were in the midst of a staring match.

And it was vicious.

"Let me tell you something else, since you're being so very receptive, *Gwen-do-lyn*. This is no dream," he shouted. "At dawn your bandages will be removed, and I will see your eyes for the first time. And when I've had my fill, and *only* when I've had my fill, we will say our vows. You will be wed to me. You will carry my name, you will bear my children, and I swear to you and God above, you will live here with me—*FOREVER*."

Her hair blew back from his tirade. *Gimme a break, Mr. I'm Your Ruler.* Like she was scared, *ha.* She wasn't scared at all. In fact, now she knew the truth. She crossed her arms over her chest and remained silent. With deliberate nerve, she stuck her chin out, purposely instigating him. Well it was her dream, wasn't it?

"You've one more chance to answer me, lass. And trust me, you'll not want to push me that far."

Gwen heard the change in his voice. It was the most chilling tone she'd ever heard. She meant to placate him, but she got carried away again. "Well, *Greylen*, you've only proved one thing, so your little tirade doesn't scare me in the least. This is a dream, so pinch me, you big oaf. Better yet—*bite me.*"

Gwen couldn't see the look on his face, obviously, but she sensed something had changed. Like all the air in the room had been sucked away and all that was left was this malevolent energy, which unfortunately, she had helped to create. She was about to make a run for it when Greylen pulled her against him with such force, he took her breath away. He kissed her—and took her challenge. He bit her.

"I taste blood. *Oh my God, I taste blood*," Gwen yelled, hitting his chest. "Greylen, this isn't a dream." For a moment, she was so excited she started jumping around on the bed. That dance that you do when you just can't help yourself.

"I told you 'tis not. *Damn it, Gwendolyn*, cease your antics—I just bit you," he snapped. "I lost control. I've never done so before, yet you're acting as though 'tis a cause for celebration." He lifted her chin as if inspecting the damage. Her lips, already swollen from earlier kisses, were more so now, and as he gently pulled upon her bottom lip, he obviously saw blood. "Sweet Jesus, forgive me," he pleaded.

What's a little love bite? Besides she knew she'd purposely provoked him. And truthfully, he hadn't hurt her. The man just had to touch her and all thinking went out the door. Which led to another mortifying thought. She was *not* dreaming. Which meant...she'd consciously behaved like a...like a...*what?* Cat in heat, woman on the edge, slut? Oh my God, she was a slut. Gwendolyn Reynolds was a bona fide slut. Could you be a slut without having sex? Hmm...oh God, you could.

Greylen grabbed her. "Whatever you're thinking, *cease*. Your mind works in the strangest ways."

"I...I acted shamelessly, Greylen. I'm not like this, I'm really not." In her desperation to make him believe her, she ran her fingers through the hair on the side of his head. "It's the drugs, and I...I thought I was dreaming." She stopped, as if another thought might be more disturbing. "Why did you say those things to me, Greylen?" she asked in a strangled whisper.

"You've not forgiven me, Gwen. I can hardly offer an explanation—"

"Big deal, so you bit me." She shrugged. "You didn't hurt me, Greylen." Then she whispered with a grin,

"Don't tell anyone, but I kind of like the way you throw me around."

"Gwendolyn," he whispered against her forehead. "If I live to be a thousand, I'll never be able to repay the liberty you just bestowed upon me. Nor will I ever fathom the way your mind works," he muttered.

"Hey." She pinched him. "That's not nice."

She could sense his smile as he sat on the edge of the bed and lifted her on his lap. "My pardon, once more, fair lady."

Gwen sat quietly for a moment. The way he spoke to her—it was like she was his lady and he, her knight. She sighed, then asked again the question he hadn't answered. "Why did you say those things to me?"

"I've said a lot tonight. Which things do you refer to?"

"You know, those *things*—about us." She couldn't repeat them herself, and maybe she hadn't heard him correctly. Maybe she had imagined it all, because he said nothing and instead, began to kiss her, gently brushing his lips against hers. She pulled away. "Dreaming or drugs? Was it all in my head?"

"Nay, love." He nudged her lips again. "I said your bandages would be removed in the morn." He nuzzled her again as if he enjoyed the feel of her skin against his own. "I said we'll be wed." Another kiss. "I said you're going to carry my name and have my children." Kiss. "And I said you'll remain here"—kiss—"with me"—kiss—"forever."

Gwen pushed away as he tried to kiss her again. She couldn't think when he touched her like that. Nuzzling was as good as kissing, especially the way he rubbed his nose and lips against her. "Why, Greylen? You don't even know me."

"'Tis no simple answer, Gwen."

"Tell me, please."

Greylen let out a long sigh, then he shifted his body and took her with him as he settled back. "There was a prophecy, an enchantment, I've been aware of for years. Its writings told of two souls who'd been born apart." He paused as if trying to gauge her reaction, but she was busy tracing circles upon his chest while she listened. Before he could continue, she asked a question.

"Like, you were born in Scotland, and I was born in the States?"

"Mayhap," he offered. "The prophecy foretold these souls would find each other one day. And once they touched, they'd be joined forever, soothing the male's lonely heart—"

"Do you have a lonely heart?"

"Nay, love." He placed his hand over hers. "No more."

She smiled. "I'm sorry. Will you finish now?"

Greylen continued as Gwen went back to tracing upon his chest. "'Twas written the prophecy's culmination would occur during the midst of a terrible storm—a storm on the eve of their shared birthdays."

"Greylen," Gwen whispered.

"Aye, Gwendolyn?"

"Was yesterday your birthday?"

"Aye, and yours as well."

Gwen couldn't answer, her throat had closed and her eyes filled with tears again. Could what he said possibly be true? *A prophecy? About them?*

"Gwendolyn?" She'd stopped tracing, and he obviously could tell she was troubled.

"Is this some sort of trick you're playing on me? I'm still on drugs, you know."

"I'd not trick you...ever."

"You really think this prophecy was about us?"

"I know it to be."

"And you're going to marry me, just because you found me in the storm and we have the same birthday?"

"I'm going to wed you so our children have the right of legitimacy."

"But what if we don't have children?"

"Since I plan to have you first of the morrow—repeatedly—and every morrow after, 'tis a very safe assumption."

"But what if you don't like me?" Gwen argued. "What if you think I'm hideous once you see my entire face?"

Greylen laughed. "You're beautiful, and I do like you."

"What about..." Gwen bit her bottom lip before she continued. "About...well, Sara seems to think I have a slight problem with my temper," she said in a rush.

"Slight? *Slight?*" he repeated. "Love, 'tis no *slight* problem you have. Your affliction's quite severe."

"It's not that bad," she muttered defensively.

"Not bad?" He laughed. "You've the temper of a wild boar...stuck in a mud trap...starved for days...about to die."

By the time he finished, she was laughing so hard, her face was buried in her hands.

"Tell me your family name, Gwen?" he asked when they became quiet again.

"Reynolds," she supplied quickly. Gwen waited for Greylen to say something. He didn't. Finally, she reached out to him. "Are we in the twilight zone again, Greylen? Greylen?"

"'Tis a good name, Gwen. On the morrow, however 'twill be no more. Father Michael will join us. And you will truly be mine."

"Greylen?"

"Aye, Gwen."

"Do you promise?" She hadn't meant it to come out as a plea. And regretted the words the moment she'd breathed them.

"Ah, Gwen." He sighed, gathering her closer. "I solemnly promise to wed you on the morrow. And I vow to make you so completely mine you'll not lose your glow for days. And I never break my word."

Gwen felt a slow, lazy smile cross her lips, she knew exactly what he implied. She laid her head against his chest and ran her fingers down his arm when she felt something wet around his biceps.

"Greylen, what's this?" she asked.

"I suffered a wound."

"You suffered a wound?" she repeated. "What in the hell does that mean?"

She sensed him smiling at her words.

"I don't stutter, love, nor do I speak in riddles. And good God your mouth's atrocious."

"*Whatever*, Greylen," Gwen said dismissively. "I swear the drugs your mother's been giving me have affected my judgment."

"Aye, Lady Madelyn can be quite high-handed where her potions are concerned," he quickly agreed. Then as if another thought crossed his mind, "Think you that's the problem?" He sounded like he was relieved by the possibility.

"What problem?"

"*Your mouth?*"

"If it helps you sleep at night, then yes, I'm sure that's the problem. Now, will you get the supplies Anna's been using for me? This needs to be re-dressed."

"You're serious?"

"I don't stutter, Greylen, nor do I speak in riddles," she mimicked.

Greylen sighed as he stepped from the bed. Gwen was standing when he returned. "Get back in bed, Gwen, I'll change the dressing myself."

Gwen crossed her arms over her chest and started tapping her foot. "*I'll* re-dress *your* wound, Greylen. I need to make sure it hasn't swelled. Tell me how it happened."

"A simple accident," was all he said.

"Sit, Greylen. Now," Gwen ordered when he didn't move.

Once he settled, Gwen worked expertly with covered eyes. She found the edge of the gauze and unwound it, then carefully brushed her finger over the surface of his skin. She mentally counted each of his twelve stitches, then tested the skin for swelling before reaching for fresh gauze and the jar of ointment. In seconds, she had his arm wrapped again.

"Are you in pain?" Gwen asked. "I know how to get my hands on some pretty good *potion* as you call it, and I'm willing to share," she teased with another grin.

"The only pain I have will be fixed on the morrow," he promised, grabbing her quickly around the waist and pulling her back on the bed. She shrieked in surprise and laughed as she snuggled against him.

"Greylen?"

"Aye, Gwen?"

"If this *is* a dream, don't wake me. It's the best one I've ever had."

He spooned her body, then wrapped his leg over her. "'Tis no dream, Gwen," he promised, "just a matter of time, love. Just a matter of time."

Greylen had just fallen asleep when he heard footsteps outside his chamber door. He knew he'd not like the information his first-in-command found necessary to disturb him with.

"What troubles have you?" Greylen demanded.

"The king's men wait in the great hall."

Gavin's voice was grave, so Greylen knew he'd not be pleased with the news. "Their purpose?" he asked. At his hesitation, Greylen pressed harder. "Out with it."

"There was an attempt on our sovereign's life. The offender's to be tried two days hence."

Their king had taken the habit of not judging for high treason unless his barons were present. Greylen, being one, was honor bound to appear.

"They came by ship?" Greylen asked, knowing already 'twas the only way they'd arrive in time.

"Aye. You're to leave within the hour," Gavin told him gravely as if anticipating what was to come.

"Fetch the priest, Gavin. I'll be wed before I go." Greylen felt his stomach turn when Gavin didn't move. "I said fetch the priest. I promised to marry Gwendolyn on the morrow and I'll not leave until I do."

"'Tis not possible," Gavin stated, his expression sickened.

"Explain," Greylen ground out slowly through his teeth. "Your life depends on the answer." And right now, Greylen meant every word.

"Father Michael was called to administer last rites. He knew to be back by dawn, and Duncan and Kevin went with him to ensure he'd not be delayed. 'Tis three hours before dawn, the king's men leave within the hour."

Greylen felt as if he just received a fatal blow. He rubbed his hands against his head, noxious pressure threatening to overpower him.

"How close are our ships?" 'Twas his only hope now.

"They're still in port."

"Nay!" He grabbed Gavin's shoulders, shaking him as if the action could somehow change the facts. "They're to be on their way."

"There was a discrepancy with the shipment," Gavin explained. "Word came yesterday."

Greylen swore under his breath and went to his bed. Never more dreadful of a task, he tried to wake Gwen. "Gwen…Gwen, wake up, love," he murmured with a gentle touch. She didn't respond and he tried again. "Gwendolyn," he bid with more force. 'Twas no use, she was out cold.

But he told her all the same. "Gwen, I must leave. The king's men wait, love. I'm called to court. I will marry you just as soon as I return. The moment I come home, I—" His words fell short as he dared not promise her again. But he did kiss her. He poured his entire soul into that one kiss.

Reluctantly, he went to his wardrobe and gathered what he needed for his journey. Once dressed, Greylen placed his sword in its scabbard and slipped his dagger into his boot. He stood at the bedside and gave Gavin his orders.

"You'll stay behind. I'll trust no one but you to see that Gwendolyn's kept safe."

"You've my word, Greylen."

"Ian and Connell?" he asked.

"Below stairs, ready to accompany you."

"I'll seek Lady Madelyn and the privacy of my study. You'll find a letter for Gwendolyn atop my desk. See it to her the moment she awakens."

Moments later, Greylen left. Each step he took was harder than the last. His only thoughts were that he'd broken his word. He failed her.

She would hate him come morning.

CHAPTER EIGHT

It wasn't a dream.

No matter how many times she tried to think differently, the reality was the same. She was not dreaming.

She wasn't lying in an unconscious state hooked up to an IV. She wasn't hallucinating. Nor was she insane. At the moment, she was just tired and truly beyond thought.

She stood before the window in Greylen's chamber, able to do little more than stare as the sun made its descent. Silent tears streamed down her face, and the soft rustle of parchment whispered in the air. In one hand she held the letter Greylen had written the night before. The other fingered a wooden medallion Gavin had placed around her neck only moments ago.

It meant more to her than anything she had ever had.

Strange how in just a little over twelve hours, it was the link to her future that now gave her courage. Not her bracelet, which was the only link to her past.

So many things were clear, now that she could see.

And though the scenery of northern Scotland and the sea that surrounded it looked no different, she knew "she wasn't in Kansas anymore."

When she had awoken that morning, she had sensed something was wrong and had known instinctively that Greylen wasn't there. It shouldn't have come as a surprise. It seemed to be the only way she awoke at Seagrave. She decided, however, that if she awoke to that feeling one more time, she'd kill someone. And after today's revelations, Greylen was at the top of her list. That is if he didn't get himself killed first.

But at the time, she'd only thought that she'd been a fool. She'd believed him last night, when she'd never trusted anyone. The conviction in his voice, the way that he touched her—she truly believed him. No matter how crazy what he had told her seemed to be, he made her believe. Then he held her as they fell asleep. And she knew there wasn't anywhere she'd rather be.

Greylen and his family had awoken emotions in her, emotions she'd never felt before.

She had felt someone sit next to her on the bed. "Good morning, Gwendolyn." It was Lady Madelyn. "I'm going to remove the bandages now," she had said softly.

Gwen remained silent. There was only one question she wanted to ask. And she already knew the answer. Greylen wasn't there. Her hand kept moving across the sheets where he'd lain last night. They were cold. He hadn't been next to her for hours.

Lady Madelyn placed a warm cloth over her eyes after the bandages were removed and instructed her to lean back. Gwen gladly complied. She wasn't ready to open her eyes. Truthfully, she was scared. She finally pulled the cloth away, and for the first time saw Lady Madelyn, Anna, Isabelle, and Gavin.

They were pretty hard to miss. They were all staring at her from different positions around the bed. Each wore a cautious smile, but Gavin addressed her first. He came forward and knelt by her side. "Good morn, Lady Gwendolyn," he said in a gentle voice, which seemed rather odd. The man had to be close to Greylen in size.

Gwen could tell he was uncomfortable. And for a reason she couldn't explain, she couldn't allow him to feel that way. So she did what she did best. She put on a brave face and spared his feelings at the expense of her own. "I'm a big girl, Gavin," she assured. "Out with it."

Gavin smiled at her words, though she wasn't sure why.

"Our laird was called away last night," he said.

"Of course he was, Gavin." Gwen braced herself for whatever he might tell her, managing a fake smile.

That he tried to offer comfort with his explanation was clearly evident. "The king's men arrived in the early-morning hours. Greylen had no choice but to go with them. He tried to wake you, but you were unresponsive."

"I've been adding powders to your tea, Gwendolyn," Lady Madelyn interrupted. "They cause deep slumber."

Gwen nodded, aware of the effects of what she'd been taking. She looked back to Gavin.

"Greylen told me of his promise," Gavin continued. "He demanded that I fetch Father Michael. But he'd been called away not to return until dawn to perform the ceremony joining you to Greylen."

"He was really going to marry me?" Gwen asked. It was easy to believe him last night. But now, everything seemed different.

Gavin's smile turned arrogant. "Aye, my lady, 'twas always the plan. Our laird would never make a promise he'd not intended to keep, especially to you."

"Well, it seems your *laird*, as you call him, has only done what I've come to expect from people over the years. I'd like to return to the inn now. Will you take me once I've dressed?"

He looked insulted by her suggestion. "Lady Gwendolyn, you cannot leave. 'Twould mean my head."

"I'm sure you're exaggerating, Gavin." Gwen looked to Greylen's mother. "Lady Madelyn, could you please explain to—" Gavin's title escaped her. "To your son's *whatever he is*, that it's not appropriate for me to stay any longer?"

Lady Madelyn came back to the bed. She was so beautiful, regal actually. Her auburn hair was swept back and secured with jeweled combs. Oddly, she wore the most incredible long dress. It was the deepest shade of blue with bell sleeves that fell open to the sides. She looked straight into Gwen's eyes. Speaking in a gentle but serious tone, she said, "I'm so very sorry, Gwendolyn, but what Gavin's told you is the truth. You cannot leave."

Gwen didn't want to argue with her. But in true Gwen fashion, she did. "Why not?"

"Not only is there nowhere for you to go, but you belong to my son now. The formality of your marriage is just that, a formality, my dear."

There it was again, her fictitious marriage that was just a formality. Maybe she was pregnant too. *Oh yeah, they never had sex—and she wasn't married!* "Lady Madelyn, as much as I'd love to stay, I can't. Spare me whatever dignity I have left." Which at the moment, Gwen thought, wasn't much.

"Gwendolyn, if Greylen's men let you go anywhere, he'll kill them without hesitation. You must believe me," she warned.

"Isn't that a little dramatic?" Gwen asked. "I know he saved my life, and you've shown me nothing but kindness, but you can't think to keep me here." *Were they insane?*

"Why don't you dress and come below stairs. Anna will help you," Lady Madelyn offered. Then she stood, obviously done with the conversation.

She'd been dismissed!

"That isn't necessary." Gwen's voice caught. She was close to tears and needed desperately to be alone.

"Gwendolyn." Isabelle looked upset as well.

Gwen pushed her own feelings aside. At the moment, Isabelle's took precedent. The day she'd spent with her was one of the best she could remember.

Gwen stepped from the bed—and fell into Gavin's arms. My God the bed had to be three feet off the floor. Feeling like a complete idiot, which wasn't a stretch right now, Gwen murmured a thank-you. She held out her hands and smiled at Isabelle. She was absolutely stunning. Graceful beauty at its finest. She had a willowy frame and a face that matched. Long and delicate with the most stunning blue eyes and long blond hair.

"Please don't worry," Gwen told her, mortified that her voice cracked.

"Gwendolyn, you mustn't leave," Isabelle whispered. "*Please*. Greylen will return soon."

"I can't stay, Isabelle," Gwen whispered, shaking her head. Her heart constricted as she realized the dream she'd embraced for only the shortest of time was now shattered. The one in which she had a family to care about. A family who cared about her.

Isabelle and Lady Madelyn left the chamber and then Gavin addressed her again. "Lady Gwendolyn?"

Gwen gave him her full attention now. She couldn't help it. The man was handsome. Well over six feet tall, with thick, dark hair cut just below his ears. He wore a beige linen shirt tucked into black trousers and tall black leather boots polished to a high shine. And he had penetrating blue eyes. A second later, Gwen shook her head. "Is that a sword, Gavin?" *Why in the hell did he have a sword strapped to his back?*

"Aye, my lady," he answered. "I'm never without it."

"Why in God's name would you carry a sword?" Gwen asked, completely stupefied. Though she had to admit, she enjoyed the slight irritation her question caused.

"For protection, Lady Gwendolyn. My duty is to see you're unharmed. How else am I to accomplish this?"

Gwen gave him her best were-you-born-on-another-planet look. "Don't you believe in using your words, Gavin?" she asked and then laughed at his expression.

Oh yeah, he was fun to irritate. She liked him.

Gavin ignored her question. "I've a letter from Greylen, Lady Gwendolyn. He bid me to see you had it the moment you awoke this morn," he explained, holding it out to her.

Gwen gasped, grabbing the letter from his outstretched hand. "Thank you, Gavin. And please stay close by. I might get a paper cut and you can stab the offending paper for me." She scrunched one eye, giving him her best perturbed look before turning to Anna. "Anna, could you show me to the bathroom, please? I can't seem to remember which direction we went yesterday."

"'Tis the door across the chamber, my lady," she said, motioning with her hand. "May I help?"

Gwen politely declined, then walked to the far end of Greylen's chamber. She was not only shocked by the enormity of the room but taken with it as well.

The appointments were unlike any she'd ever seen. All of the furnishings were made from dark polished wood and the oversize chairs were covered with a rich, dark tapestry. There was a sitting area in front of the window and two stately armoires situated along the far wall. They stood on either side of the bathroom door, a door with ornate brass fittings that had been made from the same wood as the trim.

She had to push it with both hands before it finally gave, and she stepped inside, grateful to be alone. She leaned against the frame, sank to the floor, and cried. Despair so deep it stunned her.

It took a good five minutes before her control returned. She remained on the floor, looking at the letter in her hand. It was written on a deep-colored parchment. The initials "GMA" were pressed into the burgundy wax seal. It was a beautiful monogram, and Gwen felt tears again as she ran her fingers over the letters. Call her a fool, but she couldn't help wondering what Greylen's middle name was.

She was scared to open it, so she didn't. Instead, she held it to her heart and looked around the room. It was quite large and furnished as handsomely as his bedroom. An alcove was to her right, where a large chair and table had been placed in front of a small window. To her left was a chest of drawers with thick towels, a porcelain basin, and dark valet on top. Another chest was in front of her, but this one had two basins with a towel stand between them and a large framed mirror above. The door next to it, she supposed, led to a private toilet room.

An oriental rug covered most of the floor. She noticed the richness of its pattern and felt the expensive silk threads beneath her feet. The walls were constructed from large pale stones finished with dark trim. And tapestries hung from brass rods, covering the walls with their warmth. The room was magnificent.

Done being a coward, Gwen moved to the chair in the alcove. She pressed her face against a plaid that hung over the back. It was Greylen's scent. She hugged it in front of her and carefully broke the seal to the parchment. Tears again. His writing was beautiful, the letters perfect. And she smiled at the ink smeared in spots from left to right. He was a lefty.

She began reading...wondering what he would tell her. How he would break her heart.

Again.

My dearest Gwendolyn,

'Tis with the deepest regret that I find myself leaving you. Never have I broken my word and that you are the one I have failed pains me as nothing before. Though I tried to wake you, 'twas no use. Hear my plea now, Gwendolyn. I will return to you, I will have you as mine for the rest of my days, if you will only still take me.
My heart is in your hands, Gwendolyn, where it shall remain forever.

Yours,
Greylen Allister MacGreggor

He wanted her. Greylen really wanted her.
But why?

If only she could remember what they'd said last night. She recalled some of it, but it didn't make sense. More importantly he was gone. She had to go back to the inn.

With somewhat of a plan, Gwen decided to get dressed. She needed desperately to use the bathroom and struggled with the heavy door until it opened. Then she stood there shocked. It was an old-fashioned garderobe. How could a family with so much wealth not have indoor plumbing? She stared at the stone bench built into the wall. It had a wooden seat and she knew if she looked down, she'd see running water at the bottom.

In the end, it wasn't as bad as she thought. But the crude toilet paper wasn't even close to Charmin. She must've been on some powerful drugs to have missed that yesterday.

She walked to the mirror, relieved that her face showed barely any marks. Those that were left were only a shade or two darker than her natural skin color. She washed her hands in the basin filled with fresh water, careful of the cloth on her right hand. She unbuttoned her shirt and pulled it away. She still had bruises from the seat belt, but they seemed to be fading.

She didn't see any supplies to change her bandages and her clothes were nowhere to be found either. Taking a deep breath, she pulled the door open, hoping Gavin had left. She'd listened to enough outrageous statements for one day.

Anna waited just outside, her arms loaded with clothing. "I thought you'd like to dress."

Gwen scanned the room relieved that Gavin had in fact left. "Do you have my clothes? These look nothing like the ones I wore," Gwen said, looking pointedly to the bundle in Anna's hands.

"'Twould not be proper, Lady Gwendolyn. This dress should do nicely till we fashion you a suitable wardrobe."

"Anna, I have my own clothes," Gwen reminded her. "And please stop calling me Lady Gwendolyn."

"'Tis only proper," Anna returned.

"Proper?" *My God.* "Nothing is proper about my stay here."

"Try to understand," Anna said softly, taking Gwen's hand. "We've waited so long, and the plans are set. You must listen to reason. Greylen's men will not let you go. They cannot."

"My God, Anna," Gwen exclaimed. *They were crazy.* "Just give me what you have. I'll get my clothes later."

Anna smiled. "You'll do no such thing. I'll help. 'Tis my duty."

"*Whatever*," Gwen said. She was tired. They'd worn her down already.

Anna led her to the fireplace and removed Greylen's shirt. Gwen stood naked before her, completely unashamed and completely distracted. She could see Greylen's entire room from where she stood. And it truly was enormous.

Each space had to be at least thirty feet across and just as deep. The fireplace area was filled with tables and chairs and another rich-looking rug. The fireplace itself was larger than any she'd ever seen. The hearth was made from the same stones that the castle had been constructed with, and the mantel from the same wood as the trim.

The sleeping section lay just beyond the space she was standing in, and to say his bed was gigantic would be a gross understatement. The mattress *was* three feet off the floor and encased in a masculine frame. A dark-burgundy quilt lay on top of ivory sheets and decorative pillows covered most of the headboard. There were nightstands on either side, with candles and glass-covered oil lamps. And the sconces on the walls flickered like they had candles in them too.

Didn't they have electricity? "Anna, may I ask a question?"

"Of course, anything you wish," she offered, continuing to clean Gwen's abrasions.

"I noticed there wasn't indoor plumbing in the bathroom, and there are no lights."

"I don't understand, Lady Gwendolyn. Our plumbing surpasses the standard and the candles are lights," Anna replied with a confused look on her face.

"You're kidding, right?"

Anna put her hand to Gwen's forehead, pursing her lips. "You feel cool, Lady Gwendolyn, but mayhap you should rest again."

"Not a chance. I've rested more than I have in years. I just need to go home." She couldn't stay here any longer, but home... Gwen covered her face as tears filled her eyes.

"Lady Gwendolyn, you are home. Let us take care of you now." Anna hushed, pulling her into her arms.

When Gwen wiped her eyes, Anna finished dressing her wounds. She used a thick paste from a small clay pot and spread it with a flat wooden stick. Gwen picked up the pot and smelled the substance. It was the same she'd used last night for Greylen. "Anna, what kind of ointment is this?"

"'Tis a mixture of herbs we grow in the garden."

"*Really?*" Gwen asked in surprise. "You don't believe in doctors or pharmacies?" Anna looked puzzled again. Gwen felt uneasy.

Anna helped her into a crushed velvet dress lined with soft linen. "Whose are these?" Gwen asked after Anna placed slippers on her feet that fit perfectly.

"Isabelle's," Anna answered. "You'll have your own in no time. Now, let's get you downstairs so you can break your fast."

"Aren't you forgetting something?"

"Whatever do you mean?" Anna asked, looking to the now empty table that once held the clothing she'd brought in.

"*Underwear*, Anna?" How could she not think of it? She'd thought of everything else.

"I was leery of the bloomers. They might bother the bruise over your hips."

"*Bloomers?* What about my thong?"

Anna placed her hands on her hips. "If you mean that piece of string we found in your trews," Anna chastised, "'twas destroyed. Greylen was none too gentle when he undressed you."

"*Humph*," Gwen squeaked, sorry at once that she'd missed it.

Gavin bowed to her as they stepped from the chamber. "Oh please, Gavin, enough already."

He didn't reply, which was good. Gwen was too busy looking around. She could see the openness of the foyer below and walked to the banister before peering over. A beautiful rug was in front of the stairway and the wide steps led up to a spacious landing adorned with a large window. From the landing, the banister curved to either side and more steps led up to a walkway perfectly symmetrical on both sides. Large double doors were set into the sidewalls, three on either side.

At the bottom of the stairway she passed two massive doors. And the archway to her right opened to a room like she'd never seen before.

The ceiling was at least thirty feet high, and gorgeous tapestries hung everywhere. A large fireplace with ample seating was in front of her. And to her right was a dining area with a long mahogany table and buffet. Candelabras had been placed at various points across each and there were small bowls with fresh flowers in between. To her left was another sitting area. Large sofas with ornate pillows and various-size tables were everywhere. And there was a piano that looked new, but antique at the same time.

But what struck her most was that despite the wealth the room represented, it held a quality of warmth. She envied this family for knowing such a luxury. Warmth, not wealth.

"Gwendolyn, please join us," Lady Madelyn called from the table. She sat facing the openness of the room and Isabelle sat across from her. Gavin pulled out the chair next to Isabelle. "Lady," he offered, motioning to the chair.

That was it. "Gavin, if you don't leave me alone, I swear I'm going to hit you." Gwen's hand formed into a fist and she watched Gavin hide a smile. They were all smiling, holding their hands in front of their faces. Did they think she was stupid? She saw what they did. Shooting Gavin another dirty look, she sat in the chair. Her situation got worse, Gavin took the seat next to Lady Madelyn. Directly across from her.

"Shouldn't you be standing behind me, Gavin? Guarding me with your sword?"

"Greylen's men always dine with us, Gwendolyn," Isabelle explained. "But only two at a time as they rotate their duties."

Gwen gave a snort but didn't miss the softness in Gavin's eyes as Isabelle justified his presence. So he liked Isabelle, huh? Interesting, very interesting.

"Isabelle, I'm going to write down my phone numbers and address so we can keep in touch. After breakfast, however"—Gwen looked at Gavin—"I insist on returning to the inn."

Gavin stood so fast the chair he'd been sitting on fell. "Lady Gwendolyn, I've told you more than once, you'll go nowhere. And if I have to, I'll sit on you myself to see the task done. Do I make myself clear?"

My God, the man sounded like Greylen when he was irritated. "Don't have a tizzy, Gavin. Just take me back to the inn," Gwen shouted, standing to enforce her point.

"A *tizzy*?" he asked, his eyes narrowed and threatening. "Explain your meaning?"

"An outburst," Gwen said with relish. "More to the point, a *fit*—much like the one you're having now."

"You're daft," he bit through clenched teeth.

"I am not," she bit back.

"Aye, you are."

"No, I'm not."

"Are."

"Not."

Gavin's fists hit the table. "You're as stubborn as he. I swear you deserve each other." His eyes narrowed again as he stared her down, his hands still fisted on the table. "I've my orders, Lady Gwendolyn, and I will see them through. You are to have anything, *anything you so desire*—but leaving here is not an option."

"This is ridiculous. Lady Madelyn, Isabelle, I've lost my appetite. Excuse me." Gwen left the table muttering a few choice words when Gavin followed. She went straight for the front door and tried repeatedly to open it. It wouldn't budge. She kicked it, turning at the sound of Gavin's chuckle. "Your door is stuck." She kicked it again.

"Allow me," Gavin said with a flick of his wrist. The door opened effortlessly.

Gwen turned away in disgust, just in time to catch Isabelle watching from the archway.

Isabelle ogled her current nemesis. Well, at least someone liked him, because she didn't anymore.

Gwen stepped through the doors. Men stood on either side and bowed to her. "What is going on here? Get a life, people." Holding the material of her dress, she walked down the stairway into the courtyard.

She stopped after a few steps, faltered actually, inhaling a deep breath audibly. She turned from left to right, shaking her head before closing her eyes. *Be different, please be different.* She opened them again.

It wasn't.

Gavin stood behind her. His hands were on her shoulders and held her steady, because she was shaking. "Should we go back inside?" he asked.

The warmth had returned in his voice, and she was sorry she'd pushed him before. "Gavin, tell me what's happening," she whispered.

Gavin led her back inside and didn't stop until they were in the great hall again. She was relieved to see it was empty.

"Lady Gwendolyn, tell me what you find so troubling?" he asked after he sat her in a chair in front of the fireplace.

She looked at him like he had just sprouted horns. "What I find so troubling, as you put it, is *everything*."

Gavin walked to the table beside the fireplace. He picked up a decanter, then poured some of its contents into a goblet. "Let's try again," he offered with a smile.

"This isn't the time to get me drunk. I just witnessed a scene out of a history book." Gwen stood as she said it, and Gavin sighed before setting the goblet on the table. He took hold of her arms and sat her down again. Damn, she should have taken more of that potion.

"Drink first. Then I'll explain," he ordered, placing the goblet to her lips.

Gwen grabbed it from his hand. She drank it down. "I'm waiting," she demanded.

Gavin took one of the chairs and placed it in front of her. He sat, leaning forward, close enough that their legs almost touched. "Do you know why you're here, Lady Gwendolyn?"

"Greylen saved my life and brought me here. Is there more?"

He cursed, much like Greylen did the night before. "Did he tell you *anything* of the prophecy?"

"He told me about a prophecy last night, but I can't remember everything he said. I've been taking that potion, and now..." The brandy started taking effect. *Ahhh*, it helped.

"The prophecy, Lady Gwendolyn, foretold your coming. We've waited years for its culmination."

"Yeah, yeah…on our birthdays, I know. I remember that much."

"'Twas written you were of a different time, Lady Gwendolyn," Gavin said clearly.

"Greylen said we were born apart, Gavin. I was born in the States and he was born here."

"Mayhap—"

Gwen cut him off. "*Mayhap* is what he said. What in the hell does that mean?"

Gavin cursed again, but she could tell it wasn't directed at her. No, she had a feeling his anger was directed at Greylen. "Aye, you were born apart, but 'tis more than just that."

"Then what? What aren't you telling me?" *Why couldn't he give her a straight answer?*

"Lady Gwendolyn—"

"Stop calling me Lady Gwendolyn," Gwen hissed, cutting him off again. "Just spit it out." She took his shoulders, trying to shake him. But in the end, she only shook herself.

"You're of a different time," he said slowly, his eyes penetrating with each word.

"*I'm what?*"

Gavin shook his head. "This is maddening. Pray tell," he said, grinding out his words, "exactly what don't you understand?"

"I understand nothing!"

"You are daft."

"Daft? *Daft?*" Oh, she was going to hit him. Hard. "I am not daft, Gavin. I do however have a problem trying to make sense of whatever it is you're trying to tell me. You suck at explaining."

"Then listen well, Lady Gwendolyn," he said through clenched teeth, coming closer to her with each statement. "You are not of this time. There are no phones, whatever that may be. There is no inn. And this is not the twenty-first century."

"You're a nutcase," Gwen hissed, pushing away. She walked back to the door, and on the third try, it finally opened. But when it did, the sight hit her full force again. Gwen closed the door. Gavin's words repeated in her head.

She knew he was behind her, but she didn't turn around. Instead, she leaned her head against the door. "You don't have a phone?" she asked in a whisper.

"Nay."

"The storm didn't wipe out your power or the phone lines?" Again it was a whisper.

"Nay."

"You said I'm not of this time. What did you mean?"

"Simply that, Lady Gwendolyn. This is not the twenty-first century."

"If this isn't the twenty-first century"—Gwen's hands fisted next to her head before she asked the next question, and she laughed as she said the words—"what century is it then?"

"'Tis the sixteenth century, my lady."

Gwen made a strangled sound. "What year is it?"

"The year of our Lord…fifteen hundred and thirty-six." He said it clearly, catching her as she crumpled.

"*Potion...*" Gwen screamed, beating against his chest. "I want potion!"

"You've just had brandy," Gavin reprimanded, grabbing her hands.

"You're messing with me, right?"

"If you mean tricking you...nay, I fear not."

Gwen started laughing.

"You find this amusing?" he asked as he set her before him.

Gwen regarded him with a smile. "As a matter of fact, I do," she replied. "I told Greylen I was dreaming last night. And I am." Thank God, she could still rationalize in her unconscious state.

"You're not dreaming, Lady Gwendolyn," he said. "Can you not believe?"

His question surprised her. She thought about it. "*Believing* is what got me into this mess in the first place."

"Explain."

"What? Now you're my therapist?" she said with a sneer, but Gavin only stared. "Oh what the hell," she muttered. "I *believed* I would find what I was looking for if I came to Scotland. No." Gwen shook her head. "I can't explain it. I just had to leave. I had this feeling that if I didn't, I would never find what I was looking for."

"And what was it that you looked for?" Gavin asked seriously.

Gwen stared at him. What had she looked for? She knew at once what she'd been looking for. "I think I was looking for Greylen," she whispered.

"Then it seems everything has worked itself out."

"*Are you insane?*"

"You found him, didn't you?"

"In the sixteenth century? *Come on.*"

"Can you not see that which is in front of you?" he asked.

Gwen's eyes widened. "Oh my God…I'm one of those people," she cried. She grabbed his shoulders. "I hate those people."

"Pray tell, which people would those be?" he asked wryly.

"The ones who can't see what's in front of them." *Damn him.* "Gavin, what you're telling me isn't possible."

"And as I've already said, I fear 'tis exactly as I've told you."

"So what I just witnessed outside, and the antiquity of this castle—"

"Seagrave Castle is the finest in the Highlands, Lady Gwendolyn," Gavin corrected, cutting her off. "And as to what you saw outside, I can only surmise 'tis different to you because you're not of our time. 'Twas written so in the prophecy."

"So it's normal that this castle has no electricity or indoor plumbing?"

"I know not of electricity, but I can assure you our plumbing surpasses the standard."

"Yeah, so I've heard. Trust me, it's not even close."

"Furthermore, there's nothing antiquated about this castle, you'll not find another finer."

"In the courtyard"—Gwen put her head in her hands, replaying the scene in her mind—"it's a village out there. People don't live like that anymore," she whispered in disbelief.

"Explain to me what is so different," he prodded gently.

"The clothing for one. Women don't dress like that anymore, even in Scotland. Oh my God." She pulled at her dress. "Dress like this. And people's courtyards are quiet and peaceful. They're private. This courtyard is alive with activity—mothers and children, men with weapons. There're stables and what looks to be a chapel. And I saw beyond the wall, there were cottages and men fighting *with swords*. This does not exist. I spent three weeks discovering everything I could about Scotland, and I swear everything I've just seen *doesn't*."

"Everything you witnessed is very real. And the men, women, and children of this clan live a life known to few in the Highlands. Their laird provides well and protects with honor. In return, his people work hard and live quite happily." He paused, as if waiting for a reaction. When she didn't reply, he continued, "Does anything else bother you?"

"You bother me, Gavin." Well, she had to take it out on someone.

"Lady Gwendolyn, I've been nothing but forthright and respectful to you," he countered.

"Forthright maybe—but respectful—*yeah*..." Gwen rolled her eyes.

He sneered, taking the bait. "Very well, my lady. Mayhap you should make some more outrageous requests to leave. And please, do use your acidic tongue."

"Did you say I have an *acidic* tongue?" Gwen demanded in false outrage.

"Aye, you've a foul mouth. 'Tis the truth and you know it," Gavin hissed. "Don't have a *tizzy* as you so put it, my lady."

"I'll have all the damn tizzies I want, Gavin—back at the inn."

"This is the only 'inn' you'll ever know, Lady Gwendolyn. I suggest you get used to it…for you shall never leave."

Lady Gwendolyn remained quiet as Gavin helped her back to her chamber. 'Twas a first, and he found that he missed the quickness of her comments—even those caustic in nature.

He now understood Greylen's perplexity with her dialect. His commander, however, failed to mention the details of her foul mouth. She was actually quite entertaining when riled, and he wondered if Greylen felt the same.

He led his mistress to bed, ordering that she rest away the brandy's effects. Then he told her he'd be outside the doors. She'd clutched his hand before he could leave. "I'm not dreaming, Gavin," she said softly, as if saying the words aloud would somehow help.

"Nay, lady," he agreed. "Mayhap if I told you—"

"*Mayhap* you could tell me anything," she begged, cutting him off. "Please," she added with a smile, squeezing his hand.

Taken aback, Gavin returned her smile. He'd not seen this side of her. With her guard down, she was quite different. He wanted to ease her, perhaps help her to see the rightness of her being here. "I swore my allegiance to Greylen fifteen years ago," he began. "From the first, there've been but a handful of days I've not been with him. The most disturbing of which, the days a betrothal was set before him. I never understood his reluctance to marry but witnessing the events that occurred each time..." Gavin shook his head, pained by the memories. "Greylen wasn't hasty in his refusal, but he'd demand that his intended be brought before him." Gavin looked directly to his mistress, imploring his words. "In all those years, I'll never forget the look on his face as he held each woman's shoulders and stared into her eyes. He carried an emptiness for days after such occurrences."

"But if the prophecy foretold my coming, why would he look to someone else?"

Gavin gave a crooked smile. "We're all open-minded, Lady Gwendolyn, but we are speaking of a prophecy," he reminded her. "We know not who wrote it, or for that matter, when."

"Did he ever believe in it?"

"You misunderstand. He *always* believed. On occasion" —Gavin qualified with a shrug—"he thought mayhap to outsmart the prophecy and find you sooner."

His mistress snorted. "Talk about arrogant."

"Aye." Gavin smiled. "He is that."

"Is there more?"

"Greylen told me of the writings five years ago," he explained. "I believed as well, lady," Gavin said quickly. "And he told me." He hesitated before revealing yet another confidence. "He told me he'd know you at once. He said he'd had a dream of you for years. The same dream each night—"

"I had the same dream."

Gavin was surprised, not only at her words but also by the tears she quietly wiped away. "Upon the eve of his thirty-second year, we told the rest of our men: Duncan, Ian, Connell, Kevin, and Hugh. We've planned for your arrival every day since."

"Does anyone else know?"

"Aye, Lady Madelyn, Isabelle, and Anna. Rest now," he ordered. "You've had a taxing morn."

"Will you stay? I don't want to be alone. *Please*."

"Should I call for Lady Madelyn? Perhaps Isabelle?" he asked, alarmed by her tone.

His mistress sat up at once. "Given the choice, who do you wish I'd have with me?"

The way the question was spoken shocked him. Did she bait him? "I've no idea your meaning, mistress," he returned, masking his expression.

"*Humph*." Her facial expression matched her verbal disbelief.

"Get some rest, *now*," he ordered, unnerved by her perception—and the brow she aggravatingly raised. Then he heard her response as he walked to the fireplace.

"'Oh what a tangled web we weave…when we first practice to deceive.'"

Gavin reached for his hair, a habit that became worse over the ensuing days.

Gwen couldn't sleep. She couldn't stop thinking of the things that happened this morning. Not only what she'd seen, but also her conversation with Gavin. How could it possibly be true? *It was crazy.*

It was, wasn't it?

She knew she wasn't dreaming or trapped in unconsciousness and lying in a hospital bed. Nope, she had to give that one up. She was one of the most rational people she knew. Okay, so it was a conceited thought. But, damn it, objective rationalization had gotten her through life. At least that's what she told herself.

If this *was* real, if somehow she *was* in a different time… She started laughing. She couldn't believe she was rationalizing *that*. But she had to. Didn't she?

She hadn't seen any phones earlier. No outlets or anything else for that matter that could be considered modern. And the scene in the courtyard added credence to everything else. Then there was the way Greylen and his family held themselves, their speech, their clothing, their formality.

Where was Greylen, damn it? She missed him. No, she *needed* him. Two days in the man's presence and she felt a connection so deep it was astounding.

And he left her.

She must have dozed off for a while, and when she awoke, she called to Gavin. He answered from the area by the fire. "Please call me Gwen. I can't stand this 'lady' stuff."

"You'll get used to it," Gavin said, approaching the bed. "Come, I'll show you the holding."

She smiled. What the hell? "May I have a few minutes?"

"Take all the time you need, *Lady* Gwendolyn," he said purposely, grinning at her dramatic sigh.

Once inside the bathroom, Gwen took her time. She went to the mirror and placed her hands on the chest. First things first. "Well, what do we do now, oh smart one?" she asked, staring at her reflection. "No quick answer, huh? Yeah, I didn't think so, brainless, and your hair's a mess."

She opened the drawers of the chest to look for a brush. Her breath caught. Greylen's shaving tools lay inside. She picked up the round bar of soap and inhaled its sandalwood scent. A short-handled lathering brush with thick, soft bristles and a long blade with a wooden handle lay next to it. There was even a stone for when it became dull.

Curious, she searched the rest of the drawers. No Gillette razors, no aerosol cans, no toothbrush, no—*great*, not one thing modernly familiar. She went back to the drawer that had a hairbrush and comb. Then she looked through another, hoping to find something to secure her hair, like an alligator clip or a ponytail holder. Instead, she settled for a thin strip of leather she took from a pile in one of the drawers. Then she grabbed the plaid from the chair in the alcove.

When she stepped back into the chamber, Gavin's look stopped her. "Have I done something wrong?" she asked.

"Nay," he said quickly. "I only wish…" He paused and smiled. "I only wish Greylen were here to see you. He'd be pleased you wear his plaid, and you look fetching in Isabelle's dress."

"A romantic as well as a torturer," she replied, rolling her eyes. "How refreshing."

Gavin grinned, seeming to like her again. He ushered her out of the chamber and down the stairs. They entered the great hall where Lady Madelyn and Isabelle were sitting before the fire.

"Gwendolyn, are you feeling better?" Isabelle asked. Lady Madelyn remained quiet, though looked to her with concern.

"I am, thank you," she answered. "Gavin's going to show me the holding today. It seems I'll be staying awhile."

"May I come, Gavin?"

"Not today, Isabelle."

Gavin's tone was so tender that Gwen gave him a look of disgust. "Excuse me, how come you never speak to me like that? I only get ordered and bossed around." They all laughed at her remark, but Gwen's observation was dead-on. Gavin was soft for Isabelle.

"Come, lady, we ride." He offered his hand.

"Ride what?" Gwen asked, pulling her hand back.

"Horses, lady. What else?"

"I don't ride horses," Gwen said.

"No matter. You'll ride with me."

"I've never been on a horse in my life. And I'm not getting on any of the ones I saw earlier. They're enormous."

"You've ridden on a horse before, you just can't remember."

"How would you know?"

"I was there, my lady. Greylen carried you upon one from the shore, and his beast is larger than those in the courtyard."

"Why doesn't that surprise me," Gwen muttered to herself.

Anna entered the room carrying a leather bag. "'Tis filled," she said, handing it to Gavin. "Make sure she eats well." Anna ended her instructions, frowning as if not pleased with Gwen's current weight.

Gavin retrieved the bag and took her arm. As he opened the door, Gwen closed her eyes. Then she took a deep breath.

"'Twill be all right," Gavin assured. He continued to hold her arm as they walked through the courtyard. She shook the entire time.

"Everyone's staring at me," Gwen whispered, moving closer.

"They're aware you're here, lady, and you wrap yourself in the MacGreggor plaid." He waited a moment. "Besides, by now 'tis common knowledge their laird saved a helpless lass from the water."

"I'm an incredible swimmer, not helpless," Gwen said rather indignantly.

"I could tell," he replied dryly.

Gwen shot Gavin a nasty look before pulling away. She walked to the stables to the right of the keep. She stopped when she reached the front, then turned to look at the castle now to her left. She gasped.

It was magnificent.

It stretched wide across the beautiful land and stood probably four stories high. Stone steps with a marble or limestone balustrade led to the front doors. And decorative emerald green shutters adorned all of the windows, each with flower boxes beneath. To the left of the castle was the garden Anna had spoken of earlier. And to the right, directly across from the stables, was a simple one-story structure. It had a beautiful wooden door and large stained glass windows.

She assumed it was the chapel and decided to ask Gavin about it later. For now, she wasn't speaking to him. Her inspection was interrupted when the current bane of her existence stopped before her. He held the reins of his horse, and the bag Anna had given him was secured to the saddle.

"How did Anna know we were leaving?" she asked without thinking. Damn, she forgot she wasn't talking to him.

"We're not leaving," he corrected. "I'm merely showing you where you are."

"*Whatever*," she replied, brushing off his imperial tone. "You didn't answer my question."

"Anna came to check on you while you rested," he explained. "I told her I'd be showing you the holding." He grabbed her waist, and a second later, she was sitting atop the saddle with Gavin behind her.

They left the gates of the courtyard and traveled down a wide path. There were cottages on the left and fields where men were engaging in various states of swordplay on the right. They continued past a lake, riding quietly for over an hour.

Gavin helped her from the saddle, then held her while she gained her stand. She gave him a warm, genuine smile. "It's more beautiful than anything I've ever seen," she said. He nodded his agreement and handed her a small bag. Pointing toward the trees, he told her she could see to her needs.

"I'm impressed, you've thought of everything."

"Not everything," he remarked. "I'd not expected Greylen to be called away last night."

His candor humbled her. "Was he surprised too?" she asked.

"*Surprised?* Furious was more the case."

"Do you think he'll return soon?"

"Mayhap in less than a week. It depends whether he rides or sails."

"Is he in danger?"

"He was called to court to be present for a trial, lady. He's in no danger."

"I guess I'll have to take your word for it. Excuse me now, I'm going to the trees," she said with as much dignity as she could muster.

When she returned, Gavin had laid a blanket on the ground. The items Anna packed were spread out on top. "I'm starved," she confessed. "You annoyed me so much at breakfast, I forgot to eat." She sat across from him and they ate from an assortment of cheese, fruit, and dark bread. The cup she drank from was made of baked clay, glazed, and etched with an intricate pattern. She took a large swallow, choking as it went down. Gavin laughed and pounded her back.

"What is this? *Beer?*"

"'Tis ale. I'd not thought to warn you."

Gavin offered to fetch water, and she was just about to say yes when she thought better of it. She chugged the rest of her ale instead, and his too.

As they rode back, Gavin pointed to various areas explaining the purpose of each. There were pastures for sheep, cattle, and horses. All separate and each had men watching over them.

When they reached the stables again, Gwen followed him inside. They were glorious. They really did value their beasts. There were stalls on both sides and clean hay piled high in the back. The floors were immaculate, and the wooden gates weren't rough but sanded to a smooth finish. After Gavin finished tending to his horse, he began leading her back to the castle.

"Is that a chapel?" Gwen asked, pointing to the building across from them.

"Aye, would you like to go inside?"

"Do you think anyone's there?"

"Nay, Father Michael came back early this morn. I'm sure he's asleep."

At her nod, Gavin led her to the door and walked in first. A moment later, he came back. "'Tis vacant. I'll wait for you outside," he offered before closing the door behind her.

Gwen stood in the doorway, looking at the most charming chapel she'd ever seen. To her left was a table with candles. And in front of her was a floral runner that led to the pulpit. The altar stood one step off the rest of the floor and was covered with large pots filled with plants and flowers. Beautiful polished pews were on either side of the room, and she counted each of the ten rows. Its smallness only added to its appeal.

Gwen had always hated churches, but not because she didn't believe. It was the families that made her uncomfortable. They seemed so together, whether in pain or joy, and she envied them. Secretly, she hoped one day she'd find happiness. To join a church with a family of her own and share that togetherness she always yearned for.

She still wasn't sure what happened. If the things that Greylen and his family had told her were true. But if there was even the smallest chance that they somehow were, she wouldn't take it for granted. She was in too deep already.

She picked up a candle and lit the wick from one that already burned. Then she ran her hands along the tops of the benches as she made her way toward the altar. She sat on her feet and entwined her fingers. And she just sat there not sure where to begin. But she looked up and saw the large wooden beams that ran from one end to the other. Every last detail was perfect here.

Her words came easily then. "Okay, so this is the way I see it. Somehow, I'm here. I don't know how it happened, but if what Greylen and Gavin said is true, I think I know why." Gwen paused, frowning at what had escaped her until now. "Please take care of Sara and Mr. MacGreggor. I know she'll assume I drowned in the accident, but she was all I had left." *Oh, Sara.* A tear slipped down her cheek.

Would she ever see her again? She was suddenly hit with another revelation—Mr. MacGreggor. She'd found him outside her apartment five years earlier and had taken him in without hesitation. Oddly, she hadn't had him more than a day before she started calling him by that name.

It took Gwen a minute to continue. And when she did the words came from so deep within, even she was surprised to hear them voiced. "Please let me stay here. It's the most enchanting place I've ever seen, and I love the people already. I've been so good for so long, and I've worked hard my entire life. I don't want to go home. *I want to stay*. Please keep Greylen safe. Bring him home to me." She quietly whispered amen and wiped her tears as she stood. Gavin was standing in the doorway.

He looked at her so solemnly. "I meant not to intrude. 'Twas concern which brought me within, when you'd not come back out." He walked to where she stood and knelt before her. "Forgive me, Lady Gwendolyn. I overstepped my bounds. I'll relieve myself of your watch immediately."

"No, you won't. You're Greylen's best friend. You should know the truth."

He seemed astounded at her graciousness and took her hands in his own. "He will return," he implored. "You must believe me. The prophecy's come true. *This* is where you're meant to be. *This* is your home now, Lady Gwendolyn."

Gavin continued to remain by Gwen's side. He, in fact, refused to be relieved until morning, much to the surprise of Greylen's men, whom she'd met that afternoon. His loyalty to her meant more than he'd ever know.

They dined that night with Lady Madelyn, Isabelle, and Duncan. They spoke of things clearly insignificant, obviously avoiding any subjects that might cause her unease.

Afterward, they sat by the fire while Isabelle played the piano—the harpsichord—in the corner. The music was haunting, and Gwen watched as Gavin repeatedly stole looks at Greylen's sister. He seemed so taken with her, and Gwen sensed that his feelings ran very deep.

Anna came in later and asked Gwen to accompany her upstairs. She had a bath waiting by the fire and washed Gwen's hair before helping her dress. Gwen smiled sadly as Anna held open another of Greylen's shirts. Then she led her to the hearth and brushed her hair. Anna asked if she'd like her to stay, but Gwen declined. As soon as she left, Gwen walked to the nightstand to look for the letter she'd placed there earlier. She couldn't find it and instinctively opened the top drawer. Someone had placed her letter inside.

When she picked it up, she saw a wooden medallion attached to a thick leather cord. She snatched it immediately and sat on the bed. The dark polished wood had a design etched on its face. A dragon—fierce and beautiful at the same time. She turned it over and saw Greylen's initials. Gwen walked to the door to ask Gavin about it. He stood just outside and smiled when he saw her.

"Nice bedgown, lady," he remarked dryly.

"Shut up, Gavin." She laughed, taken by the sparkle in his eyes. "Could you tell me about this, please?" she asked, holding the medallion before him.

He took it in his hand, fingering the etched design. "Greylen's father made it for him years ago," he explained. "The dragon is his crest, lady, for he slays all that comes before him."

Gwen rolled her eyes. "That's very comforting, Gavin," she replied sarcastically. He turned her around and tied it behind her neck. She took a deep breath, strangely calmed by wearing it, then regarded Gavin once again. "Come back inside, Gavin. I'll not have you stand for the rest of the night," she ordered, pointing toward the door.

He had come in and took a seat by the fireplace, affording her a modicum of privacy. She had walked to the window, catching her breath at the sky alight with more stars than she'd ever seen.

She stroked the medallion as she held the letter, staring at the sea beyond the cliffs. She forgot to wipe the tears from her eyes before she turned to say good night and get into bed. Thankfully, Gavin made no mention of it. He quietly said good night as she curled beneath the covers.

❧ CHAPTER NINE ❧

When Gwen awoke it was still dark. She knew it had to be somewhere between four and five in the morning, and she groaned as she stretched the aches from her body. She rolled over and hugged the pillow. The room was cast in shadows from the fire, and she could see Gavin's profile where he sat by the hearth. She felt safe with him and was glad that he'd stayed last night. Not that she'd left him a choice.

She was about to call out to him when she heard the door open. She smiled as Isabelle crept toward the bed. Candle in hand, Isabelle returned her smile and practically beamed when Gwen pulled back the covers and patted the mattress.

"Good morn, Gwendolyn," Isabelle whispered softly after she lay down next to her.

"Good morn, Isabelle," Gwen mimicked.

Isabelle laughed. "I'm so glad you're awake."

"Me too. I missed you yesterday."

"I saw you many times yesterday, Gwendolyn," Isabelle corrected.

"I know, but we didn't have any time alone."

"I suppose you're right," she agreed. "How did you lose your guard, Gwendolyn? The only time there's not been one posted was the night before last."

Gwen was about to tell her she was wrong, but curiosity got the best of her. "Why didn't I have a guard the second night if I did on the first?" she asked.

"Greylen was with you, Gwendolyn. You need no guard when he's about."

"But wasn't he with me the first night?" Gwen was under the impression they'd slept together that night. He'd told her so.

"Aye, he was, but Mother added a sleeping potion to his wine that night. Even my brother sought the guard of his own men knowing his abilities had been jeopardized."

"So normally he wouldn't seek the guard of his men?"

"Nay, he'd not. My brother could hear a pin drop on the other side of the castle, mayhap as far as Edinburgh."

"His senses can't be that heightened, Isabelle," Gwen said, rolling her eyes.

"Aye, but they truly are," Isabelle argued. "Greylen's abilities are known throughout the land, Gwendolyn. He's our king's most skilled champion. 'Tis whispered he's the fiercest warrior in the realm."

Gwen hoped she was exaggerating. "Are you sure you're not confusing him with someone else?" Gwen asked. Isabelle only shook her head, her eyes were wide, and she was looking at Gwen like she were crazy. "Are you ever frightened for him, Isabelle?"

"Nay." Isabelle scoffed. "'Twould be a grave insult, Gwendolyn. He's invincible."

Gwen couldn't believe the way Isabelle spoke. It wasn't the conviction in her voice that bothered her. It was the complacency she heard, like Isabelle was bored with a topic that had worn out its welcome. But if all that had happened were true, Gwen knew, Greylen's life was on the line every day. The thought was terrifying.

"How *did* you lose your handsome guard?" Isabelle asked. "You never told me."

"I di—" She tried to finish, but Isabelle interrupted her.

"He's wonderful, isn't he?" she said wistfully, then quickly changed her mind. "*Nay*—he's the most insufferable, perplexing man ever," she rushed with a frustrated laugh. "No matter how I try, he treats me always as his laird's..." Isabelle's expression changed as if she'd never spoken of it aloud. The revelation must have come as a hard blow because her barely whispered words were filled with hurt when she continued. "Gwendolyn...he no longer treats me as such. In company he's respectful, but when alone, 'tis more...like I'm a bother. I always thought—oh, Gwendolyn, I should have seen it soon—"

"Good morn, Isabelle," Gavin called from the chair by the fire. His tone was curt.

Isabelle went rigid at Gavin's words. Her anguish was clear only to Gwen as she continued to face her. "Good morn, Gavin," she returned quietly.

Gwen couldn't help but be impressed. The way Isabelle held herself together was amazing. "I'm sorry, Isabelle," Gwen whispered. "I tried to tell you sooner, but you wouldn't let me finish." Gwen felt awful now that she hadn't stopped her, but she'd been so surprised by what Isabelle was saying. She had assumed that Gavin returned Isabelle's feelings. Was she the only one who saw it? Was she wrong?

Isabelle finally sat up and looked toward Gavin. "Gavin, did you show Gwendolyn the study or library yet?" she asked.

"Nay, think you she'd like to see them?"

"Of course she would," Isabelle said quietly, stepping from the bed.

Gwen shot Gavin a nasty look and mouthed "be nice," pointing her finger in accusation while Isabelle fussed with the bedcovers. Then, as if the exchange with Gavin hadn't taken place, Gwen asked, "What are you two talking about?"

Gavin stood and walked to them. "Come, we'll show you," he offered.

"I'll get something for you to cover yourself with, Gwendolyn, 'tis too early to dress."

As Isabelle walked to the bathroom, Gwen watched Gavin stare at her. She wore a beautiful white satin nightgown and matching robe tied low around her neck.

"What's wrong with you?" Gwen hissed.

Gavin's head snapped in her direction. "Pardon?"

"Don't act stupid, Gavin. If you hurt her, I swear—"

"I'd sooner die than hurt her."

"You're a little late, Gavin, you already have."

Their conversation came to an abrupt halt as Isabelle returned carrying Greylen's robe. Gwen noticed it in the bathroom yesterday and was happy that Isabelle had chosen it for her now. She slipped it on and stopped herself just before she brought the material to her face. She was about to inhale his scent. Grateful she'd saved herself in time, she covered her heated face by tying the belt around her waist. She waved her hand at the slippers Isabelle held out. "I'll go barefoot," she insisted.

Isabelle looked to Gavin. "Gwendolyn mustn't go barefoot throughout the keep, 'tis highly improper."

Gavin threw his hands in the air. "She wears Greylen's shirt and covered herself in his robe. *Whatever*," he replied, apparently happy to throw the term back at Gwen.

Isabelle took Gwen's hand and led her downstairs. They turned and walked past the archway that opened to the great hall. Narrow tables were situated along the hallway walls and sconces flickered, casting a soft glow. Isabelle stopped at the first set of doors they came to. Gavin leaned against the far side of the doorframe, facing Gwen as Isabelle turned to her. "This is my brother's private study, Gwendolyn. The *war room*, as I call it."

Isabelle's eyes lit up as she said it, and Gwen grabbed her cheeks to kiss her. "You're delightful, Isabelle." Gwen noticed that Gavin smiled at her words. Obviously, *Mr. Mixed Signals* agreed.

"Come, let's go inside." Isabelle pushed the doors, but they wouldn't budge. "Gavin?" Isabelle placed her hands on her hips and tapped her foot impatiently.

He smiled and reached into his pocket removing a key. "Allow me, ladies." He unlocked the doors and pushed them aside. "Wait a moment while I light the wicks."

Gwen stood in the doorway as Gavin brought the room to life. Her chest tightened as each lamp was lit, her heart pounding as she stared at a room that had to be the perfect reflection of Greylen. She could picture him working within. Worse, she could imagine herself sitting inside while he did.

Gavin finished and stood to the side, but Gwen seemed rooted to the floor. Isabelle finally grabbed her hand and pulled her in.

From where she stood inside the doorway, a large mahogany desk sat directly in front of her. A high-back leather chair behind it, and two in front. Behind the desk were polished wood shelves filled with leather-bound books and window seats built within each side.

Narrow tables sat on either side of the doors with oil lamps, ashtrays, and knickknacks. To her right was a large round table with seven chairs and to her left was a sitting area with a settee, as well as more chairs and tables. The stone floor was covered with an expensive silk rug, its pattern woven with dark threads, which were highlighted with gold. The walls were paneled in the same rich-colored wood as the desk, but they were covered from floor to ceiling with framed maps. The ones to her right were filled with tacks and markers. The ceiling was paneled as well.

Gwen brushed her hands over everything as she walked slowly through the room. She didn't miss a single item. When she stopped behind his desk, she looked at Gavin. He nodded, and she sat in Greylen's chair. She ran her hands over the desk and the items on top. There was a large burgundy blotter and matching trays filled with parchment and scrolls of paper. A quill and ink cup lay in the center, and brass tools scattered all around. There was a compass and something that she knew measured distance on a map, and a magnifying glass as well. The desk had three drawers, each of them with brass handles and a lock.

"Would you like the key, lady?" Gavin questioned.

"Nay." She shook her head. The word came so easily, and she saw Isabelle and Gavin smile at each other. "I meant no, Gavin. It's all right."

"Come, Gwendolyn, you must see the library," Isabelle exclaimed, clapping her hands.

"'Tis even better."

Gwen had no idea how they could top this room, but Isabelle's excitement was contagious. They waited just outside the doors as Gavin extinguished the lamps. And sadly, Gwen felt a loss that she had to leave.

"You may return anytime you wish, Lady Gwendolyn," Gavin told her, sensing her reluctance. "You need only ask. Isabelle, however, is correct. You'll be more pleased with the library."

They walked farther down the hallway and stopped at the room next to the study. Isabelle swatted Gavin's arm impatiently. "Go and light the wicks already. Hurry," she demanded.

He turned to look at them. "Remain here until I've finished."

It was an order, and Gwen wondered why he felt the need to be so stern. She was further surprised when he closed the doors behind him. A few minutes later Gavin came out, leaving the doors slightly ajar. "You may go in now, lady."

Gwen turned as she entered the room. The doors closed behind her. *They left her alone.* When she turned again, she was completely unprepared. Her hands came to her face and the air rushed from her lungs. Her eyes suddenly filled with tears and she stood there, staring at the incredible image in front of her. It was a portrait. The room was filled with them.

In a trance, she walked across the room, stopping in front of the massive likeness of Greylen, Isabelle, and their parents.

It must have been painted years ago. Isabelle appeared to be a child of no more than eight, and they were posed in front of the fireplace in this very room. The portrait was surrounded with a thick gold frame that sat atop the mantel. It was so large it had to be life-size.

Lady Madelyn was seated in a high-backed chair. She wore a deep-purple dress and her hair was swept back atop her head. Her hands held little Isabelle in front of her, who was dressed in a plaid skirt and white shirt with soft ruffles at the neck and wrists. Her shoulder-length hair curled sassily at the ends. Greylen's father stood to Lady Madelyn's left, a sword hanging from his waist. He wore a white linen shirt, black breeches, and tall polished boots. He looked so proud, and Gwen couldn't help but wonder what had become of him.

Greylen stood to his mother's right. He was so handsome. Just what she pictured when she had touched him. But there were no traces of the lines that she knew to be on his face now. This was the picture of a young man just discovering the world. She saw it in his features, in the twinkle in his eyes, and his wide genuine smile. His skin was bronzed from the sun and his eyes were so dark she wondered if they were truly black as the painting suggested.

He was dressed the same as his father but seemed much more carefree. His shirt was open at the neck and the sleeves had been rolled up, revealing his forearms. He held the hilt of his sword in his left hand, its point next to his boot. If this likeness were true, he had to stand well over six and a half feet tall. He was built just as she imagined. His shoulders were broad and his body long and powerful. And though she couldn't see the muscles through his shirt, she knew their form personally.

She sat in front of the fireplace, smiling offhandedly that Gavin lit it for her. She had no idea how long she remained on the floor staring at the painting, but for the first time in her entire life, she knew that this was where she truly belonged. She didn't want to be anywhere else. Ever.

After a while, she walked along the edge of the room. The wood floor was stained with a soft color, but the most beautiful feature was the intricate pattern the craftsman had designed around the rug that lay in its center. The colors in this room were softer, too, whites and beiges with subtle splashes of gold, burgundy, and blue in the pillows and drapes. There were bookshelves and paintings everywhere, and she looked at all of them. The more she saw of this family and their home, the more she wanted to be a part of it.

Strangely, she felt she already was.

Gwen began extinguishing the lamps at the far end of the room as she made her way toward the door. She checked the fire and placed the screen in front of it, though it was low enough now that it wouldn't cause any danger unattended. As she opened the door, she looked back once more at the portrait above the fireplace. She stepped from the room, a sad smile on her lips as she looked to Isabelle and Gavin. They wore their own sad looks, and she wondered why.

"Thank you, the both of you. I never imagined…" When she couldn't finish, Isabelle wrapped her arm around her shoulders.

"Don't cry, Gwendolyn. Greylen will come home soon."

"I know, I'm sorry. I just…I'm acting foolish." She really wanted to tell Isabelle that she missed Greylen, but she couldn't, not in front of Gavin.

"Come, ladies, back to the chamber. 'Tis still an hour or so before we can break our fast." Gavin's order was soft, though he looked at neither of them.

Gwen knew something had happened when she went in the library. He had no trouble speaking to them directly before. "Why don't I make breakfast for us?" Gwen offered. "I love to cook and I'm starving."

"If you're hungry, lady, I can wake Anna."

"You'll do no such thing, Gavin, I'm perfectly capable. And that woman deserves her rest. Besides, cooking makes me feel better, and trust me, I need to cook right now." Concerned for Isabelle, Gwen turned to her. "Isabelle, you seem awfully quiet, are you all right?"

"Aye, Gwendolyn, I'm fine," Isabelle assured her, then looked at Gavin. "Gwen's right, Gavin. There's no reason to wake Anna, and I'm hungry as well."

The look Gavin gave Isabelle was frightening. It was almost devoid of expression save the intensity of his eyes and a slight tic that marred his cheek, most likely from clenching his teeth so tightly. Gwen could almost feel his anger. She knew she could fix the situation if she could just get them into the kitchen.

"Gavin?" Gwen prompted sweetly.

"Aye, lady?" He sounded as if he knew he would not like what she was about to ask.

"Didn't you tell me that I was to have *anything* I so desire per your laird's instructions?" She had him now, and he knew it. Gavin gave her the same look he'd just given Isabelle, and it took all of her courage to defy him. "Come on, Isabelle, show me the kitchen," Gwen said, holding out her hand and leaving Gavin no choice but to follow them.

They continued down the hallway, then walked through the swinging doors at the end. "Oh my God," Gwen exclaimed, "this kitchen is fabulous." She turned to them. "What would you like for breakfast?" she asked. "I can make omelets, French toast, pancakes," then she added with less enthusiasm, "I suppose oatmeal, if that's what you'd like."

"What's an omelet, Gwendolyn?" Isabelle asked.

"Do you like eggs?"

"Aye, we have them all the time."

Isabelle sounded bored with her reply, and Gwen set her straight immediately. "An omelet is made with eggs, but filled with potatoes, cheese, onions, and ham."

"That sounds delicious," Isabelle exclaimed, her eyes bright once again.

"Well, what do you say, Gavin?" Gwen asked, turning to him. "You game?" Damn, he was tough, his face was completely expressionless.

"I'll leave it to the two of you," he answered. He walked away and sat at the large table on the right side of the room.

"Fine, just sit, Gavin. Isabelle and I will make you a meal you'll never forget." Hoping to give Gavin a few minutes alone, Gwen asked, "Okay, Isabelle, help me gather the ingredients?"

"The pantry's on the left, and the cellar's below," Isabelle explained as she walked to the door and opened it.

Floor-to-ceiling shelves were filled with all kinds of foods: spices, nuts, dried fruits, and an assortment of canisters that Gwen began to open. There was flour, sugar, oats, and things that she had no idea as to what they were. There were large burlap sacks on the floor, and she opened those next. She hoped her curiosity wasn't obnoxious, but she just couldn't seem to help herself. The first sack she opened had potatoes in it, and she took out two, handing them to Isabelle. She looked in the one next to it and found onions. Gwen jumped up and down again. "This is great, you have everything we need."

She already knew they had eggs and cheese, and the only thing missing now was some bacon or ham. She came out of the pantry intent to bring Gavin out of his stupor. "Gavin, is there any meat we can use?" she asked. He raised a brow but remained quiet.

Gwen tried again. "Something like bacon or ham. You know smoked meat, from a pig." Gwen made an oinking noise, and he finally smiled, shaking his head as he stood.

"Aye, lady, we've smoked meat—from a pig."

He walked past her, and she followed him. He picked up the wooden door built within the floor of the pantry, then proceeded to go down the steps to the cellar.

Gwen went back to opening sacks while Isabelle waited patiently by the door. There was one pushed far into the corner and Gwen pulled it out. She screamed happily when she saw what was inside.

Gavin came up, meat in hand. "Good God, lady. Your screams have probably awoken the entire holding."

"Gwendolyn, what is it?" Isabelle asked.

"What is it you ask? *It* happens to be coffee, and I can't live without it." She danced around in a circle, smelling the beans she held in her hands. *She had coffee!*

"It came on our last shipment," Gavin explained, "but we'd no idea of its use. Though it smelled wonderful, all of Cook's attempts left us…let's say, *very* unsatisfied."

Gavin seemed to be easing into a better mood much to Gwen's relief. "Gavin, you're in for a real treat." She smiled, and then frowned when she looked at his hands. "Where are the eggs?" she asked. Didn't he remember they were making an omelet?

"I forgot." He sighed, giving her the small slab of meat.

"Thanks," she called behind him before adding, "We need cheese, too, that soft orange one we had yesterday would be great." Gwen smiled at Isabelle. "Come on, let's get started."

They placed the items on the large island in the center of the kitchen. An enormous wood-burning stove ran along the back wall. It had two separate surfaces on top, one that looked like a large griddle while the other had various-size burners. There was a large fireplace, as well, with iron handles and rings set within the sides that she supposed were for roasting.

Figuring she had a couple minutes, Gwen took Isabelle by the shoulders. "What happened, Isabelle? Everything seemed fine when I went in the library, but when I came out, everything had obviously changed."

"Gwen, h-he…" A tear slipped from the corner of her eye, and Gwen wiped it away.

"Tell me, Isabelle, I won't break your confidence, I just want to help."

Isabelle tried again, this time whispering her words. "He held me, Gwendolyn. He pulled me against him, and we rested along the wall. My back was pressed to his chest and his arms held my waist. I could feel his head, Gwendolyn, it leaned on mine. We remained that way the entire time you were in the library."

Gwen's heart went out to her. "Oh, Isabelle, I'm sorry. Gavin probably feels guilty. He'll come around, just give it some time." Their conversation came to a quick stop when they heard Gavin close the cellar door. They busied themselves cleaning vegetables.

Beautiful wooden cabinets lined the walls, and Isabelle showed Gwen where the dishes and utensils were kept. For such an imposing room, it was just as charming as the rest of the house, especially the island where they stood. It only needed flowers. Then it would be perfect. There were three sinks, too, and each had a water pump and a drain.

They had plumbing after all.

After a while, the silence became deafening and Gwen had had enough. She wanted to enjoy her time with Gavin and Isabelle, and that's just what she intended to do. "Gavin, would you light the stove for me and put some stools around the island?" she asked. "That table's too big for just the three of us."

Gavin quietly went about the duties that she asked of him, and Gwen turned to Isabelle next. "Isabelle, why don't you set the table, but find a fry pan and a small boiling pot first."

"She's bossy isn't she, Bella?" Gavin asked with a soft smile.

"Aye, Gavin, she is," Isabelle replied with a cautious smile herself. "But we are going to keep her."

"Aye, Bella," he answered, returning her smile. "We are."

Their exchange hit Gwen so hard she almost cut herself. *They were in love with each other. Deeply in love.* Gavin obviously had a reason for keeping his distance. But Gwen was determined to find out what it was. Then she would put an end to it.

Thinking of how to approach him when she had the chance, Gwen put the fry pan on the stove and added the meat she'd cut into small pieces. She walked to the cabinets again, digging around. "Yes!"

"What have you found now, lady?" Gavin asked dryly.

"A new job for you," she answered with a smile. She handed him the bowl and pestle, then scooped some coffee beans from the canister she'd placed them in earlier. "Not too fine, Gavin," she instructed, "or we'll be drinking mud."

Gwen went back to the stove, adding diced potatoes and onions to the pan. Then she boiled water for the coffee.

"Isabelle, will you find some teacups and grab the sugar, too, please?"

"She's bossier than I ever imagined, Gavin." Isabelle laughed.

"Hey, hey, hey," Gwen said defensively, "we're almost done, and I promise you'll be happy. Gavin, we need one more thing, please."

"Aye, lady, what else can I get for you," he muttered with a sigh. "I swear, next time you're hungry, you're waiting for Cook or Anna."

Gwen was relieved that his normal tone was back now. "The last thing we need is cream for the coffee," she promised. Then she added the ground coffee to the boiling water and the eggs to the fry pan. When the eggs set, she added some cheese and turned her attention back to the coffee. She placed a cloth over each mug and carefully poured the liquid through. She wanted their first coffee experience to be a good one—coffee addicts liked company.

Gwen went back to the stove and folded the huge omelet before cutting it in three pieces, the one in the center larger. Then, using a towel, she brought the pan to the island and served the largest piece to Gavin.

"Isabelle should be served first, lady," Gavin instructed softly.

"I'm sure that would be appropriate, Gavin. But you didn't sleep last night and you deserve a good meal." With her free hand she reached out and held his chin. "I expect you to relieve yourself after breakfast," she ordered.

If Gavin seemed humbled by Gwen's display, then Isabelle's expression could only be described as shock, but her words explained their reaction. "Gwendolyn, you sound just like my brother." She laughed. "Not that Greylen would have shown any tenderness with such a command. More the like, he'd have knocked Gavin to the ground with his demand." Gwen smiled at her explanation, then Isabelle asked, "Should we say grace?"

"I have a better idea, but first we have to add sugar and cream to our coffee and pray that it tastes good," she said, laughing. Then Gwen did something she always wanted to do. And it was the perfect opportunity to bring Isabelle and Gavin closer together.

She held out her hands and smiled as they took them. Gwen explained that they would take turns stating something they were grateful for, and she offered to start. She was having more fun with them than they would ever know. Especially since Gavin and Isabelle had entwined their fingers, instead of just clasping their hands as they did with hers. *Progress. Definite progress.*

"I'm thankful I have both of you. You've each helped me so much, and I'll treasure whatever time we have together." Gwen's tone was very upbeat, hoping they'd play along. "Okay, Isabelle, it's your turn."

Isabelle stole a quick look at Gavin before turning back to Gwen. "I'm thankful you're here, Gwendolyn. This has been the most wonderful morn I've ever had."

Gwen squeezed Isabelle's hand and noticed, from the corner of her eye, Gavin did the same. "Okay, Gavin, your turn." She expected a fight and was surprised when he answered quickly.

"First, allow me to explain something, Lady Gwendolyn, and I will try my best not to *suck* at it. Your time here is infinite. I swear it on my life," he said emphatically. "Now, as to something I am thankful for...I am thankful this torture is almost over, for I truly believe that you can cook."

"I'll cook for you whenever you'd like." Gwen grinned as she reached for her coffee. Then she closed her eyes and moaned as the warm liquid slid down her throat. When she opened them again, Gavin and Isabelle were both staring at her like she'd lost her mind.

"Go on." She waved her hand. "I dare you both to try it and not like it as much."

Gavin took a small sip, then more as his eyes widened in surprise. "Lady Gwendolyn, first thing this morn, you're to show Cook how you made this."

"I told you," Gwen returned. "Now try your omelet."

They devoured their omelets, and Gavin and Gwen each had another cup of coffee after their meals. Together they cleared their dishes and placed them in the sink. But when Gwen tried to wash them, Gavin threatened to sit on her again, telling her that she'd done enough already.

The sun had just started to rise as Gavin hurried them upstairs. Since they were still in their nightclothes—

or Greylen's, in her case—she could tell Gavin hoped to avoid being seen by any servants who might be starting their duties.

When they stepped inside Greylen's chamber, Isabelle told Gwen she was going to dress and would meet her in the great hall. Gavin quickly excused himself and followed after her.

The halls were still dark with just the soft flicker from the sconces, and he caught Isabelle just as she reached the steps of the landing. "Bella, wait," he whispered, reaching for her arm. She looked up, her blue eyes wary and so disconcerting in their depth.

"I'm sorry I upset you earlier. 'Twas never my intention. I shouldn't have…I shouldn't have touched you, Isabelle. 'Twas wrong and I seek your forgiveness." He felt as though his honor was at stake and hers as well.

Earlier when Isabelle had started to follow Gwen into the library, he'd pulled her back. He'd reached around her waist with one arm while closing the doors behind Gwendolyn with the other. "Gavin, why—" Her words stopped when her back came to rest against his chest.

"Shh, Isabelle," he'd whispered in her ear. "Allow Gwendolyn to see this herself."

He hadn't said more and assumed Isabelle would have allowed Gwendolyn to live the rest of her days in the library, so long as he didn't make her move.

He didn't.

Isabelle didn't ask him what had changed his inhibition toward her, and neither spoke of it then. Gavin kept backing up and pulling her with him until his body rested against the wall. His arms wrapped around her waist as she leaned against him and he gathered her even closer. They stood facing the library doors. He had closed his eyes, and sensed Isabelle had done the same. They had remained that way the entire time, silently enjoying the embrace that each of them had only dreamed of.

"You owe me no apology, Gavin," she whispered, bringing him out of his reverie while continuing to stare at him.

"I can offer you nothing, Bella." He all but choked on the words.

She reached for the lock of hair that had fallen to the side of his face, stroking it between her fingers before brushing it back. "You've more value than you know, Gavin," she whispered.

Then she turned and walked slowly back to her room.

❦ CHAPTER TEN ❦

As adjustments go, it could've been a lot worse.

But truthfully, it wasn't that bad.

Gwen found a place among Greylen's family in the long days that followed. She fell easily into a routine and truly enjoyed herself in this place she now called her home. And though she battled endlessly with Gavin, she was grateful for the bond they had formed.

She awoke early every morning and later had breakfast in the great hall with Isabelle and Lady Madelyn. She acquainted herself with Greylen's men-at-arms and though she liked them all, it was Gavin with whom she felt most comfortable. After that first night he'd stayed in her chamber, as it was now referred to, he changed his rotation of duties. He slept after dawn and saw to his duties in the afternoon. Then he would resume her guard after their evening meal.

No one ever mentioned that she, Isabelle, or Gavin ate lightly at supper. For now, they enjoyed the habit of sneaking to the kitchen when everyone retired. Gwen made wonderful meals late every night, and they sat around the center island of the kitchen, always holding hands before speaking of something that they were thankful for.

She hadn't seen Gavin approach Isabelle again. Instead he stole looks at her when he thought no one watched. Sometimes when they retired to Gwen's chamber, she and Gavin would sit by the fire and talk quietly, while other times they didn't speak at all. Gwen knew they relished the time they spent together, each it seemed for different reasons. Yet there seemed no mistaking they shared a common bond: contentedness.

During the day, Gwen spent time with Lady Madelyn, and walked along the paths throughout the holding and those around the keep. She visited the chapel, as well, and Greylen's men always gave her privacy to seek her solace alone. She met Father Michael and liked him at once. He was a wise man, old in years, and he often prayed with her. They spoke of the loneliness she'd felt with her family. The happiness she found in what she now assumed as her home. And Father Michael continued to assure her that if she was true to her heart, God's plan could only follow.

She almost laughed in his face the first time he'd said it. But she hoped he was right. She loved it here. She loved Isabelle, Lady Madelyn, Anna, and Gavin. And she loved Seagrave and all of its people. She'd finally found a home, a place where she belonged.

And it was worth everything she had to give up.

She missed Sara, but she had her bracelet, the gift that Sara had made for her. She missed Mr. MacGreggor, too, but she knew that he'd be loved and cared for. She missed alligator clips, blue jeans, and tacos. Well, she missed a lot of things. But they weren't things that she needed. Honestly, she had everything she needed. Except for Greylen.

He was constantly on her mind, especially when she sat behind the keep. The view from atop the cliffs became one of her favorites, and she stayed there in the afternoons. There were benches and flower gardens, and she loved discovering her way through the endless passages within.

Isabelle remained by her side most of the time and left only to join her tutor, who came in the afternoons to see to her studies and lessons on the harpsichord. Gavin could always be found in Greylen's study before supper, and she would join him, poring through the volumes of Greylen's books while she sat on the settee.

One afternoon she was elated to find empty journals along one of the shelves and asked Gavin if she might use one. He showed her how to dip the quill in ink, his surprise obvious when she'd used her left hand.

"I know, Gavin, he's a lefty too. I could tell from the letter he wrote to me."

"Would you like to sit at the desk, my lady?"

"Nay, Gavin, I'll use the window seat instead." They exchanged a look when she answered, but she didn't correct her words. She was becoming more like them every day.

In fact, it was the window seat in the study where she sat on the eighth day after Greylen's departure when riders approached the holding. It was just before their evening meal and she watched as Gavin went to greet them in the bailey. By the time he stood before them, Duncan, Kevin, and Hugh were already at his side. One of the riders dismounted while the other six remained. After what seemed an eternity, Gavin finally turned, calling orders to the men as he strode back to the keep. Gwen hurried from the study and nearly bumped into Isabelle. They waited in the hallway, and Isabelle took Gwen's hand as they looked worriedly to Gavin when he entered the foyer.

"'Tis a missive from Greylen," he explained. "He calls for two hundred men."

"I don't understand," Gwen said. She was shaking and felt Isabelle do the same.

"Greylen was called to witness a trial. The accused attempted to take the life of our sovereign. During its course, the weak man crumbled and implicated another." Gavin spat the words, clearly disgusted by the cowardly act.

"Do you ride as well?" Isabelle asked calmly. But Gwen knew it was an act. She'd already lost the feeling in her hand from Isabelle's grasp.

"Nay, your brother orders that I remain. Duncan will ride with our troops and the king's men who brought the missive. Greylen awaits their arrival, satisfied to have three men-at-arms and the king's men as well. He's confident their charge will be swift and only calls so many to make his point. The game is over." Gavin began walking toward the study, then turned after a few steps. "Lady Gwendolyn, I'll see you now. *Alone*."

Isabelle and Gwen shared a worrisome look before Gwen squeezed her hand and followed him. It was only when he closed the door that she noticed the package in his hand. It was wrapped in a plain cloth, the size of an overly large book.

He held it out to her. "'Tis from Greylen. Would you like some privacy?"

"Nay, Gavin, stay." Gwen sat in her favorite spot atop the settee and slowly unwrapped the cloth. She was surprised to find a beautiful rose-colored velvet bag beneath, further hiding the contents.

"He'd not want anyone to know for whom it was intended and covered it plainly," Gavin explained. "Only his missive informed me 'twas a gift for you."

Gwen untied the gold braided cord and held her breath as she looked inside. It was a carved wooden box inlaid with large, colorful jewels. She carefully pulled it out and ran her fingers across the top. The stones were set deep within the lid, and the craftsmanship was outstanding. She slowly opened the top and smiled at Gavin. There was a letter inside, sealed with his crest. The infamous dragon.

Gavin watched as she held the missive to her lips, obviously happy to see the delight it brought his "mistress" as he always referred to her. As if affording her some privacy, he walked quietly to the window behind the desk.

Gwen broke the seal and held the parchment with both hands.

My dearest Gwendolyn,

I seek your grace once again. My journey has been delayed, though I should return by month's end. You must make Seagrave your home, Gwendolyn. I pray you forgive me once more.

Yours,
Greylen Allister MacGreggor

"Gavin, may I write back to him?"

"Aye, lady, but you've only a minute. Our troops are always ready to travel and will leave shortly."

Gwen ran to the desk and picked up a quill while Gavin unlocked the drawer to her left and removed Greylen's initialed seal. "Tell me when you've finished. I'll show you how the letter is sealed."

Gwen reached for the parchment in the tray at the corner of Greylen's desk. There was so much she wanted to tell him, so much she wanted to say. She did the best she could to express how she felt. *Be careful what you wish for, Greylen.*

"Lady Gwendolyn, the men must leave," Gavin told her only a minute later. He came to her side and removed the glass from the oil lamp. Then he placed a stick of burgundy wax in the flame and instructed her to fold the letter in three. As the hot wax dripped along the seam, he handed her a brass instrument. She saw the initials embossed at the end and smiled as she pressed it into the wax. They couldn't have been more appropriate.

When Gavin left, she picked up the gift that Greylen had sent to her. She settled in the cushions of the window seat, hugging the letterbox as she stared at the garden.

Days later Gavin was ready to rip out his hair strand by strand. His lady's current request was outrageous.

"Explain to me your meaning again, Lady Gwendolyn," he asked through clenched teeth as they sat before the fire. Isabelle had already changed into her bedgown as she did every night before they went to the kitchen. And he swore she did it on purpose, driving him mad to see her as such. His mistress changed as well before these *raids*, as she referred to them, donning his laird's shirt and robe.

"I need to exercise, Gavin. I'm going crazy, and my bruises and cuts are completely healed." As if sensing his discomfort at her request she went on, "But, if I continue to do nothing, I'm going to lose my mind."

"Ladies don't exercise, mistress. They take strolls and see to household duties," he purposely corrected. He was pleased with the response he received as Isabelle covered her mouth with her hands, barely suppressing a laugh.

"Gavin, I need to run, I need to do sit-ups, I need to start boxing again. Please."

"You cannot think to run, lady, I've made myself clear. You will remain here." *God but she had a thick skull.*

"You misunderstand, Gavin. I don't wish to run away. I like to run distances. It helps me think, and I miss the feeling of invigoration it gives me."

"I thought you preferred Lady Madelyn's potion or brandy," he remarked dryly. "Don't think I've not seen you run for the decanter after something's unsettled you."

His mistress smiled. "Okay, so I admit I still have a hard time with certain things. Trust me, Gavin, you would too. But it's not the same as running. And, besides, it's a much better vice." She stood a little taller, her eyes gleamed, and her smile lifted but a touch. "Would you give up training?" she asked. "Doesn't it help you clear your mind and make you feel invincible?"

Damn, she had a point. "Where would you do this running?" he asked. He shook his head, disgusted that he'd even considered it. Greylen would have his hide. But Gavin would kill him first, with his bare hands, for leaving this to him.

"I could run in circles around the castle, or down the path through the cottages. I don't care, Gavin. I'll run up and down the steps if that's all you'll let me do." She grabbed his hands and said, "I'm begging. *God, this sucks.*"

"What of this 'boxing' as you call it?" Damn, he did it again. How did she always make him see her way? His stomach turned as her face lit up and a wicked smile crossed her lips.

Double damn!

"Ready for some fun?" she asked mischievously.

"Nay, lady, I'm truly not," he said, shaking his head.

"Too bad, Gavin, hold your hands up in front of you and I'll show you what boxing is." She moved toward him, throwing her robe to Isabelle, who sat watching with obvious glee.

His mistress gave him what she referred to as a "dirty" look as he rolled his eyes and held his hands out. "Nay, not like that," she said. "Palms out and up, in front of your chest, please." He complied, begrudgingly. "Thank you, *very kind* sir."

Gavin had no time to respond, for his mistress made a perfect fist with each of her hands and began jabbing at him. First with high straight punches, then she swung low from the waist. And he found himself moving his hands, catching her every blow.

From the corner of his eye, he saw Isabelle watch in wonder. The same look he knew he carried himself as Gwendolyn beat relentlessly upon his hands. He hadn't realized that she was just getting started, until he sensed the excitement and adrenaline coursing through her body. 'Twas a feeling he knew well.

Gavin laughed as she began a routine of punches mixed with sidekicks, astonished as his mistress continued, stronger than before. He moved his arms, now pushing her further as they both became embroiled in the game. 'Twas long minutes later she ended with a reverse kick, bowing to him, her face flushed from exertion. "That was great, Gavin."

"I've not seen *anything* the likes before," he admitted with a shake of his head. "Your moves were graceful and quick. You've the heart and body of a warrior, Lady Gwendolyn. I commend you," he praised, returning her bow.

She must've been pleased for she reached up and kissed his cheek. "Thank you, Gavin." Assured she'd made her point, she added, "Can I run in the morning?"

"Aye, lady," he conceded. "But you must always have your guard. If you'd prefer, you may wait, and I'll accompany you in the afternoon," he added, disbelieving that he'd done so.

Anna, too, had to get accustomed to Gwen's strange habits and requests. The first of which was her use of Greylen's razor to shave her legs.

The shock on Anna's face was priceless, and when Isabelle saw what Gwen did, she asked if she could do the same. Gwen gave her that wicked smile that she'd become famous for, the one that sent Gavin, Anna, and Greylen's men into fits. Isabelle returned the smile and cast aside her dress before jumping into the enormous tub with Gwen. Anna almost fainted, but Gwen and Isabelle only laughed. Then with all seriousness, they went about Isabelle's new lessons.

Gwen was responsible for Anna's next mental crisis as well. It occurred when Gwen asked for her clothing back. Though Gwen knew that she tried, Anna didn't have a good enough reason to refuse her. She went to Greylen's bureau and removed them from the bottom drawer. Gwen was thrilled to have her running shoes back and hoped that they'd last forever. Anna gave her new laces since the others had been destroyed. Greylen had apparently used his dagger when he removed them from her person.

But Gwen's next request, Anna flatly refused. "Absolutely not, Lady Gwendolyn, you've an entire wardrobe at your disposal. The clothing fashioned for you is beyond compare and known to only the very wealthy."

"Anna, I love everything you've made for me. My dresses, and the robe that matches Greylen's, even the slippers and sandals. But I can't exercise in a dress, Anna. And these bloomers are—well, just forget what they are." Gwen took Anna's hands, pleading her case. Thankfully, Lady Madelyn entered the chamber. Gwen knew she'd see reason. Greylen's mother was exceptional and her understanding boundless.

"Lady Madelyn, I'm trying to explain to Anna that I need clothes similar to these so I can exercise." Gwen held up the clothing in her hands to show Lady Madelyn what she was referring to.

"What exactly do you need, Gwendolyn?" Lady Madelyn asked. "I'm sure it can't be that unreasonable." She looked at her perplexed servant. "Anna, she insists on wearing Greylen's shirt instead of the lovely bedgowns, and I know she never uses the bloomers or undergarments."

"I need pants similar to these," Gwen explained. "I'll only wear them when I run or box." She held the pants up in front of Anna. They were her tight-fitting capris. "A drawstring waist would be fine, they don't even have to be as snug, I just need pants, *please*."

"Very well, lady," Anna said with a sigh. "I'll see to it myself."

"Anna, I'm not quite done," Gwen said, biting her lip.

"Oh my." Anna sat on the trunk at the end of the bed, fanning herself.

Gwen hoped she wouldn't faint at the forthcoming request. "I need underwear, Anna, not bloomers. And I need a bra. Underwear fits tightly and only covers your bottom and front." Gwen drew lines with her hands along her body, showing Anna exactly what she was talking about. "And a bra supports your breasts."

Anna smirked. "You needn't cover your breasts, child."

"Anna, if I only wear pants and Greylen's shirts tied around my waist, my breasts will show clearly through. Everyone will see them." Gwen pulled the shirt she was wearing tight across her chest to prove her point.

"Oh my." Anna began to sway.

Gwen rushed to her side. "I don't mean to cause you discomfort, Anna. Even a band of cloth I can tie behind my back will do, or something similar to a halter." Gwen drew lines once again to explain what she meant. "If you can't make underwear, we can fashion thongs instead," she teased.

"That's quite enough, child," Anna admonished, swatting her bottom. "Underwear you shall have. I know your measurements well enough—but you'll not have that string you speak of. Is that understood?"

"Aye, Anna, thank you."

As Anna left the room, Greylen's mother settled herself in one of the chairs in front of the window. "'Tis a beautiful view, Gwendolyn," she remarked.

"Aye, Lady Madelyn, it is."

Lady Madelyn smiled so warmly at her that Gwen found herself sitting by her feet, looking up at her.

"You're a true delight, Gwendolyn. I count myself lucky to gain a daughter such as you."

"That's yet to be seen, Lady Madelyn."

"Do you doubt my son's intentions, Gwendolyn?"

"Nay, Lady Madelyn." Gwen sighed. "I doubt life itself."

"Oh, Gwendolyn, you mustn't worry so. Whatever happened before you came to us was meant to be. Just as is your being with us now."

Gwen rested her head on Lady Madelyn's lap, feeling a mother's love for the first time as Lady Madelyn stroked her head and hummed to her softly.

After a while, Lady Madelyn spoke again. "When Greylen returns, you'll be mistress of this castle, Gwendolyn, and I think you shall have an idyllic life. Though there is the matter of your strong wills." She laughed softly. "I fear you'll come to blows many times over."

After her short time with Greylen, Gwen worried that Lady Madelyn's words couldn't have been truer.

✤ CHAPTER ELEVEN ✤

Greylen stood with Ian and Connell as his soldiers advanced in the distance. He'd left Stirling Castle two days after his missive had been dispatched to Seagrave. Then rode three more to the area where they made their camp. Though he'd wanted nothing more than to return home himself, he had matters to discuss with his king and knew if he stayed to see to them now, his presence wouldn't be required until at least summer's end. That is, barring any situations such as the one they now found themselves in.

By the time the men were settled and had finished discussing their plans, 'twas well past midnight. Twelve days had passed since he'd left Seagrave and Greylen was anxious to hear what had taken place in his absence. More than anxious. He waited patiently for the men to bed down, then saw personally to the placement of guards around their encampment.

At last able to speak to his men-at-arms, Greylen walked with them to the lake at the base of their camp. The moon's reflection shone brightly atop the water casting a glow as they stood beneath a canopy of trees. They formed a close circle, Ian and Connell by his side and Duncan in front of him.

"I will have details, Duncan. Now," Greylen ordered, crossing his arms over his chest.

"All's well at Seagrave," Duncan said quickly. "I'd have informed you earlier otherwise."

"Those are not details, Duncan. You'll tell me how Gwendolyn fares," he demanded.

"Lady Gwendolyn fares well. Though, at times, she does make a run for the brandy."

Greylen raised a brow. "Think you she has a problem?"

"With spirits, nay." Duncan scoffed. "A small *shot* she calls it." Then he smiled. "'Tis enchanting."

"Explain, Duncan," Greylen bit out, irritated by Duncan's *enchantment* with his lady.

"Well, first, your lady becomes unsettled. 'Tis the only time she reaches for it."

"And *what*, pray tell, unsettles my lady?" Greylen asked through clenched teeth. He was ready to throttle the man.

"Well..." Duncan shrugged. "There was the time she helped your mother tend one of the children who'd fallen ill. It seems she's quite the practiced healer, and her way with the boy was amazing. When we left the cottage, however, she cursed her way back to the keep, muttering something about not being able to help as she should. Then there was the time she happened upon the butcher." Duncan laughed, a hearty belly laugh. "I think she's not seen how meat goes from pasture to table. But..." He smiled looking pointedly at Greylen. "Your lady becomes most upset when your fighting skills are bandied about. Nothing sends her to the decanter with more speed than a tale of you in battle. The transformation's astounding," he exclaimed before quipping the order in which it occurred. "Unsettling news, muttering curses, brisk walk to the brandy, her hand held in gesture to be left for a moment's peace. Then, finally, she turns with the most serene of smiles upon her face."

Greylen tried not to smile, appeased at last with information and not surprised in the least at what that information was. "Continue, Duncan," he instructed, his hands now clasped behind his back.

"She spends most of her time with Isabelle and takes her morning and evening meals in the great hall. She walks throughout the holding and visits the chapel in the late-morning hours, often speaking with Father Michael when he's present."

"What of her reaction to my departure?" Greylen asked.

"I wasn't privy to the telling but was told she handled it with grace."

Greylen ignored the last of Duncan's statement. No doubt, Gwendolyn bit Gavin's head off when he informed her of his absence. He asked now of the former, for his men met daily to discuss all, significant or not. "Gavin didn't inform you of what transpired?"

"Nay. Though we saw her that day, Gavin remained her only guard until the following morn."

"And your time with her after?" Greylen asked.

"There's not much to tell. Our guard duties have shifted. Kevin, Hugh, or I follow her only in the morn and afternoon. And during those times, she's shown us nothing but respect and kindness. Your sister and Lady Madelyn are always by her side, and her only time alone is when she remains behind the keep while Isabelle seeks her lessons," Duncan revealed easily.

"What of her night guard? Does no one watch her then?" Greylen demanded. His hands fisted by his sides and the muscles in his face tightened.

"Gavin's with her. He assumes her guard from late afternoon through morning. As I've said, he's changed our rotation. He now sleeps in the morning and sees to the men and ledgers in the afternoon. He's done so since the night you left," Duncan explained.

"Why has he assumed such a position, Duncan? 'Tis not reasonable." As Greylen voiced the question, a feeling unknown began to stir through his veins.

"Lady Gwendolyn prefers his guard. Since that first morning, Gavin remains her solitary shadow from dusk till dawn." Duncan paused, but when Greylen didn't reply he continued, "She refuses to allow him to stand beyond her doors and orders that he sit within the chamber till morn. 'Tis most likely why he retains the night shift alone."

"*YOU LIE*," Greylen accused, pulling his man within an inch of his face, his reaction so fierce that his hands ripped Duncan's shirt.

"I speak the truth, Greylen. She's as strong-willed as you. And her orders just as serious."

"She's a *woman*, Duncan." The statement came in a roar. "She doesn't give orders, nor would my trusted friend stay within *my* chamber."

"I speak the truth. I would not lie."

Greylen was furious at what he'd heard and threw Duncan against the tree behind him. Ian and Connell grabbed his shoulders, pulling him back. Greylen was in the process of shaking them off when Connell's next words stopped him.

"Gavin pines for Isabelle, Greylen. Not your lady."

Duncan confirmed what Greylen just heard. "'Tis the sorry truth of it, Greylen. Gavin's feelings for Lady Gwendolyn run deep, but he protects her tender heart *only*, and helps her through the nights. She has a pain in her eyes that's unreachable. Yet *he* is able to help her as no one else can."

"'Tis not his duty to help my *wife* in such ways," Greylen shouted, realizing now the feeling that consumed him. Jealousy. Gavin was the one who was with her, helping her, and it ate him alive. His men showed no surprise that he'd referred to Lady Gwendolyn as his wife, for in truth, 'twas only the formality of the priest's words that were absent.

"He allows her to know you as you cannot."

"Explain yourself, Duncan," Greylen demanded, his fury barely held in check.

"He treats her as mistress of the castle, as he should, but includes her in everything. He gives in to almost all of her demands."

"'Tis not helping, Duncan." Greylen made the reply through clenched teeth.

"She finds comfort with him because he allows her to be herself. They yell and slam doors. And I swear to God above, sparks fly throughout the holding when they're about. She's just like you, 'tis the sorry truth you make me confess. But 'twas Gavin himself who placed your medallion around her neck the first night you were gone. And 'tis Gavin who allows her to enter your study whenever she wishes. 'Tis you they both miss, Greylen. Gavin's your most trusted companion, your truest friend, and he's become Lady Gwendolyn's as well."

"Leave me," Greylen commanded. Then he spoke without turning as he walked toward the water. "We break camp before dawn. I'll not wait longer."

Furious with the information he'd received, Greylen stripped his clothing and entered the lake. He swam its width twice before making his way back to shore. His anger at last under control, he secured his breeches and sat by the water's edge recalling what Duncan had told him.

What really plagued him, he realized, was that he should be the one with Gwendolyn. That was the true heart of the matter. He knew Gavin would never betray him, nor would he jeopardize the life he'd found at Seagrave. He trusted his first-in-command with his life and his family's as well. And Gavin took his responsibility with a seriousness that at times left him humbled.

Gavin would walk through the fires of hell before endangering his position among them. And now Greylen also knew that what Connell had said was true. Gavin did in fact pine for Isabelle—it had been so for years. He was a fool, how could he not have seen it?

Gavin had always doted on Isabelle, but over the years, he had become more distant with her. He'd stopped calling her Bella as he had since the first day he met her.

And he'd ceased to chase after her when she playfully tried to gain his attention. He rarely sought the comfort of women, though they constantly tried to gain his favor. And he did so, only now, after being well into his cups, carrying the foulest of disposition for days afterward.

Why had Gavin never broached the subject with him? He of all people would understand his friend's plight.

Was it the past he never spoke of?

Greylen knew he ran from something, though he knew not from what. He never questioned Gavin of his past, and in fact knew him only as Gavin the Brave. A more appropriate moniker could not have been. Now, however, Greylen decided 'twas time to talk to his friend. Love was indeed too precious, and if 'twas Isabelle whom Gavin sought, by God, he'd have her.

At last back in his right mind, Greylen headed toward camp. He nodded to the guards posted around the perimeter, then inspected the weapons and horses and checked the well-being of his men. Satisfied they'd be rested by dawn, he made his way to the fire. His men were talking quietly, awaiting his return.

"I owe you an apology, Duncan. But damn your telling was twisted," Greylen told his man with a smile.

"'Tis I who am sorry…for jumbling the facts. You had me in such a state, I forgot to give you this," he explained as he held a sealed parcel before him.

"The camp's secured. Other than the guards, we're the only ones awake. Seek your rest, 'tis but hours before we march." Greylen made the order as he took the parcel in his hand. His men left him to his solitude, bedding down behind the tree Greylen sat against.

He opened the envelope and spilled the contents atop his lap. There were two missives and he chose the thickest first, affixed with Gavin's insignia: the hawk. 'Twasn't a letter as he assumed, but instead an account of the days Gwendolyn had spent at Seagrave. There were seven entries in all, each shorter in length as the dates progressed.

Eleventh of June,

Read this through, lest you reach the wrong conclusion. I now sit within your chamber and your lady rests within your bed. She wished not to be alone and I swear she ordered I not remain beyond the doors.

She handled the news of your departure with dignity, though a sadness lies beneath she tries to hide. She insisted on leaving the holding so many times, it became apparent she knew not her place. Her further shock at her new surroundings was very real. I was forced to speak of the prophecy, though loosely, and we seem to have come to an unspoken understanding.

I find I am unable to leave her guard and will not do so 'til the morrow. Your medallion lies upon her heart, and your letter within her hand. She stood before the window and watched the setting sun. For a moment, 'twas you who I saw there, as you often wondered of the destiny the writings foretold.

Twelfth of June,

I've changed my rotation, not allowing another to stay within your lady's chamber. She's healing nicely and has been inside your study as well as the library. Her reactions to both were telling and her emptiness at your absence is written across her face. Yet I am the only one she allows to see it, for I think she knows I, too, have carried such pain. She stood by the window once more before taking to your bed, always stroking the medallion until sleep claims her.

Greylen was surprised that his friend revealed such information of himself, and its telling nature. He also understood now that what Duncan had told him was true. Gavin and Gwendolyn had formed a bond in his absence, yet he was jealous no more.

Thirteenth of June,

'Tis day three of your absence, and your lady's a creature of habit. Isabelle remains her constant companion and your mother seeks her company in the library after supper. Her will knows no bounds and she tries my patience repeatedly. Yet, once again, 'tis forgotten when I watch her approach the window at night.

Fourteenth of June,

Your lady's truly perplexing. She smiles gleefully at the simplest things, such as today when she found a blank journal to use among your books in the study. Then she has the nerve to stare me down when I correct her of the simplest impropriety. You should be home on the morrow, 'tis a day I'm grateful for.

Greylen began to smile as he read the next entry. It broadened as he continued.

Fifteenth of June,

Sir, your absence is vexing. My hair is thinning and it seems she rules in your absence. There's no listening to reason where your lady's concerned. By the time she's done shaking her head at me, the leather strip of yours she uses to secure her hair is completely loose. If you're not heard from soon, I shall gladly begin locking her within her chamber myself.

Sixteenth of June,

I've found my first gray hair this morn, and it should be yours. Damn your sorry hide.

Seventeenth of June,

You shall be hanged from a rope…and I will beat you myself…as I light the logs I imagine beneath your feet.

Greylen laughed aloud at the last entry, pleased to know that Gavin truly did have a new friend. And though Gavin's agitation was apparent, Greylen enjoyed the knowledge that Gwendolyn pushed him as she did. That was the woman he knew for only two short days. God how he missed her.

He folded the letter and reached for the other. 'Twas only one page and when he flipped it over, he was surprised to see his initialed insignia pressed within its seal. Isabelle and his mother each had their own. Only one other would need the use of his.

He held his breath as he spread the parchment, looking at the delicate script before his eyes. A bark of laughter escaped with the first of her words.

Dear Greylen,

You'll be happy to know, I've decided not to kick your ass. And in light of the details you failed to mention before you left, I hope you realize the sacrifice I'm making. If you don't come home safely, however, I swear I'll reconsider. On a more pleasant note, I love the gift you sent me. Thank you.

I've also taken your advice. I've made Seagrave my home. But it's not the same without you. Please come home to me, Greylen. Please come home and kiss me again.

Forever yours,
Gwendolyn Anastasia

PS: We're low on brandy.

Greylen's smile could've lit the night sky. He was wed. And he held the evidence in his hand. Feisty wench, she'd get an earful when he returned. But he couldn't have been more pleased, nor did he expect differently from her.

He read the letter again, overcome by the same emotions. A sharp bark of laughter at her feisty reprimand, a smile of sublime pleasure from her honest gratitude, and her wish for him to return quite simply pierced his heart.

But what struck him most—and now seemed all too clear—was her vulnerability.

She hid it well.

He'd not deny she was strong-willed, nor quick with wit. True enough, she was. But he'd seen through her bluster from the very first, 'twas a safeguard from hurt. She might come through the gates fighting, and so far, had on almost all of the occasions they were together. Yet she always surrendered to him.

In gesture and touch, in passion and exhaustion, she always surrendered.

She had begun to trust him, and her tenderness was the reward. She wanted to believe but with his absence had doubt. He read it in her letter, her fear for his safety cleverly written in her admonishment. Not to mention her not so subtle message, *you left me*, which she'd underlined.

The woman had a way with words.

Thank God he could see through them.

CHAPTER TWELVE

"Kevin, I'll not ask you again. Have a seat," Gwen demanded, waving to the chair once more. "*Now.*"

Kevin took great pains to look around the room and seemed relieved no one was about. He must have realized he didn't have a choice and did as she ordered.

"I'm sure 'tis nothing, Lady Gwendolyn. We should be back at it on the morrow," Kevin said, referring to the run Gwen knew he'd come to enjoy.

"Are you sure this is the leg, Kevin? I thought you favored the right?" she asked as she ran her hands over said leg. Gwen was sure he muttered "damn" under his breath.

"Aye, lady, 'tis the left," Kevin grumbled.

Not sure what to believe anymore, she decided to check both. "Well, it seems okay, but you're probably right. A day of rest and you'll be fine." Gwen held out her hand for her morning guard and smiled when he couldn't help but laugh at her.

"You mock me?" she joked, placing her hands on her hips.

"Nay, lady, I apologize," Kevin said, taking her hand. "Thank you, for helping me stand."

"I'm sorry, Kevin. I guess it was pretty stupid, seeing as you're about three times my size." She laughed.

"Your compassion is endless, Lady Gwendolyn. I meant no insult."

"Oh stop it," she muttered. "You didn't insult me. Just give me a minute and I'll change."

Once inside the bathing chamber, Gwen removed the pants Anna had made for her to exercise in. They weren't as tight fitting as her capris, but they were comfortable and suited their purpose.

Of course, Anna hadn't been happy when she noticed Gwen folded the hem halfway up her calves. And she had a complete fit when she noticed Gwen also rolled the waistband over. Apparently, it wasn't appropriate to show the outline of one's bottom and legs. But breasts were an entirely different story.

Every dress she had now fit so tight across her chest, no wonder Anna scoffed at making her a bra to wear beneath. There was no room. Still, Anna did make her some bikini-style panties and a few bra-like undergarments too. And they fit perfectly. Some were fashioned in the shape of a halter that tied behind her neck and back. While the others were just a plain wide band she could wrap around her chest and tie wherever.

Removing the rest of her clothing, Gwen hung Greylen's shirt on the same hook as her robe. Even though she had her own now, it was Greylen's that she chose to wear.

She left the rest of her exercise clothes on the chest of drawers next to the door. She'd use them later, after Gavin made her beg him to go jogging. She knew that he secretly enjoyed the days she waited until he was able to join her, but he definitely took pleasure in making her grovel. She didn't mind, though. He was a great runner and pushed her further than she ever imagined. Plus, she enjoyed her time with him more than anything.

Gwen grabbed one of her favorite day dresses from the drawer in the chest. It was the one concession that Anna had given easily, allowing her to keep most of her clothes in here. It was more convenient than using the bureau in her room, as this was where she changed. Someone was always in her room, and she preferred it that way. Besides, her bureau was filled with beautiful gowns and things that she didn't know if she'd ever use. Things, for that matter, she didn't know if she'd ever figure out what in the hell they were.

The dress she chose today was deep green and much like the one she'd worn of Isabelle's until her own wardrobe had been finished. It had three-quarter-length sleeves and a low, scooped neckline that stretched tightly across her chest. It cinched at the waist, then gave gradually to the floor-length hem. She enjoyed wearing these dresses each day. They made her feel feminine despite her narrow frame.

The last thing she picked up was a pair of leather sandals the cordwainer—translation: shoemaker—had made for her. They were very comfortable. The man had a true talent. Gavin had shown him her running shoes and he'd been able to fashion shoes for Greylen's men with soles just as supportive, yet flexible. And though the materials he used were vastly different, they worked quite well. Gavin, Kevin, and Hugh had no problem pacing her.

In truth, she had no problem pacing them.

Finishing her routine, Gwen brushed her hair before tying it with one of Greylen's leather straps. She had a drawer filled with ribbons and hair combs of her own now, but she preferred to use his things. She also had a drawer with makeup in it too. And another—okay, so she'd taken over three drawers, so what? The chest below the mirror had nine. The left side was Greylen's; the ones in the middle contained towels, soaps, and other various toiletries; and she used the ones on the right.

Her top drawer held the makeup she'd pilfered from Lady Madelyn. It wasn't what she was used to, but it worked. She didn't need much but living without eyeliner—no way. And she had so much fun showing Greylen's mother and Isabelle how to apply the subtle dark line simply by wetting the brush. She'd shocked them further by adding the powder Lady Madelyn used on her cheeks to the base of her healing ointment. It made a great lip gloss.

Modern conveniences aside, life was good. She'd never had anyone to share such things with.

Gwen smiled, remembering Gavin's look the first time he'd seen Isabelle wearing the new makeup. Isabelle had the nerve to place her foot on the dining room chair and lift the hem of her dress as she told him what else she had learned. "Gwendolyn also showed me how to shave my legs, Gavin. I've become quite proficient," she said, running her hand up and down the length of her calf. Gavin barely spoke during dinner and it took him close to an hour to act somewhat normal again.

Gwen was still smiling, thinking about that particular incident as she refastened Greylen's medallion around her neck. She wore it all the time, even when she ran, and checked constantly to make sure it hadn't come loose. He seemed to be all around her, but the longer Greylen was away, the more scared she was of his return.

She'd learned so much about him, but still, she barely knew the man. And worse, he didn't know her at all. No question, she'd felt the connection they had. But what of everything else? Would it be enough? What would she do if it wasn't?

She shook her head, willing the doubts from her mind. There was nothing she could do about it anyway, and if there was, she wasn't sure she wanted to find out. She stroked the medallion once more, then left the chamber and her insecurities behind.

She waited as usual in the great hall with Kevin or Hugh until Lady Madelyn and Isabelle joined them to break their fast. She sat before the fire and enjoyed the coffee Cook always had ready atop the buffet. She'd already had a cup with Gavin earlier, but Cook knew she could drink the stuff all day.

Since Gwen was still in the habit of waking early, Cook left the canister of coffee beans and mugs on the island. She also left a pot for boiling water on the stove.

Every morning when she was just beginning to awake, Gavin would stoke the fire and light the wicks throughout the room. They'd say "good morn" at the same time as Gwen put on Greylen's robe. Then they'd race downstairs to the kitchen.

She and Gavin would work quietly at first. Gwen always filled the pot with water while Gavin lit the fire beneath the burner. Then they'd fight over who could better crush the beans. When the water finally boiled, they'd add the coarse grounds and wait anxiously for the delicious brew. They took their filled cups upstairs until Gavin's replacement came.

Sometimes they'd talk by the fire or stand in front of the window to watch the sunrise. Kevin or Hugh would arrive just after and knock gently on the door, then Gavin would relieve himself of her guard.

Gwen missed him during the day. She'd truly come to depend on him. And she knew he liked having her around too. She could tell he waited for her to come into the study in the afternoons, and it wasn't until she'd settled herself on the settee that he'd immerse himself in the ledgers he continually pored over. They seemed to have an unspoken understanding, a need of each other with Greylen's continued absence. She wondered if Greylen knew how lucky he was to have someone like Gavin in his life for so long. Somehow, she sensed that he did.

Her thoughts were interrupted when Isabelle and Lady Madelyn finally came downstairs. They had a wonderful breakfast and Gwen was surprised when they both excused themselves afterward.

"Isabelle, won't you take a walk with me this morning?" Gwen asked.

"Oh how I wish I could, Gwendolyn. But my tutor's coming early. He insisted I read the latest volume he gave me."

"Very well." Gwen sighed. She kissed Lady Madelyn on the cheek, then whispered to Isabelle, "Come find me later," kissing her as well.

Gwen walked along the paths that led to the cottages. She stopped several times to talk to the women who were going about their duties. She knew most of them by name now. She inquired of their families and always took the time to ruffle their children's hair or hold one of the babies that reached out to her. She asked Kevin again if his leg was all right and he continued to assure her he was fine, each time looking over his shoulder as if to make sure no one had overheard them.

When Gwen started for the chapel, Kevin stopped her midstep. "Lady Gwendolyn, you're unable to visit today," he said, placing his hand on her arm.

"Why not?" she asked.

"'Tis being repaired, lady."

"What on earth's being repaired? It was fine yesterday."

"Father Michael noticed water seeping through the floor, lady. 'Twill be fixed on the morrow."

"Fine." Gwen sighed. Then she added in a mutter, "'Tis a sorry day indeed."

Gwen spent the rest of the morning and early afternoon in the garden behind the keep. She would have gone inside but everyone seemed completely occupied today. So instead, she wrote in her journal and watched the waves crash upon the shore.

Isabelle loved to tell her stories of the early-morning ritual she and Greylen enjoyed. Apparently, they used to sneak out of the keep just before dawn. Then they'd run along the beach and climb the rocks as they watched the sunrise. It was a habit Greylen still kept, though Isabelle confided she'd stopped accompanying him long ago, sensing his need to be alone as he walked the shore and looked to the sea.

Gwen hadn't been down to the shore yet. Gavin and Isabelle had offered to take her many times, and truthfully, she would have loved to see it, but she was scared. It wasn't the narrow paths or the steep descent that worried her. It was the water itself. She had no desire to tempt fate. She had come here in those waters—and she'd not let them take her back.

Disappointed that Isabelle never came for her that afternoon, Gwen waited until she knew Gavin would be in the study. She needed to run more than ever, and her frustration was reaching its peak.

"Good afternoon, very kind sir," Gwendolyn said sweetly from the doorway.

"Aye, 'tis a fine day indeed, Lady Gwendolyn." He smiled, waving her inside. "Your tone, however, is much too compliant. It makes me wonder what you might be wanting?"

She laughed aloud. "Oh, Gavin, I have a feeling you know exactly what I want."

"Might that make me fortunate or not—that I know you so well, lady?"

"You'll have to tell me," she replied with a small smile.

"'Tis a fortune—and you know it." His tone had become very serious, as if somehow saddened.

"Kevin couldn't run this morning and…I was hoping you'd join me this afternoon."

He made a very audible sigh. "'Tis quite impossible," he teased, obviously waiting for the argument she'd begin.

"*Impossible*, I think not, Gavin." Gwen made the statement haughtily, then clearly challenged him. "Tell me then, why?"

"'Tis not your place to question me," he hissed as his eyes narrowed.

The remark didn't bother her at all. "Yeah, right. You live for my questioning you and if you make me wait…" Gwen tried to think of something to irk him. "Well, I guess we can just sit here and talk. Oh, I know—let's talk about Isabelle."

It was perfect. They'd be running in no time.

"Get your clothes," he said through clenched teeth. "I'll meet you in the courtyard."

"Don't pretend you don't want to, Gavin," she said over her shoulder. "I know better."

"You've five minutes," he called to the open doorway. "I'll dismiss the idea entirely if you're not ready."

"Isabelle, please. We've still to finish the headpiece," Lady Madelyn admonished as her daughter watched Gwendolyn and Gavin leave the courtyard.

Gavin had awoken her late the previous night. He'd told her he heard riders approaching and was forced to leave Gwendolyn unattended for the first time, locking the chamber doors as she slept. There'd been no call from the guards, so he knew 'twas his own men who returned. Greylen had sent the soldiers ahead to ensure that all would be ready for his arrival.

"Gavin, what is it?" Lady Madelyn had asked when he'd awoken her.

"Greylen returns on the morrow, lady," he answered with a smile.

"Oh, Gavin, 'tis about time."

"Aye, lady, 'tis."

"How shall we manage with Gwendolyn?" Lady Madelyn asked. She left the details to Gavin. He knew her better than anyone, and their friendship bothered her not in the least. In truth, she was pleased they had each other; they were kindred souls. Besides, she knew Gwendolyn was already in love with her son and that Gavin loved her daughter.

Gavin told her of the plan he'd formulated. And though she felt badly about the lies they would all have to tell her future daughter, she knew 'twas for the best. Gwendolyn would work herself into a fit otherwise, and she could only imagine the fights she'd pick with Gavin throughout the day.

What Gavin had said was best—they'd wait until the very last moment to inform Gwendolyn.

"Why don't you wake Isabelle?" Lady Madelyn asked. "She'll be so pleased." She knew her daughter would be excited by the news, especially if it came from Gavin. But Gavin had turned away. "Oh, Gavin." She sighed. "I hope one day you'll see the fault of your actions, or lack of them."

Gavin had turned again. "I would never bring dishonor to this family," he had vowed, looking into her eyes.

Lady Madelyn had taken his face in her hands. His pain had been so clear in his eyes. "Gavin, you could never dishonor this family," she assured him. "You've been a part of it much too long. You must lay to rest what scares you so."

"I've no fear, lady." Obviously undone by her words, his statement was little more than a rasp.

"Don't you?"

"I'll see to Gw—Lady Gwendolyn," he'd corrected.

"Aye, she is more Gwendolyn to you, is she not?" The formality didn't seem right between them.

"Aye, lady, she is. I'm blessed to have a friend such as her, just as I am blessed to have you all." He had kissed her cheek, and only doing so because they were alone.

"We're equally blessed, Gavin," she'd replied, kissing him back.

As Lady Madelyn watched him leave, she pushed aside her concern for the man whom she thought of as a son. She had no choice. There was much to be done. She'd awoken Isabelle a short while later and they worked throughout the rest of the night, with Anna by their side.

"Gavin, is something bothering you?" Gwendolyn asked between breaths as they paced each other. "You're not your usual temperamental self."

"Nay, I have much on my mind is all."

"Isabelle, maybe?"

"Isabelle's a part of it, my lady," he finally answered, realizing this was the time to broach the subject of Greylen's return. Their run was almost finished and by the time she knew, she'd not notice anything. 'Twas the reason they'd delayed her run in the first place.

Gwendolyn stopped immediately. As if thrilled that he might be open to discussing the topic she was so anxious to get to the bottom of. She placed her hands on her knees, catching her breath before she spoke again. "I'm all ears, Gavin. Out with it." She smiled from ear to ear. He returned it in kind. "Gavin," she exclaimed, "I've never seen you like this. Tell me already."

"Isabelle will be very pleased this eve," he teased, smiling even more.

Gwendolyn hit his arm. "Damn it, Gavin, don't make me beg. What have you planned?"

Gavin laughed aloud. Then he looked at her with an expression so serious that he could see she held her breath. "Greylen comes home, Gwendolyn. He's on MacGreggor land already." Her smile fell. Then she did too.

"I'm gonna be sick, Gavin." She was on her knees, clutching her stomach as she rocked back and forth.

Gavin knelt by her side instantly. "You should be happy, not sick, Gwendolyn." Had he been wrong to wait?

"I just need a minute."

Gavin stayed next to her, rubbing her back until her breathing returned to normal. But when she looked up, his heart nearly stopped. She had a look of despair such that he'd never seen. And then she confided in him. "I'm scared, Gavin."

"Of what? This is what we've waited for."

"I know," Gwendolyn cried. "But what if...what if it doesn't work? What if he doesn't like me?"

"Surely you jest," Gavin said. He was shocked that she'd even think such a thing.

"Jest? You think I *jest*, Gavin? It's been over three weeks since he left. What if he changed his mind?"

"You're out of your mind, Gwen!"

"Am I?"

"Aye, you are. That you'd even ask such a thing is completely out of your character."

"Put yourself in my place, Gavin. Wouldn't you be just a little unsure?"

"Nay," he cried. "I was with him that night, and it all but killed him to walk away from you." Angered, he grabbed her shoulders and made her look at him. "You'll get yourself together *now*, lady, and hold your head high as you so naturally do. I've never known a woman stronger than you, and your insecurity will cease." Gavin knew he was being harsh, but he couldn't stand to see her this way.

"You must trust me, Gwendolyn." He loosened his hold, but when she still seemed unsure, he pulled her into his arms, and she rested her head against his chest as he continued. "Greylen will love you, Gwen, as he always has, as we all do. He's the most honorable man I've ever known, and he'll be thrilled with you. Every vexing oddity you possess, every outrageous demand, every annoying nuance, every— Did you just pinch me?"

"Aye," Gwen confessed, obviously feeling somewhat better, and smiled once again. "Thanks, Gavin."

"You're welcome," he replied, giving her a squeeze.

"You need a bath, Gavin," she told him. But her actions belied her words as she held him closer.

"You could use the very same yourself. Shall we finish our run?"

"Aye." She nodded and pulled him back as he started to run ahead. "Gavin," she said. "How much time do I have before he's here?"

Gavin stared at her for a minute—then he turned and ran as fast as he could. "Two hours," he called behind him. "*Mayhap.*"

He never looked back, because he knew if Gwen caught up, she would surely kill him now.

❦ CHAPTER THIRTEEN ❦

She was wearing a wedding gown.

Gwen couldn't seem to let go of the statement that kept repeating in her mind.

My God, she was wearing a wedding gown!

She and Gavin had returned over an hour ago, neither speaking a word as they had continued their run. He just as quietly led her to her room, squeezing her hand before leaving her in the care of Greylen's mother, Isabelle, and Anna.

They had a bath waiting by the fire, and she obediently removed her clothes and stepped inside. They washed her hair and then brushed it as she sat on the hearth. They talked of really nothing. Just chitchat to ease the tension they knew she felt.

Lady Madelyn applied her makeup with expert hands, a subtle hint of liner around her eyes, a brush of rouge atop her cheeks, and a fine coat of gloss across her lips. Anna continued to brush her hair and explained that she'd wear it down for Greylen's return. Lady Madelyn helped her stand, and Isabelle smiled, holding the gown that had been lying on the bed.

"It's beautiful, Isabelle," Gwen said quietly.

"We worked on it most of the night, Gwendolyn. I hope you like it."

Gwen was touched, but, because she was so nervous, she couldn't quite come up with the right words. "How could I not? It's even more special since you made it yourselves."

Anna took Gwen's robe and Lady Madelyn eased the dress over her head. It was made of ivory silk crepe and fell straight to the floor. Very straight. The square neckline rested just above her breasts, then angled to her shoulders. There was a wide border edged with gold threads and an intricate design of perfectly joined ovals that swirled within.

Sheer chiffon sleeves fell from her shoulders, resting perfectly on her thumbs. The bottom of the sleeves, however, angled to a pointed V and stopped midthigh. They were nothing short of romantic.

Anna placed a belt around her hips and pulled one end through the hidden loop sewn behind the other. When it was secure, she pushed it down to accentuate her narrow hips.

Isabelle tightened the gold laces that started above the belt in back and ended a few inches below her shoulders. Of course, once Isabelle was finished, the bodice fit so tight across her chest, the outline of her breasts was visible. Her nipples showed clearly through the material, and when Anna noticed, she placed her hands under the neckline, adjusting not only Gwen's breasts but her nipples as well.

Then she stood back and smiled at her work, obviously satisfied.

It was one of the most ridiculous moments of Gwen's life. But it helped break the tension and they all laughed together.

Lady Madelyn went to the bed again and picked up a beautiful headpiece. It was made from a simple gold braided cord with four long, delicate strips of ivory tulle attached to the back. She placed it on Gwen's head so the front rested above her forehead and the sides angled down to the back.

Gwen laid her hand on Isabelle's shoulder while Anna placed beautiful strapped sandals, fashioned with a delicate heel, on her feet. The thin leather straps were covered with gold chiffon. They were actually quite saucy, Gwen thought as she looked at them.

"Well, do I pass?" Gwen asked, biting her lip. They had stepped back to admire their work and were smiling from ear to ear.

"Aye," they exclaimed together, obviously thrilled with the result.

"Come, Gwendolyn, we'll go to my chamber so you may see for yourself," Lady Madelyn offered, taking Gwen's hand.

They walked hand in hand and didn't stop until they were in front of the full-length mirror in the corner of the room. Isabelle and Lady Madelyn watched Gwen stare at her reflection. They smiled at her reaction.

"You've outdone yourselves," Gwen said with tears in her eyes. "I've never felt more beautiful in my entire life."

"You are beautiful, Gwendolyn," Lady Madelyn said softly. "What the eye can see...and in your heart as well."

"Please don't cry, Gwen, you'll ruin the makeup Mother has applied."

They had applied their own makeup and had their hair done before she'd returned with Gavin. Gwen helped them now, lacing the backs of the dresses after they slipped them over their heads. Each wore a dark-purple dress that scooped low in front and had been embroidered with the same pattern as on her wedding gown. When they finished, Lady Madelyn had asked if she'd like to go downstairs and wait in the great hall.

"May I stay, just for a few more minutes?" Gwen had asked. She needed some time to herself and hoped that they would understand.

"Of course, Gwendolyn, take whatever time you need," Lady Madelyn had replied.

Gwen looked at her reflection in the mirror again before walking to the window. She was terrified of what came next. Terrified of seeing Greylen, really seeing him for the first time. She said a quick prayer, hoping everything would be all right. She imagined how it would've been had he not been called away.

She saw Gavin ride into the courtyard. He was alone and quickly dismounted. He wore a crisp beige linen shirt tucked into black trousers and tall black leather boots. He looked to the window where she stood, smiling as he took the steps.

He was coming for her.

Gavin knocked softly against the open door. His breath caught audibly when she turned. "You look beautiful, Gwendolyn."

"I feel like a sacrificial lamb," she said, covering her nerves with sarcasm.

"No sacrifice shall be made today, Gwen. You'll know the truth of it soon enough."

"You look handsome, Gavin," she said genuinely. She smiled, taking the hand he held out to her.

"Our soldiers march, Gwen. They'll be here soon."

"Did you see Greylen?"

"Aye, by the lake. He stopped to bathe and change before entering the courtyard."

"I think I'm gonna be sick again."

He gave her a warm smile and stepped closer, holding both of her hands now. "You'll be fine, Gwendolyn. Tell me how I can help."

"Will you still be my friend, now that Greylen's home?"

"'Tis something I fear as well," he said honestly. "No doubt, I'll miss the time we spend together."

"So will I, Gavin," Gwen whispered, looking down.

Gavin lifted her chin. "That night Greylen pulled you from the water…I pledged an oath to you, Gwen. I swore then my life for yours. And I'd do so willingly. Not because 'tis my duty, but because you've become a friend such that I've never known before. But my best friend comes home to you now. He's the brother I always wished for, Gwen. He's the man who will make all of your dreams come true."

Gavin held her a moment longer, then stepped to her side as his eyes fixed on the distant rise. "Come, Gwen, 'tis time."

"I can't seem to move."

"There's nothing to fear."

"That's easy for you to say; you're not the one wearing a wedding gown."

Gavin smirked. "He's very subtle."

"Yes, quite," she agreed dryly at his sarcasm. "I can't go down there, Gavin," she whispered, suddenly serious. "I can't do this in front of everyone."

He sighed as he brushed his fingers through his hair. "Very well then," he conceded. "But stay by the window, you'll not want to miss this."

❦ CHAPTER FOURTEEN ❦

My God, he was right.

It was one of the most magnificent sights of her life. A procession of such pageantry her breath caught at the display. Her hands splayed the window of their own accord, her heart beat so rapidly she feared it would burst.

Hundreds of soldiers filled the path, and they rode in perfect symmetry, their lines seemingly endless. A squire held a flag high in the air, and it danced in the soft, warm breeze, an ebony dragon emblazoned in its center.

The procession continued, until the last of their lines finally topped the crest. The crest high atop the slopes of Seagrave. The crest where one man remained.

He stayed there alone, like a true hero who chose to protect rather than be protected. His dark hair blew in the wind, his bronzed skin aglow beneath the rays of the setting sun. His name whispered from her lips as her forehead pressed to the glass, for even at such a distance, his presence was omnipotent.

That young man whose image she'd memorized above the fireplace in the library—that young man ready to conquer the world—was no more.

This man had already seen the world.

He'd lived through its wonders and atrocities alike, and God help her, prevailing dominance radiated from every inch of his form. His force seemed to draw her, like some kind of gravitational pull, and at that moment, Gwen knew she would sell her soul just to be with him.

He remained completely still, watching as his soldiers continued down the path. They passed through the open gates, and amid another beautiful display, formed two lines on either side of the courtyard. Only then did he finally nudge his mount forward.

He rode through the line of men and stopped in its center. Then dismounted, looking to the steps where his family stood with his men. A boy came forward, lifting his palms high in the air, and Greylen unsheathed his sword, placing it upon his steady hands. He ruffled the boy's hair, a warm smile on his lips. Then he turned his gaze to the window where she stood.

It was a flash of such intensity, a look so chilling, Gwen gasped and stepped back. Her heart seemed to break from that look in his eyes, the hurt he'd shown her for only a second. Furious with herself for being such a coward, and knowing now, too late, she should have been there for him, she ran from the room.

She clutched at the banister with both of her hands, practically tumbling down the stairs in her haste. She grabbed at the door, tears streaming down her cheeks as she fumbled with the latch and pounded in frustration before it finally opened. She pushed her way through Gavin and Lady Madelyn atop the steps, and Greylen's men at the bottom. Then she stood completely still, relieved, and at the same time terrified, that he hadn't moved.

Greylen released the breath he held, his eyes closing as Gwendolyn's presence washed like a balm through his soul. Soothing the ache, the plummet of his heart when he realized she wasn't there. But then she'd come after all. And quite determinedly too.

He'd heard her cry as she won her battle with the door, throwing it open with such force, Kevin, who must have been leaning against it, nearly fell inside. Then she'd pushed her way through a score of people, stopping short with some distance still between them. And then the world seemingly faded away, till 'twas only just the two of them.

He shook his head, disbelieving she was real and thinking mayhap she was just a trick of his mind. But then the vision started toward him, flawless beauty with waiflike strides.

Gwendolyn.

Her name, but a whisper in his mind for weeks, released now from inconceivable depths. It became a battle cry as his head lifted to the sky. A call answered as hundreds of swords were unsheathed and raised in silent support.

Then he closed the distance. Determined, pensive strides quickening to match her own. His arms opened wide a scant second before she threw herself against him, and he crushed her in his embrace, overcome with such emotion he fell to his knees, taking her with him.

He cupped the back of her head as his arms pressed her to his chest. And he kissed her. This woman who ruled his very heart. This woman who owned his very soul. He branded her for all the world to see, kissed the very breath from her. Tasted each tear upon her lovely face while hushing her whispered apologies with those of his own. Which was a feat in itself considering his people's ridiculously loud cheers.

He finally pulled away, gripping her shoulders to bring her within an inch of his face. Staring at her so intently she couldn't look away, staring into the depths of the one thing that had always eluded him. "My God." He breathed, resting his forehead against hers. "They're green." His words brought fresh tears to her eyes. He smiled, shaking his head as he wiped them away, and kissed her again. He would have continued, too, if not for another bout of resounding cheers from his people.

"You'll have me, Gwendolyn," Greylen demanded.

"Have you? Greylen," she whispered, looking down, "you're stuck with me."

Greylen shook his head and lifted her chin. "I'd give everything I have to be stuck with you."

"Really?"

"Aye." He nodded. "Really." He pulled her into his arms again and squeezed her as she sighed. "God, how I missed you, Gwen."

"I missed you too." She smiled and squeezed him back.

He stood with her but did not release her. She continued to lean against him, her question muffled against his chest. "Did you get my message, Greylen?"

His joy was so great, he laughed. "Which one?" he asked.

"I only wrote one letter, Greylen." Her tone and expression lay somewhere between perplexed and annoyed.

"Aye." He grinned. "One letter, riddled with messages."

"I wouldn't say it was *riddled*," she denied.

"You'd not?" he argued.

"I'd not," she denied again and placed her hands on her hips.

He took a menacing step toward her and leaned down, purposely crowding her space. "Say you we start with the one I think of most importance," he challenged in a voice thick with victory.

She didn't retreat but couldn't seem to stop herself from fetchingly biting her lip. "Which one would that be?" she asked imploringly, as if begging him to get it right.

Greylen stared her down. He wanted to throttle her. *Which one would that be?* "You left me," he barked.

He would have sworn she'd feel victorious that he understood; however, she put a finger on her chin to feign a memory lapse. "*Really*, did I write that?"

"You know damn well you wrote it," he shouted. "You underlined the words." Good God, he *was* going to throttle her. "And you threatened to kick my ass—again."

"Only if you didn't come home safely. Oh my God." She started running her hands over his entire body. "Are you hurt?" Happiness seemed to give way to fear and her inspection turned frantic.

"Gwen." Greylen grabbed at her roving hands. She seemed completely panicked. "Gwendolyn," he called again, this time with a gentle shake. She finally looked up, and her expression stopped his heart.

"Tell me you're not hurt," she cried in a whisper. "Please...tell me..."

"Ah, Gwen...I'm sorry I left you," he said, pulling her into his arms. "I'm fine, love, I swear it. I came home safe." That seemed to make her cry again, and he held her a moment longer before asking, "Better?"

"That depends," she answered, her expression both cautious and hopeful as she looked up. "Did you stop by the store and get more brandy?"

"You've depleted our *entire* supply?"

"So it seems." Gwen sighed.

"Did Gavin tell you 'tis all gone?"

"Yes," she admitted, looking down in shame. "I'm sorry, Greylen, but you have no idea what I've had to deal with," she said in her own defense. "The little boy—I just needed some Motrin. But we don't have any. And then... then the butcher, oh God, do you know how they..." She couldn't finish. "Well, it's *disgusting*. This isn't funny," she yelled, poking his chest. "I had to listen to stories, too, Greylen. Stories of you—and your *frigging sword*."

"Shh," he hushed, pulling her against him. "I'm good with my sword, Gwen," he assured her. "And as for the other things, I'm sorry I wasn't here to help you. But *you'll be happy to know,*" he said, using her words, "we have plenty of brandy, a cellar full."

"That liar! I swear I'm gonna—"

Greylen kissed the last of her threat away, knowing exactly what 'twas. Then he held her a moment longer. "Come," he said, wrapping his arm around her shoulders. "There's much to be done."

They walked to the steps together and their smiles returned as Lady Madelyn, Isabelle, and Gavin met them in the courtyard. Greylen greeted his mother first and kissed her cheek. "'Tis good to see you, Mother."

"'Tis good to see you, my son," Lady Madelyn replied, touching his face.

"Isabelle, have you behaved in my absence?" Greylen asked his sister.

"You expected less?" she returned with a demure smile.

"Aye, Isabelle," he replied dryly. "Now that Gwendolyn is with us, I fear I do."

"In that case, mayhap there was an occasional lack of propriety."

Greylen looked to Gwen, resigned as he shook his head. "So I've heard."

Grateful she had the decency to blush, he turned to Gavin next. "Gavin, you've done well in my absence." Greylen placed his hand on his first-in-command's shoulder. "But from now on, I'll see to Gwendolyn. *Understood?*"

"And he won't lie about the brandy," Gwen muttered.

He and Gavin both shook their heads. "Good luck," Gavin remarked, pulling him into a quick embrace. "You'll need it."

Greylen acknowledged his words, knowing the truth of them, then turned back to Gwen. "Are you ready?" he asked.

"Ready? For what?"

"To be my wife."

"*Now?*" She asked it as if he'd gone witless.

"Aye, *now*," he answered in the same tone. "I'll not wait longer." When she seemed to dig her heels into the spot where she stood, he took her hand. "Come." It took no more than a small tug before they were walking toward the chapel.

As the line of soldiers parted, revealing the chapel and Father Michael waiting in front of its entrance, she gasped. Flowers all but spilled from the windows and steps. He was pleased to see Gwendolyn did not miss the effort of everyone's labors as they made their way inside.

Once situated, Father Michael gave a warm smile and began the ceremony immediately. "Dearly beloved, we are gathered together here in the sight of God to join together…"

Greylen stood to Father Michael's right and Gwen to his left. Somehow Gavin was now between them, obviously torn between following his commander's direct orders to leave Gwendolyn to him or to protect his mistress, who chanted under her breath "ohmygod, ohmygod, ohmygod" again and again. Then Gavin had the nerve to reach for her hand.

"Release her hand, Gavin. *Now*," Greylen bit out. He fixed Father Michael a look while motioning with his hand...*on with it, man!*

Father Michael cleared his throat and moved right to the vows. "Wilt thou have this woman to be thy wedded wife, to live togeth—"

"I will." Greylen's sharp command cut off the priest's words as his eyes implored him to continue. It took the priest a moment to register the alteration, then he pulled himself together and looked to Gwendolyn. Her lips still moved, though now, in silent litany while her hands visibly shook.

Father Michael began the vows again, this time to Greylen's bride. "Wilt thou have this man to be thy wedded husband, to live together after God's ordinance..."

Gwendolyn continued to look at Father Michael, her lips slightly parted, his words seemingly meaningless. Father Michael finally stopped speaking and cleared his throat. He gave Gwendolyn a warm, beseeching smile, then did it again, as if 'twould somehow pull her out of her reverie. Then he did it again!

"Your words, Lady Gwendolyn," the priest finally prompted.

"My words?" she asked.

"The vows, mistress—wilt thou..."

When Father Michael leaned forward yet again, Greylen sighed audibly, shaking his head. His *astute* bride was in shock. She had no idea what the priest asked. No doubt she'd bite his head off for pointing out the obvious, but the responsibility was his—not Gavin the insolent, who was about to intercede. Greylen pushed the aforementioned cad out of the way, sorry he'd not fallen down the steps when he'd done so.

"Gwendolyn, look at me, love," Greylen ordered when he stood in front of her.

Look at him. Was he serious? She could do little else. God he was handsome, and he kept calling her "love"—with that voice. She was so warm, surrounded by so many people, in the tiny chapel aglow with what must be hundreds of candles. And there were so many beautiful flowers everywhere, it smelled wonderful. She wasn't even upset that everyone had lied to her all morning. How could she be when Greylen was so close now? He was searching her eyes. He really was something to look at. And, my God, there was a lot of him too.

"Gwendolyn?"

"Hmmm."

"Tell Father Michael you will, love."

"Will what, Greylen?"

"*Marry me.*"

Greylen's shout could have parted the sea, but Gwen couldn't fathom why he felt the need to yell right now. Hadn't she already told him that she would? She felt rather smug, too, pointing out the obvious to him. "Isn't that why we're here?" she asked.

Greylen's hands fisted as a tic marred his features. "Gwendolyn, the nice man asked if you'll have me. You've not answered."

"Oh my God," she shouted. She blanked out. She peeked around Greylen to tell Father Michael she would… but hesitated. "Greylen?" she finally whispered, looking up again.

"Aye," he answered in an ominous drawl.

Gwen wrung her hands together. Then stepped even closer to him, placing her hands on his chest so she could lean up and whisper. "Everything's going to be all right, isn't it, Greylen?"

She felt the tension leaving him at her question, and he gently answered, "Aye, Gwen."

"We'll be happy, won't we?"

"I swear it."

"I mean—"

"*Gwendolyn!*"

She jumped at his shout, causing Father Michael to do the same when she practically screamed "I will" to the man.

The rest happened in such a blur she was sorry they hadn't hired a photographer or videographer to capture it. Then she repeated some of the most ridiculous words and promises she'd ever heard. Vows to be "buxom and bonny" and in a way she couldn't even believe, which made her realize why they couldn't hire anyone in the first place. She was practically in the frigging Ice Age.

But Gavin did give her away, and he and Greylen placed her hand in Father Michael's. Somehow, the gesture of their three hands joined together meant as much as exchanging her vows with Greylen. Somehow, their lives were now bound together, forever.

She stared at the ring Greylen had given her, a ring identical to the one that he wore. A simple gold band engraved with the same design on her dress, swirling ovals with no beginning and no end. Father Michael interrupted her inspection when he told Greylen he could kiss his bride. *Her.* And *her* husband kissed her all right—jeez, the man was going to take her on the floor.

Father Michael announced them to the congregants, and Greylen led her from the church. He addressed his clan with a powerful shout. "I give you Lady Gwendolyn MacGreggor, your new mistress." Then he turned with a boyish grin as they cheered. "Come, wife, we've a celebration."

And it was.

An enchanting night filled with music and laughter. Bagpipes played jaunty tunes, and they danced together under the stars. Later, they sat at one of the long, beautifully adorned tables set between the chapel and the keep, now laden with platters as they drank to endless toasts. Anna and Lady Madelyn hadn't missed a single detail and Cook truly outdid herself.

But the best part of her night was when Greylen held her in the midst of people swirling around them, oblivious to everything as he rested his forehead against hers. "That I'm dancing with you, and we celebrate our joining—it fills my heart, Gwen."

They were the sweetest words she'd ever heard, and she'd kissed him in front of everyone. Quite thoroughly too.

She stood with Lady Madelyn now, barely able to listen as she met Greylen's look. He was with his men on the other side of the courtyard, staring at her as they continued to talk. He must have said something to dismiss himself because his men walked back to the festivities and he toward her. The look in his eyes. The way he carried himself.

My God, she was married to that man!

Greylen looked at his wife as he made his approach. In truth, he'd been unable to take his eyes from her the entire night. She was breathtaking. His mother kissed her cheek before heading in Isabelle's direction, and now his wife stood alone staring back. He couldn't close the distance fast enough.

"'Tis time to go inside, Gwen," he said, stroking her cheek when he reached her.

"Wouldn't it be rude for us to leave now?" she asked.

"Nay, wife, 'tis expected."

He took her hand and walked with her toward the keep. Then he cradled her in his arms, carrying her up the steps and through the main doors.

"Greylen?"

"Aye, love."

"That was a wonderful evening." She sighed, rubbing her face against his chest.

"It still is, Gwen."

Greylen turned atop the landing and walked toward his chamber, which he'd not been within for weeks. He carried her to the fireplace and set her down before the hearth. Then knelt to add more logs, offering her a smile when he turned. She was biting her lip again. Shaking his head, he filled a goblet with wine, then took a drink as he stared at her. Then he placed it to her lips, tilting the glass until 'twas empty.

"You think to get me drunk?" she teased.

"Nay." He shook his head. "I think to ease your nerves." He smiled mischievously before tossing the glass into the fire. She laughed, sensing his playfulness. Then he removed her headpiece and pulled her into his arms. "God, how I've waited for this," he whispered, closing his eyes.

Music still played in the courtyard and the sounds carried to their chamber. He rocked Gwen in his arms, so grateful to finally be with her. She held him back, her head resting upon his chest. He was determined to take things slow, though if their last time together was any indication of how the night might progress, they'd be abed in seconds.

After a few quiet moments he asked, "Would you like more wine, Gwen?"

She gave a small laugh, as if she'd considered it. Then her look became deadly earnest and she shook her head. "No, Greylen. I want you to kiss m—"

He didn't give her the chance to finish. He cupped the back of her head and covered her mouth. He joined their lips from every angle possible, then tilted her face, moving her so she would open for him, and she did, moaning as his tongue swept inside. Her arms wrapped around his neck and her fingers tangled in his hair. The pleasure he felt 'twas immeasurable.

She seemed stunned when he pulled away moments later. Judging from her expression, mayhap annoyed was a better description. He hushed her pout with another kiss, then turned her to untie the laces of her dress. There were many, and as he slowly pulled each free and let them fall from his hand, he kissed her. Her lovely back... The delicate slope of her neck... Then the soft curve of her shoulder. She moaned then, a gesture he rewarded with a gentle nip. Her back completely exposed, his fingers ran the length of her spine and her body reacted to his touch with a tremor. Then she was in his arms again, the feel of her bare skin igniting his desire all the more.

Long minutes later, he broke their kiss. Another instance for his wife to express her displeasure with a disgruntled look. He was intent, however, to divest her of her dress, and saw to the matter at once. He'd already removed her belt as he'd kissed her before, leaving her undress but only one step away. His hands covered her shoulders and his fingers pressed her skin as he pushed the sleeves down. The weight of her dress fell to the floor where it lay pooled at her feet.

Stunned by the vision before him, he took a step back. Unable to stop himself, he found he stood there, taking to memory his wife's every measure. And good God, if she didn't stand proudly before him as if emblazoned by his stare. Every part of her was lean and toned, yet utterly feminine. Her breasts were small, their fullness so enticing he ached to reach out and touch them. Her stomach was flat, her hips narrow. He'd never been with another like her, yet her form made him burn unlike any before. His hands fisted—he closed the gap.

His arms snaked behind her back as his hands cupped her head to keep her still, and then he kissed her in a way he'd never kissed another before. This kiss was subjugating and purely carnal. 'Twas the most evocative experience he'd ever had, holding his wife's naked body against his clothed one. He had a need to dominate her, yet he felt her give at every turn, moving as he wanted her to while she pressed her body fully against his. It seemed she gladly, willingly, gave in to his every command. He needed her abed or he'd surely take her on the floor.

Here.

Now.

He felt the loss of her lips for only a second as he swept her off her feet. Then he cradled her in his arms and kissed her again. He laid her atop the covers, lowering her head to the softness of the pillows, and broke their kiss just to look at her again. Her swollen lips and body lay naked before him...naked but for the sandals upon her feet, saucy, gold-covered sandals he'd not noticed before.

His hands fisted, and he stood. *He had to slow down.*

He'd contrived this night forever, but *damn* if his noble intentions weren't falling to the wayside. He began extinguishing the wicks throughout the room, watching her as he carried out each task. And, good God, if she didn't watch him back.

I've plans, Gwendolyn, and you're helping them all to hell.

He filled another goblet, drained it, then filled it again.

He brought it to the bedside. "Another drink?" he asked. Gwen nodded and just as before, he held the glass for her. She smiled and moved over, patting the mattress. He gave a laugh, shaking his head. "Are you not skittish at all, woman?"

"Not yet," she replied. "Come here," she all but begged.

Greylen lay beside her, running his fingers down the side of her face and neck. Gwen closed her eyes and made the most intoxicating sound. It went straight to his groin. She made it again, but this time, he took it. He covered her lips as it formed in the back of her throat, wondering if he might die from the pleasure it gave him. His hand brushed across her stomach and thighs. Then slipped beneath each knee and he removed her sandals one at a time.

He placed her hands over her head and made sure to give her a pointed look indicating she keep them there. She nodded her agreement. "Take your shirt off, Greylen," she whispered against his lips. She smiled as he ripped it from his body, then laughed as his boots flew across the room. But when he laid his dagger atop the nightstand, the strangest expression came over her. 'Twas as if his habit was something she might cherish for the rest of her life. Where that thought came from, he'd no idea.

She sighed when he took her in his arms again, rubbing his back and pressing him closer. He pulled back and shook his head. Had he not just ordered, albeit silently, to keep her hands safely off his person and above her head.

She tilted her head with a look of mayhap dare, and damn if she didn't purposely take her time. Stretching her arms high about her head and so enticingly, his hand followed their movement, stroking her from hip to shoulder. He realized then, 'twas exactly what she wanted.

"Well played, wife."

"Kiss me again, Greylen."

"You please me more than you'll ev—"

"Greylen?"

"Aye?"

"Shut up and k—"

So emboldened by Gwen's actions, he'd not been able to curb the power and force with which he began to feast upon her once more. Seconds later, he realized he needn't have feared for she met him kiss for kiss and touch for touch. Then their bodies were moving together, their sounds louder as they found the perfect rhythm. That slow, torturous grind he'd felt with her but once before, the night he'd been called away.

His need of his wife now bordered on madness. Lost to the sweet taste of her mouth, the exquisite contours of her body, and the moist heat they created as he rubbed himself between her thighs. His well-intentioned plans— dust.

Cease, man, cease.

Battle, MacGreggor, think battle. Blood...putrid stench... haunting screams...ahhh.

Victorious, he rolled, taking Gwen with him. He pressed her against the mattress and lay on his side. Done playing games, he trapped her beneath his leg. Then he caressed her entire body, stroking her from shoulder to thigh. He covered her breasts, kneading their fullness with his hand, listening to her responses as he took her nipple between his finger and thumb, caressing, then squeezing with more pressure as her moans became desperate.

Then his lips were on the side of her face…grazing her neck…rubbing the swell of each breast until at last he was taking her in his mouth, sucking and scraping and biting as she continued to writhe beneath him.

His hand ran the length of her inner thigh, pushing her wide. Then Gwen's hands were tangling in his hair, stroking his neck, the width of his shoulders… *'Twas too much*. He looked up, his eyes turning harsh before she whimpered and placed her hands behind her head again.

Gwen's whimper was real, but not because of Greylen's stern look. She wasn't scared of his aggressiveness, she liked it—*she loved it*. His smoldering eyes nearly sent her over the edge. Her body pulsed, begging to be touched. His dominance only inflamed her. Playing with fire, she reached for him again…so close to touching him, then he trapped her wrists in his hand. He growled and pinned her to the mattress with his leg, then spread her wide with his knee. She lay helpless beside him, halfway beneath him, and she'd never felt more alive in her entire life.

Her husband stared at her outstretched body, his hand stroking her as her hips strained against him. She begged for his touch. Just when she thought she couldn't wait another second, his fingers pressed within her folds, sliding down her center. He hissed through his teeth as he skimmed through her wetness. She moaned as his hand slid back up and he spread her with his fingers, gliding atop her most sensitive flesh, stroking and circling over and over, again and again.

He removed the weight of his leg, allowing her to move her hips. Her moans, now short cries as she came closer to her orgasm. Powerless but to yield, Gwen began to break. Her wrists were still trapped in the circle of Greylen's fingers, her arms stretched far above her head. Her lips were now besieged by sensuous pulls and tugs with his teeth. Then his finger moved inside her, deeper and faster, again and again, as his thumb circled above with more pressure. Her cries of release surrendered against his lips, mixing with his husky groan as she shook from her orgasm.

His ministrations turned gentle now and didn't stop until her pleasure was complete, then he broke their kiss and held her passion-glazed eyes as he stepped from the bed.

Gwen watched Greylen remove his trousers, staring at the most incredible male body she'd ever seen. He was at least six feet six and made of solid steel. If she didn't know better, she'd swear he'd kill her. But she did know better, and after years of torturous dreams making love to this man, she was ready for satisfaction. Ready to give herself to the only man she'd ever have. The man she'd waited for her entire life.

She held out her hands, a gesture that must have surprised him, for he smiled, shaking his head. Then he came back to bed and slowly moved over her, the feel of his skin making her sigh as he settled atop her. That feeling of coming home, this had to be it. Covered by her husband's body—tracing the side of his face as she moved her foot along the length of his calf—she knew she was finally home.

Her husband held his weight on his arms as he looked down at her. He kissed her before leaning back, then encircled her waist and pulled her toward him. He spread her wide and laid the base of his erection completely against her. His eyes closed, and his head fell back—but this time, Gwen hissed. Then her husband began stroking his entire length against her till her cries started anew. Her head moved atop the pillow as her hands pressed the headboard to push herself against him.

"Greylen, please...I need you...*please*."

"Shh," he said, hushing her. "I know, love, almost." He continued to stroke her, spreading her farther to place the tip of his erection against her innermost folds. Then his fingers rubbed her to another orgasm but seconds away. Her head fell back. She pulsed against him. "Look at me, Gwen. *Now*." His command came with such ferocity their eyes locked. He entered her.

He thrust himself completely inside. The resistance of flesh as he entered, the tear of what must have remained of her hymen, took her completely by surprise. Greylen remained motionless, as if waiting for her to adjust to him. He lifted his head. "I'm so sorry, Gwen." His words were filled with anguish.

"It doesn't hurt anymore, Greylen." She said the words in such a way, she thought to soothe him. Then she motioned with her hands for him to come to her.

He gently shifted his weight as she untangled her legs and covered her with his body. Then he held her head in his hands, stroking her face with his thumbs. "I didn't know," he whispered, shaking his head.

"I didn't tell you," she whispered back. "Kiss me again, Greylen. Make love to me, please."

He did kiss her again and then heeding her words, he began to move inside her. The sensation was like nothing she had ever felt before. He pushed slowly at first, but when she began tilting her own hips, meeting each of his downward thrusts as she brought herself up, it seemed he gave in to the moment completely. He whispered in her ear as he drove inside her—burying himself again and again, deeper and deeper as she clutched his shoulders and held him to her with her heels.

She cried his name again and again as her body became feverish and taut once more. "I've got you, love. Just hold on to me. Ah, Gwen—" He thrust one final time, holding her tight, his breaths ragged against her neck as his body shook uncontrollably atop hers.

She held him tight, never had she imagined making love would feel like this. She was suddenly overcome with emotion.

"Am I hurting you, Gwen?" Greylen lifted his head and asked. He must have felt her shake, then realized her entire body was trembling. He shifted his weight, swearing under his breath as he looked down. Tears spilled down her face. "Ah, Gwen, I did." He cursed again, gently separating their bodies before pulling her against his chest. Then he held her as she cried.

"I'm so sorry, Gwen. I never meant to hurt you, love. I won't touch you again. I—"

"*What?*" She was on her knees in a second. "You won't touch me again? Then you…"

She pointed her finger at him, and her husband grinned, his eyes gleamed brightly like he was calculating a tactical defense.

"…might as well pick up your frigging sword and march back into battle, you sorry—" Gwen shrieked as Greylen grabbed at her with both hands. She laughed as he wrestled her beneath him. Then he kissed her laughter away and held his head just above hers.

"Are you sure I didn't hurt you, Gwen?" he whispered in the darkness.

"Yes, Greylen, I'm sure."

"What made you cry, love?" he asked, kissing the corners of her mouth.

"It's a girl thing."

"Would you be willing to share?"

"Not on your life," she cried, shaking her head.

"Then I can touch you again?"

"*Oh, God, yes.*"

"And I can stay right here? Even if I crush you?"

"Oh, Greylen...you crush me so good I wouldn't want you anywhere else."

"God, you're amazing," he whispered.

He smiled, and she returned it. She ran her fingers through his hair and rubbed her face against his, feeling like it was the single most enjoyable thing in the world to her right now. And in that moment, she'd never felt closer to anyone. There was something in his eyes that said he felt the same. Then he confirmed it.

"I love you, Gwen."

"I love you, too, Greylen."

❧ CHAPTER FIFTEEN ❧

His wife slept like a babe, wrapped in his arms the entire night. After they made love, he kissed her for nearly an hour. Slow reverent kisses that left no part of her face untouched. She returned each one in kind, her fingers stroking his hair while her feet caressed his legs. He finally wrapped her body from behind, lulling her to sleep as he nuzzled her shoulders and neck.

She stirred now and turned in his arms, sighing as she rubbed her face against his chest.

"Good morn, wife," he offered with a squeeze.

She smiled. "Good morn, husband," she mimicked.

Greylen pulled her up until her head lay next to his, her blush visible even in the soft light from the fire. "What's this?" he asked, running his finger down her cheek.

"It's called being self-conscious," she said softly, closing her eyes.

Self-conscious? This from the woman who gave herself with wanton abandon. "Gwendolyn, you displayed not a shred of self-consciousness last night," he reminded her in a voice rough with sleep.

"Shh, I'm going to kiss you now, just to shut you up." She finished with an "mmmm," then rubbed her face into his neck.

"Sore?" Greylen asked.

"Do I have to walk today?"

"Nay, I'll carry you."

"Greylen," she whispered. "I can still feel you inside me."

He groaned and rolled on top of her. "I'll carry you for a fortnight," he promised while kissing her laugh away. But he stopped a moment later when she tensed. "Don't move," he told her, stepping from the bed.

When he returned he was wearing his robe, hers in his hand. He soaked a small towel in the basin by the fire, then sat next to her again. She moaned in relief as he pressed the cloth between her thighs. "There's something I wish to show you. Are you rested enough?" he asked, as if it were an everyday occurrence to carry on a conversation as he tended to his wife so intimately.

"I thought you were going to make love to me," Gwen said with a pout.

"I am. But you've an hour reprieve."

He helped her from the bed and held her robe. Then he tied the belt himself. "I'll dress and find you something to wear," he told her as he began walking away. Then he turned as she stretched, a move which spanned her entire body, from the tips of her toes to the ends of her fingers. "You do that every morn?" he asked.

"It's a stretch, Greylen. I do it every time I wake up."

"You'll nap then—often."

Gwen laughed as she walked to the bathing chamber, and he left her to her privacy. He dressed in comfortable breeches, a linen shirt, and sandals. Then he stood before his wife's wardrobe, searching through the hanging dresses, and even the drawers below. But he found only gowns. Gowns, frivolities, and night-robes.

He stepped in the doorway to ask of her clothing. She was brushing her hair, a drawer on the right side of the chest opened. He couldn't seem to move. He just stood there, stunned, as his wife tended to her personal care in their private chamber. He leaned against the wall as she opened and closed drawers. Watched as she secured a leather strap in her hair and washed her face. Then she took something from another drawer and dipped it in water before rubbing it against her teeth.

"What do you do, wife?" he asked.

She removed the handle from her mouth and held it up, displaying rows of small bristles. "I'm brushing my teeth," she explained. "That cloth you use obviously does a great job, but this is better." She pointed to his drawers on the left. "There's one in your top drawer."

Curious, Greylen walked over and opened the drawer. She was right. An instrument exactly like the one she used lay next to his shaving tools.

"I asked your mother to have them made," Gwen continued. "She liked the idea so much, now everyone uses them."

He watched her a moment longer, then began doing the same. "You're right, Gwen," he said. "This is better."

Then he couldn't help teasing her as she bit her lip. "Your mind labors, wife. What is it?"

"I don't know." She shrugged. "It just seems so…" She turned, as if searching for the word.

"You're beautiful," he told her, reaching out to caress her face. "And the word you search for is *intimate*."

"You're right." She sounded surprised.

"I'm always right."

She rolled her eyes and walked to the chest next to the door. Then she took something from the valet and turned to him. "I've been wearing your medallion. Do you mind?"

Mind? He loved that she wore it. He tied it around her neck, then hugged her from behind. "I was distracted before. Where are the rest of your clothes?"

"Behind me." She motioned with her head. "It's before dawn, Greylen. Where are we going?"

"I told you, I wish to show you something."

"Will anyone be there?" she asked.

"Nay, only us."

His wife smiled, obviously pleased by his statement. Then she proceeded to slip on the smallest item of underclothing he'd ever seen. She put on drawstring trews next, similar to what he wore, but she folded the waistband. Then she'd the nerve to look shyly into his eyes. *Shy was dead and buried, Gwendolyn.*

"I—you're not leaving, are you?" she asked.

Was she daft? "Not on your life," he replied, mimicking her words from last night. She muttered something as he continued to stare at her. And in truth, 'twas all he could do. He simply stared in wonder. *Wonder of why in God's name Anna fashioned clothing completely unacceptable for his wife.*

Fascinated, he decided to inquire later.

He watched as she let her robe fall and reached for another item of clothing he'd not yet seen. She slipped the small swath of material over her head, pushing it down until it covered her breasts, then tied what was left behind her neck. When she reached for her shirt, his arm wrapped around her waist, pulling her back till his erection pressed snuggly against her bottom. "I would have you now but for the time," he whispered against her ear.

"Can it wait?"

"I'm quite disciplined, Gwendolyn." The remark came out harsher than he intended.

Gwen turned in his arms. "I meant what you have to show me."

Greylen smiled. "Nay, it can't wait, but I'll have you within the hour."

In truth, he wanted nothing more than to make love to her again, but he'd waited too long to share this moment with her. She took his shirt from behind the door and rolled the sleeves before tying the sides at her waist.

"You need shoes," he grumbled...*and a dress and proper undergarments. And I need you—beneath me, on top of me, and beside me.*

"We're going outside?" she asked, putting on her sandals.

"Aye, love, you'd have dressed differently otherwise?"

"Of course, I'd have dressed differently."

He suspected there was much more to her answer, yet dawn approached quickly. He held out his hand and she took it, then together they left their room. As he reached for the front door, Anna called out.

"I knew you'd be going early, so I made something for you to take."

Greylen thanked her and took the pouch. Then he led Gwen down the steps and headed toward the stables. Once inside, he went for his black, stroking his neck as he brought him from the stall. He placed Gwen's hand beneath his, repeating the motions along the horse's neck, when James, the stable master, approached them.

"Would ye be wantin' me to saddle 'em, sir?"

"Nay, James. Take a few hours before you begin your duties."

He continued to guide her hand with firm, sure strokes. Then he introduced them, though his horse had not a name. Gwen laughed, and as God was his witness, he was truly enchanted. He kissed her before moving her safely aside so he could see to the saddle. He saw from Gwen's expression she was pleased that he praised the animal, stroking not only his neck but also his flanks. Then he secured the bag and laid a plaid over the front of the saddle.

"'Tis a short ride, Gwen. I'd hoped the plaid would help." He made the statement after he lifted her atop the saddle and noticed her grimace. Gwen gave him a look, one that let him know she didn't appreciate being embarrassed. But he only smiled and settled behind her, one arm around her waist, the other holding the reins.

He rode toward the back of the keep and stopped atop the cliffs, looking to the sea for a long moment, before nudging his mount forward again. Halfway down the narrow path, he made a soft clicking noise and halted their descent. "Gwen?" He squeezed his wife's midsection. "Gwendolyn?" he tried again.

"What?" she finally answered.

"Do you fear heights?" he asked.

"No," she whispered.

"You shake, love, and your fingers dig into my arms. Something frightens you and I wish to know the cause."

"I'm sorry. Did I hurt you?"

"Nay." He shook his head. "But you'll tell me what troubles you."

"I don't want to go down there, Greylen. I...I don't want to go down there."

"Look at me, Gwen." He waited for her to turn and then gently wiped her tears. "Don't fear the water," he said softly. "It brought you to me." She started to say something, but he couldn't hear the words, just the agony in her voice. He circled her waist and turned her in his arms.

She burrowed against him. "I love it here, Greylen," she whispered. "I don't want to go back."

"I'll never let you go, Gwen, and I swear to you, I will always keep you safe." She only nodded and he kept her in his arms. She clung to him as they made their way down the path and as he slid from the saddle. Still she didn't let go.

"You can open your eyes, love," he whispered. "We're far from the water." His reassuring tone must have helped, for she finally lifted her head from his shoulder and slowly opened her eyes. 'Twas another full minute before she untangled her legs and he could lower her to the ground. But he continued to hold her, waiting until she was ready to let go.

She stood facing the cliffs, a massive wall alive with vegetation. Then turned to look down the beach, the entire shorefront cast aglow in the predawn light. Natural rock formations jutted from the sand and gentle waves washed upon the shore. "It's beautiful," she whispered.

Greylen smiled as he took her hand, then started down the beach. They walked a short distance before he spread the plaid and motioned for Gwen to sit. She removed her sandals and scooted to the center, where she sat hugging her knees. He removed his sandals as well, but sat facing her, his legs wrapped around her body. 'Twasn't long before she graced him with a smile.

"What's in the bag?" she finally asked.

"Food and drink, wife. You must be hungry?"

"I'm starved," she exclaimed. She grabbed the bag and removed the items Anna had packed, rattling off each as she placed them on a linen square. "Let's see, we have bread, cheese, fruit, yes—oh God, I love her."

Greylen laughed as he reached for the cheese and bread and asked what pleased her so.

"You'll have to wait and see," she teased, opening the canteen and moaning from the aroma she inhaled.

Greylen laughed even harder. "It can't be that good, wife," he argued.

"Oh, Greylen, it's *sooo* good." She poured the drink into a tall mug and came to him on her knees. Then she tilted it to his lips, blowing on its surface before he took a sip.

'Twas a moment that he would remember forever.

Undone by her care, he obediently took a sip. Its flavor and warmth completely overshadowed by her attentiveness. "What drink is this?" he asked.

"*This* is coffee," she explained. "I found it in the pantry, and Gavin's already ordered your captain to acquire more."

"I knew he'd be useful one day," he muttered.

They ate in relative silence while sharing the coffee between them. Then Gwen poured the last cup and handed it to him so she could put the items back in the bag. He motioned for her to sit between his legs and wrapped his arms around her waist, taking sips when she brought the coffee to his lips.

Then the soft glow shone on the horizon. Greylen stretched his arm, pointing to the east, silent as the importance of this moment swept through him. He'd watched this sunrise his entire life, for years waiting to share it with the one who would be his. He knew he would love her, whomever she was, but the depth of his feelings for Gwen was more than he ever imagined.

He took the empty mug from her hand and placed it on the sand, then leaned back and shifted to his side, laying Gwen beside him. "I would have you now, wife," he bid.

"Then have me, Greylen," she whispered.

Greylen kissed his wife and caressed her body, removing first her clothing and then his. He stroked her with his fingers, enthralled by her surrender. Then he entered her with care, holding her eyes until they closed to the pleasure of being joined again.

He took her slowly, each motion unhurried as he pushed himself deeper inside, and more frenzied as they became lost in their passion. He told her again and again that he loved her, overwhelmed by emotions again. When Gwen at last tightened around him, calling out his name, hers tore from his lips with one final thrust. They lay on the beach a long while after, silent at first and then talking quietly as he held her in his arms.

"Do you miss your home, Gwen?" Greylen asked cautiously.

"I would miss this one more." She made the admission with a sad shake of her head.

"You'll never leave here, Gwendolyn," he vowed. "You're forever mine."

❧ CHAPTER SIXTEEN ❧

When they returned from the shore, Greylen carried Gwen upstairs and laid her in bed.

"Get some rest, Gwen, I've much to see to," he said, reaching for the covers.

She wanted to tell him she didn't need to rest, but she couldn't spoil the moment. "Stay with me, please, just for a few minutes," she whispered. He smiled and lay beside her. She didn't remember him leaving.

She awoke to noises, and for a moment, she worried it had all been a dream. But as she rolled over, she smelled his scent. He was really home. Funny how that one word, *home*, a word that had always filled her with sadness and longing, now only filled her with happiness.

Anna was quietly putting their room back in order and had brought a tray with fruit and coffee. "There's a bath by the fire, child," she called softly.

"Thank you, Anna." Gwen sighed happily. She was definitely enjoying her new way of life.

"I'll see to the sheets while you soak yourself," Anna said, stepping toward the bed.

Gwen felt her cheeks warm immediately. Good Lord! "I'll do it, Anna."

"You'll do no such thing," she admonished, stripping the sheets as Gwen stood.

"Let me help then, please," Gwen insisted. But she turned when Anna pulled back the covers, revealing small spots of blood.

"You're wrong to shame yourself, Lady Gwendolyn. 'Tis an honor you give your husband."

"Anna, *please*." While of course Gwen knew this, it was still a very personal topic. She grew up when everyone was on this kick about chastity and abstinence until marriage. She'd liked the idea, and honestly, good Lord, it was worth the wait. Anna shooed her to the tub, and she blissfully complied.

Gwen stuck to her usual habits during the day. She missed Lady Madelyn and Isabelle for breakfast but walked through the paths with Kevin. Obviously, she still needed a guard, even if he was a liar. At least he blushed when she asked about his leg.

"'Tis a miracle, lady. I seemed to be completely recovered," Kevin lied again.

There was no mistaking the warmth in his eyes—his whole disposition, as a matter of fact. Something struck her that she'd never fully considered. Based on their actions, Greylen and his men always put her welfare first. Whether they had to lie to do so or not.

She finally caught up with Isabelle late that afternoon, and they sat together on one of the benches in the gardens behind the keep.

"Greylen took me to the beach this morning," Gwen told her as she twirled a flower between her hands.

"I'm not surprised."

"It's really peaceful. The sound of the water and the rock formations are almost magical."

"Did you watch the sunrise together?" Isabelle asked.

"Aye, we did." Gwen sighed, remembering the poignant moment when Greylen directed her attention to the rising sun.

"Well?"

"Well, what?" Gwen laughed.

"Gwendolyn, you're my sister now, you must tell me everything."

Gwen only smiled. "I saw you dancing with Gavin last night," she said, not subtly changing the subject.

Isabelle shook her head. "It felt wonderful to dance with him, but once again, he treats me as always, Gwendolyn."

"He'll come around, Isabelle, just give it some more time."

"I'm eighteen, Gwendolyn. I've been waiting since the first time he smiled at me and called me Bella." She sighed. "I must see to my studies. We can speak more at supper."

For the rest of the day, Gwen waited for Greylen to return. But when Anna came to the library and announced supper, she knew he wouldn't be joining them. She loved these dinners so much, but tonight she kept looking to the archway. Her behavior didn't go unnoticed and before she knew it, Lady Madelyn was explaining Greylen's countless duties. "He must check with the tenants, meet with the border patrols, and likely spend hours in his study. His responsibilities are endless, Gwendolyn."

"I must seem selfish," Gwen admitted, more than a little disappointed with herself.

"Nay, daughter, *selfish* is a word I would never use to describe your behavior."

"Thank you, Lady Madelyn."

"You may call me Mother, Gwendolyn. If you so choose."

It was more than she could take, so many changes and all so fast. She felt overwhelmed and quietly excused herself. She kissed Isabelle good night and then Lady Madelyn, making sure to whisper "Good night, Mother" in her ear.

Back in her chamber, Gwen changed into one of Greylen's shirts. She thought to lie down and wait for him, but awoke to strong, warm lips as Greylen sat on the bed beside her. *He was back!* She hoped her smile and touch conveyed just that.

"I'm sorry I woke you," he whispered.

"I hope you're not that sorry. Are you coming to bed?"

"I will be if you continue—ah, Gwen." He groaned. "I've ledgers to see to."

"You must be exhausted, Greylen," she said, brushing her fingers through his wet hair.

"I'm fine," he assured her, giving her another quick kiss before adding, "Go back to sleep, love. I'll be up later."

"Can I sit with you in the study?"

"You'd sit with me…while I work?" he asked.

"Of course," Gwen said quickly.

It seemed to take a moment for him to realize what she offered him. "Come then. I'm going to have Cook prepare something. Are you hungry?"

"You haven't eaten?" She grabbed his shirt. "Are you frigging *kidding* me? Supper was hours ago, Greylen. You must be starved."

He smiled and shook his head, as if pleased by her outrage on his behalf. "Gavin and I just returned, Gwen. We hadn't the time before now." He finished his explanation as he moved an errant strand of hair behind her ear.

"Don't wake Cook, Greylen. I'll make you something."

"To eat?" he asked, as if unsure he understood her correctly.

"Yes, to eat," she clarified, rather put off that he questioned her.

He pulled her close. "You mean to tell me, besides your proficiency of foul, colorful words in a handful of languages, your rampant, behavioral outbursts, and…" He grinned. "Well, your husband's complete captivation, you prepare food as well?"

"Ooh, such a mouthful. Aside from your last comment, you're lucky I still have that newlywed glow. Or maybe it's all that 'love is blind' stuff."

"Should I be offended?" he teased.

Gwen shook her head. "Not if I'm not." She laughed. "But I would love to cook you dinner," she said more seriously.

"Would you cook for Gavin as well?" he asked cautiously.

Gwen laughed even harder this time. Gavin obviously hadn't told Greylen of their late-night kitchen raids. He'd have to find that one out on his own. And, apparently, very soon. She stood on the bed and asked Greylen to turn around.

He did as she asked and seemed surprised when she wrapped her arms around his neck and pulled herself onto his back. She placed a kiss on his cheek, and as she glanced up at him, he closed his eyes as if he enjoyed holding her so. She rested her chin on his shoulder and hugged him as they left the room.

When they reached the landing, Gwen stopped him. "Go to Isabelle's room, she'll join us."

"She'll be asleep, Gwen," he insisted.

"Trust me, she won't."

He shrugged and took the stairs that led to the other hallway. Gwen knocked lightly on the door and it opened immediately. Isabelle greeted them with a smile. "Shall we go for a raid?" she asked.

Gwen laughed. "Aye, to the kitchen."

They stopped to fetch Gavin, who sat in the study. Feet atop the table, he held a stack of papers, wet hair dripping on his shoulders.

As if sensing that he was being watched, Gavin looked up and smiled. Gwen could only imagine his happiness at the sight before him. His commander and best friend, holding his new wife on his back. Gwen's head rested on Greylen's shoulder. She was grinning and assumed Greylen was too. Isabelle stood beside them, wearing a white bedgown covered with a matching robe, her toes peeking out from beneath. From watching him look at Isabelle now, Gwen surmised he was remembering what it had felt like to dance with her last night. For a band of well-schooled liars, they had some of the biggest hearts she'd ever known.

"My wife informs me she can cook," Greylen said. "What know you of this, Gavin?"

"Aye, she can cook, Greylen. You're in for a treat, my friend."

"Well, get up already," Gwen ordered with a smile. "We have work to do."

Once in the kitchen, Gwen went straight to the cupboards. She removed the pots and pans while Gavin lit the fire beneath the stove. Isabelle walked to the island and set the plates that were stacked next to a vase of flowers.

"Look, Gwen," Isabelle called with a smile. "Cook left four place settings."

"I noticed," Gwen replied as she took utensils from hooks above the counter. "She's the best." Gwen noticed, too, that Greylen was just standing by the island, watching them as if a bit surprised that they had a routine.

"Well, what do you think my husband would like?" Gwen asked as she turned to Isabelle and Gavin. "Rabbit, chicken, steak, fi—"

"Steak!" Isabelle and Gavin laid claim to the dish in a shout. As always, they were thrilled to sample the meat that Gwen seared to perfection on the stove.

"Is that all right with you, Greylen?" she asked him. "It's different from what you're used to," she explained.

"But your sister and Gavin said it's much tastier than the roasted cuts Cook prepares."

Greylen just looked at her. He couldn't speak. She really meant to cook for him. Joyfully.

"Are you okay?" Gwen asked, placing her hand on his arm. He continued to stare as she pulled a stool from beneath the island and instructed him to sit. Then she squeezed his hands before returning to the stove.

"Isabelle, get your brother some wine and pour some for the rest of us," Gwen instructed. "But remember, only one glass for you. Gavin, will you grab some potatoes and onions—never mind. I'll get them, just fetch the meat from the cellar."

Greylen drank the wine Isabelle set before him, looking to his wife, who stood before the stove. He realized only now that she wore just his shirt, and his sister, her nightclothes. Gwen leaned down to check the fire beneath the pans, swatting her hair as it fell in her face. His smile broadened as he watched her, and he almost laughed aloud when he heard her curse. *Good God, she was a walking paradox.*

She looked to her wrists and cursed again. He had no idea what she hoped to find, but the sight of her... by God, she was fetching. She walked toward him and lifted his wrist, smiling as she saw the leather cords he'd tied there. Their purposes were many and he always kept them handy. She removed one and looked at him as she pulled back her hair. He braced her hips between his legs and whispered in her ear, "I love you, Gwen." He was rewarded with a smile that lit her entire face.

"I love you too," she whispered back. Then she disappeared into the pantry.

"Your wife's a wonderful cook," Isabelle said as she sat across from him. "Just wait."

"And just how often has she cooked for you, Sprite?" Greylen questioned mildly. In truth, however, he was becoming a little suspicious.

Isabelle gave a delicate shrug. "Well, aside from the first time, which was the morning after you left, I suppose every night."

"*She cooks every night?*"

Gavin and Gwen stepped from the pantry, each laden with items. Greylen went immediately to help his wife, making sure his contemptuous look was fixed only on Gavin. "She cooked for you *every night.*"

"*Aye,*" Gavin taunted, "each meal more delicious than the last. 'Tis a shame you missed it."

"Gavin," Gwen yelled. "If you can't play nice, then don't play at all."

Greylen shot Gavin a triumphant look, for Gwen had come to his defense. Then he realized he'd acted like a lad whose mother had just defended him. *Good God, what was happening?*

"Greylen, sit down and drink your wine," Gwen ordered. "Isabelle, help me cut these potatoes. And Gavin—*behave.*"

"Ah, my bossy mistress has found her tongue."

"You call my wife bossy?" Greylen asked the question with more surprise than outrage. Gwen had been nothing but compliant since his return, hadn't she?

"Enough," Gwen exclaimed.

"'Tis good to have you home." Gavin clinked his goblet with Greylen's.

Greylen spoke with Gavin as Isabelle helped Gwen. And though he held his end of the conversation, he couldn't take his eyes from his wife. She added meat to one pan and potatoes and onions to another, and to another a mixture of greens. She had rolled his shirtsleeves above her elbows and the bottom edge of her shirt rested just above her knees. Her hair had loosened about her face, and she continued to blow it back in frustration. Her attention elsewhere, she'd not take the time to fix it. Without thought, he stood and stepped behind her. "Be still, wife," he ordered, untying the leather strap. Then he ran his fingers through her hair and pulled it back before retying it.

She remained completely still for a long minute. Finally she turned. "I can't believe you did that," she said as if truly shocked.

"You needed help," he told her.

"But, you fixed my hair," she told him as if he wasn't the one who just did so.

"Aye, wife, I fixed your hair."

"You fixed my hair, Greylen."

He sighed, shaking his head. "Let me help you to understand, love. *I. Fixed. Your. Hair,*" he teased with infinite slowness. Then he turned to Gavin and Isabelle.

"You're right." He shrugged. "She's daft."

They laughed as he reached out and brushed his fingers down Gwen's face.

"Greylen fixes everything, Gwen," Isabelle said matter-of-factly as she poured more wine. "'Tis always the way of it."

Gwen still looked stunned but mouthed "thank you" to which Greylen mouthed "you're welcome" before he sat down again.

Greylen resumed his conversation with Gavin as Gwen filled their plates. She served him first and he looked at the meal she set before him—perfectly seared meat covered with mushrooms, potatoes fried with onions, and greens sprinkled with spices. Then Isabelle placed a basket of bread between them and sat next to Gavin, across from him and Gwen. They took one another's hands and Isabelle and Gwen reached for his. He obliged, expecting to say grace.

"Isabelle, why don't you begin," his wife said.

"I'm grateful you're my sister now, Gwen," Isabelle said quickly and with a smile. Greylen saw that Gwen squeezed her hand, then she looked to Gavin, who began with the same words. "I'm grateful...not to be outnumbered any longer." His teasing remark caused Isabelle to laugh, and Gwen smiled too. Then his wife looked directly into his eyes and her quiet, simple words that followed touched his heart in a way that he'd never imagined. "I'm grateful you're home."

Greylen never took his eyes from her nor did he hesitate. "'Tis I who am grateful, Gwen, to have a wife such as you."

He picked up his goblet and tilted it toward his wife's. Then he held it before him and gestured to Gavin and Isabelle.

Eager to sample the foods that Gwen had cooked for him, he quickly tried everything. His eyes closed after each bite. "Good God, my wife can cook." He sighed, shaking his head.

'Twas a new experience, eating in the kitchen. And one he enjoyed immensely. They talked for the longest time and, in fact, had two more glasses of wine before they finished. Isabelle and Gwen cleared the island and washed the dishes, then Gavin put them in the cupboards. Greylen stood as well, bringing his goblet to the sink before extinguishing the fire beneath the stove.

"Gavin, see Isabelle to her room," Greylen ordered. "I'll wait in the study."

Gavin tried to keep his face expressionless, but he clearly wasn't pleased with the order, "Come Bel— Isabelle." He made the correction quickly, then walked toward the doors and held them open.

Gwen shot Greylen a questioning look. He returned a conspiratorial wink. She had to cover her mouth to keep from laughing and turned quickly so Gavin wouldn't see. After they left, Greylen held out his hand and when she took it, he gathered her in his arms.

"Thank you, Gwen."

"You're welcome, Greylen."

"I still have work to do. Should I take you upstairs?"

"I'd prefer to sit with you, if it's all right."

"Aye, I'd prefer it too."

Gavin's mood matched his gait as he led Isabelle down the hallway. She'd had two cups of wine, more than she should have, and swayed from its effects. She tripped over her nightgown as she started up the steps, forcing him to reach out and hold her waist and shoulders.

"Oops." She giggled.

"Ah, Bella, you're going to make me carry you, aren't you," he uttered, shaking his head.

She nodded, laying her head on his chest as he cradled her in his arms. Neither spoke a word as he continued up the stairs and stopped outside her door.

"Carry me inside, Gavin," she whispered.

"Nay, Bella." Then he shook his head again, realizing she'd not make it herself. He carried her to bed and laid her beneath the covers. Then he forced himself to turn quickly and leave.

"Gavin?"

"Aye, Bella," he asked without turning.

"I love you."

His entire body tensed. "'Tis the wine, Bella."

"Nay, Gavin, 'tis not," she whispered.

He left without looking back, slamming his fist against the wall outside of Bella's chamber. She was all he ever wanted. And the one thing he could never have. His past would always haunt him. And his secret, if revealed, would destroy everything he'd fought so hard to achieve. The very family he'd give his life for.

His mood was no better when he returned to the study. Greylen sat behind his desk while Gwen read on the settee. He picked up the papers he'd been looking through earlier, then sat across from Greylen so they could discuss the matters which needed immediate attention. 'Twas another hour before they finished.

"First light, Gavin, we round the herd along the northern border. We're behind schedule," Greylen said quietly.

Still out of sorts, Gavin only nodded and dismissed himself as he looked to Gwen, who had fallen asleep. What he wouldn't give to be as such with Isabelle. His chest tightened at the thought.

The pain was no better back in his chamber. 'Twas an empty bed he sat on as he laid his blade atop the bedside table. He stared at it for hours, wishing instead that the last of his nighttime ritual would end as he pulled the covers aside and gathered Bella in his arms.

Sadly, he knew 'twas a dream he would never have.

❦ CHAPTER SEVENTEEN ❦

Gwen awoke in her husband's arms. She felt better than ever. Greylen was an incredible lover, and contrary to the nasty rumors that circulated through the hospital, she wasn't an ice queen after all. She loved sex. She loved intimacy. She only realized now she'd never had the opportunity to experience it. Odd, she'd spent her entire life in the twenty-first century surrounded by people, and now, after only a few short weeks at Seagrave, with Greylen's family, the difference was striking.

She considered attacking her husband, then scrapped the idea to go for a run instead. It wasn't that she didn't want to make love; she did. But if they made love now, her run would be out of the question. She'd be useless, at least for the morning.

Yep, run first, sex later.

She carefully untangled herself from Greylen's embrace, then changed before slipping out of the chamber. She'd just put her hand on the latch of the front door when Greylen's voice startled her.

"Where do you sneak to, *wife?*"

Gwen turned, surprised by his tone. "I'm not sneaking anywhere, Greylen. I'm going for a run."

"Explain, then, leaving without telling me your intentions?"

"Greylen, I thought you were sleeping, and I didn't want to disturb you."

He looked at her like she were crazy. "Gwen, I can hear a pin—"

"Don't tell me," she cut him off, holding up her hand. "As far as Edinburgh, right?"

"That's correct. And you'll go nowhere." He crossed his arms over his chest to emphasize his point.

"Greylen, I didn't exercise yesterday," she explained. "And I really need to now. I'll only be gone an hour. *Please* be reasonable."

"*Reasonable*," he shouted. "'Tis still dark, and you go alone."

Really? He had the nerve to try that one? With a straight face no less. "Greylen, when I open this door will there be guards on either side?"

"*Your point?*" he asked, as if realizing his mistake too late.

"I won't be alone then, will I?" She said the words softly, aware from his expression that he'd drawn the same conclusion.

"Nay," he said quietly. "I will." He shook his head, as if disbelieving he'd said it aloud.

Gwen just stood there, shocked. My God, he didn't want to be alone. This beast of a man, *her husband*, didn't want to be alone. She smiled sympathetically, good Lord, how could she not. She knew how it felt to be alone. It seemed she'd spent the entirety of her life, until recently, feeling just that. Wasn't that what she'd just realized earlier? She'd either been alone, or alone in a crowd.

As she walked to him, her heart melted even more. "I'm sorry," she conceded, placing her hands on his chest. "I'll go later." After all, it wasn't like she didn't have time on her hands. Being stuck in the sixteenth century had its advantages. Of course, she belonged to a well-educated and wealthy family, which happened, she'd bet her life on, to help immensely. She wouldn't fool herself because, she knew without a doubt, it would really suck otherwise.

"Nay, I'm acting foolish. I'll go with you."

"You will?" A run with Greylen? In all her life she never really thought she'd find someone to share everything with. She'd imagined it, of course. She'd hoped for it, like deep down in that magical place where fantasy lived. But to actually feel it and live it. Wow.

"Aye," he confirmed, taking her hands to bring them to his lips so he could kiss the palm of each. "Tell me the way of it."

"It's simple, Greylen. You run."

"You call that exercise?" he teased.

"Don't knock it, you might like it," she muttered, squeezing his hands.

"I'll just be a moment. Should I wear the new shoes in the wardrobe?"

"Yes, and comfortable pants. And one of those knit shirts," she added, excited that he was joining her.

Gwen heard him a few minutes later. Her mouth fell open as he came down the stairs. *Crap!* How in the hell was she supposed to run next to *that*? He looked *way* too good. With every step he took, his muscles flexed clearly beneath the thin material of the clothes he wore.

She was screwed.

"Problem?" he asked, as if noting her expression.

"Nope," she replied quickly.

"You lie, wife." He grinned, wrapping his arm around her waist and bringing her in close. "And not very well."

"Trust me, Greylen, you'll never know."

"Gwendolyn," he drawled. "You know I have ways to make you talk," he warned against her lips.

"Hold that thought," she whispered. "You can extract the truth from me later."

"You're insatiable, wife," he said as he opened the doors. He nodded to the guards who stood outside, then followed her down the stairs.

"Ready?" she asked, eyes bright and filled with joy.

"Aye," he replied.

There was something in his eyes, something she'd come to notice when they spoke. This softening in his features in response to her, as if he'd do anything for her. It was unmistakable, and, honestly, she felt the same. He paced her as they jogged through the gates and down the path that separated the cottages from the practice fields. She started getting warm as they headed toward the lake and took off her shirt, tossing it to the ground.

Greylen cursed as he looked at her. She could only imagine what he must be thinking. It really wasn't much different from what she would've worn back home, shorts and a sports bra. So what if it was a homemade halter and something close to joggers pushed low on her hips and the hem cuffed to her knees. He cursed again. Poor baby.

"Take your shirt off, Greylen, you'll feel much better." He pulled it off but held it in his hand. "Drop it, we'll get 'em on the way back."

"I swear, Gwendolyn, if this is your normal habit," he warned as he glared at her, "my men are dead."

"We'll put an ad in the paper and hire new ones," she suggested with a smile.

It was about ten minutes later, as they circled the lake that Greylen turned to her. "I enjoy your run, Gwen."

"It's my favorite," she said. Then she added reflectively, "It keeps my spirit alive."

Greylen stopped immediately, pulling her back as she ran past. He lifted her chin as she caught her breath. "I keep your spirit alive now, Gwendolyn—since the night I clutched your body beneath the water—and 'tis mine alone to safeguard."

Greylen's tone was filled with possession and Gwen had no doubt that he believed what he said. For a moment, she almost conceded he was right. They'd never talked about that night, and she needed to know what happened. "Was I breathing when you pulled me from the water, Greylen?"

He closed his eyes, obviously recalling that night almost a month ago. "Nay."

Greylen didn't say more, and his silence scared her. "What happened, Greylen?"

He let out a long breath as he looked to the lake, then took her hand and began walking again. "We waited in front of the keep, not knowing how you'd come." He closed his eyes again, stopping where they stood and shook his head. "I heard your cry, Gwen, through the most terrible storm I've ever witnessed. There was a flash of lightning, and I swear I heard you." He stopped again, looking down at her. "I swam to you. I saw your struggles and watched you go under. You were an arm's length away, maybe two." As if consumed by emotions of that night, he grabbed her arms and brought her in close. "You never resurfaced!" His words were an accusation, and his voice was filled with the terror he'd felt.

"I tried to get to shore, Greylen, I couldn't." She was lost in her own feelings of what happened that night, reliving that fear and seeing it, too, in him. "I couldn't do it." She started crying, then became angry when he didn't seem to believe her.

He pulled her into his arms. "I know, love...I know." His tone was soothing now, as if he hadn't meant to speak so harshly. "I searched the water till I found you, Gwen. You were completely lifeless."

"How long was I under?"

"Long minutes...three...maybe four before we resurfaced."

"You stayed under that long?" she asked, glancing up to him.

"I'd no choice. The current. You'd have been lost."

"*How*, Greylen, it's imposs—" She didn't finish. They just exchanged a look. *Impossible* had little meaning anymore.

"When I finally held you, there was this force of energy that swept through our bodies. I'll never forget it, Gwen. It gave me the strength to endure, and I think it started your heart anew. It couldn't have beaten so long without air. Not for the time it took me to find you and reach the shore."

"But it was beating?"

"Aye, barely." He rubbed his fingers through his hair, as if willing the feelings away. "I gave you breath till the water released from your lungs. 'Tis a wonder your ribs didn't break from the pressure I used."

"How did you know what to do?"

"Logic. And I swore they'd not have you," he said, grabbing her shoulders. "I brought you back myself." He was lost again in emotions from that night. "Your life, your very spirit, I fought for as never before—and 'tis forever mine, Gwendolyn." He must have realized he was gripping her out of fear and anger, and he pulled her back into his arms.

Gwen leaned against him. "How did this happen, Greylen?"

"I've no answer, Gwen," he said, shaking his head. "I only know, I've waited years to have you."

"I used to dream about you, Greylen," she whispered. "Every night, I had the same dream over and over again. I couldn't make out your features in the shadows. I couldn't feel the heat of your lips or body. I couldn't even hear the sounds we made. You made love to me again and again, but I never felt what I feel now. I always woke up with this giant ache that never went away."

"I suffered the same, Gwen," he whispered.

"You had the dream too?" she asked, wiping her eyes.

"Aye."

"They started on my twenty-third birthday, Greylen. How old were you?"

"Eight and twenty, on the eve of my birth as well."

"That was five years ago for both of us. Why do you think it happened at the same time?"

"My mother told me of the prophecy when I was three and twenty," he explained. "I always repeated the words in my head, but one morning as I watched the sunrise, I recited them. The dream started that night."

She smiled. "You unlocked the dream."

"Aye, I suppose I did."

"You stole my heart and body, Greylen, even then."

He pushed the hair from her eyes. "Why didn't you tell me, Gwen?" he asked. "I never would have—"

She pressed her hand against his lips as her face heated profusely. "I wouldn't change the way you made love to me for anything, Greylen," she said, cutting him off. She so did not want to have this conversation. Ever.

He didn't press her further, then Greylen gave her a squeeze. "Let's go to the shore. 'Tis almost dawn."

"Race ya," she said, smiling as she pulled away.

He grinned. "You haven't a chance."

Gwen's smile widened. "Give me thirty seconds," she called, already running ahead.

Gwen heard Greylen's laugh, then felt his powerful strides as he closed the distance. He didn't pass her but ran by her side until they reached the back of the keep. Taking advantage of his fair sportsmanship, she sprinted ahead.

The path was only fifty yards away and she pushed herself as never before, so hard she knew it had to be a personal record.

She should've known better, Greylen was right behind her. She turned to look at him—*big mistake*. His grin was wide, and she shrieked as his hands reached, grabbing her waist. They fell to the ground. Her husband took the brunt of the fall, then rolled her beneath him.

He smiled as she laughed and caught her breath. "You'll pay for unscrupulous conduct, lady."

"Promises, promises, husband," she quipped.

"'Tis a promise you can be sure of," he vowed, covering her lips. "I'll have you again, and you'll not exercise for days when I've finished."

He helped her up, and then carried her on his back down the narrow path. They left their shoes on the sand, walking hand in hand along the shore's edge as the water rushed over their feet.

"Come in the water, Gwen."

"Are you crazy?"

"Nay. I wish to feel you naked."

"It's freezing."

"'Tis the middle of summer, love. The water's not overly cold."

Pointing her finger to the sea, Gwen couldn't help but argue. "I've been in that water, Greylen."

"Weeks ago, in the middle of the night, during a storm," he explained, lifting her chin. "You doubt me?"

"Oh, fine," she muttered, pulling her face away. She untied her halter and started for her pants, but before she could finish, Greylen hauled her against him. His hands ran down her bare back, cupping her bottom as he kissed her.

"Greylen, do your men keep watch from above?"

"Nay." He told the lie looking directly in her eyes.

She wasn't stupid, his men always kept his guard, and now, they always kept hers. Since Greylen's return, however, they'd been more discreet. She wondered where they stood atop the cliffs, knowing they wouldn't actually watch them, but she had no doubt they would remain there all the same.

He took her hand and led her into the water, stopping when it reached his chest and her shoulders. Then, still holding her hand, he slipped beneath the surface. When he came back up, he must have taken note of her look, the one that telegraphed her fear. "I'll not let go," he promised and pulled her against him.

She placed her hands behind his neck and wrapped her legs around his waist. After a few moments of his physical reassurance, she leaned back, slicking her hair as he supported her from beneath and glided her across the surface.

"I think you owe me something," she reminded him, running her fingers through his hair.

"And you'll be paid in full," he replied.

He kissed her, taking the very air she breathed. His hands moved down her body, stopping beneath her thighs. His fingers pressed into her skin until his erection slid between her folds.

He held tight to her center spreading her farther as she moved across his length. Her cries turned desperate as his finger slipped inside. She climaxed almost instantly from the dual assault. Wrapping her fingers around his width, she guided him inside. He held her thighs, pushing her back and then pulling her against him again and again, moving her so fast she ceased to keep up with him. She called his name as she tightened around him, and he released with one last thrust.

Gwen clung to his body, though he fully braced her. "You win, Greylen." Her words came in gasps as her head fell back. "I'll be lucky to walk tomorrow, let alone run."

Later she would realize that Greylen waited to respond, determined that she understand the significance of his words when he spoke them. Because when she looked at him again, he made his point clear. Very clear. "Hear my words, Gwendolyn, for I'll not say them again. I *always* win."

There was no boast in his voice, yet the way that he looked at her chilled her to the bone. His whole demeanor spoke of authority and possession. And then he kissed her, a kiss he chose to take rather than give.

Under normal circumstances, she would never submit to such tyranny. Never.

But, then, these were not normal circumstances.

And besides…her spirit was already his.

"I've another long day, Gwen," Greylen told his wife as he began to shave. They were in their bathing chamber, standing in front of the chest.

"Will you be back for supper?" Gwen asked, pushing herself up on the chest.

"Too early to tell," he replied, watching as she scooted before him and took the brush from his hand.

"Is there anything I can do?" she asked, lathering his face.

"Such as what?" he returned, his heart all but melting as she picked up the razor and began to shave him.

"Help you or your mother somehow?" Gwen asked, tilting his face to the side. "There." She smiled, wiping the remaining soap away with a towel. "Perfect."

Greylen leaned down to kiss her. "Thank you."

"You're welcome."

"Gwen," he began, back to the matter she broached. "You may do anything you choose."

"I'm a little limited, Greylen."

"You doubt your abilities?"

"It's not my abilities I doubt, it's how I can be useful."

"Being here is useful."

"Greylen, you're home now and we're married—"

"And I thought you were daft," he teased. "You're quite astute."

"Stop it." She laughed. "I'm serious. I need to do something. I can't just sit around all day."

"What did you do before?"

"Before you came home or before I came here."

"Both."

"I…" She shook her head. "You wouldn't believe me."

"You don't trust me?" he asked.

"Yes, I trust—"

Greylen grabbed her chin. "Why do you answer yes and no to me, yet, always aye and nay to my family and men?"

She seemed surprised by his question. "I don't know," she answered honestly. "Maybe I'm more comfortable with them. We've had more time together."

"Then you've found your first task. Find your comfort, immediately."

"You're kidding, right?"

"'Tis not something I find humorous, Gwen."

Their conversation was interrupted when Anna knocked on the door, informing them a bath had been filled in front of the fire. Greylen lifted Gwen and gently placed her on the floor. "Come, love, I've time for a quick wash."

"What are you doing today?" Gwen asked, grabbing her robe and his shaving tools.

"We're branding the cattle and horses. After the spring births, 'tis a task we've usually seen to by now."

"Why didn't your men take care of it while you were gone?"

"'Tis something I enjoy." He shrugged. "Rounding the animals from pasture and marking them."

"Yeah, sounds like fun," she teased and stepped into the water. "Could you stop by the store on your way home tonight?" she asked playfully.

Greylen smiled. "And what would I get for you at this store?"

"Oh, the list is endless." She laughed. "Tacos, doughnuts, Diet Coke." Her eyes got wide. "How about a smart TV, and a Netflix account? We could cuddle in bed and eat popcorn and Milk Duds."

He shook his head. "You'll tell me of these—" He lost his train of thought as she placed her foot over the rim of the tub and covered her leg with soap from his lathering brush. She reached for the razor using long, upward strokes.

"I've a busy day, Gwendolyn," he yelled.

"So, what in the hell did I do?" she yelled back.

"You're distracting me," he growled.

"I'm shaving, Greylen," she informed him with a smile. "I do this every day too."

He groaned and pulled her on his lap. Then he took the razor from her hand and gently ran the blade from her ankle to her knee.

"Now, 'tis I who thanks you, husband." She obviously chose her words carefully.

Greylen dried her as they stood by the fire. He dressed as Gwen sat on the trunk at the end of their bed. He turned to say good day—images reeling through his mind as he stared at her. Images of the night he'd pulled her from the water, images of locking her satchel inside the very trunk she sat upon.

He'd all but forgotten its existence. Now, however, its presence unsettled him. He walked to her as she stood up on the trunk, a tremor causing him to kiss her quickly and take his leave.

He was shaking by the time he leaned against the closed door outside of their chamber.

From an ominous chill that ran the length of his spine.

Gwen had another long day. *Big surprise*. After breakfast with Lady Madelyn and Isabelle, she gave serious thought to what she could do. She already helped Lady Madelyn when someone was injured or became ill, which, thank God, didn't happen often.

It was a good thing she was married, she decided. She could only imagine trying to support herself being the village doctor. She'd probably live in a shack filled with animal bladders and other gross things people would try to pay her with. *Ugh*.

"What bothers you, daughter?" Lady Madelyn inquired as she embroidered in the library.

"I don't know what to do with myself." Gwen shrugged.

"'Twill come in time," Lady Madelyn said to her, smiling over her work.

"I noticed the children watch as their parents tend chores. Do you think I could teach them a game?" Gwen asked.

"Of course," Lady Madelyn said quickly. "Though they, too, study in the late-morning hours."

"I know but maybe they could play in the courtyard after they finish."

"Gwendolyn, you needn't ask my permission." Lady Madelyn scoffed. "'Tis you who are mistress now."

"Lady Madelyn—*Mother*," Gwen corrected after receiving a disapproving look. "This castle runs itself.

I wouldn't know the first thing of doing it, nor would I interfere."

"You could show Cook how to prepare the meals you and my children enjoy, not to mention Gavin."

"You've found us out, have you?" Gwen said with a laugh.

"Aye, dear." Lady Madelyn smiled. "And though I'd never intrude, I've heard you're quite the cook."

"Well, I guess I can start there, but would you help me with something else?"

"Of course."

"Greylen was wearing a pair of calfskin breeches this morning. Do you have more of that material?"

"Aye, we've a room full of cloths and supplies."

"If I explain what I need, would you make something for me?"

Lady Madelyn listened to Gwen's instructions and informed her she would be done after their noon meal. Gwen left the library and sought Cook next, delicately broaching the subject of recipes. Thankfully, Cook was more than happy to listen to her suggestions.

Finding a new purpose was easier than she thought.

Gwen spent the rest of the morning knocking on cottage doors along the path. Connell had her guard today, and he stood quietly as she explained to the mothers what she wished to do. He helped her place flags at either end of the courtyard. "What of this, Lady Gwendolyn?" he asked, holding up the item that Lady Madelyn had fashioned.

"*This* is a football, Connell. The children will be placed on teams and they'll throw it to one another while trying to outmaneuver their opposing teammates and bring it through the goals."

"Truly?" he asked in surprise. "Do men play as well?"

"Aye." Gwen laughed. "Men play this game as well. In fact, they probably enjoy it more."

As she waited for the children, Gwen saw riders approach. It was Greylen and his men herding the cattle. They had removed their shirts and her husband began circling the animals, his voice thundering as he brought them closer to the corral behind the stables. He wore tight caramel-colored pants, rough leather boots, and a white band tied around his forehead. He looked like a cowboy—no, maybe a pirate. Ah, who the hell cares, either way, he was hot!

Once the animals were inside, the men handed their mounts to the boys who came to help. They sat on the fence, allowing the animals a few moments of peace.

"What will they do, Connell?" Gwen asked, watching the men drink from canteens, their legs swinging beneath them.

"They'll inspect them for disease and injuries, then brand the young calves," he explained. "We see to fifty or so at a time until all of the herds have been checked."

"How many do you have?"

"*You*," he corrected, "have over three hundred cattle, and close to fifty wild horses on the land."

"Is that a lot?" she asked.

"In cattle, our numbers are low, but the horse count is high. Our men take good care of their steeds, and of the three hundred currently in use by soldiers, none show any signs of abuse."

The children began filling the courtyard. Their mothers sat close to the keep, working on clothing or holding babies on their laps. Gwen explained the game to the boys and girls, while trying to divide them fairly. When she finished there were two teams of nine and cheering squads for each team.

It began as a mess, but as time progressed, the boys and girls took to the game. She told them only a touch from an opposing teammate would stop the play, and she watched carefully that no one became rough. Before long, the game was in full swing, and they learned to pass the ball and run like the dickens for the flags claiming a goal. The mothers and small children cheered for both teams, and Gwen saw that her husband and his men had come to watch as well. She smiled from across the courtyard, waving as Greylen returned her smile.

"May we join your game, wife?" he called over the field.

"Aye," she called back. "But as long as the children play, a touch calls the play over."

"Very well. Connell, join us."

Greylen, Hugh, and Ian joined the team on the left, while Gavin, Duncan, Kevin, and Connell joined the team on the right. Her husband picked up the ball and turned it in his hand.

"A football," she called. "Cowhide filled with sand. Do you need me tell you how to play?"

"Nay, we've watched long enough."

They obviously had, and it was the best game she'd ever watched. The men were fabulous with the children, lifting them as they came close to the goals and then racing them across. When the children began to tire, they sat with their mothers, and now only Greylen and his men remained. Gwen held up her hand and came on the field.

"Now that it's just the men"—she smiled wickedly—"let's change the rules."

They beamed and waited impatiently for her to continue.

"To stop a play, you can tackle the opposing teammate with the ball," she explained. "You can also rush the quarterback, the one holding the ball at the beginning of each play."

Greylen grinned and moved to stand before her. Her hair was filled with the flowers that the children had picked, and she was wearing a deep-blue gown. Judging from his look, her husband approved. "You've found good use today," he said, reaching out to stroke her face.

Gwen smiled, distracted as Greylen touched her. "We have to toss a coin to see who goes first," she explained once her brain started functioning again.

"I've no coin upon me," Greylen said.

"Nay, you don't, but I do." She flicked it in the air and then caught it in her hand. "Call it, husband, heads or tails?"

"Tails," he drawled. He watched as she flipped the coin on her forearm before taking her hand away.

"Shocking, husband. *You win*," she said suggestively.

"Is it?" he asked, raising a brow.

She didn't answer but reached up and kissed him before she left the field.

It was the most violent game of football she had ever seen. They played for at least an hour, and the more forceful they became, the harder the children cheered. She actually breathed a sigh of relief when they finished, and Greylen walked to her as his men went back to the corral. He was covered in dirt and had scratches on his shoulders and cheek.

"Boys will be boys," she said, shaking her head as he placed the ball in her hand.

"'Tis no boy who'll seek your bed later, lady."

"Ah, more promises, husband. What's a woman to do?"

He smiled at her taunt. "Begin praying now, love, for mercy."

"I want no mercy, Greylen."

"Remember your boast later," he warned.

Then he turned and followed his men.

❦ CHAPTER EIGHTEEN ❦

Greylen stood atop the battlement, the very place he found himself every afternoon, watching as his wife played games with the children or walked with Isabelle. Oftentimes, he'd just stare at her as she sat on the steps reading a tome she'd found in the library or his study.

The past week had been...magical. He cursed. *Magical? Good God, get a hold of yourself, man!* He tried to think of another way, then cursed as he threw his hands in the air.

"Problem?"

Gavin. Damn!

"Nay," Greylen answered. "Be on your way."

"On my way?" Gavin laughed. "I think not. Your wife tells me you've been in the study. I think not again."

"Leave, Gavin. Now."

"As your first-in-command, I should see what has you in such a state," he said, walking toward the outer wall.

"You're fired. Now, be on your way."

"Fired?"

"Aye, *fired*. Dismissed, relieved," he quipped in explanation. "My wife tells me we can advertise for new men all the time."

"Does she now?" He rolled his eyes as if not worried in the least. "I'm more than familiar with the term. Your wife threatened me with the same. Repeatedly," he said as he continued farther out. "Speaking of your wife, would she be the fetching lass in pale green sitting atop the steps?" He leaned over.

"I could push you," Greylen muttered.

"Aye, you could," Gavin returned with a grin. "But then I'd fall on your beautiful wife."

"Be gone, Gavin." Greylen sighed.

"Shh, Bella just came outside."

Greylen shook his head and rolled his eyes. "You can't hear her, you fool."

"You're the fool, Greylen," Gavin said as he turned again.

Greylen raised a brow, wondering if Gavin's body would clear his wife's if he pushed him to the left.

"Mayhap." Gavin guessed his thought. "But is it worth the chance?"

"Don't you have something to do?"

"Not more pressing than this." Gavin smiled. "Speak, Greylen. What troubles you?"

"I'm not troubled, Gavin." *Damn the man—be gone already.* Greylen crossed his arms over his chest and looked down at Gwen. "I'm not troubled," he said again, this time under his breath. "I'm enamored with my wife," he admitted with a sigh.

"And I ask you again—what is the problem?"

"Look at me! I'm watching her like a lovesick boy." Greylen threw Gavin to the ground when he started laughing. "I wake with her in my arms every morn, Gavin. Run with her before watching the sunrise on the beach. Then I think of her the entire day as I tend duties." He rested his face in his hands, then looked to Gavin again. "We—you and I," he said, motioning with his finger between the two of them, "eat the meals she joyfully prepares for us every night, no matter the hour we return. And I watch her as she sits within the study after, sleeping as I work. I—" The blow hit with such force, Greylen stumbled back.

"I can see how horrid your life's become," Gavin spat.

"What's wrong with you?" Greylen shouted, grabbing his man's shirt. When Gavin remained silent, Greylen narrowed his eyes. "You can have the very things I speak of, if you cease being a fool with my sister."

"I've duties to see to," Gavin said.

"She loves you, Gavin. You love her. What are you waiting for?" Greylen pleaded with his friend. "You've no idea what's it like," Greylen whispered. "When I carry her from the study at night and she's sleeping in my arms… good God, Gavin, I feel like I hold all the answers of the world in my hands."

"I'll see you in the fields," Gavin bit out, shaking off Greylen's hold.

Greylen grabbed his shoulder, turning him around. "Gavin, I'd not find another with more honor than you.

Nor would I be more honored than to have you as my brother."

"I'll see you in the fields," Gavin stated again, his face expressionless.

Then he turned and walked away.

"I'll be home for supper tonight," Greylen told Gwen the next morning. She was sitting before him on the chest shaving his beard.

"You know I've been here almost five weeks and we've never shared dinner together in the great hall."

"I'm sorry."

"I wasn't looking for an apology. I'm glad you'll join us," she said quickly. "Gavin too?"

"Aye, why do you ask?"

"Isn't it strange that he's never approached Isabelle?"

"Not strange, wife. Suspicious is more the like," he answered. In fact, he had thought of little else since his confrontation with Gavin. And he was sure now that whatever kept Gavin from his sister must be far-reaching indeed.

"Why hasn't she married, Greylen? She's old enough."

"She's always refused any suitors, and I'm certain now 'tis Gavin that's kept her from doing so. Besides, my father saw that she has her own wealth. In truth she needs not to."

"But she loves Gavin."

"Aye, and he loves her."

"*Well?*" she prompted, hitting his chest.

"Well, what?" He laughed.

"Do something. You fix everything—remember?"

"'Tis hard to change someone's will, Gwen, especially one as strong as my first-in-command."

"Not really. They just need a little push. Well, only Gavin needs the push."

"I've tried to broach the subject, but he refuses to listen," he said, shaking his head.

"Ahh, don't shake," she hissed, pulling back the razor. "Has Gavin admitted his feelings?"

"Nay, he stares at me like I've sprouted horns."

"I know that look."

Greylen rolled his eyes. "I'm not surprised." He sighed. "Dress for dinner tonight, wife." He squeezed her thighs.

"You're kidding, right? Greylen, I dress every day and every night."

"I'm aware that you dress, Gwendolyn. I'm suggesting that you do so appropriately."

"*Appropriately.* Gee that's such a big word, I don't think I understand."

"You understand precisely," he said, bringing her closer. "You could take the Eastern Hemisphere with an army at your disposal."

"Aw, that's so sweet."

"'Twas an insult," he muttered.

"Take it back," she cried with a laugh.

"Nay." He shook his head. "You drive me mad, woman."

And she did. Pliable in his hands one minute, and Armageddon in the blink of an eye. His wife was intelligent, loving, and mindful; foul-mouthed, headstrong, and downright feisty. She openly questioned his authority, and good God, her looks alone could raise the dead. Not to mention that finger of hers. She'd start pointing, and he'd seek escape. Or fight back if necessary.

He'd tried to change the way she dressed, but his attempts were futile. In truth, they were explosive. One morning, he'd even gone to the trouble of choosing a gown for her to wear while she'd finished in the bathing chamber. Then he called to her that he'd meet her below stairs.

He'd waited at the head of the table in the great hall, facing the archway. His mother, Gavin, and Duncan sat to his left and Isabelle to his right. He'd just taken a sip of coffee when his wife entered—the contents spewed from his mouth.

Gwen, *his wife*, was not in the dress he'd carefully placed on the bed, but in the clothing that she'd come to him in. A tight white shirt revealing her arms, most of her chest, and the outline of everything beneath. And her trews, good God, her trews were the tightest pair of anything he could ever remember. They clung to her so low he could see her navel.

And she was barefoot as well.

She'd smiled as she approached the table, where everyone, save he, had covered their mouths and laughed. "Good morn, everyone," she'd said sweetly as she looked to them. Then she'd turned to him. "Greylen, *husband...*" she had begun, her voice forced honey.

He was going to nail her...against the wall, on the floor, to the door, the bed.

"How nice you took the trouble to instruct me on what I should wear," she'd continued, his thoughts now returning from those of her imminent defeat, a triumph he could all but taste. "I just wanted to be sure," she'd said, standing beside the table now, her hands running down her body for emphasis, "*this* wouldn't be your first choice?"

He'd stood so fast the chair fell. He'd grabbed her, his hand a vise around her arm as he pulled her from the room. The laughter behind them had been so out of control by that point, they'd beat out their enjoyment upon the tabletop.

By the time they'd entered their chamber, he had been so furious he could barely speak.

"How dare you, wife!"

"How dare I? How dare *I*?"

He backed her to the door, his look causing her retreat with every step he took. "I thought to be helpful," he shouted, blocking her escape.

"You—did—not!"

"Apologize—now."

"Never."

"You'll pay for your insolence," he warned, an inch from her face.

"Oh God, Greylen!" She'd grabbed his shirt. "Make it quick, I'm almost there."

He hadn't made her wait at all.

He'd ripped the clothes from her body, then threw her to the floor. Kissing her savagely as he'd pressed himself against her, and in such a state that he was beyond thought, he had ground his hips roughly between her thighs, barely unfastening his breeches enough to free himself before plunging inside.

He'd loved to hear her beg and beg she had done— again and again. He'd released with a shout, hearing his name escape his wife's lips.

The next incident happened two days later. He'd been unable to run with her that morning, and when she had approached Hugh, who had her guard, he'd informed her 'twas forbidden. Greylen couldn't say why he chose that particular word, but he insisted Hugh use it knowing his wife would be furious.

She had still been in her robe when she'd stormed the study. "I was about to change for my run," she hissed, steam nearly coming from her ears. "But was told you *forbid* it."

Greylen had looked to Gavin and his men at the table. "Leave us," he'd ordered in an ominous tone, eyes narrowed on his wife. He could taste victory again, body and mind reeling with anticipation.

Gwen had waited till the doors closed. "Listen, caveman, I need to run and you can't stop me," she shouted, approaching his desk, her strides determined, her look furious.

"I did stop you, wife," he'd corrected.

"I'll go in my goddamned robe if I have to, Greylen! Where are my clothes?"

"Don't jump ahead, *sweet*. Repeat the term you used to describe me—*now!*"

"It was caveman," she'd yelled, leaning over the desk.

"*Caveman?*" he'd bellowed as he stood. "As in prehistoric beast?"

"Aye. You seem to be a direct descendant," she'd spit in his face.

She'd jumped back as he swept everything atop his desk to the floor. Then she had run for the door as he'd vaulted and gave chase. He'd caught her as she reached the latch, grabbing her wrists and pulling her back.

"Sit down, *love*," he'd commanded, pushing her, though she complied. She'd trembled beneath his touch, as desperate as he. His hand behind her head, fingers clutching her skull, he'd laid her atop the empty desk, untying the belt of her robe with his teeth.

"You provoke me on purpose, wife," he'd growled.

"Maybe," she'd said in a breathy voice. "Do you?"

"Aye," he'd whispered, covering her mouth, his hands rough upon her body. Tasting and biting every inch of her, he'd sat in the chair again. Grabbing her legs, he'd dragged her closer and kissed the insides of her thighs. Then he'd spread her with his thumbs and feasted on her with his mouth.

"Let go, wife," he'd whispered, moving his finger inside. She had, but still he had continued to make her surrender once again. He'd stood, slicking his hand with her wetness before covering himself. Then he'd watched as she did the same, moving her hand on her body before wrapping her fingers around his erection. He'd growled and pushed her back, entering her with such force they both cried out.

It took less than a minute—they'd released together and lay panting. "Brassy wench," he'd grumbled. "You do provoke me on purpose."

"Aye, Greylen," she'd admitted with a grin. "I do."

"Greylen. *Greylen*." Gwen rubbed his cheek, pulling him out of his reverie.

He shook his head and grinned. "Sorry."

"You were a million miles away." Gwen smiled.

"Nay." He leaned in and kissed her. "Come," he said, circling her waist and helping her from the chest.

She sat on the trunk at the end of their bed, sipping the coffee that Anna had brought up earlier. Their servant knew when they left in the morning, and on each occasion a hot bath and coffee awaited their arrival.

"So, what's on your schedule today?" she asked as he dressed.

"We ride the southern border. MacFale's been tampering with the posts again, though he's not desecrated anything."

"*Desecrate* is a strong word, Greylen. Is he that bad?"

"Aye, he enjoys inflicting pain—on people and animals."

"In that case, I don't want you playing with him, understand?"

"Aye." He laughed. "I'll only play with my men—and you." He laughed as he left the room, hearing her call out "good answer."

Gwen poured another cup of coffee and went to the landing. Wrapped in her robe, she sat on the berth waiting for Greylen and his men. They met in the study every morning, discussing whatever it was they talked about, and then together they'd head to the front doors.

Watching them was her favorite part of the day, and she smiled as she heard them coming down the hallway. Then they appeared. Seven of the most wonderful men in the entire world.

They were all huge, with dark hair of varying lengths and incredible bodies. Today they wore ebony-colored breeches and light-colored shirts. Their swords were angled across their backs and cylinders filled with quivers were thrown over their shoulders. But what appealed to her most were their eyes. No matter what trouble they *thought* she caused, it was only respect and concern that they looked to her with. And no matter how many times they lied straight to her face, she knew they did so only to protect her.

"Boys," she called playfully, rewarded with seven smiles as they turned. "Don't forget, we're having pizza tonight for dinner. Pick it up on your way home, okay?" They all nodded, clapping her husband on the back before heading out the door. Greylen, however, remained, holding her gaze the longest. Then he turned to join his men.

CHAPTER NINETEEN

His wife dressed for dinner.

She looked resplendent in pale blue. Her hair was secured with a jeweled clip he'd gifted her with just that morn and her legs were crossed as she sat before the fire in the great hall, her foot rotating provocatively. The cordwainer must've had a fit fashioning her sandals. More to the point, she must've had the fit bending him to her will. The sandals were delicate and similar to those she wore the night he wed her. The heel on these, however, had to be three inches longer, and no more than a spike. His appetite increased...for her.

She turned and smiled, as if she was pleased by his appearance. He and Gavin were both dressed impeccably in white linen shirts and black trousers tucked into tall, polished boots. Their hair was still wet, having bathed in the lake before entering the keep, a habit after their long days.

Greylen walked to Gwen and brought her hand to his lips. "You look beautiful," he said.

Gavin poured wine and handed a goblet to each of them before placing the last atop the harpsichord for Isabelle.

"Greylen, come play with me," Isabelle called.

"Aye, Sprite, something lively," he dared.

"You play, Greylen?" Gwen asked, surprised.

"One of my many talents," he teased.

Gwen snorted. "My God your ego knows no bounds." Then she turned to his first-in-command. "Gavin, come dance with me," she called. "We'll teach my monger husband and his saucy sister how to move to such music."

Gavin drained the contents of his goblet and then bowed ceremoniously before taking her hand. He led her to the center of the room and Gwen smiled. "Follow my lead, kind sir," she said. She proceeded to teach him what she called a "two-step." It wasn't long before Gavin was twirling her around the room, and when the music ended, he kissed her hand.

"My turn," Isabelle called, standing.

"Perfect." Gwen smiled. "I'll play while Gavin teaches you the steps."

'Twas rather odd that when Gwen sat next to him, she just stared at the keys with a look upon her face that belied her seconds earlier enthusiasm to play. 'Twas another long moment before she whispered an explanation, "You know, it's really rather stupid, but somehow playing the piano in the past always made me sad, more alone than I actually was." She turned to him. And when she bit her lip, he ran his finger down the side of her face.

"A stroke for courage, love." When his wife's eyes filled with tears, he asked, "What's this?"

She reached up, cupping his face with her delicate hands to bring him closer. "Everything I ever wanted is right here in this room, Greylen," she whispered for his ears only.

Good God, he loved this woman. "I'd not find the words to say it better." He kissed her, then motioned with his head to the keys. "Play, sweet."

It took but a moment for her to find the right placement, and then she laughed finding her stride, shocking them all as she played beautifully.

Greylen studied Gwen's hands, adding to her delight when he followed beside her. She gave him an incredible smile, which he returned. And now he was the one who was laughing, having more fun than he could ever remember.

Anna came in and announced dinner, and as he glanced up, he couldn't help but notice the warm look she exchanged with his mother. When he and Gwen finished their piece, Gavin escorted Isabelle and their mother to the table. He and Gwen remained where they were.

He shook his head as he stared at her. "You never cease to amaze me, Gwen." He laughed as she worried her bottom lip between her teeth. "One day, love, I'm going to bite it for you," he warned.

"You already have," she said, rolling her eyes.

"Don't remind me," he growled.

"I like it when you bite me." She grinned.

They laughed their way to the table and Greylen held her chair. He remained standing, raising his glass ceremoniously. "To the first of many joyous nights together.

May the warmth that fills this chamber last throughout our lifetimes." They touched their goblets together before drinking to his toast.

"Greylen, how did you learn to play the harpsichord?" Gwen asked as they began to eat.

"My father and I sailed to Italy years ago," he explained. "We happened to be at court when we saw the instrument. My father was so taken with the invention, he commissioned its construction for our home."

"What became of him?" Gwen asked.

"He died five years past, peacefully in his sleep."

"I'm sorry," Gwen said, taking his hand. She repeated the sentiment to his mother and Isabelle.

"We had a good life together, Gwendolyn," his mother said quickly. "He loved his children more than anything and saw that they had all the world could offer."

"Tell me more," Gwen prompted softly.

"When the children were young, he doted on them constantly. Greylen could always be found beneath his desk in the study, the same that's there today. Even when he was a babe just crawling, Greylen sought his father's presence. And though Isabelle came much later, he showed her the same affection. She loved to be bounced on his lap and dance for him before supper."

As Greylen recalled the memories, he took note of his wife's look of longing. 'Twas the same look which Gavin wore, a look he'd not taken note of before. He did so now, realizing he must get to the bottom of the puzzle.

"As Greylen became older," his mother continued, "Allister took him everywhere. They sailed the seas together and traveled to council meetings. He wanted his son to be aware of the world around him, human nature as well. And though it pained him to send Greylen abroad to continue his studies, Allister knew the importance of learning and expanding one's mind."

"He must have been a great father," Gwen said wistfully.

"He was," Greylen said, squeezing her hand. "What of your parents, Gwen?"

"My parents were nothing like yours," she answered. "You were lucky to grow up in a loving home. It was all I ever wanted. My world is so different, *people* are so different."

"Circumstance may change, Gwen, but people and their motivations remain."

"Do you always have to be right? It's *sooo* annoying."

"Annoying you happens to be my favorite pastime."

"Really, I could have sworn it was something else." She let the innuendo hang and turned to Gavin. "Gavin, what of your family?" she asked.

Greylen knew if Gavin could take Gwen outside and beat her, the time would be now. She'd voiced the question no one had the nerve to ask. Greylen was shocked to hear Gavin answering. "I, too, dream of family, Gwen, but only in the years since I've held your husband's guard. I was lucky to know a mother's love, and, at one time, mayhap a father's."

"What became of them?" Gwen prodded.

Greylen knew that he wasn't alone in holding his breath. His sister and mother had to be as well, for they'd never heard Gavin speak so freely.

"My father still lives, but he's a weak man and I chose to leave. I studied abroad until I joined my king's ranks in service, and 'twas there I was lucky enough to find a man of honor."

"Do you have any other family?"

"None I would speak of. I turned my back years ago—and the devil himself couldn't make me look upon them again." He spat the words, his anger barely contained.

"I'm sorry, Gavin."

"Nay, Gwen." He shook his head. "'Tis I who am sorry, for I left much behind. Though I'd not take for granted what I've gained in the years since."

The conversation lightened as servants cleared the dishes. And after another hour or so by the fire, Lady Madelyn excused herself, kissing each of them before leaving. Greylen stood a short while later and held out his hand to Gwen. They left Gavin and Isabelle sitting across from each other in the chairs before the fireplace.

Gavin finally looked to Isabelle. She leaned against the side of the chair, her feet tucked beneath her. "What I wouldn't do for things to be different, Bella," he said, staring into her eyes.

"Imagine they are, Gavin, just for a moment," she whispered. "What would you do then?"

"You'd be mine already, Bella. My babe would grow fat in your belly, and I'd care for you as I've only dreamed."

Isabelle left the comforts of the chair, taking those few steps until she stood before him. "Dance with me again, Gavin?" she asked, reaching out. "Please."

He stood and pulled her in his arms. Then he moved her about the room, imagining the music they listened to earlier. Imagining the life he feared could never be his. Gwen had opened a myriad of emotions tonight, and he was surprised he answered her questions. But somehow, spoken aloud, the memories seemed to lessen those that forever haunted his mind.

"Come, I'll walk you to the stairs," he whispered, brushing the hair from her face.

"Will you kiss me, Gavin?"

He couldn't seem to stop himself tonight. He reached out and held her face and then he slowly leaned forward and covered her lips. He remained perfectly still, feeling as close to heaven as he'd ever been.

He held her hand as they walked to the stairs. Then with his foot atop the step and his hand on the banister, he watched as she made her way. She turned at the landing, but just before she reached her door, she leaned against the railing.

She mouthed the words *I love you*.

And he was lost.

His hand covered his heart as he closed his eyes. When he opened them again, he looked at her. He looked at her until he was sure that she understood, first, that he accepted her words, but more importantly, that he would love her until his dying breath.

Moments later, he left the keep. Damning himself with each step he took. Knowing that his freedom to have her would destroy the life he now knew.

But what once was enough…

His hands reached for the sky as his roar echoed through the night.

❧ CHAPTER TWENTY ❧

"For God's sake, Gwen, what are you doing?" Greylen asked, shaking his head. He was dressing and she was lying on the floor.

"Sit-ups, Greylen."

"Ah…your simple exercises, wife. To run you simply run, and to do sit-ups you sit up. Is that the way of it?" he teased.

"Aye, it is, and these sit-ups keep my stomach flat and tight. Something that I can honestly say pleases you," she said, continuing her crunches.

He straddled her body. Grinning, he pushed her to the floor. "What would please me more is your belly filled with my babe, and an end to your thusly named exertions."

"Really?"

"Aye, *really*," he answered. "Don't you want children?"

"Of course, I just… We just never talked about it," she stammered.

"Nay, we only rut like animals two or more times a day." He laughed, then kissed her.

"Oh my God, Greylen, I could be pregnant."

"Aye, love, we should know in a matter of days."

Greylen made love to her again, as if proving his point before leaving with his men. Gwen still continued to watch them every morning, calling out playfully as they stood in the doorway. Today, however, she realized she forgot to tell Greylen something and ran downstairs. When she'd opened the door, they were exchanging coins. They looked guilty as hell.

"What's this?" she asked, hands on her hips.

"These are called *coins*, Gwendolyn," Greylen said, holding one up. "We use them to purchase things."

"I know what frigging coins are, you idiot. I meant, what in the hell are you doing with them?"

"She has the foulest mouth," Greylen said to his men, like she wasn't standing right in front of them.

"Answer me, husband," she hissed.

"We're trading them." He grinned.

Gwen's eyes narrowed. "Do I look like an idiot? Because I'm not."

He laughed.

She gasped as it hit her. "You're betting on what I ask for in the mornings, aren't you?"

"Ah, Gwen, don't be angry. You'll be happy to know, I always win."

"And you'll be happy to know, I'm gonna kick your ass." She came at him no-holds-barred, and he wrestled her to the ground seconds later.

"Give," he said, smiling above her.

"Like I have a choice?"

"You always have a choice, Gwen. You can either make nice or I'll make you make nice, for all the world to see," he warned suggestively.

"You'd touch me and make me beg in front of your men?"

"I'll kill them after. Then we'll put an ad in the paper and hire new ones."

"I'll give," she grumbled, knowing she'd surprised him by conceding so quickly.

Greylen shook his head. "Too easy, love."

"I swear, Greylen." Gwen took great pleasure in lying to his face. "I give. Now help me up, you overgrown bear."

He stood, taking her with him. Gwen kissed his cheek as if nothing had happened and then told his men to have a nice a day as she walked away. "Greylen, can I see you for a moment, please?" she called without looking back. She knew he'd feel at least somewhat contrite and would oblige her request. She was already on the steps when he reached her, and she turned so that they almost touched, her face just before his.

"Do you remember making love this morning, Greylen?" she asked wistfully.

His eyes narrowed. "Aye."

"I can still feel you inside me," she purred, covering her breasts with her hands, "hot, thick...and so hard. I swear I'm wet right now."

She took immense satisfaction in the hiss that escaped his lips as his eyes clenched shut. Well, that and the fact that her husband was rock-hard with six men standing directly behind him.

"Well, have a nice day," she said cheerily before sauntering away and closing the door.

Seconds later the door splintered in Greylen's wake, his roar sending her screaming up the stairs. He caught her at the landing. Her dress ripped down the back as he carried her toward their chamber over his shoulder. He took her against the wall, thrusting again and again as she cried his name, releasing with a shout that shook the very rafters.

He explained the wager he and his men made as they sat in the study, quite pleased with himself that he'd won every morn.

"Was it worth it, Greylen?" she asked him.

"Every frigging coin, love," he admitted, kissing her.

Another week passed and as she sat on her perch, she heard Greylen and his men coming down the hallway. Though they still laughed and smiled as they took to the front doors, she knew that troubles were occurring more frequently. And of late, her only request was that they come home safely. It was really all that mattered now.

Somehow the realization changed everything, and she found herself enjoying life as she never had before. She was comfortable with the drastic changes, and confident that she and Greylen would be happy forever.

It lasted until dinner.

Playing music and sharing a meal with Greylen, Isabelle, Lady Madelyn, Gavin, and tonight, Duncan, she opened the can of worms herself, sipping coffee from an exquisite porcelain cup. *Stupid frigging cup.*

"Do you know people pay millions of dollars every year, just to have a cup of coffee?" she asked.

"Millions, Gwen," Greylen argued, shaking his head. "It cannot be."

She rolled her eyes. "There are people who are millionaires many times over."

"In truth, Gwendolyn?" Isabelle asked.

"In truth." She nodded. "And there are stores everywhere that sell anything you can imagine." She decided not to mention the internet or Amazon.

"Do you miss your home, daughter, your family?" Lady Madelyn asked as they stared at her.

"Honestly, Mother, I don't. I love it here...and my family is gone. My parents and my aunt were all that I had, and they died over two years ago."

"The prophecy spoke of your mourning, Gwen," Gavin said.

"You'd think"—Gwen glared at Greylen—"my husband would have told it to me by now."

"You'd think," Greylen growled, "*my wife* would know her place by now."

"You've shown me often enough," she muttered back.

"Please recite it, Greylen," Isabelle pleaded, then rolled her eyes for emphasis. "Or I may vomit from your love-play."

Gwen refilled their goblets as Greylen continued to glare. It killed her to pretend indifference. But she'd be damned if she let him see it. *Insufferable beast.*

Greylen watched his wife. The woman was practically bursting at the seams. He finally laughed. "Sit, *wench*, you'll have your words." He waited until she took her seat again, then he touched their goblets together and began.

"To the greatest Highland clan he is born..." He winked at his mother.

"From a different time, first she must mourn..." He squeezed Gwen's hand, then stood playing the grand storyteller.

"Two souls forever joined, still so far apart..." Hand over his heart he looked to his audience, caught in the words himself as they came from his lips.

"Yet the reason is clear, she mends his broken heart...

"A great storm will rage, the eve of his thirty-third year...

"On her twenty-eighth, when the path is then clear...

"Once they touch, 'tis forever, their bond is the key...

"Once together, they shall remain...for infinity."

Isabelle stood, clapping in excitement, while Greylen bowed before looking back to Gwen. His eyes narrowed as he noted her demeanor. She sat completely still, a blank stare on her face. Then she reached for her goblet and drained its contents.

"Again, Greylen," she said, looking to no one, her tone flat and her voice tight. She clearly braced herself for the retelling.

He had no idea what upset her, but he'd never seen her as such. He began again, less boastful this time, and watched her intently with each word he spoke.

Her face remained impassive until he recited, "Yet the reason is clear, she mends his broken heart…"

Gwen stood so quickly the chair fell. Her goblet empty, she reached for his and drained it. "If you'll excuse me," she said.

Then she was gone.

She was halfway up the stairs when he caught up to her. "Gwen, what's wrong?" he asked, taking the steps three at a time to keep pace.

"I…I—" She stopped only a second to look at him. "Oh God, Greylen, *I can't.*"

"Can't what, Gwen? What's upset you?" he yelled as she continued up the stairs to their chamber.

She paced the floor, wringing her hands. Then she stood in the center of their room and stared at him in a way she never looked at him before. She began shaking her head again.

"I'm going for a run," she said, looking to the floor.

"'Tis dark, Gwen, and you've had three glasses of wine," he reminded her. "You'll go nowhere."

"You don't understand, Greylen," she yelled, looking up once again. "It doesn't matter. I've gotta get out of here." She turned to the bathing chamber, clothes flying once she stepped inside. Everything from the chest emptied as she searched without reason. Then she dropped to the floor, rummaging through the pile. Her entire body shook as she removed her gown, the bodice ripped in her haste. She re-dressed in her running clothes, then stood panting, her hands fisted so tight her knuckles were white.

Good God his wife was going to blow.

He kept his voice calm and made no move to approach her. "Gwendolyn, come by the fire, love," he called softly. As she walked past him, he shouted, "You're not leaving."

"Watch me!"

Afraid to upset her further, he followed her to the steps. He realized she meant to go outside. "*Gavin*," he bellowed, "the door."

Gavin jumped to his orders, barely in time. Gwen moved quickly, but Greylen was just a second behind. He watched in fascination as Gwen stood before Gavin, fixing him with a stare Greylen had seen before—his. *Good God, but if looks could kill.* She spoke then, words Greylen knew she meant for him but were thrown in Gavin's face instead. "Fine, I'll use the stairs."

Furious, Greylen entered the great hall. "Come, my wife provides entertainment." He clapped. Then he sat in the entryway with his mother and Isabelle while Duncan and Gavin stood sentinel at the doors. The entire time, Gwen never looked at him. She raced the stairs at least twenty times, all but trying to kill herself, her pace was so fast.

She knelt when she reached the landing that time and banged on the stone with her hands. She came down the stairs again and looked only at Gavin. Breathless, she walked to him and reached for his hand. Then she backed him to the open foyer, begging him with her look.

"Gwendolyn, nay." Gavin shook his head at her. "Not now—not here."

Gwen shook visibly, her eyes pleading. Greylen watched intently, at least clear in this, Gavin knew whom not to serve. Confirming his thoughts, Gavin looked at him as if silently beseeching forgiveness. For what, Greylen knew not.

"*NOW*," Gwen shouted, obviously angered that Gavin wavered.

Gavin shook his head, not in refusal it seemed, mayhap just to rid his confusion. He brought his hands before him where they remained in wait. Gwen made no move, then Gavin's eyes narrowed, and he began to circle her. She followed with her head, her hands finally fisting.

Greylen's head tilted to the side, his own eyes narrowing as he took in the scene before him. His wife, in a stance clearly meant for battle. His first-in-command displaying the actions he himself had begged for on countless occasions. Yet this time, '*twas his mistress whom he served*.

Unsure, he stood, his mother pulling him back. "Let her find some solace, Greylen," she pleaded. "She's so like you."

'Twas those words that finally broke through. His wife was in fact like him. Strong and determined. She used her body to work through the things which plagued her most. From the corner of his eye, he saw Anna at the end of the hallway and motioned with his hand for her to prepare their room. She'd swiftly see to a bath by the fire. His full attention on the center of the entryway, he waited, his own hands fisted as well. Gavin began to circle his wife, taunting her with a stare, moving his arms as he readied himself. And still Greylen knew not what for.

Then it began, and the display took his breath away.

His wife engaged, hitting Gavin's palms with quick punches, straight, and then from below. She grunted as she delivered each blow, while Gavin threw her hands back, harder after each assault. They became embroiled in a game, the likes of which he'd never seen before. And he almost smiled with pride.

She was amazing.

She kicked at Gavin's arms from the side now, turning to deliver more from behind. Gavin's defense was harsh, throwing aside each of her blows, and now both made sounds as they battled. It continued for endless minutes, no finish in sight. Finally, he could take no more.

"*ENOUGH,*" he shouted, standing to move before her.

He grabbed Gwen's arm and led her from the room. They spoke not a word as they ascended the stairs and entered their chamber. He led her to the tub and removed her clothing before lifting her into the water. She remained silent, staring into the fire as he washed her. Then he wrapped her in a towel and placed her on the hearth.

He stood before her now, arms crossed over his chest as he waited for an explanation. She finally looked at him.

"I—" She shook her head.

"You'll tell me, Gwen, now."

"I—"

She started crying, silent tears at first, but then she became consumed, head on her knees as her body shook. And still he didn't understand, but he knelt and wrapped her in his arms.

"I—" She still couldn't finish.

"Your knowledge of letters needs work, love. Shall I employ a tutor?" he joked softly, pulling back to look at her.

She gave a laugh. "'Twould be very generous of you."

"I'd give you the world, Gwen. You know it to be true. Please talk to me," he pleaded, unsure what else to do.

"Greylen, I...I—"

"Good God, Gwen—we've gotten that far already—*you what?*"

"I mend broken hearts," she whispered.

"I know, Gwen, you've mended mine already."

"No, Greylen, that's not what they meant."

"What *who* meant?"

"*The prophecy,*" she shouted. "I truly mend broken hearts, Greylen."

"You're an enchantress," he accused. "How many hearts have you soothed—and how?"

"Greylen, you're not listening. The reason I'm here is to mend your heart—*literally.*"

"But you already have, Gwen."

"No." She shook her head. "Greylen, I have the knowledge, *the ability*, to fix a heart. 'From a different time...the reason is clear, she mends his broken heart'— Greylen, I was sent here to fix your heart!" As if unbidden images reeled through her mind, her fingers tangled harshly in her hair.

Her entire body shook as she walked to the window. She stared at the blackened sea as Greylen stood behind her. He divested her of her towel and wrapped her in her robe. "You're shaking," he said softly, pulling her against him.

"I won't be able to help you, Greylen."

She began crying again and he turned her. "If what you say is true, then—"

"I have no instruments, Greylen. Even if I had my bag, it wouldn't be—" She gasped as he tensed. "Where is it, Greylen?" she demanded in a shout, hitting his chest with both of her hands.

He walked to the trunk at the end of the bed and withdrew a key from his pocket. He removed the lock before lifting the lid. "I feared 'twould change what happened," he offered, raising the bag and holding it out to her.

Gwen hesitated, then she grabbed it. She hugged it to her chest and knelt on the floor, rocking back and forth. He sat before her, then wrapped his legs around her and tilted her chin. "You truly mend broken hearts?" he asked.

She nodded cautiously.

"Explain," he asked, feeling more ignorant than he ever had. "Please."

"I…" She released a breath as if wondering where to begin. "I'm a surgeon, Greylen, a doctor who operates on people." She stopped, it seemed, to gauge his reaction but continued when he remained expressionless. "I'd just completed my residency and signed a contract"—she must have realized he didn't understand and explained—"to become a doctor you have to go to medical school, it's a four-year program after you've completed another four-year program. Then you work at hospitals under the supervision of other doctors until you complete your residency."

Greylen nodded and she continued, "I always knew what I wanted to do, from the time I was just a little girl." She smiled. "I was obsessed with being the best at everything."

Greylen was so overcome with pride. As he listened to her talk of her past, 'twas rather difficult not to pull her into his arms.

"I finished high school early. Usually you're eighteen, but because of my birthday being early and..." She paused a moment and shrugged. "And I guess this consuming drive I had, I was sixteen when I started my undergrad program. I finished that early, as well, and then went to med school."

"My God, Gwen. How did you accomplish so much, so quickly?"

She shrugged in an attempt to remain indifferent, but her voice held a quality of despair when she quietly answered. "School was all I had, Greylen."

Greylen saw the tears in her eyes, at once suspicious of what she left out. "What do you mean 'twas all you had?" he asked, determined to understand what she wasn't saying with that admission.

"I had my aunt Millicent," she said quickly. "She was wonderful, Greylen." Her eyes lit up as she spoke about her. "We took trips together, and she always told me how proud she was of me."

"What of your parents, Gwen?" he insisted as she continued to avoid the issue. It took her so long to answer, for a moment, he thought mayhap she wouldn't.

"My parents were...busy." The last word was spoken so low, and, worse, to her hands.

"*Busy*," he nearly shouted, outraged on her behalf.

"It wasn't their fault," she said defensively. "They were trained just as I was. They were the leaders in their field, Greylen. I was poised to take their place."

"But what of you, Gwen?"

"I...I...worked hard," she stammered. "I—"

"Did they never praise your efforts, Gwen?"

"They...they expected me to be the best," she finally said. "I don't think they ever realized..."

He lifted her chin so she would look at him. "Realized what?" he prodded gently.

"I just wanted them to be proud of me, Greylen. I tried so hard to make them notice." She choked on a sob. "I—I'll never let our children feel so alone and unloved."

He cursed, pulling her into his arms. How could she have been treated so badly? She gave of herself so completely, she loved with her entire heart, 'twas a wonder she'd not been permanently damaged by their neglect.

"What's in the satchel?" he asked, hoping the turn in conversation would ease her distress.

"Not enough, Greylen." She shook her head.

"Shh. No more worries." He soothed her, wiping another tear as it slipped through her lashes. "Come now, I wish to see what my amazing wife has thought to bring with her." She started to scoot from his lap, but he pulled her back, lifting her chin again. "I am proud of you, Gwen. For all that you have accomplished. And I would have told you so often, I would have." He would have given her everything she needed, love and affection, things that she obviously lacked from her parents. He understood her vulnerability now. Why she hid behind her bluster. "I am sorry you were alone while I was not."

Gwen lost it then. She threw herself against Greylen, sobbing openly as he whispered soothing words in her ear. She'd kept it in for so long and sharing her feelings with him—and that he understood—seemed to make everything better. Greylen loved her and he made her feel safe.

She finally stopped making a complete idiot of herself and left the comfort of his lap. She reached for the plaid at the end of their bed and with shaky hands opened the Gore-Tex bag. She was terrified that if water had somehow seeped inside, her instruments could be ruined. Her fears, however, were unfounded.

She ran her fingers over everything and could only imagine what her collection of essentials looked like to Greylen. There were shiny instruments in leather cases, glass vials of varying sizes, and an old iPhone and speaker. Something caught her eye, and she reached back inside the bag. Stunned, Gwen held up the garment she'd retrieved, staring at it, truly confused.

"Trust me," he hissed. "You couldn't be more bothered than I."

"These are my marathon shorts, Greylen. I don't remember packing them." She couldn't imagine how they go inside, but there they were folded, neatly at the bottom.

"Tell me 'tis an undergarment."

"Sorry," she said, scrunching her face. He seemed angry she'd ever worn them. "I wear them when I run a race. They bring me luck," she added in justification.

"You run races in those? With others present?"

She barely looked up. "I'm sorry, Greylen, but they were made from my favorite pair of jeans, and I've worn them every time I've needed to feel alive again."

"We'll discuss this later," he bit out in an angry tone. "What of the other things?" Gwen knew her husband was trying to control his rage, but he was failing miserably.

"They're instruments my aunt gave me when I started med school. She called it the quick-fix kit." Gwen smiled as she ran her fingers over all of the items again. "I can numb your pain, stitch you up, and I can even listen to your heart, but that's about all," she said, shaking her head. "This is my old iPhone," she explained, holding it up along with her mini speaker. "I kept it just so I could use it for the music. These are extra battery packs since I always seemed to have a problem with charging cords. And *this*, Greylen," she said, holding up a mini bottle and removing the top, "is vodka, sweet blessed vodka."

Greylen stopped her before she could drink. "What is it, Gwendolyn?" he demanded.

"It's a strong liquor, and the ones I have happen to be top of the line. You've never tasted anything like it."

He watched as she drained half the mini bottle and then closed her eyes. "Much better." She sighed, holding it out to him. "Try it."

Greylen took it from her hand, smelling the drink before taking a sip. "I've tasted it before. But not so refined."

"Well, we have twelve more." She counted. "Oh God, I packed thirteen." She groaned, reaching for another bottle before crawling into his lap.

Greylen held her, rubbing her back. "Do you feel better?"

"*No.* Do you?"

"Nay."

She reached up to brush the hair from his face. "Well," she said, then sighed. "I'm getting drunk."

"Drunk? As in sotted?" he asked. "You can't be serious?"

"Oh, but I am," she said, finishing the bottle. "Join me, Greylen. It'll be our last party before, whatever."

Greylen must have sensed she was trying to stop the endless, horrid possibilities running through her mind. His large hands engulfed her frame, bringing her close enough to rub his lips against her. He sighed and said, "Give me a bottle."

"How about some music?" she asked.

"You wish to go below stairs *now*?"

"I have another surprise, Greylen."

"I've truly had enough already, Gwen." He shook his head.

Gwen could feel for him, she really could. Here he was once again confronted with things he couldn't quite understand, or things that should be beyond his compression, and the man stood firm. Actually, he stood proud and tall, and she found herself ridiculously lucky to be married to him. She picked out a playlist, said a quick prayer, and waited.

He was smart, that husband of hers. He grabbed the phone out of her hand first and then the speaker, somehow knowing they were connected. "Never leave home without it." Gwen laughed as she watched him turn both in his hands.

"How does this operate?" he asked.

"I don't have a clue." She shrugged. "It would take me days to even try."

Gwen took back her iPhone and the speaker, then stood and held out her hand. "Come by the fire, Greylen."

He picked up the remaining bottles and followed her to the sitting area. Gwen placed the speaker on the hearth while Greylen sat on the floor, leaning against one of the chairs. She could tell he enjoyed the music she chose. She watched as he listened to the lyrics, obviously hearing tones and sounds he'd never been exposed to before. They had eight bottles of vodka left, and Gwen finished the last in her hand.

"Come on, catch up," she prodded. "In fact, you're bigger than me. Drink two."

Her pout must have been infectious because he smiled before draining the one in his hand and then another. She sat in his lap, holding his free hand. "I'm scared, Greylen," she whispered.

"I've told you, Gwen, I'll always keep you safe."

"But I need to keep you safe too."

He didn't seem to have a ready answer, other than to hold her. And strangely, the night turned pleasant. They remained by the fire, drinking and listening to music. Gwen excused herself for a moment before returning.

"Will you dance with me?" she asked, holding out her hand.

"Don't you know?" he asked, shaking his head. "Anything, Gwendolyn, anything."

He stood and opened the seventh bottle, drinking half before holding it to her lips. "Open, love," he whispered, watching as it emptied in her mouth. He kissed her, only to stop a moment later. "What's rock and roll?" he questioned in reference to the lyrics.

The Uncle Kracker version of "Drift Away" was playing now, one of her favorites. "It's a type of music. I'm not sure if they were referring to getting lost in music literally, or if they meant it more metaphorically, like getting lost in the music of someone's soul. I'd choose the latter, Greylen. I want to get lost in you." She took his hands and showed him how to dance to the beat of her music.

They remained in front of the fire it seemed like forever. Gwen was having the time of her life, her worries forgotten as she enjoyed a night she had only dreamed of—dancing with her husband and listening to her favorite songs by a roaring fire. And the alcohol, well it was definitely beginning to impair her judgment.

"I must call for a guard," Greylen said, shaking his head. He was watching her as she danced on the hearth to "You Sexy Thing" by Hot Chocolate. She bit her lip as he walked backward, obviously unwilling to take his eyes from her. Opening the door, he bellowed in demand. "Guards." Not happy with the response, he called again, "GUARDS!"

Obviously satisfied by slamming doors, he gave her his full attention now, kneeling in front of the chair as he drained another bottle. Then he crawled, as a predator before her, growling as he untied her belt with his teeth and dragged her beneath him. She laughed and he smiled, then he gave her a look that indisputably took her breath away.

They enjoyed a night as never before. A night in fact that they would never speak of. They stayed awake for hours, laughing, dancing, and drinking in between the most incredible sex they had to date.

It took them five hours to find their release, and every inch of their chamber was subjected to explicit carnal knowledge. Their demands were implicit, and they used not only their own hands but also each other's. Gwen ran shrieking from Greylen's clutches so many times she finally lost count of how often he wrestled her beneath him. By the time they lay exhausted by the fire, they were covered with marks of love, bruises, and scratches.

They awoke hours later, holding their heads, knowing smiles given and returned.

"I'll be useless today, wife."

"We have to run, Greylen. It's the only thing that will help," she croaked, her throat sore from screaming and laughing so much.

"You are so incredibly, terribly, terribly daft." He groaned, closing his eyes again.

"So I've been told," she muttered as she stood.

"Good God, Gwendolyn," he cried. "Are you in pain?"

"No, just my head," she assured him before looking down. "Greylen!" Her arms and thighs were covered with bruises and there were marks all over her body where he'd feasted on her skin. She looked at him now, the scratches on his shoulders, arms, and thighs, and he, too, was covered with red marks. *From her own display of feasting.*

They walked to the bathing chamber together, shaking their heads as they looked in the mirror.

"Mother will have my head, wife. I beg you, cover yourself completely till you've healed."

"Anything, Greylen," she replied, using the words he so often told her last night.

They finally dressed, dreading the run before them, but knowing it would clear their heads. They held hands as Greylen opened the door, both of them gasping when Gavin turned instantly. The look on his face so murderous, it shocked them.

"What took you five hours to find," he hissed, holding up his hand, "five!"—he waved his fingers before them—"will take me but *three seconds* when I reach the privacy of my chamber."

He turned, stiff strides taking him down the hallway. Greylen and Gwen remained expressionless as he walked away. They looked at each other at the same time, wide eyed as they covered their mouths. They were laughing as they fell to the floor in each other's arms.

✷ CHAPTER TWENTY-ONE ✷

"Play nice, boys," Gwen teased from her perch a few days later as Greylen and his men headed outside.

Greylen stopped when he reached the doors. Turning, he called back to her, "Don't cook tonight, love. I'll pick up Chinese on the way home." She smiled as he winked at her, then left to join his men.

Gwen stayed on the steps long after Greylen left. She leaned against the railing, wishing she could laugh at his comment, but she was nauseated and so dizzy that the entire stairway spun around her. She suspected she was pregnant. *Oh, you're brilliant, genius.* Of course she was pregnant. She was late and had the worst case of morning sickness ever.

She couldn't believe she had the energy to run with Greylen that morning, but she had. Now, however, all she wanted to do was go back to bed. And she did.

Anna checked on her throughout the day, bringing her tea infusions every couple of hours. Gwen started using the new brew the morning of her hangover. She'd found the mixture in one of the gift baskets from their wedding. Cook kept the canister next to the coffee beans on the island, ensuring no one else touched it. It was hers alone.

Lady Madelyn came in at some point, too, looking into her eyes and inspecting the color of her skin. "How many days have you missed your flow, Gwendolyn?" she asked, seeming confounded by the intensity of her sickness.

"Five, maybe six," Gwen answered with a smile.

"It seems appropriate," she said. "Your color, however, concerns me."

"I'll be fine, don't worry," Gwen said, reaching for her hand. "Please don't tell Greylen. I'd like to tell him myself, tonight."

"Gwendolyn, if Greylen comes home before supper and you're still abed, you'd best tell him quickly. He'll have a fright otherwise."

Luckily, Greylen didn't return early, and Gwen was able to rest for the entire day. She dressed for dinner with Anna's help and waited for Greylen in the great hall. They enjoyed a wonderful meal, but at her incessant yawning, Greylen took her upstairs.

"Gwen, are you ill, love? You barely touched your dinner?" he asked.

She smiled, then blurted out, "I'm pregnant, Greylen."

"With child?"

"*No*, with a horse, you fool," she replied, rolling her eyes.

Greylen threw his head back in laughter. He picked her up and spun her around. He must have felt her tense and quickly set her down. "I'm sorry. I only—I'm—"

"Ha. Who's the stammering idiot now?"

"Shut up, Gwendolyn. Your husband's going to kiss you. Quite senseless, I fear."

She rewarded him by batting her lashes and smiling, and he did kiss her senseless…slowly, sweetly senseless… until she swayed. "You're not well, are you?" he asked.

"I'm so happy, Greylen, but I feel horrible." She tried to make light of her symptoms. Greylen, however, took them very seriously. He helped her undress, then carried her to bed. It was the first night they didn't make love, but he covered her stomach protectively with his hand, and she fell asleep in seconds.

When Gwen awoke, he was already gone, but he'd left a note upon the table. It simply said "I love you." She tried to get up but couldn't move. Anna found her in bed when she came to tidy their chamber and cared for her throughout the day again.

Anna continued to bring the tea infusions, which seemed to be the only thing that eased her nausea. But as the day turned to night, Gwen started to think that something else was causing her sickness and knew that she had to talk to Greylen.

But she never awoke when Greylen entered the chamber that night. And the next day, she actually felt better. She made it to the great hall and had a light meal with Isabelle and Lady Madelyn. And by the later part of the week, her strength began to return, probably because she was eating more and drinking less.

On the seventh night, she awoke to pain. Pain like she'd never felt before. Her body was racked with cramps, and she was so weak she could barely cry out.

"Gwen?" Greylen came awake instantly. "Gwen, what's wrong?"

"Your mother...*please*," she somehow managed to say, tears streaming down her face.

Greylen pulled back the covers to do as she asked. His expression masked but a second after he took in the sight of his wife's body atop a small, but growing, pool of blood. He hadn't noticed how much weight she'd lost, nor had he suspected anything amiss—until now.

"I need to lift you, love. I know you're in pain," he said softly. He'd not leave her, not even for the seconds 'twould take to fetch his mother. He cradled her shaking body and carried her to his mother's chamber.

He stood by his mother's bedside, calling to her in the calmest voice he could muster. And considering the rage and terror he felt, it took everything he had.

Lady Madelyn came awake, her hands covering her mouth. "Lay her on the bed, Greylen," she ordered as she stood. "Fetch Anna, tell her to bring my bag and have the servants prepare a bath. Quickly, Greylen."

She'd needn't have said quickly, he was already halfway down the hall as she yelled the last of it.

Anna almost screamed when she came awake. Honestly, he couldn't blame her, his light-colored breeches were soiled with blood, and the look on his face was obviously one she had never seen before. "Dear God, Greylen, what's happened?"

"Gwen's in Mother's chamber," he told her. "I think she's dying, Anna."

Wanting Anna to help his mother as soon as possible, Greylen saw to the servants himself. Then he called for his men.

He placed his personal guards by the entrance doors, Kevin and Hugh outside, and Duncan within. Ian and Connell stood just beyond his mother's chamber, and Gavin all but tore his mother's door from the frame as he stormed inside.

Greylen was only a step behind him as they entered. Their first sight was his mother and Anna forcing a liquid down Gwen's throat. In her current state, she could barely push them away. Gavin went right to the bed, taking in the color of Gwen's skin, and opened each of her lids as he inspected her eyes. Greylen glanced up to Gavin, who then shook his head and said in a whisper, "She's wasted away before our eyes, and we've not been the wiser."

"Greylen, carry her to the tub," his mother ordered, not commenting on Gavin's admission.

Greylen did more than carry his wife. He climbed in with her, holding her as Anna and his mother gently scrubbed the blood from her body. Tears leaked from his eyes as he held her, knowing if she died from his negligence, he'd beg Gavin for his death.

He heard sheets being torn from the bed and looked over. Gavin was ripping the soiled coverings and wadding them before throwing them to the floor. He left the room, and Greylen had no doubt where 'twas that he went. Gavin's anger and fear were as close to his own. They would both carry the blame.

When Gwen was washed, Greylen lifted her from the tub while the women swaddled her in a towel.

"Her bleeding should stop for now, Greylen. The babe was so new—"

"I care not about the babe, Mother. 'Tis my wife for whom I fear."

"I gave her a strong dose of elixir. With luck, it should reverse the damage of what she's been ingesting." She pulled the covers around Gwendolyn after he laid her in bed. Then he sat next to her, stroking her forehead.

"How long, Mother?" he asked, looking only at his wife.

"Seven days, mayhap longer," she said and shook her head.

"I'll return as soon as possible. Call for me if she awakens."

Just as he'd suspected, he found Gavin within his chamber, tearing the sheets from their bed.

"'Tis poison," Gavin spat, anger causing his entire body to shake.

"I know," Greylen answered. "Tighten our patrols and account for each of our men's actions over the past two weeks."

As they headed for the door, Gavin said, "I won't be far behind. Where?"

"The well," Greylen called, taking the stairs.

Gavin signaled to Duncan as he left the keep. Greylen and Gavin awoke their soldiers and increased their guard. Careful not to inform them what was amiss, they placed within each group two men they trusted implicitly. Then they headed toward the well.

Greylen had already lowered himself. Kevin and Hugh were holding lanterns from above, watching as he inspected the walls for discoloration and the water for odors.

Gavin took the rope and slid down. They stood in the water glaring at each other. "I see no signs, but I want it covered just the same," Greylen ordered. "How could we not see it, Gavin? *How?*"

"We thought 'twas from her carrying," he shouted. "I'm just as guilty, Greylen."

"Did you see her body?" Greylen whispered.

"Aye. If you'd not awakened, Greylen…" He didn't finish—he couldn't.

Greylen finally gave the signal and they were pulled up, ordering a group of men to fill the well immediately. Then they stormed back to the keep and straight to the kitchen.

Greylen and Gavin lit every wick as Ian left to fetch Cook.

Gwen opened her eyes sometime later, confused by her surroundings. Then she realized she was in Lady Madelyn's chamber. "Mother," she whispered weakly.

"Aye, child, I'm here. You'll be all right, Gwendolyn, you just need rest."

"I ha—" An intense cramp made her gasp. "Speak—" Gasp. "Grey—"

"He's outside with his men," she said, gently pushing the hair away from Gwen's face.

"*Please.*"

Lady Madelyn went to the door and when she opened it, Ian and Connell stepped inside. Obviously wishing to check her condition for themselves, they walked to the bed. They took note of her skin tone and inspected her eyes.

"Connell…take me to Greylen," she whispered, holding out her arms.

He didn't refuse her and cradled her in his arms as he carried her down the stairs. As they walked through the foyer he looked to Ian. "Lady, I must lay you down," Connell said, trying to keep the anguish from his voice and failing quite miserably.

She could feel blood seeping along her legs and felt awful that he and Ian had to witness it, but she had to speak to Greylen. "Take me to my husband, Connell," she said weakly. Then she added, though the words were barely audible, "'Tis an order."

Gwen was confused when they passed the study, but when Ian held open the swinging doors, the sight before her made her aware that they already knew. The kitchen was ablaze in light, and Cook stood between her husband and Gavin at the island. Kevin and Hugh were in the process of emptying the entire pantry.

Cook, Greylen, and his men looked up at the same time. Each of them appeared horrified as they looked at her.

Greylen came forward, taking his wife from his man's arms, exchanging a look with Connell he wished never to need again. They were all in agony. Her plight tore at their hearts.

"Why are you out of bed, sweet?" Greylen smiled, pretending as though he'd not a care in the world.

"Not…buying it…husband," Gwen whispered. She reached for his face, tears in her eyes. "The tea, Greylen… the tea."

They had just been about to open the canister when Connell arrived with Gwen. Cook was sure 'twas the one thing Lady Gwendolyn had daily. And hoping to keep the wedding gift only for her mistress, she'd not allowed another to sample it.

Greylen watched Gavin lift the lid and spill the contents. They gathered around the island searching through the crushed leaves. The sight and smell confirmed 'twas a mixture of herbs used as an abortifacient. But Gwen had taken so much, it not only killed their babe, but possibly her as well.

"Find where it came from," Greylen ordered. "I'll be above stairs."

Greylen knew not to ask for guards, his men would likely sleep with them if they deemed it necessary. He carried Gwen to their chamber and cleaned her again. He could hear her try to speak, but she was so weak. "Shh, don't talk, love. Save your strength."

He wrapped her in his arms, her face pressed to his chest. He heard her whisper and it all but killed him. He bit the inside of his cheek, holding her as she cried. He cried, too, his tears falling silently to the pillow.

He kept his hand pressed firmly over her heart, willing the steady, though weakened beat to continue. He listened to each of her breaths, his body clenching in fear when she gasped with her efforts. Her words kept repeating in his mind, words she thought may be her last. "No regrets. The happiest days of my life."

They were but five weeks!

He remained motionless when his men entered his chamber, positioning themselves on the floor around his bed. They, too, felt shame and found comfort only now by guarding their mistress with their lives. He knew without looking that Gavin stood sentinel at the door. "Take the other side, Gavin," Greylen commanded quietly.

Lady Madelyn came in throughout the night, giving Gwen more of the elixir as he and Gavin held her head. He could see her sorrow increase each time she stepped over the men as they lay awake on the floor. He knew 'twas a sight she would always remember—her son and his best friend taking comfort from each other as they held Gwen between them. And their men who sought comfort, too, guarding their mistress's soul with the silent prayers that moved from their lips. He imagined she, too, prayed that night, with Anna, in the privacy of her chamber.

❧ CHAPTER TWENTY-TWO ❧

The morning hours passed in a blur. Gwen remembered waking in Greylen's arms and felt the warmth of another behind her. "I'm gonna be sick." She moaned.

"Fetch a basin, Gavin," Greylen said as he sat her up.

"Just take me to the bathroom, Greylen—quick." As Greylen carried her, she saw his men on the floor, and also that Gavin had been the warmth behind her in their bed. If she hadn't felt so terrible, she would've told them what their presence meant to her.

Greylen held her hair back as she threw up, refusing to get his mother. "You're my wife, Gwen, I'll see to you."

Dignity be damned, it was the sweetest care she'd ever received.

He tried repeatedly to take her back to bed, but she insisted on resting on the cool, stone floor. He sat beside her the entire time, rubbing her back and helping her each time her stomach turned. At some point she heard a knock on the door. "I've had Anna prepare a bath within. We'll remain in your bedchamber."

"Aye, Gavin," her husband replied.

When her nausea passed, Greylen took her into the tub. He washed her body and then dressed her as she sat on his lap in the chair. He chose only her most favorite things. A simple band of material that he tied around her chest, a pair of underwear that he'd placed thick cloths in, and one of his shirts. He brushed her hair before tying it back, and finally, he secured his medallion behind her neck.

"Thanks," she whispered, leaning against him.

"I'm sorry, Gwen."

"It's not your fault, Greylen."

"Aye, 'tis."

They stayed in the chair for quite some time. She dozed on and off as Greylen rubbed her back and kissed the top of her head. Then he carried her back into their chamber. Pallets still remained on the floor, and Gavin sat on their bed, which had been straightened and turned down again. He drank from a cup and ate from a plate of foods that sat atop the table next to her letterbox. The rest of the men were gathered around the fire, eating food she was sure Anna brought up while she disgraced herself in front of her husband.

Gavin adjusted the towel beneath her as Greylen laid her down. Then he went back to the papers he studied, leaning against the pillows.

"My first sleepover with seven men and I can't remember a thing," she joked weakly. They all looked at her, cautious smiles mixed with anguish, and her eyes filled with tears.

Then she rested between the two men she loved more than anything in the world, and they acted like it was an everyday occurrence to sit in bed, looking through papers as she lay between them. When Lady Madelyn and Anna came in to check on her, Greylen helped her sit up while Gavin adjusted pillows. She had to drink more of that god-awful elixir, but Anna handed her a mug when she finished. Gavin took it from her hand, smelling and drinking it before allowing her to have any. Anna closed one of her eyes, fixing him with an angry stare. But Gavin only shrugged.

"Well, how is it, Gavin?" Gwen asked with a smile.

"As sweet as you," he answered, touching her nose with his finger.

"If you wish the comfort of my bed, you'll not touch my wife again."

"I held not only your *wife* last night, but *your* sorry hide as well, let's not forget."

"I've held your sorry hide as well, my friend—on more than one occasion. I almost regret not letting you freeze to death while I had the chance."

"Good God, stop fighting," Gwen said as she sipped the tea infusion. "Wow, that's a great phrase, *good God, good God, good God.*" She mimicked her husband's brogue.

Just then, Isabelle walked into the room as everyone stared affectionately at Gwen. "Good God, what's happened?"

Gwen patted the bed beside her. "Come, Isabelle, were having a sleepover."

Isabelle looked around the room; pallets still lay on the floor and it was obvious Gavin had slept in their bed. "Tell me, what is the meaning of this?"

Greylen started to tell her, but Gwen interrupted him. "A *sleepover* is a party you invite only your best friends to. And you play games, listen to music, and eat snacks all night long."

Greylen and his men would have to take her words to heart, knowing she spoke them for their benefit.

"How come I wasn't invited?" Isabelle asked.

"You must have been sleeping when it started. In fact, I don't remember it either."

"Well, that hardly seems fair, sister," Isabelle said, placing her hands on her hips.

"You're absolutely right, Isabelle. Greylen, I demand a redo."

"Pardon?" He would have no idea what she spoke of.

"I said, I demand a redo. You're not a very good listener, are you?" she teased.

"Explain a redo."

"It's simple, I want another sleepover minus the... well, you know."

Greylen shook his head, his smile full of love for his wife. She knew—as well as he—that his men had no intentions of leaving. Their pallets lay on the floor, neatly made, and Gavin had obviously made camp on the other side of the bed. She would have her sleepover, whether she wished for it or not. "Anything, Gwendolyn. Anything you so desire."

"Good answer," she said, snuggling into the pillows and handing her cup to him. She called to Isabelle, who remained at the end of the bed. "Isabelle, fetch some parchment, the thickest you can find, and shears too. Then change back into your nightgown and come to bed."

Isabelle climbed onto the bed and kissed Gwen's cheek. She had tears in her eyes, for she obviously knew something terrible had occurred. "I love you, Gwen."

"I love you too. Now do my bidding," she teased, mimicking her husband's brogue again.

Greylen sat next to Gwen, adjusting her so she lay in the crook of his arm. He kept whispering he loved her as he passed papers to Gavin, who shared their written words with the men by the fire. Taking their orders, the men began leaving in groups of two, then they'd return before another two would go. Yet he and Gavin made no attempt to leave. And they'd go nowhere, not until they were sure Gwen was, in fact, making a swift recovery, as the case seemed to be.

Isabelle returned with the items Gwen had requested. She sat on the bed between her and Gavin, listening as Gwen explained what she wanted her to do. "But, Gwendolyn, we have cards already."

"I know, but those decks have fifty-six cards and I want these with fifty-two."

Isabelle made three decks of cards as Gwen requested. Then his sister read while Gwen napped, sitting very close to Gavin. Close enough to brush her leg against his. Gavin seemed to pretend not to notice, but when she stopped, Greylen watched as Gavin's leg brushed hers.

Gwen felt better by early evening and was allowed to use the garderobe by herself. Greylen still insisted on carrying her and waited just outside the door as his mother and Anna saw to her personal care.

They dined in their chamber that evening, and she had him "turn on some music." She had what she called "an extensive collection" that she'd "downloaded over the years." According to his wife, he and his men liked the "acoustical sounds and lyrics of alternative rock."

Greylen sat on the bed, alone with his wife. He had her wrapped in his arms, his lips against her forehead as they listened to a song she'd played for him before. "'Tis the music I hear when I watch you in the courtyard," he whispered, squeezing her as she nestled against him.

Later, Gwen taught everyone how to play her favorite card games. Greylen and his men were truly grateful for the new games. Within minutes, as was their want, they became fiercely competitive. "Gwendolyn, we've need of coin."

"Okay, poker it is." She laughed, patting the bed. "Come on, I'll teach all of you this game. It's what men gamble over most."

They played for over an hour before Greylen insisted it was time for bed. He and Gavin took the outside, while she and Isabelle lay between them. Greylen wrapped Gwen in his arms, facing his sister, but Isabelle and Gavin lay still as statues. His wife fixed that. "Group hug, everyone," she whispered. They laughed huddling together, and she and Isabelle were within four strong arms. "Much better." Gwen sighed.

His sister chose that precise moment to giggle.

"What humors you, Bella?" Gavin whispered.

"I never thought to share a bed with you *and them*," she whispered back.

Though Greylen was amused by Isabelle's comment, he wanted Gwen to get the rest he knew she needed. "Go to sleep, Isabelle," he whispered over Gwen's head.

"Good night, Greylen."

"Good night, Sprite."

"Good night, Gwen."

"Good night, Isabelle."

"Good night, Gavin."

"Good night, Bella."

CHAPTER TWENTY-THREE

It was another week before Gwen was allowed out of bed. If it wasn't Greylen staring her down, it was Gavin, and each remained impervious to her repeated insistence that she was better.

Lady Madelyn and Anna had assured her that the herbs she ingested had been used for centuries—their purpose when combined could prevent a pregnancy, or as in her case, stop one. Thankfully, they told her, it would have no impact on her becoming pregnant again. Gwen chose not to be bitter, and instead did her best to ease the guilt Greylen, Gavin, and their men carried.

They blamed themselves for what happened.

They never spoke of the poison that caused her miscarriage, or the fact they feared for her life. But she knew that Greylen and his men spent their days interrogating their soldiers and the inhabitants among the holding. Isabelle stayed with her during the day, leaving only when Greylen returned late at night. But she had plenty of visitors.

Greylen and his men took turns coming above stairs to make sure she was indeed improving. It was on these occasions that she'd try to get through to Greylen and Gavin, to assure them that she really was better, and staying in bed wasn't helping.

They'd look at her with true concern, listen intently to every word she said, and even sit next to her on the bed. Then they'd pat her on the head and leave.

Her food and drink continued to be sampled, and the amounts they placed before her were ridiculous. "I can't possibly eat this much," Gwen said, shaking her head.

"You've lost so much weight, Gwen, please," Greylen pleaded, filling a fork and bringing it to her mouth.

"I can feed myself, Greylen."

"Very well," he conceded. "Are you sure you're up to it?"

"Greylen, it's been a week. I'm not bleeding, I've rested more than I have in my entire life, and I've been forced to eat like a pig."

"My sweet pig you are," he teased.

"Please, Greylen, I'm really better. I'm going crazy."

"Do you promise you'll be careful and let your guard know the minute you need help?" he asked.

"We're back to my guard?"

"Need you ask?"

"I guess not," she said. "Do you suspect anyone in particular?"

"Aye, we've narrowed it to two, both have ties to MacFale."

"What will you do?" she asked.

"When I'm certain who's to blame, kill him."

"*Kill him?*"

"Aye."

"Can you do that?"

"The man came to me under false pretense, Gwen. He killed our babe. I feared you would die as well."

"You really mean to kill him?"

"Good God, Gwendolyn—AYE!"

"I just...I never really thought about what you do or that it's you who sees it through."

"'Tis who I am, Gwen. 'Tis what I do. I've protected our home, our land, my entire life."

"Just be careful, Greylen. Whatever you do, please be careful."

If only she'd listened to her own worries, if only *she* had been more careful. She never would have found herself in the situation she was now in. She'd never meant to cause her husband the anger and helplessness she knew that he must have felt. She'd acted only on instinct.

She'd been waiting for Greylen to return on the keep steps, having been doing so for the past few nights. And she always had Isabelle and her guard with her. Tonight it was Ian. It was a beautiful night. The sky was full of stars and the moon cast a glow over the entire courtyard. Isabelle had just excused herself to get her a shawl, not that she'd asked for it, but Gwen finally stopped arguing and waved Isabelle away.

Gwen was talking quietly with Ian when they both noticed a form slipping through the gates and creeping along the outer wall toward the stables. Ian placed a hand on her knee, squeezing it to indicate that she remain still and silent. From where they sat between the balustrades, they must've been concealed within the shadows. And Isabelle's departure into the keep had mistakenly led the man to believe no one was about. As the man opened the doors to the stables, Ian stood to follow. "Go inside *now*," he whispered.

Gwen watched Ian walk to the stables and reach for the latch to go inside. But for some reason she didn't go inside, she couldn't. Instead, she crept down the stairs, crouching next to the balustrade as she waited for Ian to come out. Long minutes passed before she saw smoke coming from the stables and the man who entered first leave by himself. Her only thoughts were of helping Ian. She ran.

Once inside the doors, she started crawling on her hands and knees, calling Ian's name. She saw him farther within, lifting latches to set the horses free. He turned upon hearing her, a flash of incredulity as his eyes went wide and mouth fell agape. He was covered with blood, most likely from fighting with the man who fled. He cursed aloud and ran to her, wrapping his arm around her shoulders to protect her as he herded her out of the doors. When they came through the cloud of smoke, Greylen and his men were running toward them from the bailey.

As they cleared the stable's entrance and reached the spot where Greylen and his men now stood, Ian pushed her away and knelt before her husband, meeting Greylen's murderous stare. But it was not he whom Greylen directed his anger to. It was her.

Gwen stood before her husband never more fearful in her life. Greylen's look was like none she had ever seen. His body shook so tightly it was a wonder he didn't explode. She remained silent and motionless as he grabbed her shoulders.

"What were you thinking?" he demanded. "Did you *think* at all?" He pushed her away, a roar ripping from his throat. When he finally looked down at her again, his eyes were filled with betrayal—hers.

"REMOVE HER—*NOW*."

His shout was filled with venom, the words seemed to be spat in disgust. If Duncan and Connell hadn't grabbed her arms, she would have run herself. They all but threw her through the doors, and she ran to Lady Madelyn's room.

Greylen's mother had her arms opened wide when she came through the doors. Gwen ran straight to them, crying until there was nothing left. She knew Lady Madelyn had seen what occurred, but she said nothing. She just held her as she cried, and then they walked silently to the window seat where they watched the men release the animals and douse the fire.

It took hours before they were through, and they were covered in soot and sweat. Greylen and his men had just retrieved their horses and strapped their scabbards back in place when one of their rank leaders, Alex, approached them. Their horses were led away again, and Greylen and his six men-at-arms stood together in a solid line as Alex brought a man before them. Alex pushed the man to the ground making him kneel before his laird. They formed a tight circle around the man, and Greylen nodded to Alex, who was enjoined to stay.

Greylen looked to Ian, who must have confirmed that the man on the ground was in fact the one who started the fire. What happened next was a sight Gwen would remember for her entire life.

One that made her realize Greylen's absolute authority.

Greylen took a step forward, yet all of his men took several back. He spoke words to the man whom he must have commanded to stand. And with an action so quick it stunned her, Greylen's hands were behind his shoulders, covering the hilt of his sword, and he swung the blade. His powerful sweep rent clear through the man's neck.

It was the most gruesome display she'd ever seen.

Greylen turned, looking to the window where she stood. His features were hidden in the shadows, but his message was clear.

This is who I am: a leader, a warrior, an executioner.

He was covered in blood and let forth another roar as he embedded his sword in the dirt. He turned toward the lake. He never looked back.

Gwen paced the floor in her chamber for hours, her stomach churning in knots. She finally heard them enter the keep and ran to the railing. Greylen never looked at her. His men remained in front of the doors and her husband walked down the hallway, his study door slamming with force.

She went back to her chamber, pacing again. *She couldn't take it anymore.* Intent to go to him, she opened the doors. Kevin and Hugh waited just outside. They shook their heads, beseeching her to stay.

"I'll not be scared," she said, straightening to her full, measly height.

They followed her down the stairs but stayed by the entrance where the other men stood silent. She looked at no one as she continued down the hallway. Her hands shook so badly it took three attempts to press the latch.

She'd lied before. She'd never been more scared in her life.

Greylen was in front of the window, his arms across his chest and his legs braced apart. Water dripped from the back of his head, and his sword, now clean, leaned against the wall. He made no move to turn. He made no move at all.

Greylen knew 'twas his wife who stood in the doorway, for no one else would dare disturb him in his current state. Watching earlier, as she ran to the stables, all but stopped his heart. 'Twas too much. He'd almost lost her only two short weeks ago, and that she'd endanger her life—good God, it created a madness in him he'd never felt.

Now he felt something else, her arms around his waist and her body pressed to his back. Aye, she was brave. His love for her made his heart ache.

He finally broke the silence. "Have you no idea your value?" he asked.

"I'm sorry, Greylen. I'm so sorry."

Her body shook and the back of his shirt became wet with her tears. He closed his eyes, willing his mind to let go of his anger. He pulled her around, resting his cheek atop her head as she clung to him. He finally pushed her away. "Don't ever risk your life again, for anyone. Do you understand?" He hadn't meant to shout, but he was consumed with fear.

Nodding emphatically, she whispered, "Aye. Do you forgive me?"

"'Tis not something I can forgive, Gwen," he said, shaking his head, giving her a look that brought tears to her eyes again. "Had Ian not ordered you inside?"

"Aye, but—"

"Gwen, when my men give an order, it must be followed. They can't worry about you and another problem at hand. Orders are given for a reason, wife."

"I thought he would die, Greylen. He didn't come out and smoke was coming through the doors."

"Did you see that he knelt when he emerged?" He was shouting again, furious she still didn't understand. "Have you any idea why?" he asked in a chilling tone as she shook her head. "He awaited my blow. Do you understand now?"

She gasped, stepping back. "You would kill him, because of me? Because of what I did, only to help?"

"I've never been put to the task—till tonight."

"I'm sorry, Greylen. But I wouldn't change what I did. I wouldn't let someone die if I could help them."

"Then it seems we're in a predicament. I'll take you upstairs."

"It sounds as though you have no intention of staying with me."

He gave a sarcastic laugh. "I can't sleep, Gwen. I can't kill a man and seek the comfort of my bed. 'Tis something I've never been able to do."

"Then I'll stay with you," she pleaded, tugging on his shirt.

"No."

The air released from her lungs, a sound close to a cry emitting from her lips as the impact of his refusal seemed to hit her like a physical blow. He'd never said that word before. In her own language, he turned her away.

"Come, don't argue," he bit out, taking her arm.

She let him lead her down the hallway, but when they reached the front doors, she wrenched free of his grasp. She walked to his men and stood before Ian. "I know it's not enough, but I'm sorry, Ian. I never meant to put you in such a position." She looked at each them: Duncan, Kevin, Hugh, Connell, and Gavin. "I'm sorry for the trouble I caused. I know now I was wrong." She made for the steps then, and Greylen started to follow. "Don't," she said without turning. "I know the way."

Greylen shouldn't have been surprised that Gwen chose to go alone. He was the one who turned her away. Why, then, did his heart constrict? His men said nothing as he turned back toward his study, but he didn't miss Gavin's look, the censure in his eyes.

It took less than an hour for him to come to his senses. He sat behind his desk, his hands pressed to the sides of his head. His only thoughts were of her.

How often she had come to him? How often she had given of herself? How often he had thanked the gods above for the grace of Gwendolyn in his life?

He didn't face his men as he approached the stairs, and for the first time felt unsure as he entered his chamber. Gwen didn't look up when he came in. She sat on the floor in front of the fire, staring at the flames and listening to music. The volume was so low her head rested on the hearth next to the speaker.

She looked sad, a look for which he was to blame. He sat on the floor and faced her. Still she didn't look up. "Gwen, I've done things a certain way my entire life. I've had to. But I've never regretted them...till now."

"You shouldn't have to regret your actions, Greylen," she whispered. She didn't speak for another full minute, but when she did, her words caught on a sob. "I feel so alone right now, and you're sitting right beside me. That hurts more than anything." Still, she didn't look at him.

"Look at me, Gwen," he pleaded softly.

"I'm afraid of what I'll see there, Greylen."

"Only love, Gwen," he said in a voice he scarcely recognized. "I swear 'tis only love." He sensed her struggle and damned himself for being the cause.

She finally looked up. "I hate that I love you so much. I hate it."

The words tore through his heart, and again he was unsure. He just wanted to hold her, but now it seemed this wall lay between them. And once again, 'twas she who came to him. Gwen crawled into his lap, then laid her head upon his chest. He could have squeezed her to death his relief was so great.

He held her as he sighed, feeling so very lucky to have her in his arms again and realizing now just how fearful he was of her rejection. "Will you stay with me by the fire?" he asked. He still couldn't sleep in their bed, but he'd been a fool to turn her away earlier.

"Anything, Greylen," she whispered. "Anything."

He added more logs to the fire as Gwen took pillows from their bed. Then removed his boots and laid his dagger atop the hearth as Gwen turned off the music. They still hadn't made love, not since she first told him she was pregnant. And they wouldn't tonight. But Greylen held her as never before, vowing never to allow his anger to come between them again.

Just as he was falling asleep, he felt her hands upon his face, her whisper melting his heart anew. "I love you so much, Greylen, I love you so much."

"I love you, too, Gwen. I love you so much too."

CHAPTER TWENTY-FOUR

Greylen woke Gwen as she lay in his arms. They were still in front of the fire and he held her so tightly, she couldn't move.

"I leave this morn, Gwen."

"You're going after MacFale, aren't you?" she asked.

"Aye."

"I'm sorry about last night, Greylen, I never meant—"

"No more apologies, Gwen. You acted on instinct. 'Tis only one of the many things I admire about you. But watching you run into the fire..."

"Are you still mad at me?"

"I feared for your life again and that you'd risk it... It nearly killed me. Forgive me my anger, Gwen."

"I do, Greylen. I just want you to be safe. I'm scared for you."

"You've nothing to fear. I'll send word as soon as I can."

A few minutes later, Gwen sat on the chest in their bathing chamber shaving Greylen's beard. The impact of his departure creating a sensation in her chest, like it was being squeezed in a vise. She could sense that Greylen felt the same. Their silence was deafening.

When he finished dressing, he came to her as she stood on the trunk at the end of their bed. His hands encompassed her head and he kissed her as he never had before.

It was a kiss of remembrance. Slow and more than bittersweet.

Hand in hand, they walked down the stairs and into the courtyard. She stood by his side as he secured his belongings to the saddle. Then he led her back to the steps to stand with Isabelle and Lady Madelyn. He stared at her as he brushed his finger down her face. He leaned forward and whispered in her ear words that moved through her very soul.

They were the most beautiful words she'd ever heard, though he'd spoken them before. Every time they made love it was those words that he whispered most. She wanted so much to ask him what they meant, to beg him to take her upstairs and make love to her again. But she couldn't speak. Her throat was closed, tight with emotion that threatened to strangle her.

He turned to join his men where they waited in the courtyard. Their looks were serious, and she missed so much the laughter and light she'd always seen in their eyes. She clung to Isabelle while Lady Madelyn stood behind them, a hand on each of their shoulders. She watched sadly as her husband rode toward the gates.

Greylen looked back once more before he rode through the gates. His anger was gone, replaced with feelings that were hard to fathom. He wasn't even sure if Gwen realized what she had done that morn. He would never forget.

After she shaved him, she'd walked to his wardrobe, removing the things that she knew he would wear. She'd held out each item, smoothing the material over his body with her hands after he'd put them on. Then she packed his satchel, hugging it as she sat on the trunk. He knew she held back tears, and in truth, her actions tugged at him as well. Since he was a young boy, no one had dressed him or packed for him. No one had ever touched his heart the way that she did.

He left Connell and Ian behind with strict orders to stay by Gwen's side. The order wasn't necessary, but he voiced it all the same.

They reached the MacFale holding before noon. The gates were open and they rode straight to the keep. Malcolm's father waited on the steps.

"Where's your son?" Greylen commanded, meeting the old man's stare.

"I've not seen Malcolm for weeks."

"You expect me to believe you, old man?" His shout was filled with reprimand. "He had my wife poisoned and his man set fire to our stables." Greylen nodded to Kevin, who released the remains of the man he'd killed the night before.

MacFale looked to the ground, nodding before addressing Greylen again. "Aye, 'tis Malcolm's man. But I swear, MacGreggor, I've not seen my son. Nor do I approve of his actions."

"You've defended his actions in the past," Greylen accused. "I don't want war, old man, but I'll have your land before you pass power to him."

"I have no choice," the old man argued. "He's the only son willing to take what's rightfully his."

"I'll not speak in riddles, MacFale. When I find him, he'll pay for his offenses with his life."

"Then it seems you'll have this land, MacGreggor. I'm not long for this world, and I've had no control of Malcolm for years."

"The fault is your own," Greylen charged. "He's of your blood. His evil could only come from you."

"I've bred good as well, MacGreggor, though my actions caused his leave. I only wish to right my wrongs."

"Cease your twisted words," Greylen bellowed. "Speak of what you wish."

"'Tis no longer my place. I've said my piece. Leave the man."

"Stand aside, we'll search the keep."

"Have your look. I've nothing to hide. Malcolm may lie upon the land, but the keep's otherwise empty."

"'Tis a trap," Duncan spat.

"I've three servants, all so aged 'tis a wonder I have food on my table and clean rushes on the floors. You see any men?" the old man asked, waving his hands. "There are none. Malcolm has only a handful, and they ride with him."

Greylen and his men entered the holding. They stood within the hall where Gavin shook visibly as he stared at the steps that led to the bedchambers. Assuming fury caused his actions, Greylen ordered him to stay with the old man. He took Duncan above stairs while Hugh and Kevin searched the main floor.

"I should have killed him years ago," Gavin hissed.

"Mayhap." Guy MacFale shrugged as he stood next to Gavin for the first time in years. "But your honor kept you from it."

"Nay, your weakness did, old man."

"If I could change the past, Gavin—"

"Would you?"

"You know I've tried to make amends, Gavin. My continued silence should be worth something."

Greylen and his men joined in the entrance, and then together they went below stairs. Let them search all the darkened passages. Malcolm was not there. When they came up, MacGreggor's words confirmed it. "'Tis empty, just as you said. You're lucky you spoke the truth, old man."

"I wish only for peace, MacGreggor, I've not caused trouble in years, and I've tried to keep a leash on Malcolm. He's the one who wishes you harm. They're a nasty, childish bunch."

"He'll be mine, old man. Pray you now for his sorry soul."

The elder MacFale watched sadly as MacGreggor and his men left the keep in unison. He'd made so many wrong choices throughout his life. But now, he was more determined than ever to see the wrongs of the past righted before he died.

God willing, his heir would have his land. And he'd bring it back to its former glory.

He took the stairs slowly, each step harder on his weakening body as he went to the great hall. 'Twas long minutes before he recovered from his exertion, for in truth, he had little time left. But with each breath that remained, he would seek his son's forgiveness.

Lord, it had been so very good to see him again.

Greylen and his men turned east through the forest as they approached their border. Greylen, consumed with thoughts of the confrontation he'd had with the old man, kept replaying the scene in his mind. He couldn't shake the feeling that he'd missed something. There was a message in MacFale's words, suggestive but directed not at him.

His first-in-command had him worried as well. Gavin wasn't at all himself. He seemed haunted almost from the moment they'd entered the keep. In truth, that concerned him more than not finding Malcolm.

They were so silent and so deep in thought, they heard the sounds of arrows being rent as soon as they were released. Gavin brought his horse to Greylen's, protecting his back as the attack began. The men formed a tight circle around their laird while returning fire of their own. Two men fell from the trees, but at least four more remained. Kevin took an arrow in the leg, ripping it out as their horses danced in fright.

"Fight like men, you cowards," Greylen bellowed as their attackers remained silent above.

"I've waited years for this, MacGreggor, to see the look upon your face when you crumble."

"Then come, MacFale. See the look upon my face now." Greylen's voice was chilling, contained fury simmering through his entire body as he taunted Malcolm to confront him.

Greylen felt Gavin tense at his words but didn't have time to glance at his first-in-command to understand his apprehension. They'd never shied from a fight. Gavin had never shown anything other than dauntless strength during battle. But then they'd never confronted MacFale before.

Malcolm was never called on by their king, nor had he ever been present at their council meetings. Only the elder had attended. Greylen hadn't seen Malcolm since they were boys and he didn't like him even then. Malcolm was always jealous of Greylen's skills, and rather than work to achieve the same, he became spiteful instead.

'Twas hard to admit, even to himself, but Greylen took pleasure in humiliating him, time and time again, at swordplay and fisticuffs. And ever since, Malcolm's father kept him far away, paying for his transgressions with coin and promises to leash his son's behavior.

"I've arrows aimed upon your back, MacGreggor. But I'd not miss this for anything," Malcolm taunted as he came down from his perch.

Greylen's men awaited his command as they watched the form approach. Gavin remained to Greylen's right, Kevin and Hugh behind them, and Duncan to Greylen's left.

"If you move, they'll release their weapons," Malcolm told them. But what he didn't know was that they weren't in the least threatened by another attack. With one word from Greylen, they would all be dead, and though they might suffer a wound or two, such was the price of fighting. But Malcolm had obviously piqued Greylen's curiosity. 'Twas the only reason he still lived.

"I wish only to give you a glimpse of what you've been too blind to see," Malcolm continued, not realizing his precarious circumstance. "What say you, Gavin the Brave?" he hissed as he stepped from the shadows but feet away. "Your downfall shall be even more rewarding."

At that moment it all became so clear—the old man's words and Gavin's behavior. Greylen looked upon Malcolm for the first time in years. Really looked upon him. He shook his head in disbelief, for the similarities were so close and the eyes—*good God*—the eyes were identical.

Greylen turned to Gavin, his look so bleak, so barren and filled with despair. The betrayal was nothing short of crushing. His sworn enemy—the man who almost killed his wife and brought destruction to his land—was the brother of his first-in-command.

His *friend*.

The brother of *his* soul for years.

Greylen's judgment flashed through his mind as he held Gavin's stare, his choice made in mere seconds. 'Twas the only choice he could make. But just as Greylen was about to speak, Malcolm gave his ominous order.

"Now!"

Taken by surprise again, though this time by the shock of what they witnessed, the sound of arrows rent the air as Malcolm released his dagger. Gavin jumped from his horse, placing his body between Greylen and the dagger meant for his heart. It embedded in Gavin's shoulder, but as if unfazed in his state of fury, Gavin ran for Malcolm.

Compelled by an internal sense of dread, Gavin turned as his commander fell to the ground.

"*Noooo!*"

"Your own betrayal killed your laird, brother," Malcolm boasted. He turned to flee, then with a sickening chuckle, added, "Your look is almost as priceless as when I murdered our mother."

Gavin ran to Greylen as Duncan gave chase to Malcolm and his men. He lifted Greylen's head to his lap, a blow to the back of his head leaving him unconscious. Blood seeped from the jagged wound and two arrows had found their marks, one in his thigh and another in his back. Kevin and Hugh began to circle him, their swords still drawn.

"I'm still your first-in-command," Gavin hissed. "Kill me if you must but get him home!"

'Twas a call they could not make. Gavin was in agony, and they knew he only meant to protect Greylen. Duncan was back only minutes later, sure that Malcolm and his men were gone, and he knelt beside Gavin to help tend Greylen's wounds.

Gavin had already sliced through the arrows' shafts, cutting them close to the point of entrance. He ripped his shirt, tying the material around Greylen's leg. The arrow that pierced his back had somehow deflected, and its tip rested just beneath the surface of his shoulder. Though it bled profusely, 'twas the blow to his thigh that worried him most. The blood pulsed from it and Gavin tied it again before gaining his saddle. He pulled up Greylen's body in front of him as his men lifted him from below.

They left the forest quickly, silent the entire way back. All of them with pained expressions, yet none as fierce as Gavin's. He held tight to his commander, his own wound draining with each stride his mount took, but he never loosened his hold. The strength it took to keep Greylen upright before him was nothing compared to the sickness he felt. The look Greylen had given him before they were set upon again replayed in his mind.

He could only imagine what Greylen's words would have been, had he spoken them.

He sent Kevin and Hugh ahead as they reached the first of their border patrols. And with each group of men they passed throughout the holding, their numbers increased as men joined their procession.

Gavin's pace was so determined, however, Kevin and Hugh remained in his sight as they passed through the gates.

❧ CHAPTER TWENTY-FIVE ❧

"Gwendolyn, you must tell me what you're making," Isabelle called over her work for the second time.

"I've told you it's a surprise, Isabelle," Gwen chastised. "I'll make one for you, too, but I have something entirely different in mind," she teased with a smile. They were sitting in the library with Lady Madelyn. It was still an hour or so before dinner and she had just begun to work on a garment for Greylen. A Christmas present.

Gwen had told them only a week before of how she celebrated the holiday and she'd cautiously asked Greylen if they might have a tree and exchange gifts. She was rewarded with one of his incredible smiles, and his assurance that he'd like nothing more than to begin such a tradition with her. Now, thanks to her big mouth, she had four months to make seven shirts, something naughty for Isabelle, and things for Lady Madelyn and Anna too.

Thank God she was good with needles.

They were startled as shouts rang from the courtyard and what had to be a stampede as horses and men raced toward the steps. Ian and Connell were already through the front doors by the time the ladies reached them and Gwen raced outside. Isabelle started screaming immediately and Lady Madelyn began calling instructions for the table to be cleared in the great hall.

Gwen ran straight to Greylen. She had no time for fear and immediately began a clinical assessment. He was covered with blood, unconscious, and suffered two apparent wounds.

Her assessment continued as Gavin confirmed each of her observations.

"He's been unconscious for hours," Gavin said, looking only at her. "Two arrows found their marks, one in his shoulder, the other his leg. There's a gash behind his head, but the blood flow has stopped."

She took one deep breath, then Dr. Reynolds began calling orders. "Kevin, fetch the board against the stables. Ian, there's a satchel in the trunk at the end of my bed. It's locked—*break it*. Isabelle, stop screaming and fetch a clean sheet—now, *move*. Lady Madelyn, Anna—clean the table in the great hall with antiseptic and lay your instruments on the buffet." She never took her eyes from Gavin as she rattled off each instruction. She knew he was keeping something from her. "What? Tell me, Gavin, *now*."

"His leg wound—I think 'tis mortal."

"Just—hold—tight—Gavin," she ground out between her teeth. She didn't come back almost five hundred frigging years to lose. She was the best. And right now, she was the best this world had to offer.

Kevin returned with Alex in tow, the new soldier Greylen had taken under his wing. Just as Duncan helped them brace the board for Greylen's weight, Isabelle ran outside. She was less hysterical now and helped Gwen drape the sheet over the board while Connell and Hugh took Greylen from Gavin's arms. They placed him on the board and started for the steps, listening to her instructions as they hurried.

"Carry him to the great hall, but don't remove him. Isabelle," she called without turning, "see to Gavin's and Kevin's wounds."

Lady Madelyn and Anna were still placing items on the buffet when Ian ran into the room with her satchel. Kevin, Duncan, and Alex held Greylen on the board and she instructed Ian, Hugh, and Connell to grab the corners of the sheet as she reached for the other, but Gavin was already there, and they all lifted Greylen onto the table.

"Let Isabelle see to your wounds," she instructed Gavin and Kevin. "He'll need to be moved again." Gwen started washing her hands, shouting for everyone to do the same. She grabbed her instruments.

She started with the wound on his thigh, knowing if she didn't stop the bleeding, Gavin would be right with his prediction. "Mother, take my stethoscope and check his heartbeat. Anna, thread the needle, the one on the left side, and hand it to me when I ask." She began probing the gash in Greylen's thigh, what was left of his blood, which couldn't be much, barely pulsing from the wound when she removed the bindings. The arrowhead was embedded close to the bone and her fingers kept slipping. She forgot to breathe. *Focus, Gwen!*

She felt a strong hand on her shoulder, Gavin squeezing it reassuringly. "Gavin, stand at the head of the table, keep his neck straight so the passage stays clear to his lungs, and make sure you can feel his breath."

Gwen finally felt metal and carefully removed the arrowhead. "Anna, douse it with the antiseptic, then hand me the needle. You have to keep the wound open so I can repair it inside. *Now, Anna.*"

Anna used the liquid that Lady Madelyn assured her prevented infection, and then held the wound open as instructed. Her hands were shaking so badly they continued to slip. Duncan pushed her out of the way and used two linen strips to keep his fingers firmly in place.

Gwen began the first layers of sutures, working from the inside out. Her hair began falling, covering her eyes. "Anna, for God's sake, tie her hair back," Gavin shouted from over Greylen's head.

The tension in the room was oppressive. But Anna hurried to the task as Gwen began sealing the top layer of tissue. It was a wound that could still cause serious repercussions, especially with the amount of blood he'd lost. After what felt like hours, his worst wound was finally closed, and Gwen breathed her first sigh of relief. Then she went for his shoulder.

"'Tis too faint. I can't hear it anymore."

"I feel no breath, Gwen. 'Tis stopped." Gavin and Lady Madelyn had both spoken at the same time.

"No!" Gwen grabbed the stethoscope and listened. *Come on, Greylen!*

Nothing.

She jumped on the table and began compressions, counting under her breath. "Gavin,"—*two, three*—"when I tell you, give him two short breaths,"—*eight, nine*—"pinch his nose and make sure his tongue hasn't dropped,"—*twelve, thirteen*—"hold it with your fingers if you have to. Mother, check the vein in his neck, tell me when you feel something." She continued to count, her palms pressing Greylen's rib cage. "Again, Gavin."

Oh God, help me, please!

Where was the frigging ER!

Lady Madelyn shook her head again. Still nothing. Duncan, Kevin, and Hugh moved closer to Greylen. She could feel them behind her as she continued to lean over his body. Ian and Connell, who were on the other side next to Greylen's mother, began moving closer as well. They were chanting, all of them, and she could hear the same incantation from the courtyard outside.

Their prayers were deafening, but what Greylen needed was a shock. The thought taunted her with each compression. "Again, Gavin." Lady Madelyn continued to shake her head.

Noooo!

Her voice filled with anger and her fury unleashed. "You, stupid, pigheaded"—*two fingers over the sternum*—"sorry as all get-out"—*close fist over thumb*—"damn you to hell"—*twelve inches above…six…eight…ten…perfect*—"STAND BACK."

They all watched in stunned silence as Gwen released her blow. The sound as she made contact could be heard through her agonized cry. Then they watched as she readied for another.

"Don't you leave me," she shouted, hitting her mark again. Her fingers were numb from the impact, and she readied to start compressions again.

"I feel it," Lady Madelyn called, stopping Gwen's hands midair as she threw herself back, lest her ministrations affect the beat. Duncan caught her before she fell from the table. Then she hurried to check Greylen's breathing for herself. The sound of his heartbeat grounded her precarious balance between insane fear and utter elation.

The wound to his shoulder was repaired in minutes, the tip of the arrow easily removed. Lady Madelyn kept a count of Greylen's pulse, which remained steady, though weak, as Gwen poured antiseptic over the gash behind his head. The wound wasn't deep, but it was wide and took almost twenty painstaking stitches to close. It was another hour before she was done.

Then her head hit the table next to Greylen's. It was minutes before she finally lifted it and looked at everyone staring at her. Their expressions the same as her own. Relief. Fear. Exhaustion.

She stood slowly, and Gavin held her shoulders as she began to sway. Then he whispered for her ears only, "I've never loved you more than I do at this very moment." She covered his hand, squeezing her acknowledgment as she began with her orders again.

"We can't move him yet," she said. "Anna, prepare my chamber. Lady Madelyn, I need fresh linens and water. Alex and Hugh, scrub the board with antiseptic."

Gwen washed Greylen, each part of his body cleansed to her satisfaction before laying him against clean sheets.

Then she covered him with another clean sheet. It was another hour before she finally agreed to move him.

Though his pulse was steady, she was terrified he wouldn't wake up. He could easily lapse into a coma, and there was no way to know if he'd suffered any lasting damage. She kept reminding herself that he was strong, he was conditioned. That she was here to fix him, not to watch him die. But uncertainty still consumed her.

In a somber procession, Greylen's men carried him to their chamber on the board they used to bring him inside. The trunk that had been at the end of their bed lay in pieces outside the chamber doors. Ian had, in fact, destroyed it when he retrieved her satchel.

With the same care used below stairs, they grabbed the corners of the sheet and placed him on the bed. Lady Madelyn stood by the bedside looking at her son. "You saved his life, Gwendolyn."

"I kept him alive, Lady Madelyn," Gwen said gravely. "It's not over yet."

"He has much to fight for," Lady Madelyn whispered, touching her shoulder before leaving the room.

Gwen was left to care for her husband and sat in the chair Ian placed next to their bed. Duncan and Connell stood just outside her chamber doors while Gavin, Kevin, Ian, and Hugh called their men to arms.

They would search for Malcolm.

'Twas well past midnight when Gavin found Isabelle in the chapel. She sat in front of the altar, tears streaming from her eyes. He knew she'd dismissed Father Michael earlier, for Gavin had spoken with him briefly in the great hall as he sat with Lady Madelyn. He told Gavin he'd already been to his laird's chamber and prayed with Lady Gwendolyn before she, too, had dismissed him.

Gavin walked to Isabelle and knelt on the floor beside her. The look she gave him nearly broke his heart. He took her in his arms and rocked her against his body.

"Does he live, Gavin?" she asked, clutching him.

"Aye, Bella. Greylen's strong. He'll not die by the hand of a coward."

"Mother wouldn't tell me what happened. It must have been horrible, Gavin. The chants of our people still ring in my head."

"I must go, Bella."

"You'll find him, and you must kill him, Gavin," Isabelle demanded as she grabbed his shoulders.

"Aye, Isabelle, I will."

"Come back to me, Gavin. I'll stay away no more."

"I won't be back, Bella," Gavin said, shaking his head. "Seagrave is no longer my home."

"How can you say such a thing?" She gasped.

"I'm the reason your brother almost died. And from the look he gave me...I'm no longer welcome."

"'Tis untrue! Greylen could never turn his back on you."

"Some things can't be forgiven, Bella." He stared at the floor before cupping her face. "I will always love you,

Bella. I have always loved you." He gathered her close, kissing her with all the emotion that poured through his heart. He looked at her one last time, his eyes filled with unshed tears as he stood and left the chapel.

Gwen heard her chamber door open and looked up as Gavin stepped inside. He closed it behind him and walked slowly to the bed. She'd been told of the attack, and more importantly, of the shock it revealed. She watched Gavin look at her husband and bent to place his lips to his forehead.

"I'm so sorry, my friend," Gavin whispered. His shoulders were shaking and when he turned to her, she threw herself in his arms. She couldn't contain her sobs any longer, and they were violent in their release. She held Gavin tight, and he held her back with the same intensity.

"You saved his life, Gwen, I can't thank you enough."

"If you hadn't gotten him home, Gavin, you saved his life as well."

"I only broke his heart."

"He loves you, Gavin. And until he tells you differently, I won't believe anything else."

"I can't change who I am."

"Oh, Gavin," she cried, shaking him in despair and trying to get him listen. "You're the most honorable person I've ever known."

"I'll miss you, Gwen. I'll miss you all so very much."

"Don't go," she pleaded. "Not until you've talked to Greylen."

"I can't wait. I have to find Malcolm before he gets too far. If Greylen wishes to see me…" Gavin didn't finish, as if he believed Greylen would never wish to see him.

"I've never felt this pain before, Gavin. I can't lose you now."

Gavin gathered her in his arms again. "You've more strength than any woman I've ever known, Gwendolyn MacGreggor. I've a feeling you'll be fine."

"Oh, Gavin, I love you. I love you so much."

"I love you, too, Gwen." He wiped at her tears as his ran freely, pulling her into his arms to hold her tight. He held her a moment longer, then pressed his lips to her forehead.

Then he left her chamber and the life only she could understand how much he loved.

❦ CHAPTER TWENTY-SIX ❦

The next twelve days were the longest of Gwen's life. Greylen lay trapped in unconsciousness, first with fever and then with a stillness that terrified her. His vitals were stronger, but his mind remained quiet.

She soaked linens with a mixture of salt and sugar, slowly squeezing the liquid in his mouth, then carefully coaxing it down his throat. She talked to him endlessly and when she became too tired, his men, or Lady Madelyn and Isabelle, took over. She lost her appetite and now only pretended to eat as Greylen's men watched. They didn't argue with her but assured her that Greylen would be furious when he awoke. She prayed they were right.

But as the days stretched by, her hope began to fade.

It was on that twelfth night that she finally allowed herself to crawl into bed. His wounds were healing, and she was sure that if she stayed on the other side of the bed, she wouldn't disturb him. She laid her head on the pillow, her tears falling down the side of her face as she looked at Greylen. She couldn't imagine what she'd do without him. In only a few short months he'd become everything to her.

Her life would be meaningless without him.

Sleep came easily, her strength nearly gone as she refused to eat. Her wedding band slipped from her finger two days ago and now hung from the cord that held Greylen's medallion. Secretly, she wished to join him, to find that oblivion he rested in.

She had the most wonderful dreams that night. Greylen was well again, and they made love on the beach as they watched the sunrise. She could feel the sun's warmth on her cheek and fought to stay in the dream's embrace rather than the nightmare she'd wake to.

When she opened her eyes, it was to see a pair of solid black ones looking back.

"Haven't I told you…there are no sides to this bed?"

She couldn't answer. Silent tears came freely as she stared back at him. She covered his hand when it caressed her cheek, knowing it was the warmth she'd felt on her face.

Greylen could do little more than stare at his wife. She looked terribly pale and deep shadows lay beneath her eyes. "I'll drag you if I have to, Gwen," he said weakly. "But you've no idea how long it took just to reach out to you," he admitted truthfully. It had taken forever. He'd never been so weak, but he needed to touch her. And now he only wanted to see her smile.

Gwen did smile at his words and obeyed him instantly, carefully pressing her body against his side. Then she cried before pulling back to look at him.

"Do you remember anything, Greylen?"

"Aye, I remember it all, till a *mountain* thrashed my head."

"'Twas a boulder. A large one from the looks of it," she remarked, brushing the hair from his eyes. "It's in the courtyard, fueling the anger of your men."

"Gwen? Did you mend my broken heart?"

"Nay." She shook her head. "I only made it beat again. I fear the mending is to come."

"He's gone then?"

"Aye."

"Where?"

"To kill Malcolm."

"He thinks I hate him."

"Do you?"

"I could never hate him. I love him as much as you, if you can understand."

"I understand. I feel the same."

"I know that too."

News of Greylen's well-being spread quickly throughout the holding. Well-wishers left flowers and baked goods on the steps, and a steady stream of visitors crowded their room.

Lady Madelyn sat by his side, brushing the hair off his face as she smiled down at him. "You gave us quite a scare, Greylen."

"You should know better, Mother," he chastised with a smile. "Nothing will beat me."

"Don't let your good fortune fool you," she said seriously. "If not for your wife, your predicament would have been fatal."

"She looks worse than I," he said as he watched her walk back toward their bed. "I noticed her ring rests upon her neck. I assume she's so far gone even her fingers show the signs."

"She hasn't eaten. Greylen…" His mother looked to her lap, obviously changing her mind about saying anything. Greylen squeezed her hand and she finally looked at him again. "I believe she wished to join you."

"I'll see that stops at once."

"I know you will."

Anna came in with a tray. "Bring a tray for my wife. I'll eat only if she does."

Gwen tensed. "Greylen, I've eaten every day. You're the one who needs nourishment."

"Don't lie to me, Gwen," he hissed before glancing toward the door. "Duncan?" he called.

Duncan turned and looked only at Gwen as he spoke, his fury barely contained. "She acts as though she eats every day, but she throws her food to the fire when she thinks we're not watching." He continued to glare, as if daring her to argue. "I fear she is worse than before."

"Leave us."

Gwen sat on the bed next to Greylen, placing the tray beside his legs.

"Bite for bite, Gwen, or I'll have nothing."

"Greylen…" She started to argue but saw his look. He might be weak, but his determination and command were as strong as ever.

"You heard me."

"Very well," she conceded, "but you first."

It took forever. Gwen went slowly, spooning him broth and small bits of bread, careful of upsetting his stomach. She continued until both trays were emptied.

"Gwen, what were you thinking?" he asked. "You'd starve yourself to death had I not made it?" He'd only meant it as a gentle chide, but she turned away. "Good God, Gwen, 'tis true?"

"I don't know what I'd do without you, Greylen. This is my home. But only because of you."

CHAPTER TWENTY-SEVEN

What a difference a day makes.

'Twas a sentiment his wife used.

Greylen always had an aptitude for seeing beneath the surface, but now 'twas deeper. His perception held new qualities. And, although he was terribly dismayed with Gavin's absence, 'twas only with sheer control and authority that he handled the tasks before him.

Most important of which, the task of cleaning up the incredible mess he had awoken to. He knew Gwen had saved his life and though he arrogantly believed nothing would ever fell him, his mortality had been thrown in his face. Secondly, his wife would rather die than be without him. And, as ridiculous as that was, he could understand her fears. This was not the life she was born to, though she was born to be here all the same. In addition, his best friend was gone, mistakenly believing he'd been cast aside. And as if he needed any more grief, Isabelle was inconsolable, certain that Gavin would never return.

He took the burden on himself, determined to do everything in his power to restore the balance he and his family had known. Now 'twas his turn to make the best of their predicament. His wife needed reassurance, his friend needed to come home, and his sister... Well, his sister needed a good smack in the head.

Malcolm, he decided, could wait. Greylen knew he and his family were safe. No one could breach the land and he'd already sent missives to his king demanding justice by his ruler or at his own hand should he be lucky enough to find the miscreant first.

Greylen also sent word to the elder MacFale, requesting a private meeting. He needed to understand the reasons that Gavin made the choices he had. Now, 'twas up to him to end the bitterness that had plagued their families for years.

His men had orders to bring Gavin home. The message passed to each laird throughout the land, as well as a personal word to their ruler, should Gavin be at court. If he was, Gavin would be instructed to return to Seagrave by command of their king.

Gwen insisted that he recuperate fully before he took action. And though he knew she meant well, she didn't understand his strength—or maybe she did. Whatever the case, he'd heed her words. He needed more than anything to return her vitality to her. For someone with so much courage, his wife had a fragility that truly scared him. He had no desire to be apart from her anyway, and in fact didn't let her from his sight. The time they had now, he'd take and cherish as never before. Life could indeed be too short, and he'd live in the moments, not for them.

Compounding everything, his head still throbbed, his leg pained him, and he was weaker than ever before. But he was doing everything in his power to return to his usual physical self, and he knew that began with the right mental outlook.

The tasks he set before himself, however, left him exhausted just thinking of them.

He ordered the table from his study to be brought to his chamber. 'Twas placed to the left of their doors, across from the sitting area by the window. He'd confer with his men there, not from his bed. His wife had smiled at his determination and made a few changes of her own. She had a table brought up as well, one she placed in front of the window where they would take their meals. She also had *weights* fashioned, as she called them, so he could exercise his arms, and crutches to support himself until his leg healed.

He gave her no arguments, nor did she argue with his demand to resume his rule.

Their chamber became a central meeting place for his men, their family meals, and what would be some of the most incredible days he and Gwen would have together.

From the morning after he awoke from his battle with death, he moved as much as possible. At first 'twas only to the bathing chamber, Gwen taking as much care with him as he had with her when she'd been the one recovering. The crutches were his savior, and it eased his mind that he didn't have to lean on his men or his wife. He relished her care, though. She helped him bathe, shaved his beard, and assisted him with his dress before his men gathered in the mornings.

They spent their afternoons alone, everyone dismissed after discussions around his table and a late-morning meal with his mother and Isabelle. They sat by the fire, playing games of cards and talking quietly. Gwen insisted that he rest before supper and would lie beside him as they napped together. After supper, they were alone again, sharing their evenings and nights with just each other.

He used the weights as she'd shown him and continued to walk on his own, now using a cane to lean on. No word had been heard from Gavin, and the elder MacFale sent word he'd not seen him either. The old man did agree, however, to meet with him and would come the following week.

Greylen had just awoken from one of his lazy naps as his wife approached him, stethoscope in hand.

"Gwendolyn, if you check my heart one more time, I swear I'll beat you."

She smiled. "I just want to be sure."

"What good is it? You know I'm well. 'Tis you who still needs to mend."

"Greylen, I'm almost back to where I was."

"You've the body of a gangly boy, wife," he teased.

Her eyes widened as she tried to control a smile from forming on her face. "I can't believe you said that."

"'Tis true, you bag of bones." He smiled and pushed her to prove his point. She fell by the bed and laughed. He came before her where she lay on the floor, resting on her elbows.

"You must pinch yourself daily to find you're married to a man such as me." His words made her laugh even harder. "God how I love your laughter, Gwen."

"We need to find Gavin, husband. Your teasing has reached a new level."

"What we need is to make love. 'Tis been too long, Gwen."

"Greylen, you have stitches all over your body."

"Force or compliance, make your choice."

"Get back on the bed," she ordered, sighing. "You'll have your compliance."

"You have two seconds to divest yourself of that dress or I'll rip it from your body."

"Foreplay, so soon?" she teased. He laughed and threw her to the bed. "Greylen, be careful, your stitches."

"Take off your clothes, *now*."

Her dress was off in a second, her undergarments thrown over her head as she slipped under the covers and held them back. Greylen removed his shirt and the loose-fitting pants he wore, then held her against his body. He groaned at the feel of her. It had indeed been far too long. Weeks actually, and he had no intention of waiting a moment longer.

"Lie back, husband, while I have my way with you."

"I'll lie back, but I'll have my way with you first," he argued, leaning upright against the pillows. He lifted Gwen and held her between his legs, her back against his chest, and her feet on either side of his thighs. She made a sound of concern and moved to check the bandage covering his leg. "Shh," he hushed. "'Tis fine, wife."

He settled her more deeply against him as his lips found her neck, and she relaxed beneath the gentle touch of his hands. He nuzzled her neck and shoulders, caressed her entire body, but when his fingers slipped between her thighs and she began to move against him, he made his intentions clear. "You're not to move," he whispered, "not one muscle, Gwendolyn, or I'll stop. And I've nothing better to do than to torture you all day."

Gwen tried to heed his demands, but Greylen was merciless. He had her pressed so tightly against him that every twitch she made he felt. And he held true to his promise. His hands left her body as soon as he felt *any* movement from her. Then he admonished her lack of control with a teasing whisper in her ear. "Concentrate, love. Keep completely still. I promise you only bliss in return."

He was right. It was the hardest thing that she had ever done. Holding herself completely still as his fingers slowly stroked her. Her orgasm, when it came, was so intense she swore her brain shook from the impact.

"I told you," he whispered in her ear, chuckling from her unintelligible response. "If I don't get inside you, wife, I fear I shall die." His words were a caress and Gwen turned to straddle him. He lifted her hips, taking great care to gently push himself inside. Gwen's head fell back as he entered her, overcome by the intense feeling of having him inside her. It felt so good, but her slowness obviously drove Greylen mad because a second later she was flipped beneath him. He covered her lips at her protest, his husky reply, "You'll mend my stitches should they split," was the last thing she remembered.

They remained undisturbed that night, their passion obviously heard by the guards beyond their doors. Anna knocked at some point, though, informing them she'd brought trays with dinner. Gwen wrapped herself in a sheet before she retrieved them, her embarrassment deepening as she looked to Ian and Connell, who smiled knowingly in return.

They ate by the window, the moon bright in the darkened sky above. Greylen held her on his lap as they sat in one of the chairs by the fire, kissing for hours and rediscovering each other's bodies. They slept soundly, exhausted emotionally from what the night represented.

Homecoming. Belonging. The depth of their love for each other.

"Hold still, Greylen." Gwen laughed, swatting his hands away. They were sitting in front of the window and Gwen was trying to remove his stitches, though her husband kept grabbing her and kissing each part of her body he brought to his lips.

"You're mine to do with as I please," he teased.

"Don't remind me, you brute."

"Gwendolyn, you know I'll remind you every day for the rest of your life, and quite gladly, I might add."

"God help me," she pleaded to the ceiling, "I'm stuck with an egomaniac."

Greylen laughed at his wife's display. "You're the most pleasing wench, wife."

She poked his chest. "Gangly boy, bag of bones, and *wench*. Why I find your charm so irresistible, I'll never know."

"Fine," he relented, releasing her hands. "Have your way, you always do."

"*Ha!* My way? I never get my way."

"I'd beg to differ, love. However, you do hold the shears."

Gwen removed his stitches, pleased with the results after inspecting her work. "Come on," she said, pulling him up from the chair. "I promised you could leave our chamber when they were removed, so let's go outside."

"I'll take you for a walk," he said. "We've had little time for such pleasures."

Hand in hand, they walked to the door where Greylen paused before reaching for the latch. He turned, his expression serious. "Although these few weeks were spent here because of my recovery, they're times I'd trade for nothing. I love you more than anything, Gwen, you know that, don't you?"

"Oh God, you think I'm suicidal again."

"Nay," he began, tilting her face, "I only wish for you to know what I feel. Your lapse in judgment will never happen again," he ordered, squeezing her chin. "I'll always keep you safe, Gwen. I'll always be there for you. You must always believe it."

❧ CHAPTER TWENTY-EIGHT ❧

Greylen sat within his study, waiting for the elder MacFale. The man's ailing health had kept him from their original meeting but now, six weeks later, Greylen would at last have some answers. Gwen had been terrified he would go to the MacFale holding himself, and rather than cause her any more stress, he agreed to remain here until the man could take the journey.

Finally hearing riders approach, Greylen went to the front doors. His men had provided escort and he took the steps, greeting the old man as he began ascending the stairs. The man looked up in surprise as Greylen took his elbow and helped him.

"Until we've spoken, I'll not pass judgment," Greylen stated respectfully.

"You're a good man, MacGreggor. I see why Gavin aligned himself with you."

Lady Madelyn stood to the side as they passed through the entrance. "Guy, welcome to our home."

"Madelyn, you look well. 'Tis been too many years since we've last seen each other."

Greylen's mother said no more but followed them into the study. She sat on the settee while Greylen and MacFale took their seats, Greylen behind his desk and the elder MacFale in front.

"I have many questions and my hope is that you'll shed some light on Gavin's actions."

"I'll answer your questions," the man replied quickly. "I want nothing more than my son's happiness."

Lady Madelyn made a sound of disgust. Greylen raised a brow at her interruption.

He had never seen his mother angry before, truly angry. Yet the look on her face was revealing. "Speak, Mother." 'Twas obvious she needed no further prodding.

"I've sat back far too long, Guy," she said with barely contained fury. "You cast him aside and your wife as well. How could you do such a thing?" she accused.

"I tried to make amends," he pleaded. "I was foolish, blinded. Had I known the evil in Malcolm, I would have prevented his actions. They were merely boys, Madelyn. How could I know?"

"She tried to tell you. Allison pleaded with you. Yet all you could see was her defiance. You had your heir and you cast her aside."

Greylen remained quiet, learning far more from their exchange than he'd ever hoped.

"What would you have me do? I can't change my actions. She was so much younger than I. 'Twas easier to turn her away than accept what she offered."

"She offered you love. She offered you peace. And in return you betrayed her and let her leave. You should have never begged her to come back."

"I realized my mistakes, Madelyn. I wanted my wife back. I wanted to get to know my son. I needed help with Malcolm."

"I warned her never to return. She knew there was something wrong with him. I thank God she and Gavin had ten peaceful years away from you."

"May I interrupt?" Greylen asked as his mother and Gavin's father stared in silence.

"Aye." 'Twas a shout from them both.

"Mother, I never knew you were friendly with the MacFales," he remarked.

"I was a friend only to Allison. Your father and Guy never got along. You must've realized that from the few occasions he'd taken you there, Greylen. But Allison and I shared a friendship. We met along the border each week, and as young boys, you and Gavin played together."

Greylen's shock quickly turned to anger. "You've known all along who he was?" he accused. "Where he came from?" Good God, he wanted to throttle her.

"He left when he was five, Greylen," she justified quickly. "You were both too young to remember each other when you met again. Almost fifteen years had passed." She paused for a moment before looking at him again. "I'll never forget that day you brought him home," she said, shaking her head. "I was speechless, Greylen. Seeing the two of you together. 'Twas as though you'd never been apart."

"Why did you not say anything?" There was a quality of incredulousness in his voice. In truth, he felt like a boy begging answers.

"You've not heard the entire story, Greylen," she remarked sadly. "I remained silent for Gavin's sake. It must have pained him terribly to live so close to the home he ran from," she said directly to Guy, who sighed before finishing the tragic story.

"Allison left me when the boys were five," he began. "She would've taken them both, but I insisted that Malcolm stay with me. Gavin was far too quiet for my liking. The boy's eyes left me unsettled. I should've known the depth of his perception then, his controlled contempt. 'Twas that with which he looked to me, condemning my actions even at such a young age. You see, I treated his mother unfairly. Though Malcolm caused only trouble, I saw it as strength instead," he said regretfully. "Allison tried to give Malcolm love, but he hated her. She and Gavin shared a closeness, and Malcolm turned to me.

"I wrote to her over the years, begging her to return. I wanted to know my other son. He was the first to come from Allison's womb. My true heir. And at fifteen, Malcolm was showing signs of evil. I needed help."

"Then, they did return?" Greylen asked.

"Aye," MacFale stated, looking to Greylen, his eyes filled with pain. Greylen stood and poured a brandy, handing the snifter to the man who clearly needed a drink. MacFale drained the contents and met Greylen's stare as he finished.

"They came home for ten days—ten days of hell for both of them. Malcolm acted ever the gentleman, but I saw the looks he exchanged with Gavin. I saw the hate he cast to his mother, but I never imagined the extent of it. I'd been in my study, stirred by a cry of alarm from the hall. When I reached Gavin, he was cradling his mother's head in his lap, tears running from his eyes. He said she'd been pushed from above, knowing 'twas Malcolm who did so, but he'd only seen a shadow. I couldn't believe Malcolm had done such a thing. I didn't want to believe he'd done such a thing.

"I told Gavin he was wrong, that he had no proof. Then I watched Allison use her remaining strength to stroke her son's cheek and whisper her love to him. Gavin, my boy of only fifteen carried his mother from the keep, swearing never to return. In the same breath, he vowed to avenge his mother's murder. Too late, I realized what a fool I'd been. We could have raised them together," he cried in regret. "Mayhap then none of this would've happened. But, in truth, it had been easier to let her go when she asked. Her love scared me, and I turned to others instead."

"Where did Gavin go?" Greylen asked.

"To his mother's family. 'Tis where they lived for years. Lincolnshire, England. I wrote to Gavin repeatedly throughout the years, begging his forgiveness. I deeded all the lands that came with my marriage to him. Set coin in his name so he could live." He shook his head. "He never used it...none of it. His mother's family paid for his education at the university, and when he joined in service for our king, he used his spoils to repay them. He's wealthier now than I ever was, and of his honor, I could not be prouder."

"I'll have the whereabouts of those estates," Greylen said, reaching for parchment and a quill. "My captain will sail immediately."

"Have you heard anything from him?" the elder MacFale asked.

"Nay. We know he's tried to track Malcolm," he explained. "It seems Malcolm and his men hide in the lowlands. We've received word, however, that Gavin's set a price on his head. It's so significant, 'tis a wonder Malcolm's not been captured."

"Bring my son home, MacGreggor, if not to me then here. You gave him more than I ever could."

"If you've word from Malcolm?" Greylen asked.

"I'll turn him over. Though he'll probably kill me first."

Greylen stayed within his study long after Guy MacFale left. His ship's captain had his orders, and Duncan and Hugh sailed with him. His mother had seemed exhausted after their discussion and, truthfully, he was still in a state of shock that she'd known about Gavin all along. He smiled as he remembered her parting words, just hours ago.

"You and Gavin would run along the hills, Greylen. 'Twas your imperiled kingdom you'd both commanded proudly, puffing your little chests out. You both fought so valiantly to protect it. 'Tis a sweetness I've always remembered, especially to have watched you do so together as men. Allison would be pleased to know how close you've become."

His thoughts were interrupted as Gwen stood in the open doorway. He gave her a smile. "Come. Sit on my lap, sweet."

"I've come to trim your hair, my laird," she teased.

Greylen loved that her playfulness was back, but what pleased him more was that she seemed to glow these past weeks. He filled her in on his conversation, rubbing away the line of worry that crossed her forehead as she sat on his lap. "He'll be home soon, Gwen," he assured her, "hopefully in but a month's time."

"I hope you're right, Greylen. Isabelle's so hard to keep company. I swear if I had some Prozac, I'd add it to her tea every morning. And your hair." She sighed, running her fingers through it. "Well, your hair becomes grayer with each day that passes."

"I fear you're right," he agreed. "Does my appearance bother you, love?"

Gwen could only stare at him. Greylen had never been more appealing and that was saying a lot. His face was more sculpted now, his looks more penetrating, and his hair made her want to jump him all the time. He had enticing gray streaks now, not many, but in contrast to his black hair and bronzed skin—jeez, the man was hot.

"Greylen, I…I—You—well—" Her face was flaming as she backed away.

He laughed, pulling her against him. "For someone with all your intelligence, I find your stammering enchanting."

He muffled her embarrassment with a kiss and carried her upstairs. He sat patiently on a chair in their bathing chamber as she poured water over his head before trimming his hair. She knew he loved the way she rubbed her fingers into his scalp in a deep massage, careful of the scar along the back of his head.

"Do mine now, please," she instructed as she held the shears before him.

"Are you daft? I'll not cut your hair." He reached out, brushing his fingers through her hair.

"Please, it bothers me," she asked again.

"You ask much. What would you give me in return?"

"I'll let you in on a secret."

"You've no secrets from me, Gwen. You're completely guileless."

Her mouth fell open at what sounded like an insult. "Thanks."

"Very well," he conceded. "I'll cut your gorgeous locks. Then I'll reveal your secret myself." Greylen carefully trimmed the ends of her hair, then finally relented and cut it to rest between her shoulder blades as she'd asked.

"Well, great master, in your most arrogant, pigheaded, overlord way, tell me, what's my secret?"

"If you insist on playing games, you'll lose," he said, pulling her against him.

"Oh, I'll not lose, husband," she assured him.

"I can taste your defeat," he growled, fisting her hair in his hand and bringing her face close to his. "Tell me again the names you carelessly flaunt," he demanded.

"Master." She breathed against his lips. "Arrogant." She breathed again, this time rewarded with a slow, sensual kiss he ended with a gentle scrape.

"You've not finished, love," he prompted, tightening his grip enough to make her gasp.

"I said you were pigheaded." She whimpered in anticipation, her own hands bringing him closer.

"You've cried off the most important, wife," he accused, lowering her to the floor. "Now tell me," he hissed. "Who am I?"

"*You* are my very own overlord," she said at last, their conversation forgotten as her husband won the battle she started.

The battle she had purposely started.

Gwen stood just beyond the door of her husband's study. She paced back and forth, wringing her hands. Greylen had been right; she sucked at keeping secrets. She wanted to tell him what she'd been hiding, but she couldn't seem to get the man alone. He and his men were sitting around the table, crossing off dates on a piece of paper, and laughing as they called out dibs on future ones. She listened for a few more minutes.

Crap! They were laughing at her.

"What's this?" Gwen asked, stepping into the room.

Greylen sighed, sitting back in his chair as he looked to the door. He picked up the paper and held it before him. "This is a *calendar*, Gwendolyn," he explained like he was speaking to a two-year-old. "It's a sequence of numbers we call weeks, which comprise another sequence of numbers called months, which in turn leads us to yet another sequence of numbers which comprise a ye—"

"I know what a frigging calendar is!"

"Then why did you ask?" Her husband looked as though he was having trouble keeping a straight face.

Gwen's hands fisted. "I'll ask you again—what are you doing?"

"We're marking days, love," he answered in obvious exasperation before he continued. "It's usually what one does when working with a calendar."

"You're betting on something," she said through clenched teeth, his smug tone infuriating her. "And I want to know what."

"Betting?" he asked innocently.

Her eyes narrowed. "Betting, you imbecile. Now answer me." He remained silent, so she marched to the table and yanked the paper from his hand. Their names were scrawled over each of the days, amounts of coins written beneath them and doubling as the days progressed. She looked at Kevin, snorting in disgust as she shook her head. He lied easily, then she realized she was completely screwed. Every frigging one of them lied easily. Resigned, she picked Ian, the lesser of seven evils. "Ian, what's this about?" she demanded.

Ian turned beet red, looking to Greylen for help. Her husband remained silent. "They're days we've chosen, lady."

"Thank you, Ian," she ground out through her teeth. "I never would have guessed. What does it mean?"

"Gwen, come now, love—"

"Don't 'Gwen, come now, love' me," she snapped.

Greylen scoffed, waving his hand over the paper. "'Tis just a simple wager."

"A simple wager *on what?*" she asked again.

Greylen held her stare, then finally grumbled under his breath, "On when you would tell us you're with child."

"*Ahhh.*" Her mouth dropped open. She could tell they were holding laughter back and it took her a good full minute before she regained her control. "Greylen, can I speak with you for a moment?" she asked sweetly.

He rolled his eyes. "Like I'd fall for that again?"

"But it's important," she pressed. "It's about the baby."

"I've a busy day," he stated emphatically. "I've not time for games, wife."

"Oh, very well." She sighed. Then she left the room.

"You, my friend, are in trouble," Duncan said, clasping Greylen's shoulders as he stood behind him.

"Nay, she left easily enough," Greylen reasoned. Then realized she left too easily. He kept waiting for her to come back, but when she didn't, he assumed he escaped her wrath, for now. He couldn't hide his thoughts from his men. "She'll seek her revenge, but later."

Later, however, wasn't long. They were still in the study when Isabelle came in and handed Greylen a missive. "One of the border patrols just delivered this, Greylen," she said, handing it to him. "He said 'twas important."

Greylen took the missive and opened it immediately, hoping 'twas information on Gavin. The seal was illegible but when he spread the parchment, he recognized the script. Clever wench. He knew he shouldn't read it, he couldn't help himself.

> *Greylen,*
> *I just wanted to tell you how much this baby means to me.*

His heart warmed at her words and he continued.

> *I also wanted you to know when our baby was conceived. It was the day of the storm, the day you stayed in the study with your men, the day I waited for you in the tub by the fire...*

The room was suddenly crowded. He stepped into the hall, leaning against the wall beside the door. His body rock-hard as he read, in explicit detail, the events of that day.

> *I stood as you entered our chamber, drops of water running down my body. Do you remember how you took each one from me, Greylen? You dried me with your mouth and made me wet again with your hands and your tongue and your body.*

His hands fisted on the page as he walked to the steps, his eyes never veering from the script as he took the stairs.

You laid me on the floor, and...

Holy mother of God, she was descriptive.

You wouldn't stop, Greylen, not till I lay as a rag doll before you. You were very pleased with yourself. Do you remember?

Aye he did, 'twas in fact hard to walk at present.

You took me into your lap, and I took you into my body. You rocked me in your arms. Slow, deep motions till you could take no more. Then you laid me down again. You never left my body...

He stood inside their chamber, now aglow in candlelight. Daylight shut out behind the closed shutters. His wife sat in the tub before the fire, her back to him.

"I thought you had a busy day," she asked without turning.

"I do have a busy day," he returned, walking toward her. "It seems you need to be reminded of a few things."

"Oh?" She feigned surprise. "Did I forget something?"

"Aye." He breathed on her neck. "And this time you'll not soon forget."

He spent the next two hours reminding her of everything he did to her that day.

He took her to the brink of Eden.

And gladly went with her.

❧ CHAPTER TWENTY-NINE ❧

Autumn gave way to winter and with the passing months, Greylen threw himself into his duties. With his full strength at last returned, his mornings were spent on the practice fields. Hour upon hour training with his men, oftentimes until he was the only man standing. His afternoons were occupied riding the land, his gaze scrutinizing the horizon in futile hope that Gavin would return.

On the occasions he wasn't away from the holding in the afternoon, he withdrew to his study, with his wife. Gwen had begun to oversee many of their household chores, but on their completion, and at his insistence, she spent her time with him there. He felt 'twas imperative that she learned his system of documentation. For in light of her feelings of helplessness when he lay unconscious, he wanted her to feel move involved.

Gwen was also beginning to understand Gaelic and asked that he read and speak to her only in his native language. She always seemed to throw herself into each task, and in this, she was no different. She'd master it before long. His pride for her only grew.

On days when the time allowed, he would take her to their chamber before supper. Sometimes they would sit by the fire, while others he carried her straight to bed for a nap. No matter where they sat, however, he always undressed her, his hands roaming possessively over her body. Her stomach was rounded now, and he'd smile when she teased that she now had breasts, *real breasts*. She was so sensitive, though, he could do little more than brush his knuckles against their fullness.

She always fell asleep for a short while, sometimes embraced in his arms while he remained clothed. If he felt she wasn't too tired, he made love to her first, then he'd smile in pure male satisfaction as she instantly succumbed to sleep after their leisurely trysts.

He truly enjoyed these afternoons. In truth, the pain of Gavin's absence was only tolerable with his wife in his arms. *Life* seemed only tolerable with Gwen. He wasn't sure now how he'd lived without her before.

She still awoke early, and every morning they walked together before he joined his men. Anna had fashioned a lightweight cloak for her with wide sleeves, as it had already snowed several times. The garment, made to his specifications, allowed her to warm her hands against the cool morning air. And no matter how often he argued that she not go, her answer was always the same. She'd given up running during her pregnancy, but she'd be damned if she didn't walk. Hard.

At first, he refused her any form of exercise, but her explanation stopped those arguments cold. Gwen told him that being in better physical shape would help with her labor, thus making her birthing easier. Of course, his fear of something happening to her in childbirth was so terrifying that he made sure she hadn't missed a single day. On the occasions she was too tired to walk in the morning, he took her after supper.

Their afternoons, however, were never played with. Rather, they were never played with, until at last, one cold November afternoon, their prayers were finally answered.

Gwen had just entered his study when shouts were called from the courtyard. Gwen followed him as he walked to the front doors, and as he opened them, Duncan raced up the steps. "Gavin returns," he cried. "He crossed the border hours ago. He's but minutes behind."

Greylen grabbed his man by the shoulders. "Did you speak to him?" he demanded, his heart pounding with joy.

"Nay, he rides alone, and his look, one of such seriousness, he only afforded a nod and regal sweep of hand to announce his presence."

Greylen turned to his wife, his smile surely reflecting the joy he felt. "Wife, if you wish to greet our friend, fetch your cloak." She was gone before he finished but back within minutes and standing by his side. He pulled her against him, knowing 'twas he who took comfort from her. Good God, his knees were weak. He squeezed her as his man rode between the gates. His heart pounded as Gavin stopped before nudging his mount forward again.

Gavin Montgomery of Lincolnshire brought his mount to a halt within the gates of Seagrave. It seemed forever had passed since he'd left this land, the land and family that meant more to him than life itself.

Each day he was gone, he prayed for Greylen's life. His relief at hearing that Greylen had indeed recovered was so great he stopped at the first church that he came across. He lit a candle and sat alone in one of the pews where he silently wept.

During the first two months of his banishment, he'd tracked Malcolm. However, he lost his trail as his brother hid within the forest and later, somehow, secured passage to parts unknown. He couldn't return to Seagrave and instead went to England, where he stayed with his mother's family.

As wonderful as his homecoming had been, 'twas not the home he wanted. Holding on to some ill-begotten hope that one day he would return to Scotland, and refusing to do so as a MacFale, he petitioned his king to recognize his name as Montgomery, the name of his mother. Upon receiving written word of his ruler's acceptance, he found a sliver of peace. He was no longer tainted with a name that held only bitterness and sorrow. That same missive, however, also commanded he return to Seagrave.

Gavin took the order seriously, knowing he'd face his death at the hand of the one person he wished more than anything had been his true brother. But he'd meet his fate nobly and with no regret. Greylen had given him years that he had only dreamed of. And, in light of his imminent demise, he decided to pass his lands and monies to Isabelle. Had things been different, they would have been hers anyway.

He spent the following three weeks documenting the passing of his worldly possessions to Isabelle, securing passage aboard a ship and the long ride *home*.

Somewhere along the way, his hope began to build. He heard during his journey MacGreggor ships had been sent to his estates, men in search of the first-in-command of a mighty Highland laird. Then, as he passed through the lands toward Seagrave, he was greeted with only smiles and nods, and a few times, an occasional word that "MacGreggor would at last have peace for Gavin the Brave was back."

Gavin finally nudged his mount forward, his eyes on Greylen and Gwendolyn, who awaited his approach. He stopped when he reached the center of the courtyard and dismounted before handing the reins to James. "Sir, 'tis good to have you home again," the stable master told him with a nod.

Gavin closed his eyes. *Could it be true? Could he possibly be welcomed?*

He looked to Greylen as he began walking. Just to see him alive and well was enough if this was, indeed, to be his end. Those thoughts, however, were soon replaced with something else. Greylen's look held no disgust and Gwen wore only a smile, squeezing her husband's hand before Greylen started walking too.

His commander approached him as never before. His look pained, though not with anger. He looked different to Gavin, older, but not from the gray now in his hair. 'Twasn't agedness that made him appear so. 'Twas a change within.

God, how he had missed him.

Life seemed to repeat itself on that cold November day. This time, however, 'twas Gavin's knees that buckled, and 'twas he who fell in the courtyard. And 'twas he who would beg forgiveness. Forgiveness for not trusting Greylen with the secrets that ruled his life.

When Greylen at last stood before him, he stared down with a strained face and misted eyes. His commander's expression cut like a blade, he'd been such a fool to not confide in him. Greylen closed his eyes and shook his head as he laid a hand upon Gavin's head. When he removed his hand and opened his eyes again his full composure seemed returned, the words that followed confirmed it. "If you make me kneel upon this ground as my wife and I did so long ago, you'll have to bed me as well, my friend."

A smile tugged at Gavin's lips as he looked up. "I'll not be on the receiving end."

"Then we, indeed, have a problem." Greylen laughed, grabbing Gavin's shoulders. He pulled him up and embraced him. "Why did you leave, Gavin? Why didn't you return sooner?"

Gavin wouldn't release his hold but held his head away just enough to look in Greylen's eyes. "I would kneel before you now, Greylen, pledge to you my life again."

"Nay, Gavin, you've never been released from your vow. If I must, I will kneel before you." Greylen tightened his hold, his voice strained as he fought for control. "You never heard my words, Gavin. I'd not had the chance to speak them. You'll hear them now." Greylen never took his eyes from his man, shaking him with each statement. "'Tis *I* who am your brother. *I* am your family, Gavin, and there's not another man I'd have beside me. I swear 'twas those very words Malcolm would have heard that day."

"You'd have me back?"

"I've already said you've never been released. You'll never be released."

"Then I seek your sister's hand, Greylen. I'll be wed to her tonight."

"You'll have more than her hand." Greylen laughed. "My wife's threatened to set up a laboratory, whatever that is, and concoct some kind of *antidepressant*. Again..." He shrugged. "I've no idea, but she assures me she'll come upon something."

Gwen started walking forward as they made their way toward the keep. Gavin couldn't hide his joy at seeing her. Her hair blew softly in the breeze and her cloak opened to the wind as she approached.

"You should've seen her that day, Greylen," Gavin said, staring at Gwen. "She was amazing."

"Aye, Gavin, she is amazing," Greylen said proudly. Gwen threw her arms around his first-in-command, crying unabashedly as she pulled away. Gavin smiled as he held her face and covered her lips. "Remove your lips from my wife's face!"

"Nay, I'll kiss her again." And he did, laughing as he pushed Greylen back. "Ah, Gwen, I missed you."

"I missed you, too, Gavin."

"Enough of your love-play with my wife," Greylen demanded. "And you, Gwendolyn, for God's sake hold yourself back!"

"You're well, Gwen?" Gavin asked as he held her slightly away. His eyes widened when he noticed her expanding belly and he reached out to cover her stomach. "When?" he asked.

"Late spring," she answered with a smile. "You'll be our child's godfather, won't you?"

"I'd be honored."

"You've fondled my wife long enough. Now go find Isabelle, she's most likely crying on a bench behind the keep."

Gavin pulled Gwen into another embrace before doing the same to Greylen. Then he ran toward the side of the keep.

His breath caught when at last he saw Isabelle. She sat on a bench, her back to him as she looked to the sea. She wore a cloak similar to Gwen's, the hood about her neck, and her blond hair a mass of disarray from the incoming winds.

He stood behind her and called her name. She must not have believed 'twas him, for she placed her face in her hands and wept. He sat on the bench, his legs bent over the opposite side of hers. "Isabelle?" he said again, placing his hand on her shoulder. She slowly lifted her head, reaching out so cautiously, as if she feared her touch would make him disappear.

"Gavin, oh, Gavin," she cried.

Her hands wrapped around his neck as he held her windburned cheeks. Then he kissed her. She robbed him of his senses, and 'twas long minutes before he pulled away. He wiped at her tears, having to kiss her again before he could speak.

"We'll marry tonight, Isabelle. Say you'll have me, Bella."

"I am only yours, Gavin. I'd have no other."

Gavin and Isabelle were married that evening, surrounded by family, Anna, and Greylen's inner circle of men.

Since they only had hours to prepare, Gwen asked Isabelle if she'd like to borrow her wedding gown. Isabelle happily accepted and Anna worked for the rest of the afternoon, letting out the seams to accommodate Isabelle's slender but more curvaceous form. Gwen chose a burgundy velvet dress. It fit snugly, revealing the outline of her expanding belly and a fair amount of cleavage. Pregnancy, of course had its perks. The men dressed the same as they had for Greylen and Gwen's wedding. Beige shirts, black breeches, and tall, polished black boots. Gavin's shirt was white this time, just as Greylen had worn.

Greylen gave his sister away in the ceremony performed by Father Michael. Having waited so long to finally be together, Isabelle and Gavin were very serious as they exchanged vows. Cook outdid herself for their evening meal and everyone dined together in the great hall, sitting around the table and toasting to the happy couple.

Hours later, Greylen's men excused themselves, followed by Lady Madelyn and then Anna. Greylen looked to Gwen, and after noting the shadows beneath her eyes and saying good night, carried her to their chamber. Left alone, Gavin and Isabelle remained by the fire where they kissed. It seemed forever. But when the keep was at last quiet and kisses were no longer enough, Gavin cradled his wife in his arms and carried her up the stairs.

He was so gentle as he made love to her for the first time. He held her afterward, loving her tender ministrations as she traced her fingers upon his chest before succumbing to sleep.

He held tight to his sleeping wife for the rest of the night. He looked to his dagger atop the bed stand, the blade reflecting the fire's soft glow.

Gavin the Brave was home at last.

❦ CHAPTER THIRTY ❦

"Do you think they're mad, Gwendolyn?" Isabelle asked, her head tilted slightly to the side.

Gwen snorted, tightening her arms around Isabelle to keep warm. "Mad?" Gwen repeated. "How about demented?"

Isabelle tilted her head to the other side, considering Gwen's words. "Aye, you're right," Isabelle agreed. "Demented is more the like."

It was Christmas morning, and instead of sitting in front of a roaring fire, enjoying a rather good reproduction of eggnog, here they were, sitting on the steps in front of the keep watching the men play football.

"This is all your fault, you know," Isabelle said in a soft but accusing tone.

"My fault?" Gwen returned. "How do you figure?"

"You taught them how to play," Isabelle reminded her.

Gwen sighed. "He told me to be useful."

"And you listened to him?" Isabelle asked with a laugh. "Good God, Gwendolyn, 'tis one of the most ridiculous things you've ever done."

"Ridiculous?" Gwen repeated. "You know what ridiculous is, Isabelle?" Gwen asked, pulling away to look at her. "*You*, wearing that insanely expensive necklace that Gavin gave you."

"Do you like it? 'Tis quite beautiful." Isabelle beamed, fingering the piece.

"I'll give you that," Gwen agreed. "But you still look ridiculous."

"You look rather ridiculous yourself." Isabelle snorted. "*You* have two medallions around your neck, *and* the scarf you made for Mother."

"So what?" she argued defensively, clutching the medallion Greylen had made her. It was identical to the one she always wore, the one she was still wearing, but this one had a dragon on the front, clasping the torso of his lady as he pulled her from the water. On the back was the same inscription that was inside her wedding band. She had started to ask Greylen what it meant, but the baby chose that exact moment to kick for the first time. She spent the next ten minutes covered by anxious hands as everyone took a turn feeling him move.

"So what?" Isabelle repeated. "*So what?* Is that the best you can do?"

Gwen reached inside Isabelle's sleeves, pressing her freezing hands against the skin on the backs of her arms. Isabelle shrieked, fighting back as she did the same. Soon they were throwing silly insults at each other, and snow, too, as they tried to shove it down each other's backs. So caught up in their antics, they didn't notice Greylen and

Gavin standing before the steps now, arms crossed over their chests, regarding them through narrowed eyes.

"Problem?" the men said at the same time.

Gwen and her sister-in-law both started talking at once. "*Your* wife is insufferable," Isabelle told her brother in gasps as she laughed.

"And *your* sister is a big baby," Gwen blurted out as she laughed too.

Greylen and Gavin rolled their eyes, obviously listening with little interest as she and Isabelle ranted. Their insults were becoming more ludicrous by the second, and each scathing remark they made was belied with a hug as they gathered warmth from each other.

"Can we get back to our game?" Greylen asked impatiently.

"I told you this was all your fault, Gwendolyn," Isabelle muttered. "You just had to make them football jerseys, didn't you?"

"If I recall," Gwen said, casting Isabelle a smug look, "I made you something as well." Isabelle blushed, obviously recalling the scandalous short nightgown she'd made for her. "Had I known you were pregnant," Gwen said, then frowned. "I would have made it a little larger." Isabelle had made the announcement of her pregnancy as they'd opened gifts, clarifying the reason she had made little booties for Gavin. You'd think he would have gotten the hint.

Greylen was frowning at her now. "Yours had better be large enough, Gwendolyn," he warned, speaking of the short nightgown she had made for herself. "I intend to see it on you tonight."

"Oh, you will," Gwen promised, bringing a smile back to her husband's face.

"Can we go back to our game now?" Greylen asked again.

"Go on," Gwen said as she and Isabelle both shooed them away. "We'll just freeze while we watch you play." Their husbands didn't seem too worried and, in fact, turned as soon as they heard the word *go*.

Gwen and Isabelle huddled to keep warm as they watched the men resume their game. And lucky them, it started snowing. The men obviously didn't mind and were soaked and covered in mud by the time they finished. Their smiles were priceless, though, and the only thing besides their eyes that remained white.

After an early supper in the great hall, Isabelle and Gavin joined them in their chamber. They played cards by the fire and listened to music. It was a habit they began shortly after Gavin and Isabelle were married, and now they spent almost all of their evenings together.

Later, Greylen helped her into the black nightgown she had made, stretching the material across her belly. After they made love, Greylen laid her between his thighs, her back against his chest. He covered her stomach with his hands, willing their son to kick.

It became a nighttime ritual, lying together as they felt their baby move. In the beginning, it was a wonderful end to their days, but as the months passed and the baby grew, Gwen dreaded the movements.

"I'm sorry, Gwen. I know it must be terribly uncomfortable."

"Terribly uncomfortable? Greylen, you have no idea." She groaned as the baby turned again, feet and elbows poking her ribs. "He better come soon. He's huge already."

"You said it should be four or five weeks."

"There's really no way to know, Greylen. Some babies come early while others come late."

"And if he is too large?" Greylen asked, fear in his voice.

"Greylen, we've been incredibly lucky," she said truthfully. "We'll come through this too."

"Gwendolyn, you've more knowledge than any of us in such matters. You must use it." He squeezed her to enforce his point. "I'll not lose you."

"Aye, in the throes of labor, I'll remember that." She laughed. "I don't want to talk about it anymore, Greylen. Just make love to me. It's the only thing that makes me feel good these days." Gwen finished her statement with a disgruntled sigh.

"That *was* a compliment you just gave your husband, wasn't it?" he asked, skeptically.

"Aye, 'twas a compliment and you know it."

Making love to her husband, actually her husband making love to her, was the best part of her day, though it was becoming more and more difficult to find a comfortable position.

She knew Greylen felt the same, enjoying the intimacy they continued to share. He loved to find positions better suited to her current condition. He always seemed worried, however, that his lack of control, as he called it, when they made love, would hurt her or the baby.

Gwen didn't miss the look of unease that crossed Greylen's face now. "Oh, good God, Greylen. Stop worrying and ravish your miserable wife." Why he seemed shocked by her outburst escaped her. "I'm sorry, Greylen, please help me. I need to feel you inside me, please."

"You know I'll make love to you, Gwen. And you can count on more than a mere ravishing. I have no control where you're concerned."

Greylen lay on his side and pulled her against him, resting her leg over his hip. He calmed her with his kisses, calmed her with his hands, then entered her from the same position.

Gwen tried to push against him, almost crying in frustration as another position bit the proverbial dust. She felt big and awkward, when all she wanted was to feel consumed.

Greylen sensed her aggravation, fixing her distress by rolling her beneath him. He placed her on all fours and gave in to both their needs. His forceful thrusts penetrated so deep, they cried out in release only a minute later.

"Bless you, husband," Gwen said breathlessly as Greylen lay above her.

Greylen chuckled in her ear, his head resting on the pillow next to hers. He felt their son turn as he held her stomach beneath them. "I fear 'tis a mixed blessing, Gwendolyn."

"After *that*, you've been elevated back to hero worship," she said adoringly.

"When had I joined the lower ranks?" he asked.

"Never." She giggled. "It just sounded good." They remained as they were until their breathing returned to normal. Gwen suddenly became very serious. "You've always been my hero, Greylen, even when you weren't there."

"I'll always be your hero, Gwen, from now until forever."

Two weeks later, Greylen made true to his words. He was just returning from a successful hunt with his men when Ian rode to greet them at a breakneck pace. They'd barely halted their mounts, but Ian's words nearly stopped his heart.

"Gwendolyn calls. Her time is here. 'Tis not going well, Greylen."

His heart constricted as he spurred his black to the keep's entrance, vaulting off the beast before he came to a complete stop. Though Gwen seemed fine this morning and insisted he join his men, he damned himself now for leaving. The keep's doors were already open, and he could hear his wife's distress as he raced up the stairs.

Duncan paced in front of their chamber, holding his hand on the latch as Greylen looked to him for answers.

"It sounds bleak," Duncan told him. "All seemed fine till the last hour, then she called that we bring you as soon as possible. Lady Madelyn and Anna didn't agree with your wife's wishes, but we serve Lady Gwendolyn."

Duncan had ended his statement half in question and Greylen gave him the answer immediately. "Aye, 'tis Lady Gwendolyn whom you serve."

Greylen's heart dropped as he entered their room. Gwen leaned upright against the pillows, her eyes closed, her hair damp and clinging to her face. Isabelle sat beside Gwen, wiping her forehead while his mother and Anna sat between her legs.

"You have to pull him...please," Gwen begged, her voice taxed with exhaustion. "It's been too long." Her shoulders started shaking, and she pleaded with them again. "I need, Greylen, please, *please*."

Greylen rushed to her side and placed his hand on her face as he sat. She opened her eyes. "Greylen, help me. They won't listen."

"Tell me what to do, Gwen," he said. His words were firm, assuring her that he'd do anything in his power to help.

"You need to guide the baby's head out. You have to pull—" Her fingers dug into his skin as she grabbed his wrists, and it took all his abilities to remain in control as he watched her suffer. Then her grip relaxed as the pain seemed to subside.

He heard his mother speak quietly to Anna. "Nothing, he's not moved."

Gwen looked to him again. "He won't come, Greylen, I don't know if the cord is around his neck. I...I can't do it. He could die, help us—please, help us."

Greylen squeezed her hands before standing again. He'd been present and helped with countless births throughout his life. A child, however, was never one of them. Women always saw to such duties, yet for Gwen to call for him, he knew 'twas only his help she wanted. Determined to do just that, he washed his hands in a basin of fresh water. Then fixed his mother and Anna with a look of pure outrage. "MOVE."

They stood instantly, giving him space as he sat on the bed and placed a hand on Gwen's knee. She tried with all her might to push their babe free. Isabelle held her shoulders, forcing her to sit upright as his mother and Anna pleaded with Gwen to push. Her attempts were futile. The babe hadn't moved. Gwen started crying again. "I can't do it, Greylen. Pull him—you have to."

He knew now what she asked of him and looked to her one last time, waiting for her acknowledgment. When she nodded, he didn't hesitate. He'd be damned if he didn't do everything he could to help her, even this. He tried to be gentle as he pushed his fingers around the babe's head, yet his wife's cry said otherwise. She caught her breath and nodded again.

"Put your other hand on my stomach, and when you feel it tighten, pull."

Her next pain came only a minute later. He could feel the tightening she spoke of. His palm hid the babe from his view, but he felt his tiny head between his fingers, his soft skull covered with slick hair. He pulled with the greatest of care as Gwen bore down, then moved his hand from her stomach to catch the baby's head.

Bless her heart, 'twas all the help she needed. His son's head lay in the palm of his hand. "Oh God, Gwen." 'Twasn't even a whisper, and for all he knew the words never came from his lips. But when he looked to her again, awe turned to terror. Her skin was so pale and she was—"Gwendolyn, *noooo!*" Her eyes rolled back and her body went slack. "GWENDOLYN!"

His mother held her hands on Gwen's stomach, as Anna brushed a cloth over her face. Isabelle was crying now, watching helplessly as another cry ripped from his heart. "Gwendolyn!"

Gwen's eyes fluttered open as his mother instructed him. "Greylen, you need to guide his shoulders."

Still holding the babe's head in the palm of his hand, he helped free one shoulder and then the other. He placed his hand beneath the baby's back and continued to pull with the greatest of care. His shoulders racked as he gently squeezed his fingers around his son. Then his head fell back when his son began to wail. "Gwen, we have a son!" He looked to her, tears running down his face as he stared in wonder between the babe in his hands and his crying wife.

"Put the babe on her chest while we see to the afterbirth," his mother instructed.

He shot her a look, holding the baby closer. "Why didn't you help her?"

"Greylen, we were just about to, I swear to you. We only wished to avoid causing her more pain."

Greylen said nothing, still angered that Gwen might have suffered more than necessary, or worse, that she could have died had he not gotten there in time. He carefully moved his son, noticing now that Gwen was reaching out to hold him. He placed him in her hands and covered them with his own. He didn't let go until their babe rested on Gwen's chest.

He sat beside her and pushed the hair off her face, then bent to kiss her. They both cried again, tears of joy and relief.

"Thank you, Greylen," she whispered as he rested his forehead against hers.

"Don't ever scare me like that again." His voice shook, belying the angry undertone of his words.

"I love you too," she said. "I'm so glad you came, Greylen. I don't know what I would have done without you."

Tears still ran down her face and he brushed them away. "I'll always be there, Gwen, always. I thought I'd lost you."

"I'm sorry, Greylen. I'm so tired. I'm just so tired."

Her body slackened again, and he quickly reached out to hold the babe against his wife's chest. "Gwen? *Gwen?*"

Her eyes opened slowly, then she placed her hand on his cheek. "Shh, it's okay, Greylen. Cut the cord," she whispered. "You have to cut the cord now."

Greylen followed his mother's directions, then reached for the babe again. "I'll wash him and bring him right back," he told Gwen as she nodded and closed her eyes.

Isabelle helped him clean his son, his tiny fists smacking the air in anger. "Mother would've helped her, Greylen. She meant what she said."

Greylen had no desire to speak of it anymore and, now, in the aftermath, he was glad Gwen had called for him. "Isabelle, I delivered my own son," Greylen said softly, as if 'twas a secret he was sharing with her.

"Aye, and you did it very well too," Isabelle said admiringly.

Greylen couldn't keep his hands from his son and reached for him again. "Give me a minute," Isabelle balked. "You'll have him the entire night."

Isabelle wrapped him in a blanket and rocked him in the crook of her arm. She passed him back into his impatient hands. "He's so beautiful, Greylen."

When Greylen turned again, his mother and Anna were just finishing with Gwen. The sheets had been changed and her body washed. She looked exhausted as she faced him, but she motioned with her hands for him to come back. He placed the babe upon her chest again and called for a much-needed bath.

"Let me take a quick wash, then I'll come stay with you."

She nodded and held her hands around their son's back. He smiled before leaving her, hearing the soft mewing sounds his son made in his sleep.

Greylen sat in the tub within the bathing chamber, his head against the rim. He'd been so consumed with helping Gwen and listening to instructions, he'd merely followed orders. No questions, no hesitation. Now, however, the results of his actions were astounding. Not only was he present for the birth of his first child, he'd been the one to deliver him. *He delivered his own son.* He started laughing as the words repeated in his head. He'd delivered his own son.

He grabbed his robe, anxious to join his family on their bed. *His family*: Gwendolyn and their babe. He wanted to shout from the top of a mountain, his joy was so great.

He finally lay next to them, grateful to see the color back in Gwen's face. "Are you comfortable, love?" he asked.

"Nay." She laughed as she brushed one of her hands over Greylen's face. "Hold the baby while I sit up. He needs to be fed." Greylen helped her sit instead, letting her hold the babe while he adjusted her. He took the babe and laid him between his legs. "Open the blanket, Greylen. I want to see him again."

"'Tis what I'm doing," he said with a grin. "You've not had a chance to really look at him."

They stroked his little body, counting his fingers and toes. They laughed as the baby latched on to Greylen's finger. They finally wrapped him again and Greylen watched in awe as Gwen nursed him for the first time. Then he helped her change and swaddle him again.

He lost track of how many times they kissed him, of how many times they kissed each other, as the babe lay between them.

A cradle sat beside their bed, but they'd not place him in it. Anna now slept in the chamber next to theirs, a complete nursery. Their babe wouldn't see it for days, mayhap even weeks.

"Gwen?"

"Aye, Greylen?"

"You wish to name him Tristan, don't you?"

"We can name him whatever you want, Greylen. He wouldn't be here without you."

"'Tis Tristan then. Tristan Allister MacGreggor."

"Tristan Allister MacGreggor," she said, looking down at their son, "this is your daddy." Then she looked back to Greylen, taking his face in her hand. "My hero."

❧ CHAPTER THIRTY-ONE ❧

Tristan Allister MacGreggor was christened on a warm summer day. Gwen basked in the joy she felt from Greylen, who stood proudly by her side, Gavin and Isabelle next to them as they held their godson.

The weeks that followed Tristan's birth created a bond between Gwen and Greylen that astounded them both. From that first night Tristan lay between them—in the aftermath of his birth and everything that had happened throughout the previous year—they now had a child they created together. Their love could not have been stronger.

Tristan stayed in their chamber every night, in the cradle beside their bed. Greylen would always pick him up and hold him before handing him off so she could nurse him. He was a very large boy and it was no wonder she'd had such a hard time delivering him. Her husband told her he considered having no more for fear that she'd not make it through another, but Gwen only laughed, assuring him that the next would most likely fall out. He seemed appalled at her words, but finally laughed with her. He wasn't fooling her, though, she sensed he secretly considered leaving Tristan an only child rather than watch her suffer again.

Gwen wasn't scared at all of having more children, and in fact, her strength returned quickly. Lady Madelyn took over her duties of seeing to the keep and, other than nursing their son, Gwen really didn't have any responsibilities. Anna always kept her chamber in impeccable order and there were so many helping hands she was actually quite rested, despite waking every two hours to feed her demanding son.

Three nights after Tristan's birth, she awoke alone. She looked throughout the room cast in a glow of firelight, but Greylen and Tristan were nowhere to be seen.

She wasn't sure why she got out of bed and walked to the window, but something compelled her. The full moon shone brightly that night and she saw him immediately, her husband standing on the cliff's edge. His dark hair blew in the breeze, his arms stretched toward the sky. Their son in the palms of his hands, as if showing him to the gods.

It was a sight she would always remember. She stepped back as he turned, leaving this moment just for him. He returned a short time later and placed Tristan back in his cradle before joining her. Then he pulled her in his arms as she pretended to sleep. She listened to his Gaelic whispers, understanding everything he said. He thanked the gods for her and his son and he vowed to love and protect them for all eternity.

As the days passed, she began taking short walks and joining the family for meals in the great hall. In the afternoons, she stayed in the library, or, if Greylen was working in his study, she sat there with him.

It was on one of those afternoons as she sat on the window seat that his men presented him with a gift. They had gathered around the table and handed Greylen a wrapped package. He opened it and removed a jersey that they had one of the servants fashion. She learned later that Anna had refused to make it.

It was a jersey, identical to the one she had made for him, but when he turned it to look at the back, he fixed them with a furious stare. His men were laughing so hard their hands beat on the tabletop.

"What is it, Greylen?" she asked, puzzled by his reaction.

He turned it for her to see. She laughed so hard tears rolled from her eyes.

"You find this humorous?" he demanded, but he was smiling, too, and even laughed himself.

The jersey had large white letters on the back, but it wasn't his name that was sewn on it. No, it read Midwife.

"They have a point, husband," she choked out. "Now you'll have something to wear for my next delivery."

"Nay." He scoffed. "Gavin shall be the next," he said, turning to his first-in-command. "You'll wear it to deliver your own children."

"I still owe you a beating for setting such a precedent."

"Aye, you might, but Isabelle insists you be present." Greylen grinned. "I relish the day."

Gwen had just ordered Isabelle to strict bed rest. By the beginning of her third month, Gwen informed them that Isabelle was carrying twins. It was easy to tell, even without her stethoscope, which confirmed the two heartbeats. Isabelle had been so overcome with nausea and fatigue, and she started to show *very* quickly. Isabelle was terrified after Gwen's delivery, but Gwen assured her that she'd be fine. Gwen also offered Gavin's assistance. He had no choice but to agree.

Things became somewhat normal again. Greylen and his men saw to their summertime duties with enthusiasm, and Gwen began to exercise again. Her body was finally returning to normal and with her runs and sit-ups she felt better than ever. Greylen ran with her in the early mornings after she fed the baby. And now that Tristan was sleeping in the nursery with Anna, they left him in her care for the hour they were gone.

They were so consumed with a new baby that their birthdays and anniversary had passed with little fanfare. But Greylen did commemorate both occasions. The first being their birthdays. The night he'd pulled her from the water one year ago.

He took her to the shore and, since they only had an hour as Tristan was a few weeks old, Greylen had had everything prepared. There was a roaring fire when they arrived, and he held her between his legs as they shared the moment alone. Then he surprised her again, removing her iPhone and speaker he secretly tucked in a satchel. "I propose a new tradition, wife," he said, holding her tightly.

"Do I have to sing?" she teased, looking up.

"God forbid." Greylen laughed. "Although, when we're sotted, 'tis not so bad."

"Get on with it, husband. What's this new tradition?"

"Since it's my idea, I'll be the first," he said with a squeeze. "But I thought that every year we could each choose a song to dance to."

"I'm impressed," Gwen exclaimed.

"Shut up, Gwendolyn." He laughed. "Join your husband." He stood, leaving her for only a minute as he pressed buttons. Then he held her in his arms, moving her around the fire as he whispered the words of "I'll Be" by Edwin McCain.

For their anniversary, he surprised her with a special dinner in the great hall. His family and men were present, and Tristan joined them, passed between everyone as they took pleasure in the entire evening together. Gwen even enjoyed a small amount of wine for the first time in months. But she became so tipsy, Greylen had to carry her upstairs, teasing her as she giggled in his arms.

They made love that night for the first time since Tristan's birth. It couldn't have been a more appropriate way to celebrate their anniversary, but when Greylen first entered her, she cried out in pain. He withdrew instantly, holding her tightly in his arms. "I'm sorry, love."

"Please, don't stop."

"I won't cause you pain, Gwen."

"It's just this first time," she promised. "Make love to me, Greylen."

He entered her again, slowly this time, and must have felt her wince. He lay motionless on top of her, his arms around her head as he looked to her. She could tell he wanted to stop and took his face in her hands. Then she whispered to him, words she knew would make him understand.

They were the words he always whispered to her, the words inscribed on her wedding band and medallion. She understood them now and gave them back to him. The look he gave her was indescribable and one she would cherish for the rest of her life. Then he whispered back, "*Tha thusa gu bràth mo ghràdh.*" You are forever my love.

Her husband made love to her so tenderly that night, loving her with his body as he never had before.

Isabelle gave birth to two healthy babies before summer's end. Her delivery was long, but she came through it easily. Gavin was, indeed, present, and Greylen insisted that he wear the jersey. He did begrudgingly, though Gwen was the one to deliver Gavin's sons. Gavin sat by Isabelle, helping her through her labor, clearly wishing to be anywhere but at his wife's side. Her pain was just too much it seemed for him to bear. Greylen knew exactly how he felt.

Gwen had demanded that Gavin hold the first baby when he was born, and he did, watching in pure awe as the second was born. He cut their cords as Gwen instructed, crying like a babe as Greylen taunted. Gavin damned him for being right. But in the end, he admitted he was glad to have been there.

His nephews, Ethan and Collin, kept their mother busy. In fact, they kept everyone busy. Three babies now occupied the women during the day and the men gladly helped, too, when they could.

Greylen began to steal his wife away in the early afternoons so he could teach her to ride. He was so proud of her skills, he gifted her with a mare, prouder still when she insisted on caring for the animal herself. They rode together in the afternoons, and on the occasions that he couldn't accompany her, she was allowed to ride alone, though one of his men always followed her from a distance.

As Tristan's feedings decreased, Gwen started boxing with Gavin. Greylen even took to it himself, incorporating it in routines with his men. 'Twas Gwen's talk of marathons that intrigued him most, her constant teasing of her endurance that finally got the better of him.

He watched her as she sat on the steps one morning, her eyes narrowing as his men raised flags along the path and later rode out with more secured to their mounts. Greylen joined her, taking Tristan from her arms and kissing his belly.

"Greylen?"

"Aye, wife," he said, knowing exactly what was on her mind.

"What are the men doing?"

He heaved a sigh and rolled his eyes. "They're raising flags, love," he replied, like she'd not understand his statement.

"I know they're raising flags," she hissed. "Why?"

"I've proposed a race." He grinned, throwing Tristan in the air.

"I've just fed him," she cried. "He'll spit up all over the place."

"Nay, he'll be fine."

Gwen sighed; she obviously knew Tristan loved to be jostled by him. "Tell me of this race, husband."

"'Tis nothing really," he teased.

"You lie." She laughed, swatting his arm.

"Very well…if you must know…" He purposely didn't finish.

"Tell me!"

He threw his head back and laughed. Tristan laughed with him. "I thought to run one of your marathons," he explained. "If you're a *good wife*, and I use that term very loosely, I may let you join us."

"You *may* let me join you," she said, standing, hands upon her hips now. "I'll be joining your damn race. Wild horses couldn't stop me."

"Tristan, your mama's gifted us with yet another phrase from her sorry past."

"That happens to be a great phrase. Store it in your sorry memory bank."

Their banter was interrupted as riders approached. Greylen handed Tristan to Gwen and walked to the courtyard to greet them. They'd been escorted by Duncan and Ian. Greylen took a missive from one of the men's outstretched hands and read it. Then exchanged words with the men as Gavin rode into the courtyard. Gavin dismounted and Greylen filled him in as they headed back toward Gwen.

"What is it, Greylen?" Gwen asked as he stood before her.

"Malcolm's been captured. Our king awaits my presence to see justice done."

At first, she seemed relieved that he'd been caught, then she must have realized what he'd also said. She looked terrified. "I must go, Gwen. I'll sail on the morrow. It should only be days," he assured her, taking her hand. "A week at most."

His wife nodded but held Tristan more closely. He pulled them both into his arms. "Gavin and I have things to see to," he told her. "Would you like me to take you upstairs?"

"Nay," she whispered. "I'll see if Cook needs help before supper."

He and his men made their way to his study. There was much to see to before he left. As was their habit, they surrounded the table, standing as each took their orders. Greylen walked back and forth between the table and maps that covered the wall, marking the placement of his ships with colorful pins. The ones currently in their port and tagging the position of the others from the latest word they'd received.

Greylen knew Gwen kept busy in the kitchen that afternoon. Later, he sensed her presence and when he glanced to the doorway, he found her standing there. He smiled and was about to wave her in, but she only smiled back and quickly walked away.

They dined together in the great hall that night. Greylen knew his wife did her best to put forth a brave face, but she was clearly upset. He would try to ease her fears later, assuring her that they could at last live at peace. She'd need no further guards and the threat of Malcolm returning was finally over.

They made love by the fire and again in their bed. He brought Tristan in from the nursery so Gwen could feed him. After taking him back to Anna, he gathered Gwen in his arms, pressing her back to his chest. "I'd have you come with me, Gwen," he said.

She turned. "You'd take me?" she asked.

"'Tis what I just said," he remarked dryly, though he smiled and hugged her closer.

She shook her head. "Nay, just knowing you'd take me makes me feel better."

"Why's that, love?"

"If you feel that I'd be safe, then I know you'll be safe too."

"How is it, wife, that 'tis I whom you always worry over?"

"I know you'll keep me safe, Greylen, you always have. You've never let me down, not once. It's only natural that I feel the same."

Her thoughts were so sweet that he dared not laugh at her. But she had, indeed, saved his life before and he'd not belittle her offer of protection. "Gwen, you may move more freely now, but you must always let one of my men know where you're going. Do you understand?"

"Aye, husband, I understand. I can still run longer distances, though, can't I? You still intend to hold the race?"

"Aye, four weeks from today. We've already done two of the long runs you've talked of. You need only two more, right?"

"Aye," she said quickly, "I'll have one of the men follow when I do, I promise."

"Save the last for me," he whispered as he kissed her. "It's fun to push you faster."

"You're sick in the head, husband. Don't think for a second that I'm not aware you do it purposely. But you've only made me faster, Greylen. In fact, I'm gonna kick your ass."

He did laugh at her boast that time. "I love you, Gwen."

"I love you, too, Greylen."

❧ CHAPTER THIRTY-TWO ❧

Greylen and Gavin sailed early the next morning. They left only Kevin and Hugh behind.

Gwen missed Greylen terribly in the days that followed, but she kept busy and thankfully, the time passed quickly. She went for short runs in the morning and spent her days with Isabelle and the children. It was nice to have some time alone with her sister-in-law, and they took full advantage. Every night they ate decadent meals in her chamber, followed by girl talk in front of the fire.

The fourth morning after Greylen's departure, Gwen awoke earlier than usual and decided it would be the perfect morning to go for her long run. She fed Tristan right before she left, knowing that she had at least four or five hours before he would need her again. He'd just started eating solid foods—oatmeal and pureed fruits—and Anna gave him breakfast now in the great hall with Lady Madelyn.

Greylen's mother loved spending time with her grandson and watched him until his late-morning nap. Gwen gave Lady Madelyn this time alone, never bothering her unless she felt she'd burst from the pressure of not feeding him, or, as was often the case, her son became so fussy that Lady Madelyn had no choice but to seek her.

When she left the keep, Alex stood just beyond the doors. He'd been promoted from the ranks of the soldiers and was now training to become one of her husband's elite circle of men. He'd had her guard on many occasions and the seriousness with which he saw to his duties dubbed him the nickname Captain. Not that the term didn't apply to others in Greylen's ranks, but Gwen used the name affectionately with Alex. He was ruggedly handsome, quick with a smile, and even faster with a glare. And in her book, that meant he was in. Greylen seemed to have a penchant for surrounding himself with control freaks. Alex was no different.

"Good morn, Captain," she offered as she stood beside him.

"Good morn, Lady Gwendolyn," he returned. "Off for your morning run?"

"Aye, I'll most likely take my long one," she told him. "I'll not return for some time."

"Very well," he acknowledged. "Kevin rides just beyond the lake," he said, pointing in its direction, as if she didn't know where it was. "Make sure you inform him of this before you continue from there."

"Aye, aye, Captain." She saluted, hearing his chuckle as she headed down the stairs.

Gwen smiled as she began her run. It was a perfect morning. The air was cool and crisp, and the sun was just high enough now that it warmed her face. She started thinking of what she and Isabelle might have for dinner, trying to recall what she'd seen in the pantry and cellar. She'd spent the last two days in the kitchen with Cook going over lists of appropriate foods and recipes for Tristan. It was the first time that Cook gave her "the look." The one that claimed her daft. Feeling like a typical first-time mother, Gwen respectfully withdrew.

She had finally come up with the perfect menu when she realized she passed the lake—*way* passed the lake. She couldn't bring herself to turn around, and for the next hour hoped that no one realized she didn't have a shadow. As long as Tristan didn't get fussy, and Kevin stayed clear of Alex, they'd never know. And if they did—God help her—she was in deep trouble. And not just from Greylen. They would all kill her.

She stayed close to the forest, seeking the stream, which was a few yards within, every so often. When she finished, she headed for water one last time. She felt beyond good. There was nothing better than a runner's high. Her cheeks were hot, her legs felt like rubber, and she had to put her hands on her head to catch her breath. She was still kneeling over the stream when riders approached.

She continued to drink, all the while breathlessly explaining that she'd come clean to Greylen.

Then she heard a laugh that chilled her to the very bone.

Alex was atop the steps when Lady Madelyn came outside with Tristan on her hip. The poor lad was in a deep fit, and Alex reached out instantly to pat his back. "Good afternoon, Lady Madelyn," he called out, trying to be heard over Tristan's screams. He winced at the boy's cry before he could continue. "What seems to be the problem with our boy?" he asked in concern.

"Alex, has Lady Gwendolyn returned?"

"Returned?" His hand stilled on the babe's back. "She's not come back with Kevin?"

"Nay, Kevin's in—"

Alex was gone.

"Sir," Alex bellowed as he came into the study.

"Aye, Alex," Kevin said, looking up. "What troubles you?"

"I had the morning guard outside the doors. I was replaced for an hour to oversee the training with Hugh and returned just now."

"Your point?" Kevin asked.

"Lady Gwendolyn left early this morn. She was given my instruction to inform you of her desire to run the distance before leaving the area of the lake."

"I never spoke to her," Kevin yelled, coming out of his chair. "Are you sure she's not returned?"

"Tristan should've been fed an hour ago, Kevin," Lady Madelyn explained, having come in behind Alex.

"Alex, round the men," Kevin barked. "We'll find her, Lady Madelyn," he assured, coming to her side. "She's probably just become lost or suffered a minor injury." Both men knew she would have made it back in either case.

"Find my daughter, Kevin," she ordered. "Bring her home."

"Aye, lady."

Alex ran from the keep, alerting James to ready the horses. Then he took off for the practice fields to find Hugh. He felt personally responsible as he was the last to speak with Lady Gwendolyn. Her smile and salute replaying in his mind as she assured him that she would, indeed, speak to Kevin.

Fifteen search parties of ten set off in different directions, and fifty men stayed behind. Forty stood outside the keep's closed gates while ten remained within.

Kevin, Hugh, and Alex rode alone, taking the path they were sure their mistress ran that morning.

"Mother, what on earth's wrong?" Isabelle asked, coming into the nursery. "I've never heard him carry on so."

"Gwen hasn't returned from her run, and the men just left to search for her."

Isabelle walked to her mother, rubbing her eyes. She was exhausted, too tired to display the alarm that she felt. "When was he last fed?" she asked, reaching for her nephew.

"Anna thinks before dawn. Gwen left earlier than usual according to Alex."

"Shh, shh, shh, 'tis okay, Tristan. Mama will be home soon. Shh, shh, shh." 'Twas no use, he was in a deep fit. "Well, what's one more mouth to feed." Isabelle sighed. "Come, sweet, we'll have you asleep in no time."

"We could find a wet nurse, Isabelle."

"I'm the embodiment of a wet nurse," Isabelle declared in exasperation. "I could probably feed every babe upon the holding if I had to."

"I'll come fetch him in a while so you may rest."

"Please tell me of Gwen, Mother, as soon as you hear something."

"Of course, Isabelle."

By midafternoon, Alex's, Kevin's, and Hugh's worst fears were confirmed. Their mistress had been taken, and from the evidence they found, by force. Her medallions hung from a tree trunk and fresh blood spotted the stream's edge where she'd obviously been surrounded and knocked to the ground.

They counted five sets of tracks and followed their path. She'd tried to outrun them. Torn brush revealed the signs of her struggle as she tried to make open land but yards away. They happened on the boulder where she'd lost her fight. 'Twas covered with blood and strands of her hair. Her wedding band was displayed atop.

Kevin ordered Alex and Hugh to return. The search parties were to meet at dusk and they'd follow the trail after regrouping. Alex, however, refused to leave. "I'll not go. I'm directly responsible for her."

"Alex, you were relieved," Kevin reminded him again. "Had you been there the entire time and seen me return alone, what would you have done?"

"I would have asked the whereabouts of Lady Gwendolyn, sir."

"Precisely," Kevin ground out. "You ordered her to seek my regard, did you not?"

"Aye, sir."

"Go with Hugh, Alex. Follow his instruction."

"Nay, sir." Alex stood defiant.

"Come then." Kevin finally relented in frustration. "I'll waste no more time."

"We'll be but hours behind," Hugh assured them as he turned back to the holding.

Gwen regained consciousness surrounded by total darkness. She lay on a damp, soiled floor, confused and in pain. Unfortunately, her confusion didn't last long. Her entire body started shaking as she relived each second that they had chased her. Every blow that Malcolm delivered— first with his fists and then with his boot after she'd been knocked to the ground.

She tried to outrun them. She even tried to fight them. In the end, she was powerless. They even laughed at her. Fresh tears ran from her eyes and she reached for her medallions. She gasped when they weren't there. Then she screamed. Her wedding band was gone too.

She shuddered as she remembered Malcolm's taunts. She had no doubt that he'd see them through. They were going to kill her. And when Greylen came to collect what was left of her, they would kill him as well.

If that wasn't enough to make her want to die right then and there, she had to live with the knowledge of why. Live with *that* for whatever time she had left.

It was entirely her fault.

She had let them take her, and now she had placed her men in danger. All because she wanted to run...all because she didn't seek her guard. How could she have been so stupid? "Orders are given for a reason, wife." *Why hadn't she listened?* If only she had turned around.

Her despair lasted for hours. Then she felt her dagger against her hip, and with it, the tiniest spark of hope. She knew what she had to do, and resolved that she would.

She wiped away her tears and crawled along the damp surface. She had to be in the dungeons below Malcolm's keep, in a cell no more than ten feet wide and ten feet deep. Thick wooden posts barred the opening, secured with a heavy metal lock.

A strange calmness overcame her. The same that she had felt when she realized she had a weapon. It wasn't enough to gain her freedom, but that wasn't important anymore. She began humming as she pulled away the hair matted against the side of her face.

She had a deep gash high on her forehead and a cut across her cheek, a gift from Malcolm's ring as it ripped through the skin when he backhanded her. She didn't have any broken bones, but her body was swollen and bruised from his kicks.

After her clinical assessment, she hugged the material of Greylen's shirt, the one that he'd worn to dinner the night before he left. His scent gave her courage.

And she waited.

To kill Malcolm herself.

❧ CHAPTER THIRTY-THREE ❧

Greylen and Gavin were granted immediate entrance to Stirling Castle. They rode to the inner bailey where they dismounted and were promptly relieved of their mounts. It took some time before they reached the steps, greeted by men they'd not seen for months, and in the case of some, even years.

Once inside they were ushered to a private chamber where they awaited their king. He entered a short time later, flanked by guards, and they were heartily embraced by the man whom they'd served valiantly over the years.

They enjoyed brandy and discussed personal matters first: Greylen's marriage and the birth of his son, and Gavin's marriage and sons as well. The king's joy for them couldn't have been more apparent, and he congratulated them and gave his blessings. He did inform them that he'd already known, for news of the two most sought-after bachelors taking brides had quickly swept the land.

Turning to his guards, he called for the prisoner. It took only minutes as they knew Laird MacGreggor's reason for being present and, in fact, had already sent for him.

Greylen and Gavin stood as the door opened. They turned in unison to condemn Malcolm and seek a quick end to his life. He was held by the shoulders, his head cast down. He was filthy, and the clothes he wore were torn. His hair was just as dirty, and blood clung in patches where he'd been beaten.

Greylen walked to him, lifting his head by the chin. He stared into the distorted features, so similar to Gavin and Malcolm, but the eyes that pleaded mercy held no malice.

Worse—they were brown.

"Who are you?" Greylen demanded.

"James MacIntyre, sir," the man said weakly.

"How did you come to be here, James?" Greylen asked.

"I was overtaken by a group of men, and later found myself in a cell, accused of crimes, which I'd not committed."

"These men who overtook you, what know you of them?"

"'Twas a group of five, and they remarked on my resemblance to their leader. They spoke of their plan as they began beating me. 'Twas the last thing I remember."

Their king spoke quickly, coming out of his chair to stand next to Greylen. "He was brought here by four men last week. They stated 'twas Malcolm, and I believed them, Greylen," he said emphatically. "He does in fact resemble your man," he added in justification, looking to Gavin.

"What were they told of the bounty on his head?" Greylen asked, hoping that their plan was to await him and Gavin.

"I informed them you'd be notified," their sovereign said quickly. "And when you arrived, they could collect their coin."

"James," Greylen demanded again. "What of their plan? Have you any recall?"

"Bits and pieces," the man replied, shaking his head. "But they made no sense."

"Speak them, no matter how insignificant."

"They spoke of numbers," James began. "The days 'twould take for 'the bastard' to reach…to reach Stirling." He hesitated. "Then they spoke of a woman."

"What woman?" Greylen shouted, taking the man by the shoulders, shaking him as his face contorted in rage.

James hesitated no more. "I mean no disrespect, sir. His exact words…were…'MacGreggor's bi—'"

Greylen and Gavin were gone before he finished. They raced from the castle and straight to the stables. Their mounts gained quickly, their breakneck pace taking them with record speed to the pier.

Most of the ship's crew had been given the day to explore the port and spend their coins. And there, they would remain.

Greylen and Gavin ran up the plank, each shouting orders to their captain and the few men still aboard. Duncan and Connell went for the anchor, their hands working in perfect symmetry as they pulled the length. Greylen and Gavin took to the main mast, climbing high into the air to untie the sail. They grabbed the ropes and jumped at the same time, the white sail dancing to life as they descended to the deck below. Greylen assumed command of his vessel, calling orders as he navigated their way to open waters.

He was their captain now.

He would take them home.

Though the wind was in their favor, they had such a diminished crew that they worked endlessly for the two days it took to reach Seagrave. The entire time, barely a word was exchanged. By any of them. There was nothing to say. Their only need now was to arrive before Malcolm carried through with his plan.

Greylen and Gavin stood at the bow, their legs braced apart, their arms crossed over their bare chests, as they entered the cove at Seagrave. Their swords rested within their scabbards and they stood ready. But they knew not for what.

"They are but five, Greylen," Gavin said, as if trying to offer a modicum of comfort.

"Aye," Greylen replied, turning to look at Gavin. "And she is but one."

"She knows to have her guard," Gavin assured him.

"I relaxed her watch, Gavin. She had need only to inform them of her movements."

Gavin said nothing else. Only one man would follow his wife. Against five if they'd somehow breeched the land, they'd have little chance.

Their worst fears were confirmed as they dropped anchor. Their men were already moving for the narrow paths, riderless mounts behind them.

Malcolm was back.

Not wasting time to lower the dory, Greylen and Gavin removed their boots and climbed the railing. Daggers in hand, swords across their backs, they jumped to the water below. Ian, Connell, and Duncan followed but seconds behind.

They reached the shore minutes later, where Hugh waited just beyond the water's edge.

Greylen stood before his man, fixing him a stare that demanded answers.

Hugh began immediately. "Her medallions were found affixed to a tree by a dagger. 'Twas a struggle, Greylen. We found blood and strands of her hair, her wedding band as well," he reported, holding out the items.

Greylen grasped his wife's possessions, his heart plummeting as he waited for Hugh to continue.

"Kevin and Alex followed the tracks south. I'd just returned to gather the men when I saw the ship. The men wait in the bailey."

"Who had her watch?" Greylen demanded through clenched teeth.

"She informed Alex that she would run the distance and was instructed to seek Kevin before leaving the area of the lake." Hugh paused. "He never saw her, Greylen. Alex was relieved for a time, unaware she'd not returned until Lady Madelyn sought her to feed Tristan."

"When did she leave?"

"Shortly after dawn."

"How. Long. Hugh?" Greylen asked, enunciating each word through his teeth.

"Seven hours, Greylen. They've had her at least seven hours."

"Disband the men. We ride alone."

Greylen stormed through his chamber doors, allowing but a second of scrutiny as he took in its emptiness. He grabbed his boots, quickly pulling them in place before slipping his dagger inside. He reached within his wardrobe and removed a sealed jar atop the shelf. He opened it, spreading the blue paint across his forehead, cheeks, and more across his chest.

He left his chamber at the same moment Gavin left his. Gavin's image was an exact reflection, as he, too, chose war paint. Isabelle was holding Tristan and met him on the landing. His son began to cry, reaching out with his arms. Greylen took him immediately, hushing his cry as he hugged him. He brushed some of the paint on his son's forehead and cheeks.

"You've a wet nurse, Isabelle?" Greylen asked.

"No one feeds your son but me," she returned, clearly challenging him to argue.

Greylen nodded his acknowledgment as he handed Tristan to her. Then he and Gavin took the stairs. Their men were waiting just below the steps. Within seconds they were racing through the night.

It took four hours to reach their border and two more before the MacFale keep was in sight. Kevin waited just outside the gates, bare chested, his shirt clutched in his hand. His eyes held a look Greylen had never before seen.

"Alex has been taken," Kevin said immediately, stopping any questions that Greylen might have had. "He offered himself in return for his mistress. I've no idea where he is inside," Kevin reported, shaking his head. "I was told if I entered the gates before you arrived, they would kill her." For the first time since he began stating the facts as he knew them, Kevin hesitated. Worse, he looked down before meeting Greylen's stare again. "Greylen, she's…"

"She's what, Kevin?" Greylen demanded.

"She's in the courtyard." As if unable to report her condition to his laird, he looked down again. But he handed his shirt to Gavin before he could pass.

Greylen walked to the gates with Gavin. They stepped through with unwavering strides, no sound escaped their lips, no emotion showed upon their faces as the full moon revealed the condition Kevin could not himself divulge.

The debasement of his wife! *His wife!*

She'd been tied to a post, secured by ropes at her ankles and her wrists. She'd been stripped as well, and her body was covered with dark patches that he knew, even from such a distance, were bruises. Her face was cut and bleeding and her body shook visibly—not from the cool night air.

He'd *never* felt more rage in his entire life.

He walked through the courtyard, his eyes only on his wife. He heard his men ride through the gates and saw the doors of the keep open. But he didn't glance their way. Nothing could deter his steps as he made his way to Gwen.

He stopped in front of her and removed his dagger as he held her unseeing eyes. One so swollen, 'twas almost completely closed. She flinched as he reached out to touch her. She didn't realize 'twas him. He whispered in Gaelic, words she would know could only come from him. He watched as she at last tried to focus her gaze. He took his dagger and moved the blade across his forehead, waiting until blood covered his face. He showed her first that she was no different than he. She seemed to understand, for a tear slid from the eye she could still see from.

He stepped closer to her, molding his body to hers. She flinched in pain but made no sound. He knew it had to be excruciating but didn't stop until his body was pressed completely against her. He reached behind her to cut the ropes that held her hands as Gavin cut those around her ankles. Her weight fell forward immediately, but his body kept her upright. He would not let her topple before Malcolm. 'Twas the reason he'd stood so before cutting her loose.

Greylen pulled her with him as he took a step back. Gavin stood behind her and slipped the shirt over her head. Then Gavin wrapped his arms around her waist, his elbows bracing her hips while his forearms held her torso upright against his chest. This allowed Greylen to give his wife another piece of dignity. He secured her medallions around her neck, then reached for her left hand, gently lifting it to his mouth. He placed her ravaged fingers inside and wet them so he could return her band. She made no move, no sound at all, as he slipped it on her finger. Her silence was more frightening than any hysterical outburst could have been.

As God was his witness, he would have welcomed such a display.

He pulled her against his side and turned to face MacFale's keep as Gavin pushed his body to her other side for support. He knew his men would have easily gained entrance, and whatever struggle had occurred should be over. If their fury was even half of his, the task would've taken mere seconds. Malcolm would be the only man left when they were done. Purposely, as if on cue, his men came through the keep's front doors, dragging Malcolm between them.

Greylen waited as Duncan and Ian brought Malcolm before them. They threw him to the ground. Gwen started shaking uncontrollably as Malcolm fixed her with a sneer.

At the same time, Greylen and Gavin kicked him in the face. They waited until he righted himself. "Look at her, Malcolm," Greylen demanded. "Look at her!"

Instead, Malcolm turned away. They lowered Gwen, then grabbed at Malcolm and sat him upright. Greylen clutched the back of his head, forcing him to look at his wife.

"You shall *die* for what you've done to her. And your soul will rot in hell—FOREVER!"

Greylen threw him to the ground again but feet away from Gwen, who continued to stare unseeingly before her. She sat upon the spot where they'd placed her and had not moved at all.

Greylen and Gavin knelt on either side of Malcolm as Duncan and Ian held his arms and legs. Their daggers still in hand from releasing Gwen, they sliced diagonally through their palms. Then they joined their hands together above Malcolm's prone body.

This kill would be both of theirs.

Greylen reached behind his back and unsheathed his sword, placing its tip over Malcolm's heart. Then he and Gavin covered the hilt together and raised the blade.

Greylen felt a hand upon his shoulder at the same time that Gavin looked up. Greylen turned his face, tilting his head to look up at Gwen. He intended to justify his actions. Malcolm must die, surely she realized that. The words, however, caught in his throat.

His wife stood calmly by his side. Her fingers, hesitant at first, brushed his forehead and cheeks, then pressed deeply into his skin. With that same deliberation, she rubbed her fingers across her own face, covering herself with the paint she purposely took from him. She said not a word, but her next actions made her intentions clear. His wife extended her arms, locking her elbows as she placed her torn, bloody hands before them, palms up.

Her silent demand to be a part of this kill.

Greylen and Gavin reached for their daggers. Greylen saw and felt her push against each of their blades. They cut diagonally from one end to the other, just as they had done themselves. Then they placed her hands on the hilt and covered them with their own.

They didn't look at Malcolm as they raised the blade, only at the hands joined together in the center. Three sets of hands once joined so long ago as they stood before Father Michael. Tonight, those same hands joined again. In vengeance.

Greylen and Gavin brought the sword down with such force it embedded deep within the ground beneath Malcolm's body. They never looked at him again.

With the greatest of care, Greylen pried his wife's hands from the hilt of his sword. Then he cradled her broken body. He looked at none of his men as he walked with her from the courtyard. He only looked ahead. 'Twas all he could do.

He would look only ahead.

Alex and the elder MacFale were found badly beaten in the dungeons below the keep. Gavin ordered the men onward so their wounds could be tended. Greylen, however, rode back slowly. He was as silent as Gwen. Gavin, too, was silent as he followed behind them throughout the long journey.

Greylen turned toward the lake before entering the gates of Seagrave. He cradled Gwen in his arms as he walked into the water and held her in the shallows as Gavin washed the dirt and blood from her body and hair. She stared at the sky, silent.

Gavin left to fetch a clean shirt, and they carefully slipped it over her head when Greylen stepped from the water. The soaked shirt they had placed on her hours ago remained on the shore, a painful reminder that neither could touch.

The sun was just beginning to rise as they took the stairs. Greylen glanced to Gavin, who returned a look of sorrow so deep 'twas hard to speak.

"I'll send for Lady Madelyn," Gavin said hoarsely.

Greylen couldn't speak, he only nodded in reply and held Gwen more closely. Gavin came back mere moments later. "No one's about," Gavin assured him as he held the door. Then followed again as Greylen took the stairs to his chamber.

Greylen sat on the chair in front of the fireplace and waited for his mother. She must have been close by, for she appeared just as he settled. She placed a cup to Gwen's lips, which Gwen drank with no prodding. Gwen sat unflinching in his lap as his mother stitched the wound on her forehead. His mother began looking for other wounds, but Greylen only shook his head, silently informing her there were none to be sewn.

She left as quietly as she had arrived, brushing her hand across Gavin's shoulder as she passed him where he stood outside the chamber doors.

Finally hearing the latch click into place, alone with his wife, Greylen gave in, his roars of agony filled with despair. He was so lost in his own sorrow that he would later find out the battle being waged beyond his chamber.

That of Gavin's own battle as he beat his head upon the back of Greylen's door for each bellow that escaped his commander's lips. Of Isabelle's pleas as she knelt by her husband's side, begging him to stop. He would learn that it continued for so long that Isabelle finally collapsed at

Gavin's feet, jarred awake hours later when Duncan lifted her into his arms. He was told, his sister's last memory as she was taken away was the sight of her husband standing sentinel at her brother's door. His door now marred with Gavin's blood.

Greylen didn't know how long he remained on that chair with Gwen in his arms, but the defeat that swept through him that morning was something he had never experienced before. He had no idea what happened in those hours that they held her, only that she was badly beaten and so traumatized she still couldn't speak.

He finally placed her on their bed and crawled in beside her, holding her in his arms. She slept deeply from the potion his mother had given her, but not peacefully. She trembled and cried out, caught in nightmares he'd not been able to awaken her from.

Hours later, he called for Gavin. He had to find out what happened during the time she'd been held. His mother had already given Gwen more drink to ease her pain, but 'twasn't her body that hurt. Her mind was broken. He tried to find a spot where he could place his lips, just one tiny spot where he could give her comfort.

He finally stepped from the bed, watching in agony as Gwen curled into a ball. The move had to cause excruciating pain, yet she didn't make a sound. His mother took his place immediately, humming softly as she brushed her fingers through his wife's hair. He dressed quickly and left the chamber.

He went to the nursery first. Anna was busy with Isabelle and the babies, and he asked that she continue to keep Tristan. Gwen was in no condition to receive her son, and he couldn't subject Tristan to further upset.

When he entered his study, Guy MacFale and Alex were already waiting. Looking at them now, he was sorry that he'd not come to them. They looked as bad as his wife. His men were present as well. They would all learn what happened and live with the details as they were revealed.

Greylen took a shot of brandy before turning to Guy. "Gwen's said nothing. Were you aware of any of the actions that transpired?"

Guy closed his eyes, shaking his head as if images raced through his mind. "Malcolm and his men returned four days past. I was locked within my chamber and knew not of their plans, though I found out bits and pieces from the servants who brought my trays. They told me the men were plotting to take your wife and had been watching your patrols. They'd overheard that a race was to take place and of the long runs your wife had been taking. They were disgusted that your men boasted of her endurance and waited daily for her to seek the run that would take her far from the keep. They knew already that she had only one guard with her."

"Did you see her when she was inside the keep?" Greylen asked.

"Aye, but 'twas hours after she arrived. Your man here was already inside by then."

Greylen turned to Alex and waited for the rest. He was covered with short wounds, deep enough that they had all been stitched, and his right hand was covered with bandages so thick 'twas impossible to discern the damage beneath. Alex looked straight into his eyes and recounted the events as they took place.

"I rode to the doors alone. Kevin tried to stop me, but I'd been the last to see her, the last to have her guard."

"You had not had her guard, Alex," Greylen corrected. "The keep was your duty."

"Aye, but had I not been relieved, I would have known sooner she was unprotected."

"Did you tell her to seek a shadow before going the distance?" Greylen asked, repeating the same words Alex had, no doubt, been given countless times already.

"Aye." He remained silent for a moment, then he smiled softly. "She saluted me, sir." Alex looked again to Greylen. "'Aye, aye, Captain' were her exact words."

They all smiled, as if they could picture their mistress doing just so. Alex went on as their smiles faded. "I gave Kevin a blow to the back of the head and rode to the doors."

"What did you think to accomplish alone?" Greylen asked, though he knew he would have done the same.

"If I could get to her, and somehow free her, 'twould have been the best of it. Yet to at least be inside, I hoped to protect her and assess the countenance of the men who held her. I offered myself in return and was quickly disarmed before they led me into the great hall. Malcolm said nothing to me, but he ordered two of the men to bring her from below."

"What was her condition?" Greylen asked.

"She'd been beaten already, though not with the blow that covers her eye as I've been told. Her hands were covered with dirt and blood as if she had dug to try to free herself. She stood proudly before them, sir," Alex said. "She *never* took her eyes from Malcolm. Then he proposed a game of sorts...and laughed as he explained the rules."

Greylen waited for Alex to continue, his control fading as he watched a tremor run through his man. "The game, Alex?"

"I was brought before her, and Malcolm instructed her to watch as they killed me bit by bit. He told her if she wished to show mercy at any time, 'twould stop the game. Mercy meaning she would willingly give herself to him."

Knowing what Alex's living form bespoke, Greylen swallowed the bile that crept up his throat.

"I told her never to give," Alex shouted. "I made not one sound as they inflicted each wound, and my eyes, they never wavered from hers. I swear I showed her only strength." Alex came out of his chair, clearly as shaken as he was then. He shook his head, running his fingers harshly through his hair before he finally sat again and continued, "Then they began dislocating the fingers in my right hand, one by one. 'Twas the sound of the bones cracking that made her give. She did, though I begged her not to. I didn't see her again. They beat me unconscious as she was led away."

"He didn't take her, Greylen," Guy said quickly. "She fought his attempts as I've never seen before. It seemed 'twas her plan to get him alone, for she still had a trick up her sleeve, so to speak."

"How do you know this?" Greylen demanded, looking to him.

"I escaped my chamber with the help of one of the servants. I knew I was no match alone for Malcolm and his men, but I saw what took place from the steps above. I waited in his chamber after I heard your wife's shout of 'enough' with such force, 'twas the bravest word I've ever heard spoken. I waited behind the curtains, my own dagger ready to kill him for his atrocities. In my weakened state, though, I had to be sure I chose the right moment. She was in terrible shape, already beaten and filthy from the dank cells below. He taunted her for a time, saying things no one should speak, as he tried to break her with his words and cuts from his knife. There was a struggle, and she began fighting back, but so slight he easily overtook her. I made my move then, and she hers." Guy paused, reaching for water, as he'd barely taken a breath since he began.

"She had a dagger of her own, and she reached for it. She tried to go for his throat, but he caught her before the blade found its mark. He was so enraged he didn't see me as he dealt the blow that now covers her eye and knocked her out cold. I don't know where I found the strength, but I removed him from your wife. Had I not been there, he'd have taken her even in her unconscious state. I was easily disarmed and, though badly beaten, I had inflicted enough wounds upon him myself that he was in no state to hurt her further. As I was taken from the room, he ordered her stripped and tied to the post outside. Then I found myself in the dungeon next to your man until your men arrived and freed us."

The room became silent with the end of the events as they were told, and Greylen turned his chair to face the wall. "Leave me."

Greylen waited for the doors to close behind them. As soon as he heard the latch click into place, he spent the next hour destroying everything in his sight. It took half a bottle of brandy before he was calm enough to leave his sanctuary, but he did, and Gavin waited just outside the doors.

"Is Isabelle holding up?" Greylen asked as they stood in the hallway.

"Aye, but she wants to see Gwen."

"And my wife?" Greylen asked.

"Still in shock."

"I'm going to sit with her by the fire, Gavin. Wait until we've settled, then remove the mirror from the bathing chamber."

{CHAPTER THIRTY-FOUR}

Greylen watched helplessly as his wife lingered in a state of unresponsiveness. She'd not said a word and only continued to stare blankly before her. Though she took the potions his mother placed to her lips, she never left their bed. Worse, she always curled into a ball when he had to leave her.

His mother stayed with her the few times that he'd been called away and also while he spent time in the nursery with Tristan. When he was with his wife, sadly, he found that he was just as silent with her as she was with him. In truth, he didn't know what to say, and offered her comfort the only way that he knew how. He held her in his arms, praying for a sign of life, a reaction of any kind, be it tears or fury.

The third morning after he had brought her home, he dressed her when they awoke. Hoping some fresh air might do her good, he took her to watch the sunrise. He held her hand as they walked to the stables, noting oddly that Gwen positioned herself a step behind him and never directly at his side. She made no sounds as he lifted her atop his mount, nor any during their ride down the narrow path. She sat unmoving between his legs as they looked to the waters.

In no hurry to return, he leaned back, taking her with him. She was asleep moments later, tucked safely against his side. He'd slept so fitfully the past nights, listening to her cries, that now as the sun warmed them, he gave in to his exhaustion. Gavin's shout awoke him, alarm and a sense of dread sweeping through his entire body.

Gwen was no longer beside him, and he ran, knowing the only place she could be—the water. She was fighting her way through the oncoming waves, the weight of the dress he had chosen pulled her down as she continued even farther. He called to her over and over again, finally diving beneath the waves and swimming as he had done only once before. She didn't make a sound as he wrapped his arm around her shoulders and offered no fight as he swam with her atop his chest back to the shore.

'Twas as he lay with her in the surf, catching his breath, that she finally looked at him for the first time since he'd brought her home. But her eyes were filled with only emptiness.

His anger got the better of him. "You would leave me? You would leave your son?" She only stared back, her look more confused than he'd ever seen. "Why, Gwen? *Why?*"

She finally broke then, anger and despair together. "I don't know. *I don't know.* I don't want to feel this pain anymore." She covered her face in her hands and began to cry.

He'd not have it and grabbed at her hands, pulling them away. "Talk to me," he demanded. "I am here. I have been here, Gwen. 'Tis *you* who have not."

"I can't remember, Greylen," she shouted back. "I can't remember what he did to me. I didn't seek Kevin. *I* am to blame for everything that happened."

"Gwen, there were five of them. They would have taken you both and most likely killed Kevin had he been with you."

"I gave in, Greylen. I couldn't let them torture Alex."

"Gwen, you've never been put to something such as that. How can you blame yourself for such a sacrifice?"

"How can you ever forgive me for what I've done?" she cried. "What they've done...to me. *How?*"

"You think so little of me, that I'd cast you aside or shun you?" He had to make her see. "You fought them, Gwen. You acted without fear, no matter what you felt inside. You performed as a leader. You spared your man's life for the sake of your own. You thought to kill your enemy yourself."

"How do you know? 'Twas only Malcolm and I in that room, and I did try to kill him, but he stopped me. I don't know what else he did."

"He did nothing, Gwen. Gavin's father stopped him, and he's the one who told me of your battle with Malcolm. Just as Alex told me of your behavior as they tortured him before your eyes."

She was silent for a moment before she spoke again, her words only a whisper this time. "He didn't?"

Greylen knew what she asked and knew she needed to hear it again. "Nay, he did not. And had he, 'twould not have mattered to me. You are mine, Gwen. Nothing could shame you to me, *especially* a circumstance beyond your control."

"But you've not talked to me—you've not brought my son to me. Not even a whisper as you hold me."

"Ah, Gwen." He sighed, shaking his head in regret. "I knew not what to say. How could I promise to love and protect you in the aftermath of what happened? You suffered for hours without my protection. 'Tis *I* who have failed you."

"You never failed me, Greylen. You saved me from them."

"Is it so bad that you can't live with it?" he asked of her walk to the water.

"It just called to me, Greylen, or maybe I called to it. I don't know. But then you were there. You are always there."

He pulled her into his arms, all of the unspoken words at last put to rest. They lay on the beach a long while after, exhausted from their outpouring.

Greylen took Gwen back to their chamber where he left her for but a few minutes to have Anna fetch a tray. When he returned, their room was empty, but the doors of the bathing chamber were open. He hadn't told her of the mirror, and she'd been so drugged and dazed those past few days, she hadn't noticed when he or his mother had taken her inside.

She was standing in front of the chest, her hand reaching for the empty wall. He removed his shirt as he moved to her. Then he gathered her in his arms from behind, his bare feet encompassing hers as they stood there.

"Is it that bad?" she asked.

"You'll heal, love," he whispered in her ear.

"No wonder you've not brought Tristan to me."

"Ah, Gwen." He shook his head. "You are more beautiful than anyone I have ever known, even now."

"Nay, Greylen," she argued. "I am weak. They overpowered me so easily. And I am hideous, just as he said."

He could only imagine what Malcolm had said to her. Guy had said that his words were unspeakable, and now she believed them. "You are none of those things, Gwen. You have never been weak, and that you could think that you are hideous, 'tis only words he threw to you."

She brought her hands to her face and traced the stitches and swollen skin that still covered her eye. Then she lowered her head in defeat.

Greylen turned her around and lifted her chin. "You are beautiful, Gwen. Say it."

"I—" She shook her head and pulled her chin out of his grasp.

He lifted her to the chest and stood between her legs, taking her chin once more. "You are beautiful, Gwen. Say it."

'Twas barely a whisper, but she at last spoke the words that he had asked. "I am beautiful, Greylen."

"Aye, wife," he whispered back, kissing her gently.

"I don't feel it, Greylen. They are but empty words. And I am just as empty for needing to hear them…just as shallow."

If he could, Greylen would kill Malcolm again for what he had done to her. She was broken and defeated, and though he didn't want to hurt her, he needed to show her how much he loved her.

He wrapped Gwen's legs around his waist and carried her to their bed, lowering them both as he continued to hold her. He kissed her the entire time she lay beneath him. Kissed every part of her face, covered every scratch and bruise with his lips, and drank each silent tear that escaped from her eyes.

He knew she was in pain from the bruises that still covered her body, but he didn't stop. And he knew that she didn't want him to. He made love to her as he always had, as he always would.

'Twas only after they had made love, after she slept within the circle of his arms, that he realized every word they had spoken since he had first heard her voice that morn, was spoken only in Gaelic. Even in her anger and despair, she had spoken only his language. And though he should have been pleased, something about this change in her left him unsettled.

Tristan was brought into their room that night, happy to be with his mother again. 'Twas a rough few days before Gwen's body could meet his demands, but Greylen knew she was grateful that their son turned only to her now.

Gwen stayed mostly within their chamber and only left when he came and escorted her to meals or to sit with him in the study. The first time she sat with him as he went through his ledgers, he could sense that something bothered her, but she didn't say anything. He had to ask her first before she'd speak of it. Then she quietly explained, with downcast eyes, that the study seemed different to her and many of the items that she had always admired were now gone.

He explained that he commissioned new furnishings as well as maps that were more current than those he had had. The other ornaments and books, which she had quietly remarked were missing, he said he had packed away until their new things arrived.

Had she looked more closely she would have seen that his desk was barely held together by spikes, and the few leather volumes that did line the shelves were void of pages. He had destroyed everything else, including the maps that he'd torn from the walls. As for the trinkets that had lined the shelves and tables, those he had shattered.

But she'd not looked more closely. Not at anything.

She went only through the motions.

Greylen became more and more disturbed with his wife's behavior as the weeks passed. Though she awoke early every day, she made no attempt to resume her exercise routine. And though she took great care of Tristan, 'twas she who clung to him, rather than he to her.

Whenever he brought her to the great hall, or anywhere for that matter, he always had to retrieve her once he started to leave. He actually had to approach her and place his hand upon her shoulder, and when she would finally realize that he was there, he would then have to take her hand and lead her from the room.

She spoke only Gaelic, and worse, only if she was addressed first. She'd at least stopped jumping at loud sounds and now was rarely lost to nightmares when they slept. But her submissiveness and her complacency were killing him. 'Twas only at night when they made love that he saw glimpses of the Gwen he now missed so much. Only then did she resemble, if but barely, the woman he once knew.

He couldn't blame her for her behavior as it now was. She'd been through so much and not just in the hours that Malcolm and his men had held her. The past year had been filled with countless blessings, as well as horrible tragedies. He had to do something, though, and he knew the answer was there, he just couldn't seem to find what he was searching for.

He had just left Gwen with his sister in the library when he called for his mother and Gavin to meet him in the study. The furnishing had finally arrived, and he sat behind his new desk while Gavin and his mother sat in front of him.

"I want my wife back," he stated emphatically as he looked to them.

Gavin heartily agreed with him that Gwen was not the same, and he missed her too. His mother, however, didn't quite see things the same way. "Greylen," she said quickly. "Gwendolyn is fine. Why, she's the perfect embodiment of a wife."

"Fine?" he challenged. "You think that she is *fine*?" He was shocked that she could say such a thing. "I don't want the perfect wife, Mother. 'Tis *my* wife I want. *My Gwendolyn*."

"She is here, Greylen," Lady Madelyn soothed. "Think you she is so different?" she asked honestly.

Greylen looked at her as if she had just sprouted horns and he wanted to rip them from her head. How could she not see it? To prove his point, he yelled for his wife. "Gwendolyn."

She was there in seconds. Tristan on her hip as she stood in the open doorway.

"Wife?" he asked as she looked to the floor.

"Aye, husband?"

He fisted his hands when she didn't look up to address him. Resolved, he continued, "You seem tired this day. Mayhap you should nap before supper."

"Aye, Greylen," she agreed easily and began to turn.

He stopped her, further proving his point. "Wife?"

"Aye?"

"Your clothes, those you run in," he clarified. "I wish for you to relinquish them."

"Very well," she said quickly. "I'll have Anna remove them before I retire."

Gavin wasn't as shocked as Lady Madelyn, who finally came to realize that Gwen was, in fact, further gone than she had thought. Her shame showed on her face.

"Greylen?" Gwen asked timidly.

"Aye, Gwen." *Look at me, damn it!*

"Tristan isn't ready for his nap yet. Should I leave him with Anna?"

She looked to him now for every decision. "Nay, Gwen, leave him with me."

Gwen walked to the settee and grabbed the plaid that was thrown over the side. She placed it beneath Greylen's desk and laid Tristan atop it. 'Twas one of their son's favorite places, and Greylen kept a basket of small toys that he could hold or chew on beside the desk. She placed a few around their son and then walked quietly from the room.

Greylen swept his arm across the desk, and each of the new items crashed to the floor. Tristan laughed, loving the loud noises that his father always made, but Gwen came back into the room, staring. "Greylen?"

"'Tis only a bug, sweet," Greylen said, shaking his head. "Everything will be put to rights, love. I promise you—I will put everything to rights."

When he was sure she was gone again, Greylen picked up his son. He looked to Gavin and his mother for help.

Lady Madelyn was quick with an explanation. "She's lost her spirit, son," she stated plainly.

Greylen's eyes fixed on her instantly. How had he not thought of it sooner? 'Twas indeed her spirit, the very same he had vowed to safeguard. And now remembering his wife's words of what had always made her feel alive again, he looked to Gavin. "The race is back on, Gavin. Raise the flags immediately. One week from today, we run."

"You think she'll go?" Gavin asked. "She's not had a desire since she returned, Greylen. 'Twas her run that left her vulnerable."

"I'll begin to needle her this eve. Let us pray she takes the bait."

'Twas going better than he imagined. He sat with Gwen atop the steps that night, watching as the flags were put into place again. For the first time, she addressed him without being spoken to first.

"I thought you called off the race."

"Aye," he replied. "I did. But Alex has healed enough, and as you seem to no longer have the strength or endurance, I find no reason for the delay. The men were disappointed to have it put off. And to be honest, I'd rather you watch and cheer my win as I cross the line. Just as my wife should." He squeezed her knee with his explanation, and though she seemed to easily agree, he didn't miss the flicker in her eye. 'Twas but a second, but 'twas there as he boasted his win and insulted her lack of skill.

He spied her that very same night looking at the clothes Anna had yet to remove per his orders. She took a halter and pair of trews from the pile and hid them among her dresses. He turned so she wouldn't see his smile.

The next day he watched as she warred with herself. She stared at the clothing she'd hidden, even reached for them several times, but in the end, she always pulled back. 'Twas a start, but with only six days left, he needed help to move her along. The next part of his plan began before their midday meal.

"Gwendolyn," Isabelle called as she stepped into the chamber.

"Aye, Isabelle," Gwen answered. "I'm in the bathing chamber, come in."

Isabelle stood in the doorway, watching as Gwen bathed Tristan. She was soaked from his splashing, so Isabelle held out a towel, taking her nephew when Gwen handed him to her.

"Would you help me with something, Gwen?" Isabelle asked as she dried off Tristan.

"Isabelle, I'll help you with anything," she said quickly. "What is it you need?"

Isabelle was surprised that her brother had been so right. Gwen had no problem helping a woman. 'Twas men she now feared. Greylen had explained that if his wife could boost her own confidence, gain *any* modicum of control, 'twould help her on her way. "Will you teach me how to do sit-ups?" Isabelle finally asked.

Gwen looked at her in surprise. "I suppose I could, but why don't you ask Gavin or even Greylen? They can show you."

"I'm only a woman." Isabelle shrugged. "They wouldn't bother. Besides, they would tell me 'twas ridiculous."

"Ridiculous? Exercise is not ridiculous, Isabelle. 'Tis one of the most important things that you can do for yourself."

Isabelle wanted to laugh. Gwen had spoken words so true to herself but had yet to realize it. "Will you?" she asked again. "Please?"

"Aye," Gwen said with a smile. "I just need to change first, and you'll need to change as well. Fetch one of Gavin's shirts and come back. I'll be ready for you."

Isabelle watched from the hallway as Gwendolyn went to her wardrobe and pulled out her halter and pants. She seemed to struggle for a moment with what she should do. Then she changed and put Tristan in his cradle before she immediately reached for him again. Gwendolyn lifted the baby high in the air, then slowly brought him down. Then she did it again and again.

Isabelle turned to Greylen, who waited on the landing, flashing him the brightest of smiles. He was obviously thrilled by her smile and motioned with his hands for her to go into his room and stir his wife even more.

Isabelle lay before the fire as Gwendolyn had instructed. Then her sister-in-law showed her all of the ways to work the muscles of one's abdomen. Isabelle wanted to kill her brother. *Dear Lord, these exercises were painful.* Especially with someone like Gwen, who seemed to enjoy the exertion and the—sweet mother of God—*burn* as she called it. She'd burn the whole castle down if she had to do this again. An hour later she finally left, barely able to walk to her chamber. She closed the door and slid helplessly to the floor as Greylen and Gavin waited for her to speak.

Her voice was hoarse when she did. "I do not like to exercise," she whined, not at all sorry for her pitiful behavior. Then she grinned. "But, brother, your wife surely does. Once she started, I swear she couldn't stop. I've never done *any* of those things, and she'd not let me stop. Have you any idea how many ways there are to do sit-ups?" she asked. "Too many! And when I could do no more, she had to show me how to do squats and lunges. I shan't walk for a week."

Greylen picked up his sister and twirled her in the air. "Thank you, Isabelle," he said before placing her down again and turning to Gavin. "You know what to do?" Greylen asked. With Gavin's nod, he left the room.

That night as Greylen lay in bed with Gwen, she snuggled against him. *Snuggled.* She didn't just lie in his arms as he held her, she snuggled him, and he heard her sigh. 'Twas something his wife had done so often before, but not since she'd been taken. His eyes misted in response and he had to turn her so she wouldn't notice. He wrapped her body with his and slept as he hadn't in weeks.

The next morning, he awoke early and stepped up his plan. He crept from their bed and went to the fire, sitting as close as possible. He sat there till he could take no more. He went back to bed and pulled Gwen against him. She stirred from his heat immediately, turning and covering his forehead with her hand, as he pretended to sleep.

"Greylen, you're so warm," she whispered. Her hand moved, replaced by her lips before she pressed her cheek to his. She repeated it—twice.

Good God, how many ways would the woman check to determine he was warm?

She shot from the bed, returning seconds later. She sat beside him and placed a wet cloth on his forehead. When she ran her fingers through his hair, he slowly opened his eyes.

She looked at him with concern. "Greylen, you're very warm. Does anything bother you?"

"Every—" he started weakly, then realized that he'd gone too far as her eyes widened with fear. "Everything is fine," he corrected quickly. "I just feel a bit tired." *Better—definitely better. She took control again.*

"Well, we'll not take any chances," she said, shaking her head. "You're to stay in bed today, husband." As soon as the words were out, fear flashed across her face, as if she realized that she'd given him an order and looked back cautiously. "All right?"

"Aye, Gwen," he answered, taking her hand. "I'll stay abed. You know what's best, love."

She smiled and for the rest of the day took charge of his care. She wrote items on a list so that Cook could prepare a soup for him and left only to go to the nursery to feed Tristan. And each time that she passed through the doors, he leaped from the bed to warm himself again.

Midday, Gwen called for a bath and washed him before returning him to their bed. Her orders to the servants, wary at first, came more easily as the hours passed. Finally, Gavin came in the afternoon.

"Gwen, I need your assistance," he said, stepping into the room. "You're the only one who can help."

"Gavin, Greylen's not well," she returned, waving toward the bed. "Perhaps someone else could help you."

"Nay." He shook his head. "The men are busy training. I've begun a new boxing routine, but I can't find the right sequence."

"Go on, Gwen," Greylen pushed. "I won't leave the bed."

"Greylen, you're sick. I'm not going—"

"'Twould make me feel better," he offered her with a weak smile.

"Very well." She sighed. "But I'm not leaving." Greylen saw the angered look she cast at Gavin. His wife was preoccupied, something he'd made sure of. He knew 'twas the only reason she agreed.

Greylen watched as Gwen joined Gavin by the fire. Gavin explained that he first wished to show Gwen the routine he'd come up with, adding that he hoped she could improve it. Gwen looked to Greylen, and he nodded his encouragement. His wife turned then and bowed to Gavin.

Gavin started slowly, and though Gwen took all of his blows, 'twas long minutes before Greylen saw the fight stir within her. With its first glimmer, Gavin lashed out with everything he had, leaving her no choice but to defend herself. Greylen nodded him on, smiling now as he continued with his silent orders for Gavin to push Gwen even more. She was breathless when the sequence ended and took a drink of water before returning.

When she stood before Gavin again, her face was flush and her eyes narrowed in anger. Nay, Greylen realized, 'twasn't anger; 'twas fury. She nodded for Gavin to receive her blows, and they bowed again before she began. But this fight wasn't defensive on her part as the last had been. She was the aggressor now. In all of his years, he'd never seen a woman so enraged.

Greylen watched his wife carefully. He wasn't smiling anymore. She beat Gavin with everything she had, her anger unleashing as she finally let go. It killed him to watch her like this. He just wanted to hold her in his arms, to cushion her from all of the hurt that she endured. But he knew how much this was helping her. When she finally stopped, she turned away, looking at neither of them. She walked straight to the bathing chamber. His wife let go as she never had before.

Greylen nodded to Gavin to leave the room. Then he got up and went to his wife. She was doing exactly what he had, destroying everything in her sight. Screaming and crying at the same time. He didn't stop her. He stood in the doorway, waiting until she spent the last of her strength. He gathered her in his arms as she sank to the floor. Then he sat with her in the chair in the alcove, rubbing her back as he kissed the top of her head.

"I'm sorry," she whispered.

"You have nothing to apologize for, Gwen," he said, shaking his head.

"I've made such a mess of everything, Greylen."

"We'll clean up the mess, love."

"Nay, 'tis not this mess I apologize for. I've been hiding... From myself and from you... 'Tis *that* I'm sorry for."

They were the words he longed to hear. He only hoped that in the next few days, she would find the strength to, at last, win her battle.

'Twas something that he knew she must do herself.

❧ CHAPTER THIRTY-FIVE ❧

Gwen heard the cannon blast that began the race. She stood before the window and waited until she was sure that everyone had left the courtyard, then she slowly took the stairs. Isabelle was the only one who knew she was going and had offered to watch Tristan for the entire morning. Gwen knew it would take her hours to complete the course that her husband had set, but she needed this run.

She needed to cross that line.

It was the spark of hope that consumed her for the last three days, and it would be an accomplishment that no one could take from her. An accomplishment she knew she had to complete. And when she did, she would finally move on.

She wouldn't hide from her husband or her family anymore. She would tell them when the images or feelings of what Malcolm did to her were too much. Greylen had already made her tell him everything she remembered, when she'd broken down in their bathing chamber after she'd sparred with Gavin. And he'd made her tell him more than once. He took from her every blow, every kick, and every vile insult she described to him. Each moment of fear and despair. She knew it killed him to hear it, yet he insisted. And she knew, too, he did it because he was trying to help her. It's just who he was.

No one was about as she made her way through the entrance. In fact, it was strangely quiet. As she held the latch of the front doors, she smiled at the steps she'd already taken. No one had seen her take her shorts from the new trunk at the end of her bed. No one had witnessed her tears when she saw that they had been placed on top of everything else, and her running shoes beside them. Greylen must have put them there before everything happened, when he had first proposed this run. She had planned to run with him then. Now she would follow him, though he would never know.

She took a deep breath and opened the doors.

Oh my God.

Her husband stood just beyond the steps with his men by his side. They were eight now, including Alex, and they all smiled as they looked up to her.

Eight of the most incredible smiles all directed at her.

Greylen came forward, resting a foot atop the bottom step as he reached out with his hand. "'Tis your run, wife. We'd not go without you."

Gwen was speechless. They had known she would come, and they had waited for her. The other men had already left the courtyard, so now it was only her and her men. They were her elite circle this morn, and she was one of them.

She reached out to take Greylen's hand, and as she stood beside him, he bent to whisper in her ear. "You could have at least worn a shirt over your halter, wife." She smiled, biting her lip, and he kissed her before swatting her bottom to urge her on. "Set your pace, sweet. This journey we take together."

And as simple as that, she began. They ran from the gates together, toward the line that symbolized her freedom. Freedom that she now knew her husband had planned only for her.

It was a beautiful September day, and the men cast their shirts aside within minutes. All of the children had taken places along the trail, handing water to the runners as they passed. Halfway through, Gwen smiled at Greylen as she breathlessly called to him, "We're wealthy, husband, aren't we?"

"Aye, wife, beyond your wildest dreams," he answered. Then he laughed that deep rich sound she'd not heard in weeks as he realized her intent. She threw the cup high into the air, letting it shatter upon the ground.

And so became their habit throughout the rest of their run. Instead of gently rolling the pottery to the ground, as they had been doing, they threw them over their heads lost in Gwen's zeal.

"Go ahead of me," she called. "You deserve to finish at your own pace. It's the best feeling ever."

Greylen nodded to his men and they ran ahead, each of them racing to beat the other. But Greylen stayed by her side. He wore a look that showed his pride in her. They continued alone for the last hour; Gwen's pace increased as the last hill came into sight. When they reached the top, she stopped short.

All of the men who began with the sound of the cannons that morn, every last one of them, lined the final length to the finish line. Gavin, Duncan, Connell, Ian, Kevin, Hugh, and Alex stood facing their approach, fifty paces before the line that had yet to be crossed. Gwen shook her head, tears gathering in her eyes. *They waited for her.*

She was shaken out of her stupor when Greylen kissed her hand and pulled her forward. They passed through the line of men and when they reached the seven who waited for her, Greylen stopped by Gavin's side. "'Tis yours, wife." He smiled, sweeping his hand in the direction of the ribbon. "Take it."

Gwen started forward, but after a few steps, she turned back. This would be a win for all of them. It had to be. "I won't go alone," she said. "'Tis a win for us all."

"Is that an order, wife?"

"Aye, 'tis. *Now move!*"

They all grinned and joined her, making sure that her body broke the ribbon first. Greylen picked her up when they crossed the line, holding her high in the air as his men cheered her victory. Then he lowered her slowly, sliding her down his body until their eyes met.

She held his face, smiling through tears. "I won, Greylen. I won!"

"We're MacGreggors, Gwen. We always win."

❧ EPILOGUE ❧

Greylen sat atop a cluster of natural rock as he looked upon the festivities. 'Twas their fifth anniversary, the anniversary of their birthdays, and each year they would celebrate the same as before. The beach was alive with bonfires as the sun set in the distance. His family and men were all present as they shared in the joy of the night together.

Greylen always began these nights alone, watching from the same perch which he sat upon now. His mother was helping Anna set the tables that they had brought down earlier for a veritable feast. Tonight, however, he had a surprise, one that he couldn't wait to share with his wife. It had taken two years to acquire everything he needed, a small fortune, but by God, 'twould be worth it.

His ship's captain had happened by a sorry scene and taken it upon himself to buy a family from servitude. Greylen took the family in without question. He'd seen many such atrocities in his life and his captain had the authority, and means, to act on his behalf. The boon, however, was the family's heritage and with their help, Greylen had compiled lists of supplies that were finally purchased.

Gwen would have tacos tonight.

And knowing his wife as he did, she'd make herself sick before she was done with them. He'd probably have to hold her hair back as she retched. He'd do it, too, gladly.

His men were talking and drinking by the fire as they chose music. In truth, they were most likely fighting over the songs, but they wouldn't begin until he joined them. 'Twas the only night they had used Gwen's iPhone and speaker—and 'twould most likely be the last. But he would hear those notes and lyrics in his head forever.

Gavin and Isabelle were just making their way down the path with their children. The twins had a brother now, Guy, named after their grandsire who'd passed four years ago. Gavin had made peace with his father before his death and now lived on the land that was his birthright. He'd had the entire keep dismantled and rebuilt, an undertaking that lasted three years.

'Twas Montgomery land now, and Gavin was laird of his own small clan. He and Isabelle came to Seagrave every few weeks and would stay for days. Their children would play together, and then sleep in the nursery with Anna while the four adults resumed their practice of late-night suppers in the kitchens, or if his wife preferred, they dined formally in the great hall.

Gwen always referred to those evenings together as "date nights" and they enjoyed them immensely. They would play card games or chess, and if the women weren't with child or nursing, sometimes they just got plain drunk. They would sing to songs as they danced and listened to music, laughing so hard at their own antics Anna had no choice but to come downstairs and quiet them. Then they'd only laugh harder.

And then there was Gwen. His wife.

He was always so taken with her. Her beauty and her mind. The life they created together. She had changed so much over the years, and yet she had not changed at all. Her spirit was more alive than ever, and he enjoyed the challenge and banter that was an intrinsic part of their days. But she had adapted to his ways as well.

She spoke only Gaelic now, though somehow, she incorporated her outlandish remarks and phrases in his language. She raised their children just as he'd been reared, with love and compassion. And she never questioned his early training of their son. She had rolled her eyes, however, and quite emphatically, too, when he presented his son with a sword of his own. Tristan's first birthday seemed the appropriate time to him. And why shouldn't his son wear war paint when he learned to walk and hold the weapon he had made?

Maybe she really was daft after all.

Gwen was walking through the surf now. She wore a beautiful emerald green gown that set the color of her eyes afire. It stretched across her newly expanding belly as she now carried their third child. She held the hem on each side and also a hand of each of their children. Tristan was on her right and their daughter, Blair, was on her left. They were giggling, no doubt from something outrageously silly that his wife had told them.

His son wore taupe linen breeches rolled to the knee and a white linen shirt, and his daughter, the image of his wife, wore a white jumper embroidered with delicate roses. Her hair was fashioned just as her mother's, swept behind her head and adorned with ribbons. She was their little angel and he had delivered her himself.

Actually, she was the devil incarnate and her early arrival should have been his first clue. 'Twas yet another night he'd not soon forget.

His mother had gone to visit Gavin and Isabelle to await the birth of their son. And with Gwen's delivery still weeks away, his wife had insisted that she go. He had been in his study, playing on the floor with Tristan, who had been only two at the time, when he noticed Gwen standing in the open doorway. She bit her lip as she looked at him, which of course made him assume that she wished for a little play of their own.

"Greylen," she finally said as she remained within the doorframe.

"Aye, sweet. May I be of service?" he asked wickedly.

"I was hoping so."

"What did you have in mind, love?"

"My water broke, Greylen."

"Then send for a servant, wife. And be quick about it. I'm ready for whatever your heart desires."

"I didn't spill water, husband. The water spilled from me."

He finally took her meaning, scrambling from the floor with Tristan in his arms, holding him so tight that his son had to pinch him to break him from his stupor. "But 'tis not time," he cried, clutching the lad again.

"I'd say you're wrong," she returned with a sigh and shrug. "But I'd prefer not to argue."

"What should we do?"

She actually laughed. "I think we should have this baby. Take Tristan to Anna, Greylen. And help me upstairs, please."

"But she can help." *Was that his voice?*

"We don't need her, Greylen. And Tristan will sit with no one else."

Tristan was deposited in Anna's arms minutes later. Then Greylen took his wife's shaking hand in his own and led her upstairs.

Her labor wasn't long, and her spirits were very high. Except for the times when her contractions let loose.

"Let me fetch Anna. Please, Gwen," he pleaded for the hundredth time.

"She'll come when he's asleep, Greylen."

"Your daughter picked a fine time to come."

"What makes you think this babe is a girl?"

He gave her *the look*. The one that informed her of her daftness. "Only a girl, and more to the point, only *your* daughter could have a will such as this. You women will ruin me."

"Take back your insult," she demanded, "or I swear, you'll never get me with child again."

"Get you with child again? Are you serious?" Good God she was! "Gwen—wife, you think I would get you with child again?" He gave her *the look* again. "Not only do I sit between your legs…your attributes plain for the world to see. You have the temper of a wild boar, the mouth of a sailor, and have I mentioned—you have the body of a gangly boy…with a melon in your belly."

She had laughed at his teasing. Then she had screamed as another contraction came and his heart sank to the floor. God bless her, though, she was right. This babe came easily and by the time Anna had entered their chamber, he was holding his precious daughter in his hands, crying just as he had the first time.

He was so lost in thought as he remembered that day three years ago, he didn't see his daughter approach. But he felt her tiny hand on his cheek before he turned to look at her.

"Papa," she called in the sweetest voice he'd ever heard.

He smiled and gathered her in his arms. She placed her precious hands on his face, rubbing the whiskers that darkened his features. "Aye, angel?" he asked softly.

"Dance with Mama."

"Dance with your mama," he repeated. The children loved to watch them dance, though, they always giggled and covered their eyes as they peeked through their tiny hands.

"Aye, Papa," she said. "Come dance with Mama."

"Angel, wild horses couldn't keep me from dancing with your mama."

He carried his daughter toward the fire where her brother and cousins were waiting. Where, in fact, everyone was waiting. He sat Blair down next to the children and turned to Gwen. She gifted him with a beautiful smile, and he gathered her in his arms, holding her close as the music began.

The song was the one Gwen had chosen to dance to on the eve of their second anniversary, continuing the tradition they had begun the year before of dancing to commemorate their joining. Every year since, 'twas always "I Could Not Ask For More" by someone named Edwin McCain that they danced to first. She called it their "wedding song." The lyrics couldn't have been more perfect, and they whispered the words to each other as he moved her about the fire.

In truth, everything was perfect. And as the full moon cast a glow on the entire shorefront, Greylen stared into his wife's beautiful green eyes, whispering the words that were theirs alone. "You are forever my love, Gwendolyn."

"And you are forever mine, Greylen."

He'd reached for the plane where time has no end...
Captured a dream the gods thought to send...
The soul of his heart...
Her eyes he could see...
And forever she'd be his...for infinity.

Made in the USA
Lexington, KY
06 December 2019